LA
LUNE

LA
LUNE

GINA MAGEE
with Brittany Lammerts & Savannah Tyler

TRIGGER WARNING

This story contains content that might be troubling to some readers—including but not limited to depictions of and references to substance abuse, theological conflict, violence, suicide and death. Remember to practice self-care before, during and after reading.

This book is for those who believe in magic.

Playlist

1) "The Old Ways" — Loreena McKennitt
2) "You" — Ari Abdul
3) "Elements" — Lindsey Stirling
4) "Purple City" — Like Saturn
5) "All Souls Night" — Loreena McKennitt
6) "Dope" — Demeter
7) "The Mummers' Dance" — Loreena McKennitt
8) "Free Spirit" — Khalid
9) "Take Me Where Your Heart Is" — Q
10) "Addiction"— Doja Cat
11) "I'm Yours" — Isabel LaRosa
12) "Two Princes" — Spin Doctors
13) "Nothing More Than That" — The Paper Kites
14) "Dangerous Hands" — Austin Giorgio
15) "Delicious" — Nick Jonas
16) "The Mates of Soul" — Taylor John Williams
17) "Don't Fade" — Vance Joy
18) "Huron 'Beltane' Fire Dance" — Loreena McKennitt
19) "Inscape" — Stateless
20) "Just Say Yes" — Snow Patrol
21) "Whole Lotta Love" — Led Zeppelin
22) "Heal Me" — Relaxing Music for Stress Relief
23) "Fuel to Fire" — Agnes Obel
24) "Earned It (Fifty Shades of Grey Soundtrack)" — The Weeknd
25) "Rhiannon" — Fleetwood Mac

26) "Bigger Than The Whole Sky" — Taylor Swift

27) "Something Just Like This" — The Chainsmokers & Coldplay

28) "Intoxicated" — Black Atlass

29) "E.T." — Katy Perry

30) "Get You The Moon" — Kina (feat. Snow)

PLAYLIST ON PANDORA

https://pandora.app.link/h9930she3Db

"Where there is a woman, there is magic."
-Ntozake Shange

1

#1692

Harper

"We are officially in 'Witch City!'" Millie cheered. She was my good friend and nurse coworker at Massachusetts General Hospital in Boston and she'd invited me to go to Salem today.

"We certainly are!"

"Did you get a good shot of the 'Entering Salem' sign?"

"I got several. I plan to make a scrapbook of this entire day."

"As you should. Harper, I still can't believe you've never been here. You're from Northampton and that's only a little over two hours away from Salem".

"I know. But I told you how strict my parents were with my sister and me while we were growing up."

"I cannot imagine being that sheltered and drenched in religion."

"Well, Haley and I were. Our mom and dad had good intentions, though."

"I have no doubt they did, but I think it's healthy to question everything we've been spoon-fed to believe as children and make up our own minds about it."

"I agree and that's why I'm here with you. I wanted to check out Salem for myself and see what all of this witchy stuff is about. So many times, my parents said it was 'of the devil.' But to me, it seems like it's 'of 'Hollywood.' Nothing but a bunch of commercialized hocus pocus."

"Have you ever read any books about witchcraft or 'the old ways' as it's also called?"

"No, I've only read a few articles online but don't know what to believe. Some of the info is really out there, just like what I remember my crazy Aunt Jenny telling my sister and me. And I call her crazy, affectionately."

"You've never mentioned her to me before."

I shrugged. "No reason to. She just pops into my mind every once in a while. Like now."

"Is she your mom's sister or your dad's?"

"My mom's."

"I think everyone needs a crazy aunt. They're usually tons of fun."

"Mine definitely was."

"*Was?*"

"Yeah. I haven't seen her since my sixteenth birthday."

Millie jerked her head back. "Why?"

"My parents cut off all contact with her after overhearing what she told Haley and me."

"What did she tell you?"

"She had just finished talking about the elements—earth, air, fire, water, and spirit—and was in the process of telling us about the four directions—north, south, east, and west—when my parents barged into my and Haley's bedroom."

"Your aunt was teaching you and your sister the basics of witchcraft."

"Looking back, I guess she was."

"There's no guessing about it. She must've been a witch."

"She never called herself one."

"That doesn't mean anything."

"True."

"So let me get this straight. Your parents cut your aunt out of your life because of differing religious views and practices?"

"Yes."

Millie sighed. "That's really sad."

"I know. But what could Haley and I do? We were teenagers."

"I get that. Do you happen to know where your aunt is now?"

"No. I've searched for her on social media several times over the years, but no luck."

"Hmmm. I wish you could find her. I think it'd be a really good thing if you and your Aunt Jenny reconnected."

I smiled nostalgically. "I would love for that to happen. If it ever did, by some miracle, I couldn't tell my parents about it or they'd probably whack me off the family tree too."

"Just like questioning what you've been spoon-fed while growing up, the same applies to situations such as your parents cutting your aunt out of your life. You deserve to know the whole story."

"I already do."

"No, you don't. You haven't heard your aunt's side. Have you ever wondered why she wanted to tell you and your sister about witchcraft?"

"No. To me, she was just being her usual self, talking about off-the-wall stuff."

Millie looked over my face. "I'm going to try to find her for you. My investigative skills are more polished since I've been walking this earth fifteen years longer than you have."

"Don't waste your time. You've got better things to do."

"I want to find her for you, Harper. I can tell that it would mean a lot to you if I did."

I could feel a lump in my throat from thinking about the possibility. "It really would."

"Then it's settled. I'll start searching for your Aunt Jenny tomorrow. In the meantime, I'm going to begin showing you all the places in Salem and neighboring Danvers that hold the most historical significance, plus some fun ones. Are you ready to do this?"

"You know I am."

"You, my dear sweet friend, are about to embark on one hell of an adventure."

I nodded at Millie and then gazed out the passenger side window of her car at the old buildings and homes we were passing by. The buildings ranged from two to four stories and the homes varied in size and style. Some were modern while some appeared to be nearly as old as Salem, but they were maintained and looked immaculate.

Millie and I passed by some mansions, too, and they were stunning. Majestic. Proud. I wanted to visit as many of these different locations as possible and walk around inside them to smell them and touch their history.

Sprinkled around all the homes and buildings were trees that were still holding onto the last of their autumn foliage. The different shades of red, orange, yellow, and brown added an extra spark to this 31st day of October.

"The first place I want you to see is the Witch House. It's located in the heart of Salem. Do you know anything about it?" Millie asked.

"No. I thought about researching Salem's historical sites after we made plans to come here, but decided not to because I wanted to learn about them while I was here. I felt it'd have more impact."

"Oh, it will. You're going to feel a lot of different emotions today."

"I'm expecting to feel sadness because of the innocent lives lost during the witch trials."

"Probably anger too. I felt angry the first time that I came to Salem and toured around. Anyway, the Witch House was the home of Jonathan Corwin, who was one of the judges who conducted the trials. His house is the only structure with direct ties to them still standing. It's also creepy looking."

"Why is that?"

"Because it's painted slate black."

After parking in a lot, Millie paid the meter through an app on her cellphone and then we got out of her car. I looked down at my black boots on the pavement and snapped a quick photo of them. Since it was my first time stepping foot here, I had to do it. It was a big step for me and if my parents knew what I was doing now, they'd probably stroke out.

By the time five hours had passed, Millie and I had gone to the Witch House, the Witch Museum, the Ropes Mansion and Garden, the First Church of Salem, the Witch Trials Memorial, and Old Burying Point Cemetery. We had also ventured over to Salem Village aka Danvers, where there were even more locations directly linked to the horrific tragedy of 1692.

Out of all the places that I'd been to today, the Witch Trials Memorial affected me the most. I could barely speak while there because I felt so much sadness about what I was seeing. I got angry, too, as Millie had said I probably would.

A granite bench for each victim had been placed at the outdoor location with their name, how they died, and the date of their death engraved in it. Fourteen women and five men had been executed by hanging. One other man had been pressed to death after refusing to enter a plea, and at least five people died in jail. The horrible ending that all of those people had to face made me feel even more grateful for the time I was living in.

My feet were literally aching from all the walking that Millie and I had done but it was worth it. The street grid layout in downtown Salem was rather eccentric and incredibly interesting to explore. Going up and down the cobblestone and brick streets and sidewalks, I felt as if I'd stepped back in time. However, the commercial businesses reminded me that I hadn't.

There were restaurants, pubs, coffee and tea houses, and countless souvenir shops. Outside the places where one could eat, drink, or do both, there were umbrella tables set up for customers. Musicians here and there, sitting on fold-out chairs, entertained those who passed by.

Many of the fun locations that Millie and I visited were in the movie *Hocus Pocus*. I got to see Max and Dani's house, and also Allison's. Old Town Hall was where Winifred Sanderson sang "I Put a Spell on You" at the Halloween party and while that scene was filmed in California, the building where the party took place existed in Salem and was actually a museum.

When Millie took me to Lighthouse Point, I recognized it from *Hocus Pocus*, as well. That location was where Sarah Sanderson was seen flying her broom over a lighthouse while singing "Come Little Children." Before leaving, I told Millie that we were going to have to watch the movie together sometime. She was all for it.

We had just thanked a fellow tourist for taking a photo of us standing beside the nine-foot-tall bronze statue of the character Samantha from the 1960s TV show *Bewitched* when Millie turned to me and said, "I have a surprise for you."

"Everything's been a surprise."

"Where I'm about to take you really will be. I saved what I think is the best for last. Follow me!"

We had passed by the gothic-style building earlier and I'd wanted to go inside it then but didn't say anything to Millie. I knew she was on a mission to show me around Salem and I wasn't about to disrupt her plan.

"This is the Raven's Cauldron," she said, holding out her hand toward the bustling business. "You're going to love it more than anywhere else you've been to today."

"Why do you think that?"

"You'll see why."

As soon as I stepped through the entrance, I stopped, and my jaw dropped.

"Come on," Millie chuckled, grabbing my hand and pulling me out of the way of the steady flow of customers.

Glancing around again, I could only shake my head at what I was seeing. There was a coffee shop to my left, a bookstore straight ahead with a lounge area, and a wine bar to my right. The coffee shop was upscale with many bistro tables, chairs, and booths, and was abuzz with java junkies like Millie and me.

I was especially in awe of the ceiling of the bookstore. A shimmery celestial design of the sun, moon, stars, and planets was painted on top of a midnight-blue background. The stars trickled down the also midnight-blue walls, giving the interior of the bookstore an open yet cozy feeling. It was so dreamy looking too.

Unlike the coffee shop and bookstore, the inside of the wine bar wasn't as visible. There were two tall doors propped open with wooden barrels decorated with dried grapevines, fresh-looking grapes, and an assortment of wine bottles. I could partially see beyond those doors and noted dozens of people inside. Some of them were sitting on fancy red leather barstools while others were walking around, sipping on their glasses of wine and looking at the photos on the walls.

The Raven's Cauldron was an extraordinary place. Not only because of its appearance and what it offered customers, but also because of its atmosphere. The vibe in the air was relaxed and flowing just like the music that was playing.

"I'm sold," I said, looking back at Millie. "I could seriously hang out here for hours."

"I have on several occasions. I love that you can enjoy a cup of coffee or a glass of wine while sitting in the bookstore's lounge area, curled up with a juicy read. That's what I usually do when I come here."

"Speaking of a juicy read... I'd like to look for one before we leave. I finished my last one two weeks ago and am itching to jump into another steamy romance since my life is currently void of the real thing."

"I'll bet the bookstore has the perfect one for you, so let's go see what's on its shelves."

"I'm ready!"

While browsing through the romance section, Millie started talking to me about witchcraft again. She wanted to begin teaching me what she'd learned so far, being a "newbie" as she called herself.

"I'm all for it, especially after coming to Salem and seeing everything today," I said.

"That's great! Your first lesson in witchcraft is that it's not of the devil or evil in any way."

"I fully understand that now. I understand its basis is in nature."

"Yes. Your second lesson is that magic is real. It's all about working with nature's energy and our own to bring about the changes that we want in our lives. A spell is akin to a prayer. Whether you're sitting in a church pew or standing in the middle of nature, you're raising your energy by focusing on a specific thought-slash-wish. Then you send it off into the universe's or God's hands to take care of it."

"I've never thought about it like that, but you're right. Millie, what made you want to begin exploring all of this?"

"I became disillusioned with the faith that I grew up with. Once I began studying and practicing witchcraft, plus spending a lot of time in nature, I realized something about myself."

"What?"

"I feel everything in nature that I should've felt in church. It's like I'm finally home."

I smiled. "That's wonderful."

"And now, here's your third lesson: witches aren't all women. Some are men."

"You're joking."

"No, I'm not."

"Every depiction that I've seen of a witch was of a woman."

"You can thank the patriarchy for that—especially the hag depiction."

"Hmmm."

"What are you thinking?"

"I just had an image of a male witch pop into my head, but he wasn't wretched looking by any means."

"Knowing you, that image is probably X-rated."

"Borderline. He doesn't have anything on but a black hat and is holding a broom in front of his genitalia."

Millie and I both busted out laughing. After we got our composures back, I asked her a serious question. I wanted to know if she thought any of those accused of witchcraft in 1692 were actual witches.

"Yes, I do think some of them were," she said. "I think they secretly practiced what their pagan ancestors once did because that's what they were taught to do and it was all they knew. It was their *religion*. But those early people knew they had no choice but to outwardly go along with the religious changes at the time in order to survive. Inwardly, however, some refused to discard their pagan ways."

"I'm so thankful for the religious freedom that we have nowadays. We don't have to worry about anything."

"Yes and no. Because witchcraft is still viewed as evil by select groups of people, it's wise not to broadcast that you're a member of the black hat society. In a place like Salem, though, you don't have to be concerned. You can fly your witch flag twenty-four seven and no one would think anything of it."

I glanced up and down the aisle and surprisingly, it was still just the two of us. "Back to male witches," I said.

"What about them?"

"I would love to meet one today. I'm still having a hard time wrapping my brain around the fact that they exist."

"Understandable."

I held up my hand and grinned. "Fingers crossed for me to cross paths with a male witch before we leave Salem. It'd make my entire trip."

"Another lesson about witchcraft is that every word you speak is a spell and you just cast one by what you said."

"You truly believe that?"

"I do. Like I've already told you—your thoughts and words hold prayerful energy."

"Okay. I have another question for you. How do you know if someone is a witch? I ask only because there's nothing about you, appearance-wise, that drops clues about your black hat status. If you wore a necklace with a pentagram pendant on it or jewelry along that line, then it'd be a different story. You don't, though. So unless a person is wearing something occult-like or straight up tells me that they're a witch, then I wouldn't know they are one."

9

"That's exactly right. You wouldn't." Millie winked and then glanced over at the bookshelf in front of us, doing a double take. "And what a coincidence as you and I are standing here, talking about all of this."

"What is?"

She grabbed a book and held it up for me to see. "Have you ever heard of this?"

"No."

"I read it a couple of years ago and it's so good. I think you would thoroughly enjoy jumping into its pages."

"What's the story about?"

"A female witch whose first love returns to her life several years later and wants her back."

"Let me see the book." Millie handed it to me and I took a closer look at the front cover. Then I read the blurb on the back. "How steamy is this story?" I asked.

"Five-star steamy. There's one particular sex scene between the witch and her first love that happens in her kitchen during the middle of the night and..."

I held up my hand. "Don't tell me any more about it. I'm getting the book."

"You'll thank me later."

As Millie and I left the bookstore section of the Raven's Cauldron, she asked me if I was in the mood for coffee or wine.

"Wine," I said. "I'm interested in seeing the different brands offered here."

"They have a great selection from Napa Valley, Colorado, Texas...all over. But the Raven Crest brand is locally made by the Grey family."

"I've never heard of the brand or the family."

"Of course you haven't. The Greys are from Salem and they own this place, as well as several other businesses and properties around Essex County."

"Then I must try some of their wine."

"It's actually the son's wine. Gabriel. He makes it."

"Have you met him before?"

"Yes, a few years ago when I came here. He happened to be working in the wine bar that day and served me. I've seen him nearly every time that I've come here since then too. He's a super friendly guy and he's also one fine piece of eye candy."

"How old is he?"

"I would guess in his late twenties."

"Really?"

Millie grinned at me. "You're interested in meeting him, aren't you?"

"I am. It'd be nice to talk to some eye candy while we're here. I could have some flirty fun."

2

#captivated

Harper

As Millie and I were walking into the wine bar, I was immediately struck by all the beautiful décor that I hadn't been able to see from standing outside the entrance. Along with the fancy red leather barstools, there were also vintage armchairs and couches of all colors and designs scattered around the large room with thick area rugs in front of them. Antique coffee and end tables with antique lamps on them were other unique touches. So were the different-sized chandeliers hanging from the high ceiling—all of them giving off a warm glow.

I got caught up in looking at everything and didn't realize Millie was no longer standing by me until I turned to say something to her. I looked around and spotted her sitting at the bar with a glass of wine in her hand. However, my focus didn't stay on her for long. It went to the bartender talking to her.

Because of the big smile on his face and the animated way in which he was carrying on his conversation with Millie—using his hands—I got the impression that he'd known her for much longer than today. After watching him interact with her for about another minute, I started making my way to the bar.

"Found you," I said to Millie.

"Good timing! This is Gabriel Grey—the vintner of Raven Crest wine that I was telling you about." She motioned toward him and when I looked across the bar, he already had his eyes on me. "Gabriel, this is Harper Hewitt," Millie continued. "We work together at the hospital."

He gave me a nod and reached out his hand to shake mine. "It is very nice to meet you."

"It's very nice to meet you too," I said, mirroring his smile and giving him a nod in return.

The moment our hands touched, a bright spark shot up into the air from in between them and we both jerked them back.

"I apologize. That's what cooler weather will do for you," Gabriel chuckled.

Then we gave our handshake another try. This time, all I felt was the warmth of his skin on mine and the gentleness of his grasp.

"May I interest you in a glass of wine, Miss Hewitt?" he asked as we were letting go of each other.

"I would love one. And please call me Harper."

"Okay then—*Harper*. Do you prefer merlot as Millie does? Or chardonnay, cabernet sauvignon, sauvignon blanc..."

"Actually, malbec."

"We have several brands to choose from."

Gabriel handed me a list, but I didn't bother looking at it.

"I'm interested in trying yours. That is, if you make malbec," I said, sitting down beside Millie.

"I do make it. Give me just a moment and I will get some for you."

I nodded, and Gabriel turned to a wine rack behind the bar. Watching him, I thought about what Millie had said about him being one fine piece of eye candy. He really was. His tall stature and muscular build placed him in that category, along with his gorgeous thick hair. It was jet black, cut short on the sides and back, longer on the top, and finger-styled with what I guessed to be pomade since it was so shiny.

Gabriel's eyes were also at the top of the list of eye candy qualities and held my attention the moment I looked into them. They were the richest amber tone that I'd ever seen and they were surrounded by long lashes that made them appear lined with the blackest liner. But that wasn't all I'd noticed about Gabriel's eyes. They had an otherworldly look in them too, and it was mesmerizing.

Other things that caught my attention about the handsome vintner were his pierced ears, full cupid-bow lips, perfect pearl-white teeth, and the scruff on his face. It was as dark as the hair on his head and it shadowed his strong jawline, as well as encircled his very kissable-looking lips.

To complete the list was his voice. It dripped sex because of its depth and raspy sound. As Gabriel turned around, I was ready to hear it again.

"This is my malbec," he said.

I smiled at him and then looked at the bottle that he was holding. "I'll take a glass just going by the label. That's a beautiful crest with all the red roses and vines surrounding it."

"My sister Willow is the one who designed it. She's the artist in my family."

"And don't forget it," a woman said, walking past Gabriel behind the bar. Then she looked over her shoulder at him and stuck out her tongue.

After grinning at the woman, Gabriel turned his attention back to Millie and me. "That would be my sister."

The siblings looked identical except for their eye color. Willow's were aqua-green.

"Are you and your sister twins?" I asked.

"No, we're two years apart. I'm the oldest."

"You have really strong family genetics."

Gabriel briefly paused. "Yes, we do."

I watched him uncork the bottle of wine and pour a small amount into a beautifully etched crystal glass.

"Here," he said, handing it to me. "Try my malbec first. I want to be sure that you like it."

I swirled it around a few times, took a couple of whiffs and a couple of sips, and then looked back up at Gabriel. "That feels like silk gliding across my tongue. It is so smooth."

"Do you taste the hint of blackberry?"

"I do."

"What about the cherry?"

"Yes, that too. Also plum and vanilla."

Gabriel nodded and then asked me if I tasted the hint of tobacco. After taking another sip of his wine, I met his gaze again.

"I do taste it. It reminds me of pipe tobacco."

"So you like my malbec?"

"Very much so."

"Then please allow me to pour some more into your glass."

"Thank you."

"You're welcome," he said, dazzling me with his smile again.

After giving me much more than the regular five-ounce serving, Gabriel excused himself to wait on another customer. As soon as he walked off, I turned to Millie. She was grinning from ear to ear.

"So what do you think?" she asked.

"About the wine or Gabriel?"

"I already know what you think about his wine. Tell me your feelings about him."

To answer Millie, I acted like I was wiping drool off my mouth.

"That's what I thought," she chuckled.

"You weren't lying about his appearance but damn, his eyes. They pulled me in and wouldn't let go."

"Apparently, the feeling was mutual. Gabriel kept staring at you like you were at him."

I looked over at him, talking to the man sitting across the bar, completely in his element. He was super friendly, as Millie had said, and clearly enjoyed his work. I wondered if he'd also enjoy knowing what meeting him had done to me and was still doing.

"If only he was tingling all over like I am," I sighed, focusing on Millie again.

She snapped her head back in surprise. "Tingling?"

"Yes. Something like this happening to women that Gabriel meets is nothing new, I'm sure."

"Full disclosure—he had the same effect on me when we met the first time. I just chalked it up to him being a witch," Millie casually said and then took a sip of her merlot.

"Wait. What did you just say?"

"You heard me."

"How do you know? Did you ask him?"

"No."

"Did he tell you?"

"No."

"He's not wearing any kind of occult jewelry, so how do you know he's a witch?"

"I don't. But wouldn't it be fucking epic if he was?"

I shoved Millie on her arm. "You're such a jerk for messing with me like that."

"But it was so fun! The look on your face was priceless."

"Yeah, yeah. Back to your question... It would be fucking epic if Gabriel was a male witch, because meeting one was the main thing that I wanted today. But I'll take him like he is with that whole tall, dark, handsome, bad boy slash pirate air about him."

"Oh, I knew you would. As far as meeting a male witch, though—don't give up hope. The day is far from over."

Millie smiled and patted me on the back. When I looked over at Gabriel again, he was still busy, taking care of his customers. I liked watching him do it, too. I also liked what he had on.

He was wearing a collared, long-sleeve red shirt, black dress pants, black dress shoes, and a black bartender's apron with *The Raven's Cauldron* embroidered on it in red and white. If Gabriel took off the apron, unbuttoned his shirt a few buttons, rolled up his sleeves to his elbows, and posed just right, then he could grace the cover of *GQ* or any men's fitness magazine.

"Do you know if Gabriel is single?" I asked, focusing back on Millie.

"He said he was the last time I came here."

"How long ago was that?"

"Almost a month. Gabriel served me again and we started chatting as usual. I asked him about his relationship status, but not for myself of course. He's too young for me. I was just curious because going by his good looks and personality, I figured he had a girlfriend."

"I thought the same thing at first. But for him to look at me the way that he's been doing since I walked up to this bar, he couldn't possibly. Not unless he's the type of guy who stares at women despite having a girlfriend."

"That's not the Gabriel I know. I'd bet on him still being single."

"Maybe he's like me: a little lonely and in need of some hot and sweaty sex."

The moment I finished saying that, Willow walked by and she was smiling while cutting her eyes over at me. After she took a right through some swinging doors, I put my face in my hands.

"Oh my God, Willow just heard what I said about Gabriel," I mumbled.

"Yeah, I think she did too."

I peeked at Millie through my fingers. "If she did, I hope she doesn't tell him what I said."

"There's nothing we can do about it if she does."

I dropped my hands and sighed. "I am so sorry. I would never want to offend your vintner friend or his sister."

"Willow was smiling, so I don't think she was offended. She knows how good-looking her brother is and is probably used to hearing women talk about him in the way that you just did. And when it comes to Gabriel? I don't think he'd be offended knowing what you said about him. He's a man, and if I had to guess, he is a little lonely and in need of some hot and sweaty sex just like you are."

I looked over at him standing at the far end of the bar now, going over some paperwork on a clipboard and still looking so damn sexy. Then he unexpectedly looked up at me and tugged on his bottom lip with his teeth while grinning like a devil.

3

#familiar

Gabriel

"You felt her too, didn't you, Josephine?" I asked, reaching out to stroke the black feathers on her neck.

She craned her head toward me and cocked it to the side, eyeing me intently. Then she shook out her feathers and hopped over to her perch sitting on top of my desk. With a harrumph, she turned to face away from me.

"Oh. I'm getting the cold shoulder from a bird. I see how it is."

Josephine whipped her head back around and squawked at me for calling her a bird.

"You're right. I apologize," I said, holding my hands up in front of my chest. "You know I didn't mean it."

After making another disgruntled noise, Josephine settled down on her perch to take a nap. Then I walked over to the stained glass window in my office and stared at it while thinking about Harper Hewitt. Her last name was familiar to me, but I couldn't pinpoint why.

I sat back down at my desk to do some paperwork and had just finished it when Josephine woke up from her nap.

"Are you ready for your dinner, my love?" I asked her, and she clicked her beak twice to let me know she was.

"What will it be? Mixed nuts? Dried fruit? Both?" I continued as I opened the desk drawer that held her food.

Josephine pecked at the front of the drawer so I would open it wider and she could then tell me what she wanted. After I slid it open almost all the way, she touched her beak on both containers of what I had offered her for dinner.

"Mixed nuts and dried fruit, it is."

After filling her food dish, I watched her enjoy her meal as I swiveled back and forth in my chair, still trying to figure out why Harper's last name was familiar to me. Then my phone dinged and snapped me out of my pondering daze. My wine bar manager, Miranda, had sent me a text notifying me about a delivery that I'd been expecting.

"Excellent. That wine from New Orleans is here. Enjoy your dinner, darling. I'll be back to get you before I leave," I told Josephine. She cooed at me as she crunched a peanut.

Out in the wine bar, things were still as busy as ever. Glancing around, I noticed an attractive woman with long black hair, by one of the vintage sofas, smiling at a small child who had to be her daughter. Although the light from the chandeliers and antique lamps was dim, I could still see well enough to tell that the little girl was a carbon copy of the woman standing close to her.

Looking back at the bar, I saw Miranda speaking to a tall, blond fellow whom I immediately recognized and began walking toward.

"Mr. Kingston," I said when I reached him.

He looked up at me and matched my smile. "Mr. Grey! How are you, sir?"

I extended my hand to shake his. "I am well! I would be lying if I said I'm not surprised to see you. Do you always personally deliver your orders?"

"No, sir, I don't. But this being your first order and all, I wanted to make sure it arrived safely and on time. Plus, the missus has always wanted to take a trip up here, so I figured why not make a little family vacation out of it, you know?"

I nodded. "Well, it is an honor to meet a fellow vintner. How long will you all be in town?"

"We're planning to poke around Salem and Boston for the rest of the week before slowly making our way down the East Coast and back over to Louisiana."

Taylor looked over at the woman and little girl that I'd noticed and gestured for them to join us. The woman smiled, picked up her carbon copy, and started walking toward Taylor and me.

"That's your wife and daughter?" I asked.

"They are." Taylor beamed with pride.

"They look just alike."

"I know, but my daughter acts like me. It drives her mother crazy too."

"It's only fair," I chuckled.

"You're right about that. Mr. Grey, this is my wife, Alex, and our daughter, Autumn."

Alex gave me a nod and extended her right hand to me. "Pleasure to meet you, Mr. Grey."

"Please, Mr. Grey is my father. Call me Gabriel," I said, looking from her to Taylor. Then I held out my hand to shake Autumn's. "How do you do?"

She had her chin tucked and was shyly looking up at me from under the fringe of her long, dark eyelashes. Then she giggled, wrapped her hand around my first two fingers, and gave them an exaggerated shake. "I like your pretty lamps," she said.

"Why, thank you. Most of them are antiques, ah, really, really old."

"Like Grandpa," Taylor said as he leaned in toward his precious daughter. She giggled again, and then Taylor kissed her forehead and asked if she was hungry.

"Mmhmm," she said.

"I guess we should go find something for you to eat then."

Taylor started tickling Autumn's ribs and she squirmed around in her mother's arms, squealing and laughing at the same time.

"Okay, you two," Alex sighed, moving Autumn away from Taylor to her other hip. "We'll wait outside while you boys finish up your paperwork. It was very nice to meet you, Gabriel."

"Likewise. I hope you enjoy your time in Salem. Please let me know if there's anything that I can do to add to your stay," I said.

"Actually, do you know where we could buy some tickets for the Loreena McKennitt concert?"

"It's a free concert. No tickets needed."

"What? Are you sure?"

"Yes ma'am, I'm quite sure. The concert venue is on my family's property. I'll be out there helping run the concessions. Do you need a map to get there?"

"Please."

I looked over at Miranda and she pulled a copy of the map out from under the bar and handed it to me. "Thank you."

"You're welcome, boss."

"Okay, Alex and Taylor, you'll go all the way down here," I said, pointing to the entrance of the venue on the map. "Then you'll park here." I tapped the spot. "It is a bit of a walk from the parking lot to the seating area, so I would wear comfortable shoes if I were you."

"Thank you so much! I'm so excited! This is a dream come true for me," Alex said.

"I am very happy that I could help. Come find me when you get there so I can take care of your family's concession needs."

"Oh, you don't need to do that," Taylor said, putting his arm around Alex's waist. "You've been more than helpful already. We're happy to pay for anything we get. After all, you are running a business and we know what that entails."

"Please, I insist. It's the least that I can do after you drove all this way to deliver my order. You'll be guests of the Grey family at the event. As my mother says: 'And that's that.'"

I stood up even straighter and folded my arms as I spoke her words, imitating her whenever she recited her favorite argument-ender. We all laughed, and then Alex and Autumn began heading toward the exit—Alex shaking her head and smiling all the while.

"You have no idea how happy you've just made my wife. I cannot thank you enough," Taylor said.

"It's really not a problem. Let's finish up so you can get that little Autumn some food."

Taylor reached into his pants pocket and then handed me a form with my wine order printed on it. "Check that to make sure it's correct and also look at the crates right quick. If everything's good, then sign the paper and I'll be on my way."

It only took me a moment to scan over both. "Everything is accounted for."

"Great!"

I signed the form and gave it back to Taylor. "It has been a pleasure. I hope you and your family have a good time at the concert," I said, reaching out to shake his hand again.

"I know we will, and thank you again for your generosity."

"Of course."

After Taylor left, I turned to Miranda, who was still standing behind the bar. "How staffed are we tonight?" I asked.

"We're solid. You can go if you want. We'll be fine."

She handed me the clipboard that held the day's schedule. I nodded as I read each employee's name listed and the times they were scheduled to clock in and out.

"Okay then. Just call me if..."

"If we need help? I know. Get out of here, boss."

I chuckled at her. "Thanks. You're the best."

"No sir. I *learned* from the best," Miranda said, bowing to me.

I sighed as I rolled my eyes, and then laughed at her ridiculousness. She smirked and went back to putting away wine bottles.

Walking back to my office, I glanced at my watch. It was almost 5:00 p.m. *If we hurry, we can beat my parents to the house and snoop in the library without them knowing*, I thought to Josephine.

When I opened my office door, I saw her perched at the top of my coat rack. Then I glanced over at her bowl on my desk to make sure I had given her enough time to finish eating her dinner. Seeing only crumbs left, I raised an eyebrow at Josephine.

"Somebody is trying to get thick for winter. I'm going to have to start working out more if I'm to carry you around all season," I teased her.

She hopped down from the coat rack, onto my right shoulder, and then turned her head away from me and stuck her beak up in the air. I grinned at her and pulled the side of her head to my mouth, kissing her soft feathers.

"I love you, silly bird. Let's go get into some trouble."

Josephine squawked and fluffed her wings in excitement.

• • •

The drive to my parent's house was one of my favorites. Josephine normally preferred to fly above me as I drove, but the air had a bite in it and there was a threat of rain so she chose to ride in the car with the heated seat on for this trip.

Rounding the last bend in the road before crawling up my parents' half-mile-long driveway, I admired the colors of the leaves in the trees on the edge of their property. The vibrant colors stood out in contrast to the silvery backdrop of the New England sky during autumn.

After putting my car in park and killing the engine, I stepped out and took a deep breath. The air out here smelled different than the air in the city. Cleaner. Damper. More earthy. It reminded me of playing outside as a child. It reminded me of sweaters, wet shoes, and hot chocolate.

I walked around to the passenger side door to retrieve Josephine. After placing her on my right shoulder, I said, "Smell that? Smells like adventure." I winked at her and she clicked her beak at me in disapproval.

As I was closing my car's door, I looked up at my childhood home and took in all of its glory. It was a mansion—dark and mysterious with well-manicured flower beds full of blood-red roses. The place had been in my family since it was built. Electricity and plumbing were added after they were invented. Additional wings came along too, as the family grew, and remodels were done as ownership transferred from one generation of Greys to another. If a house could talk, this one would tell you about entertaining guests for days and also captivate you with its tales of the shenanigans that those guests carried out, as did Grey family members.

Walking up the front steps, I noticed how weathered the stones on the front of the house looked. Moss was growing on them, reaching farther up than I had ever seen it before. It added to the mystery of the house. Was it abandoned? Was it full of witches like the townspeople said? Did an old hermit who would yell at me for stepping on his lawn live here?

"I bet that's why they let the moss stay," I said to Josephine as I smiled to myself.

After retrieving my keys from my pants pocket, I inserted the well-aged skeleton key on my keychain into the antique lock on the front door and slowly turned the cast iron doorknob. The heavy oak door creaked and groaned as I pushed it open, almost as if it bemoaned having to do its one job.

The smell of the house filled my nostrils and I was instantly transported back in time for a brief moment. I could hear the giggles of children and the clomping of their shoes on the wooden floors as they ran through the halls. It felt like it had been both a few months ago and a thousand years ago that I had been one of those children giggling and running through this home. So many things had changed since those days of innocence and carefree joy.

After closing the front door behind me, I started walking toward the library. I had to pass through the kitchen and could already smell an enticing aroma in the air. I reached out to feel the oven door with the back of my hand and discovered it was warm.

"Mother baked. I wonder what's going on," I said to Josephine.

She hopped down from my shoulder onto the island, to get one of the treats from the special jar that my mother kept stocked for her. The metal lid hit the marble countertop like a drummer hitting his favorite cymbal on the last note of a song.

"Mmm, fresh maple cookies," I said, smiling at Josephine.

She clucked at me and pecked my hand as I was reaching into her snack jar. After pocketing a few of the small leaf-shaped cookies, I set one down on the island. Josephine picked it up, hopped back up onto my shoulder, and started eating her treat, making a mess as usual. I brushed the crumbs off my coat and then started down the hallway off the kitchen, toward the east wing of the house.

When I reached the library, I pulled open the French doors and stepped inside. Josephine hopped down onto the leather armchair sitting to the left of the doors, next to the fireplace.

"If you scratch that leather, Father will have you stuffed," I said, looking down my nose at her.

After shifting her weight to her left foot, she picked up her right one and slowly pulled her shiny, black claws across the seat of the chair, never breaking eye contact with me.

"Well, now you've done it! To the taxidermist with you, demon!"

Josephine squawked and then flew up to perch on the curtain rod hanging above the wall-length windows. After blowing a raspberry at her, I turned my attention to the wall of books. Everything on the lower shelves was newer and not what I was looking for, so I rolled the ladder over to the center of the wall and started climbing. Josephine clicked her beak twice, warning me to be careful.

"You're not my mother," I shot back at her, continuing to climb. She clicked her beak once more. "Yes ma'am."

When I reached the top shelf, I wiped away the cobwebs and dust that had accumulated. Then I pulled my cellphone from my pants pocket and turned on the flashlight to read the book spines.

"Spells and potions, grimoire, grimoire, herbs and medicines, grimoire, anatomy, tinctures, grimoire. Nope, nope, and nope. Where is it?" I muttered to myself.

"Where is what, son?" my mother asked.

I gasped and grabbed my chest. She had nearly startled me out of my skin. When I looked down at her standing in the middle of the library, she started cackling. Josephine did too, then flew down to alight on my mother's outstretched hand. I shook my head at both of them and began making my way down the ladder while they nuzzled each other.

"If I'd known you were coming over, I would have had the house ready for you," my mother went on to say as she was walking over to the fireplace. Then she bent down to light the artificial logs in the hearth.

"It really wasn't a planned trip. I decided to come here after meeting someone at the wine bar earlier whose last name is familiar to me. I wanted to see if I could find it in the book," I said, jumping the last few feet down to the floor.

"Which book?"

My mother was being coy with me, so in turn, I shot her the disapproving look that I'd inherited from her. "You know which book."

"I'm sure your father knows where it is. We can go ask..."

"No, that's okay," I said, cutting her off. "It's not that important."

My mother dipped her chin down and looked up at me from under her eyebrows. "You can't avoid him forever."

"I know. But I can put it off a little longer," I said, rolling the ladder back into its place.

Josephine made a noise in her throat.

"No one asked for your input," I told her.

She clicked her beak and then hopped up to my mother's right shoulder.

"Gabriel, you could be nicer to her. She does everything that you ask of her," my mother said, holding out her left arm for me to take.

"I do believe this is a one-sided case, your honor. I object," I said as I looped my arm through hers.

"Overruled."

She grinned at me, and then Josephine stuck out her tongue and ruffled her feathers.

"Women," I sighed.

4

#stranger

Harper

"So are you game?" Millie asked me.

"Sure. I have nothing else to do this evening."

"Great! It's going to be late when the concert ends, so I'm going to try to find a hotel or B&B for us. I don't want to have to drive back to Boston during the middle of the night."

"I don't blame you. Hey, let me see that concert info again."

Millie set her fork down on her plate and grabbed the flyer out of her purse, hanging on the corner of her chair. "There you go," she said, handing it to me.

I reread it, still unable to believe who the Grey family had been able to get to perform tonight.

"Loreena McKennitt," I sighed.

"That's the Greys for you."

"It seems that they'd be charging *something* for the concert."

"No. Only for food and drinks. It's their way of giving back to the community. They've always done that in one way or another."

"And the concert is being held on the Grey's property on the outskirts of Salem?"

"Yes."

"You mentioned that you went out there on Halloween last year, but not who performed."

"It was Lindsey Stirling."

"Oh my God, she's as amazing as Loreena McKennitt."

"I just thought of something, and now I have to ask how you came to be such a fan of Loreena McKennitt. Her music is Celtic/pagan-themed and I can't imagine your parents allowing you to listen to it."

"I'd never heard of her until a little over a year ago when I was searching for a romance movie to watch on Hulu one night. I came across *Ever After* with Drew Barrymore and absolutely loved it. I also loved the song from the trailer. It's one of Loreena McKennitt's and it resonated with me for some reason."

"She has so many fantastic songs. And that movie? I loved it too. I think it came out in the late nineties, if I'm not mistaken."

"Yeah, it was nineteen ninety-eight."

"Now I'm going to have to watch it again, just like *Hocus Pocus*," Millie chuckled. Then she asked me if I wanted to try to find a Halloween costume to wear to the concert.

Before answering her, I glanced around at the people sitting at the tables close by us. They already had on their costumes—all of them apparently having arrived in Salem in total Halloween spirit, ready to enjoy the many festivities.

At the table to my left sat a couple dressed up as a priest and a pregnant nun, which I thought was hilarious. The table to my right had a mom and dad vampire, along with their three vampire kids, and at the table directly behind Millie, there sat two guys. One of them was dressed up as Captain America and the other as Hulk.

"I'd be willing to get a witch hat," I said, focusing back on Millie.

"Not the whole costume?"

"No, a hat will do. I want to be able to walk around without having to worry about tripping over the hem of a dress or skirt."

"Okay. We'll go to the store around the corner."

"Pandora's Box?"

"Yes."

"It looked like a really cool place when we walked by it earlier."

"If you could've held your pee a little longer then we could've already gone in and checked out all of their cool merchandise."

"But I couldn't hold it any longer after drinking that bottle of Gatorade that Gabriel gave me."

"Oh, I know. I'm just teasing you. It was really thoughtful of him to look after you like he did. Caffeinated Gatorade *and* crackers to sober you up."

"It was really thoughtful of him. I still don't know what to think about his wine's effect on me, though. That one glass of malbec had me feeling so tipsy, and you know I'm not a lightweight."

"It wasn't the only thing that contributed to your tipsiness, Harper. It was also Gabriel. Mainly him, I think."

I grinned. "Maybe."

"I have no doubt about it. The way that you two kept looking at each other and talking, smiling, and laughing flooded your systems with dopamine and norepinephrine. Both of you were flying high and it was so much fun to watch."

"Glad you enjoyed it."

"I really did. You and Gabriel were adorable. Young lust at its best."

"I couldn't help but lust after him. He's a gorgeous man. On top of that, he's polite, intelligent, attentive, comical... I could go on and on."

"I know you could. And yes, Gabriel is all of that."

"Millie, it felt so good to feel that fire again toward someone although it was short-lived."

"Short-lived? Hell, you're still feeling it. You haven't stopped glowing."

I reached up and touched my cheeks. "What can I say? I'm under Gabriel's spell."

"As much as he's under yours."

"I wonder if he's going to the concert tonight."

"I'm still wondering why you didn't ask him about it. After all, he is the one who gave us the flyer."

"I didn't think about it because he just...overwhelms me."

"If he is there, what are you going to do?"

I shrugged. "Talk to him again if he isn't too busy. Lust after him some more."

"Say that he is there and isn't too busy and before your conversation with him ends, he asks you to go on a date. What would you say?"

"He can't do that."

"Why not?"

"Because his life is here and mine is in Boston."

"Allow me to remind you that the two cities are only twenty-five miles apart."

"Gabriel is extremely busy. And with my work schedule—well, no."

"Be honest with me, Harper. This pushback that you're doing really has to do with Daniel, doesn't it?"

I paused and then nodded yes.

"It's been four months since you ended things with him," Millie continued. "Don't you think it's time to open your heart again?"

"Gabriel is an incredibly desirable man that I will be fantasizing about for months to come after we leave here today."

"That's not an answer."

"It's not the one that you want."

"What I want is for my friend to trust the universe. It gave you a big sign today that there are still good things in life and they're there for the taking if you want them."

"The only thing that I want to take is another bite of this pizza."

Millie narrowed her hazel eyes at me. "You are so stubborn."

"And you have no room to talk."

"True. But do me a favor."

"What?"

"Be watchful for more signs from the universe. It's always trying to get our attention and show us where we need to go in life."

I told Millie that I would do as she had asked but left out that I would also be skeptical of any supposed "signs."

We finished eating, paid for our meals, and then got up to leave Bambolina Pizza Restaurant. On our way to the exit, chills began crawling up the back of my neck. As I was reaching up to rub it, I looked to my right and saw a man sitting alone at a corner table. He was familiar and then it suddenly hit me as to why. He was identical to the man who'd been randomly showing up in my dreams over the past few months.

Right before I pulled my eyes away from the stranger, he smiled at me and nodded his head once. As soon as Millie and I left the restaurant, I stepped to the side to take a moment to try to make sense of what had just happened because it was surreal.

"Harper, what's going on?" Millie asked.

"Um, remember those dreams I've been having?"

"Yes, the ones with the 'angel-man' in them, as you call him. Wish he'd show up in my dreams."

"Well, I just saw someone who could pass as his twin."

"Where?"

"Inside those doors and to the left," I said, pointing at the restaurant's entrance.

Millie smiled. "Seriously?'

"Seriously."

"So he has the same ice-blue eyes and short blond hair?"

"Dark blond, but yes."

"Sexy razor stubble on his face?"

"Yes, Millie."

"Is he tall and built too?"

"He was sitting down, so I don't know about his height. But yes, he's built from the waist up."

"Was he wearing Victorian-styled men's clothing and a black top hat like the man in your dreams?"

"Good grief, no."

"What a coincidence that would be. I've still got to see him," Millie chuckled. Then she turned to walk back to the entrance. I grabbed her arm and stopped her, though.

"You're not going back in there to gawk."

"I just want a little peek."

"I know you. You'd do much more than that. I can see you going over to that man and sitting down at his table to talk to him."

"Now, I wouldn't take it quite that far."

As I shook my head no at Millie, she started laughing and then took off toward the entrance of Bambolina's again. I was unable to stop her this time, so I just watched her.

When she stepped inside the doorway, she looked to her left and then peered back at me and shrugged her shoulders. I walked over to take a look for myself: he was gone, the corner table was clean, and I didn't know what to think.

"Millie, he was there. I swear. And we would've seen him leave because he would've walked past us."

"Maybe there's another exit here and your angel-man's twin left through it."

I sighed. "Maybe. This is all just so fucking weird."

"Good weird, right?"

"I suppose. It's got me a little unnerved is all."

Millie hugged me. "You're fine, Harper. Let's go back to my car so I can start trying to find somewhere for us to stay tonight. Then we'll go to Pandora's Box."

• • •

Millie and I tried on several witch hats and laughed so hard while looking in a mirror, making funny faces and wicked ones at each other. The hat that she decided to buy was solid black with purple tulle wrapped around the base of the cone and little purple crystal balls printed on the rest. The one that I got was glittery black with black tulle and a big silver crescent moon and star on the front.

Before we left Pandora's Box, I asked an employee to take a photo of Millie and me with our new purchases on so that I could add it to my scrapbook later. We were now on our way to the concert venue and my stomach was filled with butterflies.

"Jesus, you weren't lying," I said, pointing ahead of us. I'd just spotted the end of the long line of cars that Millie had said would be out here on this rural road.

"Get ready to settle in for the wait."

"Fingers crossed that it passes by quickly."

"I'm crossing mine too."

We had come to a standstill and were talking about next week's work schedule when someone tapped on the passenger side window, making both of us jump. To my total surprise, it was Gabriel. He smiled and waved at us, we smiled and waved back, and I lowered my window.

"Good evening, ladies," he said, leaning down.

"You just scared the shit out of us!" Millie chuckled.

"I apologize. I did not mean to."

"I know you didn't."

"I see you're on your way to the Loreena McKennitt concert."

"Yes, we are."

"I was wondering if you'd be interested in following me to a cut-through road that will get you to the concert venue faster."

I glanced at Millie to see her grinning like a Cheshire cat.

"That'd be great! Thank you!" she said. "But first, I want you to tell me how you knew it was Harper and me sitting in this car. You walked up from behind us, right?"

"Yes, I did. I also happened to see the two of you getting into this fire-engine-red Mustang in front of Bambolina's earlier, while I was running an errand. You stand out."

Gabriel looked straight at me while saying that last part and my stomach did a flip.

"Ah, I suppose my car does stand out a bit. Where are you parked?" Millie asked.

"On the side of the road, not far behind you. See the cut-through road over there and the gate?" Gabriel pointed ahead of us, to the right, and sure enough, there was a metal gate with a winding dirt road beyond it. "I'm going to pull up beside you, and then you can follow me."

In the brief amount of time that he had been standing beside Millie's car, he'd gravitated closer to it without me realizing it until there was only about a foot and a half of space between us. I could smell his cologne now and liked it. A lot. It was earthy and musky and masculine.

"Do you mind telling me the name of the cologne that you're wearing?" I asked.

Gabriel looked straight at me again and gave me another one of his perfect pearl-white smiles. "It isn't cologne."

"Then what is it?"

"A blend of essential oils that I made."

"You're into essential oils?"

"I am."

"Well, whatever is in that blend smells really good on you."

"Thank you. The perfume that you're wearing smells really good on you. I noticed it when you were at the wine bar."

"It's actually body cream."

"I smell hints of vanilla, amber, and musk."

"What about the hint of jasmine? It's lighter than the others, but it's there."

Gabriel slowly leaned closer to me as I tilted my head to the side to expose my neck. Then he breathed me in.

"Yes, I do smell it," he said, backing away. "Your cream mixes well with your body's chemistry."

He continued staring into my eyes like I was his, but neither of us said another word. It felt like time had slowed down, allowing this quiet and intimate moment that I hadn't seen coming. But it was here and it was happening and it was... Dare I say it? Yes. It was magical.

Someone in the line of cars honked their horn, startling Gabriel and me. We grinned at each other almost shyly and then he looked over at Millie.

"I guess we should go now," he said.

"One more question and then we can."

"Okay then."

"Do you always attend the concerts that your family hosts?"

"Yes."

"Huh. I've never seen you at any of the ones that I've been to before."

"I hang out in the background to be sure all goes smoothly. Help out wherever and however I can."

"That makes sense. Plus, it's a huge section of land out there."

Gabriel nodded in agreement, patted the passenger side door, and told us that he was going to get his car. As he walked off, I watched him in the side mirror for several seconds, and then looked over at Millie and sighed.

"I could've sliced the sexual tension in the air between you and Gabriel just now," she said.

"I know."

"Please tell me that you recognize this second sign from the universe."

"To open my heart to a good thing with the last name of Grey?"

"Yes."

"It would be so easy to read Gabriel showing up here as a sign to do just that, but it's nothing more than a coincidence. We're all on our way to the concert."

"Harper, I'm telling you that there's more to this."

"Neither of us knows for certain if Gabriel is single or even interested in getting to know me beyond today. He's just been having some flirty fun with me like I've been having with him. It means nothing other than we're both just horny."

"Would you like to take a bet on him being single and also being extremely interested in getting to know you beyond today?"

Before I could answer Millie, she peered over my shoulder and waved. I turned my head and saw Gabriel sitting in the driver's seat of a sporty black Land Rover Range Rover. He motioned for Millie and me to follow him, she pulled out of the line of cars and the three of us began heading toward the gate that Gabriel had pointed out.

After opening it with an apparent remote control that he had with him, he drove through and Millie followed. Once Gabriel closed the gate behind us, he led the way to an area reserved for those working the event this night. Millie parked next to him and we put on our witch hats as soon as we got out of her car. When Gabriel saw us, he threw his head back and started chuckling.

"Well, well, well!" he said. "If it isn't Salem's prettiest two witches!"

Millie and I both thanked him and curtsied, making his smile grow even bigger.

"Do you like our hats?" Millie asked him.

"Yes! Those are great! Did you get them today?"

"We did, at Pandora's Box."

"Where's your hat, Gabriel?" I teased.

"At my house."

"You didn't want to wear it on this festive night?"

"I only wear mine when it's a full moon."

"I see. Would you happen to dance naked under the full moon?"

Gabriel glanced down at my lips. "I've been known to do that on occasion."

"Interesting."

"What about you?"

"I've never danced naked anywhere except for inside my apartment when I have music playing."

"You should try it outdoors sometime, with or without music. It's quite freeing."

"Noted."

We continued looking at each other without saying anything else just like we had less than fifteen minutes earlier. Then

Millie cleared her throat and broke the trance that Gabriel had me in all over again.

"Harper, are you ready to go explore this magnificent place?" she asked.

"Um, sure. I'd love to."

"I'm going to get my cargo unloaded," Gabriel said.

"Cargo?" Millie asked.

"Wine."

"Do you need some help?"

"Thank you, but I've got a dolly for that. You and Harper go enjoy yourselves."

Vintner Grey stole a quick glance at me and then stepped over to his car and opened the hatch. Inside were several crates of wine.

"Is any of your malbec in there, by chance?" I asked.

"Yes."

"Good! I'm looking forward to enjoying some more of it. And if you don't mind, I'd like to buy a couple of bottles to take home with me."

"I can arrange that, but there'll be no charge. It's my gift to you, being that it's your first time coming to Salem."

"That's very generous. Thank you, Gabriel."

"It's my pleasure. Once you're done looking around, come see me. Both of you," he said, looking back and forth between Millie and me. "I'll have the malbec and merlot ready to pour."

5

#coincidences

Harper

People were everywhere, walking around the Grey family's property, and they were all jovial. The vibe in the air was electric and the sun had just dipped below the horizon. Twilight had arrived and the stage where Loreena McKennitt would soon be performing was ready. I was so excited too.

"You just can't stop smiling, can you?" Millie asked.

I smiled even bigger. "Nope."

"What an incredible day this has been for you."

"It truly has been."

"I've thoroughly enjoyed watching you experience Salem."

"I can see why you come back so often."

"It's a relaxing getaway for me."

"The next time you feel like venturing over here, let me know. I'd love to accompany you again."

"Will do! What's your favorite location that we visited today?"

"I actually have three: the Witch Trials Memorial, the Raven's Cauldron, and out here," I said, looking around again.

"Does any one of them lean toward being your *most* favorite?"

"That's a tough question because they're each so unique. But if I had to choose a *most* favorite, I'd go with the Raven's Cauldron."

"Because of its glorious bookstore?"

"That and the glorious bartender who served me some of his glorious wine earlier."

"Speaking of him... You never answered me about taking my bet on him being single and wanting to get to know you beyond today."

"I'm not going to either."

"Why?"

I cut my eyes over at Millie and grinned. "I'm just not."

"Could it be because you know you'd lose the bet?"

"Maybe."

"Bullshit! There's no maybe about it. You know I'm right about Gabriel on all accounts and now I'm wondering what you're going to do about it."

"Nothing other than wait and see how the rest of this evening goes."

"Don't you mean wait and see if the universe sends you another sign telling you to open your heart again?"

I stopped walking and stared at the western horizon with its mix of ebbing warm colors. Then I focused back on Millie. "It's already open."

"I knew it was. I know Gabriel's is too. It's so obvious."

"Millie, this all came out of nowhere."

"And that is what makes it so sweet. Let me finish showing you around, and then we'll go get a glass of wine."

I smiled. "Okay then."

• • •

As we were approaching the open-front building where the main bar was located, I spotted Gabriel. He was busy helping his employees fill the customers' orders of the different wines and beers being served. It was easy to see that he enjoyed his job and took a lot of pride in it, as he should have. He was a hard worker and a highly skilled winemaker.

Standing in line with Millie about twenty feet away from the bar, I kept watching Gabriel taking care of business. Then he unexpectedly looked up, smiled at me, and then went back to what he'd been doing. Several customers later, he greeted Millie and me.

"And here's Salem's prettiest two witches again," he said. "I have your malbec and merlot ready for you."

He picked up two half-full stemless wine glasses off the counter behind him and handed them to us. After we thanked him, Millie took a sip of her wine but I just kept watching Gabriel.

"Is everything okay?" he asked.

"Yes. Everything is wonderful." I held up my glass toward him and he grinned, then focused on someone or something behind me.

"Hey, Taylor, Alex, and Autumn! I'm so glad you were able to make it out here tonight," he said.

I looked over my shoulder to see an exceptionally tall man like Gabriel, holding the hand of the woman standing beside him. He was carrying a raven-haired little girl on his hip who looked identical to the woman. Just a younger version was all.

"We are too. I really appreciate you inviting us," the man said with a very noticeable Southern accent.

"Of course! How are you doing, Miss Autumn?" Gabriel asked the little girl.

"Good," she said in her sweet voice.

"Taylor, I'd like to introduce you and your family to my two friends here. This is Millie Dupree and Harper Hewitt. Millie and Harper, this is Taylor, Alex, and Autumn Kingston."

We all greeted each other and shook hands. Even Autumn's tiny one. She was adorable, not only with her manners but also in her witch costume. It matched her mother's.

"Taylor is a fellow vintner from New Orleans and was kind enough to personally deliver some of his wine to me today," Gabriel told Millie and me.

"Do you sprinkle a little voodoo into your bottles of wine before corking them?" Millie teased Taylor.

"No voodoo," he chuckled. "But Alex does cast her own spell of sorts, blessing my wine."

I couldn't tell if he was joking or serious, so I looked over at Alex to see if she was smiling like him. She wasn't. She was straight-faced and staring at me. Then she took off her hat, handed it to Taylor, and reached for the silver chain hanging around her neck.

"Harper, I'd like to give you my necklace," she said, slipping it over her head and holding it up in front of me.

"Um, why?"

"You need it for protection."

I jerked my head back in surprise. "Protection from what?"

"I don't know, but something inside me told me to give it to you. The pendant is black tourmaline. It's a stone that's been used since ancient times to shield against negative spirits and destructive forces."

I stared at Alex for a long moment. "Are you a witch?" I finally asked.

"Yes. I come from a long line of them."

"I see."

"I know all of this probably sounds really strange to you and you may even be worried now, but don't be. Giving you my necklace is just a precaution. One can never be too safe in guarding oneself against the seen, as well as the unseen. So may I?" she asked, motioning to put her necklace on me.

I nodded yes and took off my witch hat. Then Alex slipped the silver chain over my head.

"Thank you," I said, reaching up to touch it.

"You're welcome."

Alex smiled and gently rubbed my arm. As she was stepping away from me, I looked over at Taylor.

"Are you also a witch?" I asked.

"No, I'm not. The only thing magical about me is Alex and our little girl here." He tickled Autumn on her side, making her giggle.

"Well, this has been enlightening, to say the least."

Taylor and Alex chuckled, and then I heard Gabriel say my name from behind me. I turned around to see him holding up a bottle of Raven Crest malbec.

"Let me have your glass," he said, reaching out for it. I handed it to him and he filled it nearly to the rim.

"Wow. That's a lot."

"I think you need it."

"I think you're right."

"Just sip it, though. Okay?"

"I will."

"If you get light-headed like you did at the Raven's Cauldron, then come see me. I have some Gatorade and crackers here too."

"Do you always bring them out here with you?"

"No. I brought them in case you came to the concert and needed them."

We smiled at each other, and then Gabriel poured some more merlot into Millie's glass. When we tried to pay for our wine, Gabriel waved us off.

"There's no charge," he said. "And Harper, I have those two bottles of malbec set aside for you. I'm also sending a bottle of Bayou Vineyards cabernet home with you. You too, Millie. I want you both to try Taylor's wine. It is excellent."

Millie and I thanked him, and then I turned my attention to Taylor again.

"I'm excited to try your cabernet," I said.

"I hope you enjoy it. It's Alex's favorite of all the varieties that I make. She says it's smooth as silk."

"It is!" she added.

"Gabriel's malbec is also smooth as silk and so flavorful."

"Now I'm going to have to try some."

Millie and I again told the Kingstons how nice it was to meet them, then excused ourselves to start heading over to the concert stage. Before walking off, I looked back at Gabriel. His amber eyes were already on me and they were sparkling.

• • •

"So how do you feel about what happened with Alex Kingston back there?" Millie asked.

"Obviously, I was taken aback by her wanting to give me her necklace. What did it the most, though, was hearing her so matter-of-factly confirm that she's a witch *and* comes from a long line of them. I can only imagine her abilities."

"Me too."

"It's interesting to me how Taylor has just accepted who Alex is and what she does. Until I met them, I'd never thought about a witch and a non-witch co-existing."

"It's no different from one partner in a relationship attending a church of whatever denomination and the other partner choosing not to."

"Well, Alex and Taylor have clearly made their different approaches to spirituality work. You can tell how happy they are, and their little girl is the cutest thing."

"Yeah, she is. She's a daddy's girl too."

"That was easy to see and so was how much Taylor adores Autumn, as well as Alex. I would love to have what they have."

"You certainly deserve it."

"So do you."

"I've experienced great happiness, Harper. With Owen, it didn't last a lifetime like I'd hoped, but that's how relationships go sometimes. People grow apart and that's what happened to us."

"You've told me that it's time for me to open my heart. What about yours? Your divorce was over a year ago."

"My heart is open—but it's open to only me for now. I'm enjoying being single and only having to take care of myself. I don't have to pick up after a man, cook for him, wash his clothes, fuck him when I'm not in the mood, or clean his piss and shit off the toilet."

"That's true," I chuckled.

"Honestly though... If you have a partner who loves you and treats you like you need them to, then you don't mind doing domestic things for them and having sex with them when you're tired or whatever. But when your partner expects you to do all of that, it's a whole different story."

"Yes, it is."

"Enough of that. Back to Alex Kingston."

"What about her?"

"Do you like her necklace?"

"Yes! It's beautiful, but my having it isn't necessary. I don't feel threatened by anything out here. I didn't tell Alex that because I didn't want to seem ungrateful for her gift or her concern."

"I don't think she was only referring to negative spirits and destructive forces possibly being out here on the Grey's property. She meant those spirits or people could be anywhere and at any time."

I shrugged. "I'm not worried about it."

"I know you're not, but please do me and yourself a favor."

"What?"

"Keep that necklace on."

"Do you really believe it has the ability to protect me?"

"Yes."

"I'll keep it on then. For now."

When we reached the concert area, every seat was occupied except for the ones in the last three rows. Frustrated, I looked around and then saw an embankment to the left of the stage. There were people sitting and standing on it, and it was exactly where I wanted to be to take in the show. Millie and I wouldn't be much closer to the stage, but the vantage point would make up for it.

"Look up there," I said, pointing at the open area.

"Is that where you want us to go?"

"Yes."

"Then come on!"

We found a spot, sat down on the grass, and toasted each other. A few minutes later, Loreena McKennitt's band came onto the stage and began warming up, prompting everyone in attendance to rise to their feet.

"Oh my God, Millie! This is really happening," I said, shaking her arm.

"I know it is!"

"Let's take a quick selfie with the stage in the background."

"Okay. And by the way, I get a copy of all the photos that you've taken today, including the ones taken of us."

"Of course you do!"

I snapped our photo and we continued chatting and sipping on our glasses of Gabriel's divine wine. When Loreena McKennitt's band began playing the intro of "All Souls Night," I scanned the stage looking for the Celtic/pagan queen but couldn't see her anywhere. Then she appeared from the right, draped in a long black gown with her ginger hair flowing, singing in her beautiful soprano voice. Watching her felt surreal, but so much about this day had.

The song had just reached its midpoint when I became chilled all over. I couldn't understand why. I had on a sweater dress that reached mid-thigh, and also thick stockings and knee-high boots. Until now, I'd been comfortable.

"What's going on?" Millie asked, leaning over to me.

"Nothing."

"Are you sure? You have an irritated look on your face."

"I'm just a little cold is all."

Millie nodded at my glass of wine. "That's still half-full. Down it. The surge of alcohol in your system will warm you up."

She grinned at me and I did as she'd suggested. I drank every drop of what was left of Gabriel's malbec. Afterward, I told Millie that I was going to dispose of my glass.

As I was walking toward the table, chills began crawling up the back of my neck and I shivered all over. After handing my empty glass to the attendee, I thanked her and turned around to go rejoin Millie. I hadn't made it very far when someone tapped me on my right shoulder. When I saw who'd done it, I gasped and stopped walking. It was him—the man that I had seen at Bambolina's, sitting alone at a corner table. The man who looked identical to the one in my dreams.

I continued staring up at him and he kept his ice-blue eyes glued to mine. "Who are you?" I finally asked.

He didn't say a word. Instead, he stepped all the way up to me, took my face into his hands, and pressed his lips against mine. My eyes closed even though I tried to keep them open and my body froze up, making it impossible for me to get away.

Only a few seconds had passed when my lips began parting against my will, and then the stranger filled my mouth with his tongue. When I felt the heated length of it, I sighed in pleasure, shocking myself. I was confused as to why I was now enjoying what was happening. I should've been horrified as much as I was repulsed—but I wasn't.

Unable to fight my sudden and unexplainable desire for this stranger, I began kissing him in return. As our tongues kept sliding across each other's and our breathing grew even deeper, I felt the invisible restraints on my body go away. I could move around again, so I wrapped my arms around the man's waist and pulled him up against me. Moments later, my head started spinning and I stopped kissing him. When I opened my eyes, he was gone. I looked around in every direction and couldn't see him anywhere. He'd vanished like a ghost.

I was still searching for him in the crowd when someone yelled my name. It was Millie.

"What are you doing?" she asked.

"I-I don't know."

"What do you mean you don't know?"

"I mean, I just saw the man from Bambolina's."

Millie glanced around. "Where is he?"

"I don't know. He was standing here with me, we were kissing, and then he was gone. Poof."

"Hold on just a damn minute," she said, holding up her hand. "You kissed that man?"

"Yes. He initiated it and I gave in to it. I don't know why either. It's not like me to do something like that."

Millie looked over my face. "What is his name?"

"I don't know. I asked him who he was but he never answered me. It was like he knew me, though. It was the way that he stared into my eyes."

I started feeling dizzy again and took a deep breath. Then I lost my footing and fell into Millie.

"Harper, what's wrong?" she asked, holding me in her arms.

"My head is spinning."

"Shit. It must be the malbec."

"I guess."

"I shouldn't have suggested that you down it. I really didn't think it'd affect you to this degree."

"It's okay. You were just trying to help."

"Come on and stand up straight for me."

Millie kept her hand on my arm to keep me steady, and after a minute I started feeling like myself again.

"Better now?" Millie asked.

"Getting there."

"You still have a bewildered look on your face."

I shrugged. "I don't know what to think about what happened with that man. Now, I'm not even certain it was real. It feels like a distant dream."

"Do you know what I think about this situation?"

"Not a clue."

"I think your romantic heart grabbed onto an actor that you saw in *Downton Abbey* or in one of those Jane Austen movies that you repeatedly watch, or maybe a character you read about in a romance book, and you started dreaming about him. He became your angel-man. Then today, you just so happened to see someone who resembles him. Because you are intoxicated at the moment and the man from Bambolina's has, no doubt, been in the back of your mind, you conjured him up out here. You imagined him. Harper, a person doesn't just go up to someone that they don't know and kiss them. They don't disappear into thin air, either."

I sighed. "You're right. They don't. And maybe the man in my dreams did come from something I watched or read. I don't recall ever seeing or reading about someone who looks like my angel-man, though."

"I don't know what else to tell you then. Maybe you'll eventually figure out where his image came from. One day, it'll just come to you."

"I hope it does because it's frustrating not knowing. And now I'm wondering what it's going to be like when he shows up in another one of my dreams. Seeing the man from Bambolina's made him seem even more real to me, if that makes sense."

"It does."

"Speaking of real... My imagined kiss with the stranger felt that way."

Millie glanced down at my mouth. "An intoxicated mind can really trip us up sometimes. If you'd actually been kissed by someone, then your lipstick would be smeared. It's still perfect."

"Well, that's good to know. No touch-up needed."

"Are you feeling okay enough for me to leave you standing here so I can get rid of this?" Millie held up her empty wine glass in front of me and wiggled it.

"Yes. I barely feel intoxicated now. So weird. Gabriel's malbec is something else."

"That's one way to put it," Millie chuckled. "I'll be right back."

I nodded and watched her as she walked toward the same table where I'd taken my empty wine glass. Then my skin started tingling. Seconds later, I sensed someone standing behind me and turned around.

"Hi," Gabriel said, smiling at me. "How are you?"

"I'm good. How are you?"

"I'm good too. Just a little hot, but I'll cool off in a minute. It's been busy."

I looked down at Gabriel's chest. He'd taken off his bartender's apron and unbuttoned his shirt a third of the way, as well as rolled up his sleeves to his elbows. I could see sweat beads on his smooth skin and the top part of a black tattoo just below the center of his chest. I couldn't tell what the design was, though, because Gabriel's shirt wasn't unbuttoned far enough.

"There are so many people out here," I said, meeting his gaze again.

"It's the norm, especially on Halloween."

"How did you break away from the wine bar?"

"I have a great staff. That's how."

"You're lucky."

"Yes, I am. Have you and Millie been enjoying the concert?"

"Very much so. We were just about to walk back over. Care to join us?"

Gabriel tugged at his bottom lip with his teeth and grinned. "Yes, I would."

"You know, I really like it when you do that."

"Do what?"

I mimicked him, then he gave me a full-blown smile.

"Noted," he said.

"That's my word."

"Do you mind sharing it with me?"

"No, I don't mind. Is there anything else that you'd like for me to share with you?"

"As a matter of fact, there is."

"What?"

"Your time."

"What do you mean?"

"I would like to take you on a date and get to know you better."

"Okay then."

"That's my saying."

"Do you mind sharing it with me?"

"No, I don't mind. Is there anything else that you'd like for me to share with you?" Gabriel asked, using the exact words that I'd used.

"That's a loaded question," I giggled. My thoughts had just done a nosedive into the gutter.

"Should I reconsider your same one then?"

"If you wish."

The words between us came to a stop like the other times this day and we just stared at each other. Then Gabriel glanced over my shoulder.

"Millie is standing a few yards behind you," he quietly said. "She's giving us some space."

"I know. But let's not keep her waiting any longer. I'll talk to you later about where you'd like to go on our date."

I nodded and turned around to see Millie grinning like a Cheshire cat again.

"Hope I'm not interrupting anything too serious," she said, coming up to Gabriel and me.

"Not at all," I said.

"Nice of you to join us, Vintner Grey. Will you be staying or do you have to go back to work?" she asked him.

"I'll be staying."

"Great! Harper and I were about to go watch the rest of the concert. We've been hanging out up there." Millie pointed toward the embankment.

"Would you witches like to get closer to the stage?"

"Yes!" we said at the same time.

"Then please allow me to escort you."

Gabriel held out his arms, and Millie and I linked ours through them. While he was leading us through the crowd, I gave Millie a look that I knew she'd recognize. We had been working together long enough to read each other's body cues. I'd just told her to *not* mention the man from Bambolina's. I didn't really think she would, but wanted to be sure. She gave me a quick nod that let me know my silent message had been received, loud and clear.

As we were approaching the stage, a security guard recognized Gabriel and led us all the way up front. Loreena McKennitt just so happened to be coming in our direction, shaking the hands of the concertgoers to my right. Then she shook mine, smiled, and moved on to Gabriel, Millie, and the rest. When Millie looked over at me, we both squealed in excitement and our handsome escort started chuckling.

As the band began playing the intro to "The Mummer's Dance," I pulled on Gabriel's arm with mine. "This is my favorite song of Loreena McKennitt's," I told him.

"It's mine too."

"I didn't realize you were actually a fan of hers. I thought you were just playing host."

"No, I've been a fan for several years."

"I want you to know that I really appreciate all you've done, Gabriel."

"It's my pleasure."

"This is the best night of my life."

"Mine too."

6

#itsadate

Harper

After the concert ended, Gabriel, Millie, and I went back over to the main bar. There, Gabriel handed me a sack with the two bottles of his malbec and also a bottle of Bayou Vineyards cabernet.

"Thank you again for doing this," I told him.

"Of course. And Millie, here's some of my merlot and Taylor Kingston's wine. Enjoy!"

She expressed her appreciation, and then Gabriel walked us to her Mustang. She hurried around to the driver side, got in, and cranked the engine, but not before giving me a wink first.

Now it was just Gabriel and me standing here together at the rear of Millie's car, and I was feeling nervous. Gabriel appeared to be feeling that way, too, because he'd tucked his hands into the pockets of his dress pants.

"About our date... Have you heard of No. 9 Park restaurant in Boston?" he asked.

"Yes. It's French cuisine."

"So you've eaten there before?"

"Actually, I haven't."

"Would you be interested in going there?"

"Not to be rude or sound ungrateful, but no thank you."

"Okay then. Where would you like me to take you?"

"To where you make your wine."

Gabriel's eyebrows crawled up his forehead. "Really?"

"Yes, really."

"I can do that."

"I'm guessing it isn't located inside the Raven's Cauldron."

"You would be correct. It's in a building behind my house."

"Where is your house?"

"On the backside of my family's property."

"It's secluded, then."

"Yes. It's really peaceful out there."

"Sounds wonderful."

"Harper, showing you where I make my wine isn't going to take very long and I'd like to spend more than an hour with you. I would like to feed you too."

"I do believe that's the sexiest thing I've ever heard a man say."

"Which part?"

"The feeding me part."

"Noted," Gabriel chuckled. Then he pulled his hands out of his pockets and let them rest at his sides. "How about I cook a meal for us at my house?"

"Only if you let me help."

"Agreed. What do you like to eat?"

"Anything except sushi."

"I feel the same. How do you prefer your steak to be cooked?"

"Medium."

"So do I. Does a baked potato and garden salad sound good as sides?"

"Yes."

"Which salad dressing do you like?"

"Red wine vinaigrette, if you have it."

"I do. It's my favorite."

"That makes four things that we have in common."

"There are actually five."

"I missed one, then."

54

"You didn't miss it. You just weren't aware that malbec is also my preferred wine."

"Is it really?"

"Yep."

I sighed. "Something is telling me that our list of likenesses is going to keep growing."

"Something is telling me the same thing." Gabriel's eyes flickered down to my lips. Then he looked back up. "My work schedule is flexible, but with you being a hospital nurse I'm guessing yours isn't. When are you free?"

After we decided to meet on Friday at noon, Gabriel asked for my phone number and address.

"I'm happy to give them to you, but you're not coming to my apartment," I said.

"I'm confused now."

"There's no sense in you driving to Boston to pick me up, taking me to Salem, taking me back home, and then driving back. To keep things simple, I'll come to you."

"Harper, really, it isn't a problem for me to pick you up and make the turnaround trips. In fact, I insist on it. Please."

"Have you always been such a gentleman?"

"I'm just me."

"Well, I like your chivalry."

"Thank you. So you're okay with me picking you up?"

"Yes. But I'd like to ask you some questions before our date. Like now."

"Okay then."

"They may seem silly, but I don't care. I'm all about the little things."

"Ask me anything you want."

"What's your favorite color?"

"I don't have a favorite color, but *colors*."

"What are they?"

"The ones you see at sunset."

"Ah, a mix of beautiful warm colors then."

"Yes."

"Next question."

"Go for it."

"When is your birthday?"

"Today."

My mouth fell open. "You're a Halloween baby! Why didn't you say something? More than that, why didn't you go out and celebrate tonight instead of working?"

"Because duty comes first."

"No, Gabriel. Birthdays are important, and you deserve to be celebrated."

"I can always do that later. When is your birthday?"

"December twenty-fifth."

Gabriel's mouth fell open as mine had. "You're a Christmas baby!"

"I am. My sister Haley and I were both born on Christmas Day. We were twins."

"*Were?*"

"She died four years ago in a car wreck. A drunk driver hit her."

"Harper, I am so very sorry."

"Me too. I miss her every day."

"I cannot imagine not having my sister around."

"You're blessed to still have her."

"I know. Were you and Haley identical?"

"No, but very similar, like you and Willow. Our hair was the same medium brown and we had the same olive skin tone. But Haley got our dad's green eyes while I got our mom's."

"Molten chocolate brown."

I smiled and nodded yes.

"Who was born first?" Gabriel went on to ask.

"Haley was, by two minutes."

"How old are you?"

"Twenty-four. How old are you?"

"Thirty. Officially an old man today."

"Hardly."

56

Gabriel glanced over in Millie's direction. "Listen, I could stay out here for the rest of the night, talking with you like this. But you and Millie need to start heading back to Boston before it gets any later. I want you to be careful, too."

"We will."

"Will you please do me a favor? Text me when you get home."

"Okay then."

"I'm a worrier."

"I get it. I'm a worrier too.

After exchanging our contact info, I stepped up to Gabriel and kissed his cheek. Then I pulled back and looked at him.

"Happy birthday. I wish there was more that I could do for your special day," I said.

"There is."

"What?"

"Tell me what your favorite color is. It's only fair since I told you mine."

I smiled. "It is only fair, but you're going to laugh."

"No, I won't. Promise."

"It's black."

"What is it about black that you like so much?"

"Besides the fact that it goes with any other color in clothing or whatever? It symbolizes elegance, rebirth, and also mystery."

Gabriel carefully took the stone hanging from the necklace that Alex Kingston put on me earlier into his hand and looked at it. "Black is a good color for many things and has lots of symbolism and abilities. As Alex told you—black tourmaline is used for protection. It's also used for banishing evil spirits and people, as well as for grounding yourself."

"How do you know that?"

"I read a lot."

"About witchcraft?"

"Yes. And many other things." Time slowed down again as Gabriel and I continued staring at each other. Then he said,

"Before you leave, I must tell you that meeting you has made my day and my night."

"Ditto."

7

#fascination

Gabriel

After seeing Harper and Millie off, I walked back over to the venue to help with the cleanup and tear-down. My work crew had already finished doing it, though.

"Congrats on another successful event," Miranda said to me as she was closing the back doors of the wine bar delivery van.

"Thank you. I couldn't have done it without you. Tell me that you're taking tomorrow off."

"I'll think about it."

I cut my eyes at Miranda, pulled my cellphone out of my pocket, and opened the scheduling app. After clicking on tomorrow's date, I scrolled until I found Miranda's name in the employee roster and marked her "off." Her phone chimed the familiar tone from the scheduling app and Miranda glanced at the notification scrolling across the screen. Then she let out a sigh and shook her head.

"And that's that," she said in a mocking tone before having a good chuckle at herself.

"Oh, I cannot wait to tell my mother that you imitated her."

"She won't believe you. Now if I told her that *you* did it..."

I gasped and put my hand on my chest, pretending to be wounded. "There's no such thing as loyalty anymore. First, it was Josephine, and now it's you. Guess I'll have to kill you both and start over."

Miranda rolled her eyes and laughed. "See you tomorrow, boss. I mean next week. See you next week."

"Uh-huh. Next week, Stevens. Not a day sooner. Enjoy your rest."

Miranda saluted me and then climbed into the driver's seat of the delivery van and cranked the engine. After waving her off, I glanced around the empty field and couldn't see one speck of trash. My crew had picked it all up, as well as disassembled and packed away the stage and concession stands in record time. The threat of a late-night storm had them moving quickly.

I looked to the north and saw the front line of it several miles away. Lightning flickered above the clouds just as the wind picked up, and I glanced to the south to try to find Josephine in my mind. I couldn't, though, because she was still too far away. I had sent her to follow Harper and Millie back to Boston. Navigating these winding roads at night could be tricky. If an accident happened, Josephine would let me know.

As I was walking to my car, my thoughts wandered back to Harper. Her beautiful brown eyes and long brown hair, the sight of her smile, the sound of her laughter, the smell of her body cream... The woman had blown in like a storm and caught me totally off guard. And now, I had a date with her on Friday.

I had been avoiding dating anyone for the past two years, filling my time with work to keep myself occupied. Of course the universe sent Harper to me at the Raven's Cauldron: it knew it had no other option. It also knew that for me to be open to dating again, whomever it sent my way would have to be extraordinary—and Harper was.

Dating had become a sore subject for me not long after I graduated from high school. That was when my father began pushing his expectations onto me to find someone suitable to marry and have a male heir with. Even though he, my mother, my sister, and I didn't consider ourselves "traditional" witches, many of my father's expectations were rooted in tradition. Especially the one to continue the Grey name.

As my father's only son, that burden had fallen onto my shoulders. I wasn't against marriage and having a child or several children with someone so much as I was against being pushed into getting married for the sole purpose of having a son. If and when I ever gave my last name to a woman, it would be for the right reason only: she and I would be deeply in love with each other.

This subject had driven a wedge between my father and me and in turn, I'd stopped visiting him, my mother, and my sister as frequently as I used to. At my birthday dinner last year, at my parents' house, my father and I had gotten into an argument about me continuing our lineage. That tension had yet to be resolved.

While sitting at the dining room table, my father had asked me once again if I was dating anyone. Exasperated by the question that he asked nearly every time he saw me, I sighed and said, "Would you prefer I drag the dead horse into the living room so you can beat it or shall we do this in the front yard?"

My mother then put her hand on my shoulder and said, "Sweetheart, your father means well. We just don't want to see you alone any longer. You deserve love, happiness, and companionship."

I told my mother that I already had those things and did not need another person in order to feel like my life was complete. Happiness was an inside job, and I couldn't depend on someone else to make me happy. "You taught me that, Mother," I added, and looked from her to my father.

"You are twenty-nine years old, Gabriel, and you are running out of time!" he yelled as he pounded his fists on top of the table.

"I'm nowhere near running out of time."

"Yes, you are! Your mother and I have asked very little of you and your sister concerning witch traditions. We want you both to have room to become who you want to be while also staying true to our family name. I understand the pressure you feel."

"Like hell you do! Any pressure that you felt to get married and sire a male child is a pressure that you put on yourself. It never came from Grandfather, and I know that for a fact because I talked to him about this messed up situation before he died. He told you to marry Mother *only* if you were certain she was the one meant for you. Were you certain or was she just for breeding, Father?"

His face turned beet-red and his nostrils flared, then he stood up from the table and glared at me. I stood up and glared back.

"I have two more things to say to you and then I'm leaving," I continued. "The first is: you're lucky to have Mother in your life. The second is: from this day forward, do not question me about whether or not I'm dating someone. Your intrusion into that part of my personal life is what made me end my past relationships. If you stick your nose where it doesn't belong again, I promise you, Father, that I'll make it a point to stay single and childless for the rest of my life."

"Gabriel," my mother whispered, reaching for my hand.

When I looked at her, she had tears in her eyes and it gutted me. All I knew right then was that I had to get out of the house before I put my hands on my father. I never had before, but he'd pushed me nearly to the point of no return that evening.

On my way to the front door, I whistled for Josephine. Right afterward, I heard Willow begin yelling at our father. She had always been a feisty one, headstrong, and had a mouth like a sailor. I loved her for it, too, as well as for her loyalty to me.

I had almost made it to the front door when she came running up behind me and said, "Gabe, I'm going with you! I can't live here like this with Father any longer. He's such an asshole and so wrong about the way that he's been treating you about this witch tradition bullshit."

I hugged my sister and told her that I appreciated her support as always and to stay put. She didn't need to leave. The way that our father treated her versus me was like night and day since she was his daughter and not his son. I told Willow to have a slice of my birthday cake for me and then walked out the front door.

I was standing beside my car now, at the concert venue, but couldn't remember walking to it because I'd been so deep in thought. As I was fishing my keys out of my pocket, I heard Josephine squawk and looked up, searching for her silhouette in the dark.

"Where have you been?" I asked her as she was landing on top of my car. "Did you decide to take a nap on the way back?"

Josephine clicked her beak at me, hopped down to my right shoulder, fluffed her feathers, and then made a noise in her throat.

"Worried? Me? Absolutely not. I just wondered if I was going to have to find a new familiar is all. No skin off my nose," I said, smirking at her as I opened the driver side door.

She made an unpleasant noise this time, letting me know she didn't appreciate my snarky comment. Then she flew down into my car and settled onto the passenger seat.

"So everything went well during your flight to Boston?" I asked as I was starting my car. "No problems for Harper and Millie?"

Josephine squawked to let me know that everything had gone as smoothly as I'd hoped, then pecked at the heated seat button. After turning it on for her, I started the journey home and my thoughts immediately went back to Harper.

I barely knew her but what I did know about her, I liked a whole lot. Other than the fact that she was so beautiful, she was also smart and witty. Our rapport with each other came easily and I'd thoroughly enjoyed talking to her. I also enjoyed the kiss that she'd given me on the cheek for my birthday. Her lips were soft and warm, and I could imagine what it would feel like to kiss them.

My dick was starting to get hard, so I shook my head to snap myself out of my thoughts of Harper and then asked myself why I'd bothered opening the door to dating again. It was a bad idea and I knew better. My involvement with Harper was only going to complicate my life, and all because of my father. If he found out that I was dating her, he wouldn't be able to keep his nose out of it. He was predictable, and I could already see a bigger blowup happening between us. A much bigger one than last year's.

As I was nearing the road that would take me to my house, I hit the call button on my steering wheel and scrolled to find Willow's name on the dashboard display. I reached out to tap the call icon next to her name but stopped myself at the last second because it was late. I needed to talk to my sister, though, and decided to call her anyway.

"Hey, you! Whatcha doin'?" she said, answering her phone.

"Driving home from the concert."

"Oh yeah? How was it?"

"It was great. Sad you missed it."

"Me too. I'm just so freaking swamped with work right now."

"I get it. Did I wake you?"

"No," Willow chuckled. "I just made myself another cup of coffee so I could keep working."

"You're still at your studio?"

"I am. I'll crash on my couch in a bit."

"Okay then."

"Are you going to tell me what's wrong, Gabe?"

"Nothing's wrong," I quickly said.

"You know I have the most accurate intuition, especially when it comes to my big brother. So whenever you're ready to talk about whatever *isn't* wrong, I'm here."

I let out a long sigh and pinched the bridge of my nose. "I met someone at the Raven's Cauldron."

"A woman?"

"Yes—and I'm taking her on a date on Friday."

Willow squealed with excitement. "Shut the front door! Tell me everything!"

"Her name is Harper Hewitt, she's beautiful, she's smart, she's got a great personality, she loves my malbec and I'm totally fascinated by her."

"Is she the petite woman with long brown hair who was sitting at the wine bar with a friend? The woman who I let you know was wondering if you were single and was also having dirty thoughts about you?"

"Yes."

"Oh my, brother!"

"Stop. You know I was having the same kind of thoughts about her."

"Yeah, I do know."

"But I think I've made a mistake, Willow."

"About what?"

"Asking Harper out on a date."

"Fuck. This is about our father, isn't it?"

"It is," I sighed. "I really need to talk about all of this some more but I don't want to do it over the phone. Would you mind coming over?"

"I'm on my way."

8

#twosides

Harper

Millie and I made it back to Boston safe and sound. We listened to music during the drive and chatted about what an amazing day it had been. As she was pulling into my apartment complex's parking lot to drop me off, she again expressed her excitement about my upcoming date with Gabriel. Then she said, "I told you so," and I laughed. Her feelings about him asking me out before I left Salem were spot on.

Inside my apartment, I locked the front door, reset my alarm, and set down my sack of wine, purse, and new romance book in the kitchen. After that, I let Gabriel know I was home.

We continued texting each other as I got ready for bed. Laying in it now and reading back over my text thread with Gabriel, I smiled. Especially at the part where he asked if I wouldn't mind him calling me at noon the following day. Of course, I told him that I wouldn't mind at all.

After turning off the lamp on my nightstand, I Googled Gabriel to see if anything came up. I hoped to find a photo of him to save to my cellphone and later print for my Salem scrapbook. To my surprise, there were several photos, all tied to a website for Raven Crest Wine.

Each one caught my eye, but especially the one of Gabriel standing in his vineyard. It wasn't just the location, the big smile on Gabriel's handsome face, and the clusters of grapes that he was holding up that grabbed my attention. It was also seeing him without a shirt on.

I immediately enlarged that particular photo with my fingertips because I wanted to take a closer look at Gabriel's bare shoulders, muscled chest, and arms. What I wasn't expecting to see were his pierced nipples. The small hoops in them matched the ones in his ears, revealing an even wilder side of him. Now, I was even more intrigued.

After saving the photo, I pulled it up again. Gabriel was so damn good looking and was going to be my only fantasy from this night on. Watching online porn had just taken a back seat. All I now needed to make me cum like a nymph goddess was my vibrator and to look at this photo of Gabriel while imagining him fucking me.

. . .

"What time did you wake up this morning?" Gabriel asked. He'd called me at 12:00 p.m. on the dot.

"It was almost ten. I was more tired than I realized."

"You had a long and eventful day yesterday."

"Yes, I did, and it was so wonderful. When did you wake up this morning?"

"At six-thirty."

"So early! What time did you go to sleep last night?"

"Around three."

"How are you functioning with so little rest?"

"I'm used to it. Other than preferring the quiet of nighttime and wanting to stay awake to enjoy it, the full moon also affects the amount of sleep that I get. It energizes me."

"But the full moon was on Thursday."

"You are correct. However, its energetic effect begins occurring three days prior to it reaching complete illumination and continues for three days afterward."

"I did not know that. It explains why we get so many crazy people coming to the hospital every month for, yes, about a week around the full moon. Thank you for telling me about this," I chuckled.

"You're welcome."

"You know so much about this kind of stuff."

"What kind of stuff?"

"Witchy stuff."

"I told you that I read a lot, and about many different things."

"Yes, you did."

"Are you a reader?"

"I am, but mainly of romance books. I plan to start a new one today that I just so happened to buy from the Raven's Cauldron."

"Did you really?"

"Sure did. Millie highly recommended it to me."

"So that's your Sunday plan, huh?"

"Along with getting my laundry done. I've got to get my scrubs ready for the workweek."

"Are all of them black?"

"No, and I know that probably surprises you."

"It does surprise me. What other colors are your scrubs?"

"I have a set of hot pink ones, turquoise ones, and also white ones with monarch butterflies."

"Nice and bright."

"They are."

Gabriel paused for a few seconds and then cleared his throat. "Harper, I want to ask a favor of you, but before I do, know that it's okay if you don't want to do it."

"You've got me feeling a little nervous now."

"There's no reason to be."

"What's the favor?"

"Would you mind putting off starting your new book, getting your laundry done ASAP, and then letting me pick you up after it's done? I don't want to wait until Friday to see you again."

I sighed in relief. "I don't mind, Gabriel. And to be honest, I didn't want to wait until Friday to see you again either. I was dreading the days."

"So was I."

"About my laundry... It can wait, just like my new book. I have a backup pair of scrubs for when I don't feel like washing my dirty ones."

"Okay then. How soon can you be ready?"

"How soon can you be here?"

"As soon as you want me to be."

"Then I'll see you in an hour."

9

#makeawish

Harper

I was standing next to the window by my front door, looking out, when Gabriel pulled into the parking lot of my apartment complex. I kept watching him as he eased toward my building and parked in front. When he got out of his Range Rover, I smiled at seeing him again. I smiled even bigger when I saw what he was holding.

He climbed the three flights of stairs quickly, and as he was nearing my front door, I stepped away from the window. I didn't want him to realize I'd been watching him this whole time. After he knocked, I waited about ten seconds before opening the door.

"Hi," I said.

Gabriel's amber eyes were shining so brightly. "Hi. These are for you."

He handed me the red roses, more than a dozen of them, in a large crystal vase.

"They're beautiful! Thank you so much, but you didn't have to do this."

"I wanted you to have them. They're freshly cut, too."

"Really?"

"Yes. Freshly cut out of my yard. They grow wild there."

I took a closer look at the bouquet and then looked back up at Gabriel. "These are the roses on your wine label."

"Yes, they are."

"I love them. Thank you again."

"You're welcome."

"Come on in," I said, stepping back from the doorway.

I told him that I was going to put the roses on my coffee table and looked back at my front door. I needed to close it, but the vase was in my hands. Gabriel recognized my dilemma and quickly stepped toward me, reached over my head, and pushed the door closed.

He was standing directly in front of me, close enough for me to smell the essential oil blend on his skin. Between the enticing scent of it, the scent of the wild roses, plus the way that Gabriel was staring into my eyes... Well, he'd cast a spell on me once again. After a few more lingering seconds had passed, he stepped aside and held out his hand for me to walk ahead.

"This way," I said.

I placed the roses on my coffee table while Gabriel was checking out the room.

"I really like the way that you have it decorated here," he said, meeting my gaze. "It's nice and cozy with all the warm colors."

"The colors that you see at sunset. Your favorite."

"Yes. And I see your favorite in some of the decorative accents."

"My favorite color goes well with yours, I think."

Gabriel grinned. "I think so too."

"Would you like for me to show you around the rest of my cozy abode?"

"Sure. I'd love to see it."

"Okay then."

I led Gabriel into my kitchen first. He checked it out like he'd checked out my living room and again complimented me on the sunset-colored decor accented with black. The valance above the window, the canisters on top of the counter, my coffee maker, the spoon-rest on top of the stove, the glass container full of cooking utensils, and even my microwave were all a blend of our favorite colors.

Before we left my kitchen, Gabriel took the time to inspect the plant that I had hanging in the window. He gently touched some of its leaves and then looked back over at me.

"Your English Ivy is happy, and they can be rather persnickety," he said.

"It's always done well for me."

"You have a green thumb."

"It appears we have that in common."

We smiled at each other, and then I began showing Gabriel the rest of my apartment. After he'd seen it all, I asked him if he would help me with something.

"Of course," he said.

"I'm guessing you're mechanically inclined."

"I am."

"Great! I've been having a little issue with a cabinet door in my kitchen and would appreciate you taking a look at it."

"Lead the way."

After leading the handsome handyman back into my kitchen, I pointed at the cabinet door that I'd claimed needed repairing, although it really didn't. What Gabriel didn't know was that I had a surprise for him sitting on the shelf behind said cabinet door.

He opened it, closed it, opened and closed it again, then looked over his shoulder at me. "Are you sure it's this one?" he asked. "It seems to be in working order."

I was trying so hard not to laugh. "Gabriel, nothing's wrong with the door. Take a peek inside the cabinet and tell me what you see."

"There's a cake."

"I got it for you since you didn't bother celebrating your birthday yesterday."

He dropped his head and sighed, but he was smiling. "Harper, thank you," he said, looking back up at me.

"You're welcome. Now please move out of my way so I can light the candles. I hope you like chocolate."

"It's my favorite. The cake and the frosting."

"It just so happens to be my favorite too."

After Gabriel stepped aside, I carefully lifted his birthday cake off the shelf and set it down on top of the kitchen counter. Earlier, when I hurried to the grocery store to purchase his surprise, I'd started to get the "3" and "0" number candles but then decided to get a box of red individual ones instead. When I finished lighting all thirty of Gabriel's candles, I looked back up to see his eyes on me. They were still smiling, but there was something else showing in them that hadn't been there a minute ago: happy tears.

"Would you mind standing behind your cake and leaning down so I can take your photo when you blow out your candles?" I asked.

He shook his head no and after he had done as I'd asked, I started singing "Happy Birthday" while holding up my cellphone with the camera focused on him. I was actually recording him and planned to snag still images from the video later.

When I finished singing, I told Gabriel to make a wish and start blowing. He giggled like a little boy would've done, which made me start giggling. We were having fun, and I was so glad that I'd decided to get a cake for him. I'd hoped he would receive it well and he truly had.

Gabriel looked down at his flaming chocolate treat, pausing to think about his wish. I recognized the reflective look on his face. After that moment, he began blowing out his candles. It took three attempts for him to get all of them extinguished and once he had, I started clapping and cheering for him. He stood back up straight, took a deep breath, and kept smiling. Then I walked over to him, raised up onto the tips of my toes, and wrapped my arms around his neck. He hugged me back.

As I was letting him go, I turned my head to kiss his cheek as I'd done last night before telling him goodbye at the concert. This time, though, he turned his face toward me and our lips briefly met. We were both surprised—evident by the look on his face and the one I knew was showing on mine.

"I-I'm sorry, Gabriel. I didn't mean to do that. I was aiming for your cheek," I said.

"I don't mind that you missed."

I stared up at him, not knowing how to respond. Then I pulled my eyes away from his and focused on his cake. "How about you and I enjoy a slice of this now?"

"Harper?"

I took a deep breath and met Gabriel's concerned gaze.

"Don't be embarrassed," he continued.

"It's kind of hard not to be."

"There's no reason to be. We had an oops."

I chuckled. "An oops?"

"Yes."

"Okay then." I looked up at the top of Gabriel's head and then trailed down his body to his feet and back up to his handsome face. "Tell me something."

"What would you like to know?"

"How tall you are."

"Six feet-four. How tall are you?"

"With the black boots I had on last night? Five feet-seven. Without them, I'm a foot shorter than you."

"A little less than a foot with those Skechers that you're wearing today."

"You are so tall."

"So is my father. He is who I got my height from."

"I inherited my mother's, unfortunately. I've always wished I was taller."

"I think you're perfect the way you are."

I searched Gabriel's eyes and took a mental photo of the sincerity that I could see in them. Then I asked the birthday boy if he was ready to have some of his cake.

"A large slice, please," he said.

"You're absolutely having a large slice. Would you like a glass of milk to go with it?"

"If you're having one."

"I am. Cake and milk go hand in hand."

We devoured our slices and drank every drop of milk in our glasses. Then I put the plastic cover back on top of Gabriel's chocolate surprise.

"We're taking this to your house because it'd be dangerous to leave it here. I would end up eating the rest of it," I said.

"It's going to be dangerous having it at my house for the same reason."

"It's your birthday cake, though, and I expect you to enjoy every bite that's left."

• • •

Gabriel and I walked beside each other while talking and making our way down my apartment building's stairs to his car. As we were coming out of the stairwell, I looked up to see a large raven on top of the Range Rover, staring directly at us. I looked from the raven to Gabriel and noticed he was frowning.

"What's wrong?" I asked.

"I just washed my car. If there's bird crap on it, so help me God..." As soon as he finished his sentence, the raven loudly squawked and flew away. Then Gabriel shook his head and muttered "Birds!" under his breath.

"Do you not like birds?" I asked as we reached his car.

"Oh, I like them just fine. Add a little olive oil, some garlic and onion, a dash of salt, a sprig of rosemary, and set the oven to 350—they come out quite tasty," he said with a smirk. Then I heard the raven let out several loud caws. It was circling above us. Gabriel ignored it, though, and opened the passenger side door for me. Once I'd climbed in, he asked, "Would you mind holding my cake?"

"Of course not. I'll make sure it doesn't bounce around," I said.

He handed it to me and I set it down on my lap. Then he began doing something that I hadn't expected. He started putting my seat belt on me, working it around his cake and buckling us both in. When Gabriel finished, he pulled his hand away from me but in the process, his fingertips grazed my hip and I sighed.

"Are you okay?" he asked.

He was still leaning across me, staring straight into my eyes now, and his face was only inches away from mine. I glanced down at his pretty cupid-bow lips, wanting so much to kiss them. I wasn't talking about a quick peck like the accidental one that'd happened between us less than an hour ago, either.

"I'm fantastic," I said, smiling. "How about you?"

"I feel the same."

Gabriel mirrored my smile, stood back up straight, and closed my door. After walking around to the driver side of his Range Rover and getting in, he put on his seatbelt and cranked the engine.

"Would you mind if I played some music?" he asked, looking over at me.

"I would love to listen to some."

"Great!"

As soon as he finished syncing his cellphone with his car's stereo, he asked me if I was familiar with Khalid.

"Yes! I especially love his song 'Free Spirit.'"

Gabriel tugged at his bottom lip with his teeth and grinned, then looked back down at his cellphone and touched the screen. That was when the song that I'd just mentioned started playing.

"I already had it pulled up for us to listen to."

I shook my head. "How many likenesses does that make between us?"

"Ten."

After putting on a classic pair of black-framed Ray-Ban Wayfarer sunglasses, Gabriel backed out of the parking space and then we were on our way to Salem. It was a beautiful sunny day, the temperature outside was unseasonably warm for November 1st, and I wanted to make the drive with the windows rolled down. So I asked Gabriel if we could just that.

"Absolutely! I often drive with them down," he said. "I didn't think you'd be open to doing that, though. Your hair will get tangled."

"I have a brush in my purse."

"Problem solved."

We'd just reached the interstate. Gabriel quickly made his way over to the far left lane and then lowered all the windows.

"Would you mind if I started 'Free Spirit' over?" he asked, stealing a glance at me.

"No, go ahead."

"I know it hasn't finished yet, but now that I won't have to make any turns for a while, I can enjoy listening to the song without any distractions."

"You can give it the appreciation that it deserves."

"That's right!"

"I do the same thing."

With the music turned up and the autumn air blowing all around us, I sighed because I felt genuinely happy. I felt lighter in spirit, too, and knew it was Gabriel who was making me feel this way. His presence energized me. He was like my very own full moon.

When he began singing along with the song, I did too. We both kept randomly looking over at each other and smiling while holding a hand outside our lowered windows, riding the air like a wave.

When "Free Spirit" reached its midpoint, I stopped singing so I could hear Gabriel better. He was harmonizing perfectly with Khalid's voice, hitting all the high and low notes with ease, and I could only shake my head. Gabriel was full of surprises and there didn't seem to be anything that he wasn't capable of doing.

He looked over at me and motioned for me to start singing along with him again, but I shook my head no and pointed at him. He smiled even bigger and turned up the song even louder.

It was after he'd sung the lyrics, "So tell me when you're falling. No, I could never doubt our love. Can you hear me calling? Is it everything you're dreaming of?" when I started wondering about his relationship history again. I had wondered about it the day before, after we'd met. Then, like now, I was curious about the number of women that had been in Gabriel's life. How many had he fallen in love with? How many times had his heart been broken? How many hearts had he broken? When did his last relationship end?

I had dated a few guys, starting when I was a senior in high school, but nothing serious ever came of those relationships. Then I met Daniel last year. We were introduced by a mutual friend at a party and things blossomed from there. We became romantically involved with each other but never had sex. We did everything except have intercourse and it was because of me.

Although Daniel and I had come close to doing the deed several times, I never could go through with it. I wasn't a prude by any means. I just wasn't ready to give up my virginity because it was something of great meaning to me.

At first, Daniel expressed total understanding about how I felt. Then one night, he became cruel about it and asked me if it was going to take him marrying me for me to finally "fuck" him. In that heated moment, lying naked in my bed beside him, I realized it was never going to work between us. I also realized my refusal to fuck him wasn't only about me not being ready to give up my virginity.

Although I cared about Daniel a great deal, I wasn't in love with him. For me to give all of my body to a man, I was going to have to be so deeply in love with him that I found it hard to breathe whenever we were apart. I had always dreamed of having a love like that with someone. Perhaps I'd read too many romance books and watched too many romance movies and they'd made my expectations unrealistic. I didn't care, though. I was never going to settle for anything less than pure magic.

Things ended that night between Daniel and me when I told him that we were over and to get the hell out of my apartment. He left, but not before coming up to me, pointing his finger in my face, and calling me a prude bitch. We hadn't spoken to each other since then and that was four months ago. Four peaceful yet lonely months.

Gabriel had just finished singing the last line of "Free Spirit" and turned down the volume on his stereo.

"I enjoyed your mini-concert. It was wonderful!" I said.

He grinned and shook his head in disagreement. "It wasn't, but thank you."

"No, Gabriel. You really do have a great voice."

"So do you, but you stopped singing with me."

"Because I wanted to listen to you."

He paused and then focused back on the flow of traffic in front of us. "Is there any other particular song that you'd like to listen to?"

"You pick one. I want to learn more about your taste in music."

"It's all over the place."

"So is mine. Loreena McKennitt to Lindsey Stirling to Van Morrison to Taylor Swift to even some of the classical greats."

"Hold up. You're a Swiftie?"

"Absolutely and unapologetically! Her songs speak to the hopeless romantic in me."

"I get it."

"Do you not care for her music?"

"It's a little too girly for me."

"You're missing out, man," I teased. "I've got several of her songs on a playlist that I listen to all the time."

"A playlist of all your favorite songs from all of your favorite artists?"

"Yes. Do you have one?"

Gabriel nodded. "It's what we started listening to."

"Which music app do you use?"

"Pandora."

"So do I."

"That makes fourteen likenesses between us."

"This is crazy," I chuckled.

"I like it, though."

"Ditto."

"What if you and I shared our playlists with each other? They say listening to someone's favorite songs is one of the best ways to get to know them."

"I agree. Songs are tied to our deepest memories and emotions."

"So is that a yes?"

"Yes."

Gabriel shot me his perfect pearl-white smile and then turned up the volume on his stereo again. His black hair was glistening in the sunlight streaming through the sunroof on his Range Rover and I wanted to run my fingers through it. I also wanted to run them along the dark stubble on Gabriel's jawline. He was undoubtedly a classy man, but the ruggedness of his unshaven face was something that I really liked seeing. I felt the same about his Ray-Ban sunglasses. Gabriel looked sexy AF in them.

Another thing that made him look especially sexy was the teal button-down shirt he was wearing. It was collared, fitted, and hugged his muscled chest just right. The black denim jeans that he had on hugged his long legs in all the right places, but even more so to the bulge between them. Gabriel had quite a package, and I was finding it increasingly difficult to keep my gaze from wandering in its direction.

I took a deep breath and glanced down at the black leather low-top sneakers that he had on, noting how well they went with his jeans and shirt. So did the watch and ring that he was wearing. He'd had them on yesterday and I'd noticed them then, but mostly his ring because it was unique. I guessed the metal to be either black gold or titanium. Gothic crowns were etched onto the sides and the gemstone mounted in the center was large, rectangular, and had to be a garnet due to its blood-red color. Gabriel wore the ring on his middle finger on his right hand, and I wondered where he'd gotten it. If the timing was right later today, I planned to ask him about that particular piece of jewelry.

Gabriel had just exited the interstate and completely turned off his stereo this time. "We're about five minutes away from where I live," he said.

"I'm excited! Just like listening to your playlist, getting to see your home will give me a lot of insight about you."

"Just like yours did me."

"What did mine show you?"

"That your home is your sanctuary. It's where you totally relax and shut out the world."

I smiled. "You're right."

"The photos that you have hanging on your walls and sitting on your furniture let me know how much your family means to you, too."

"They do mean a lot to me. Even though Haley is physically gone, I still feel her presence, and being able to see her face in my photos makes me happy. This may sound weird, but I often talk to her."

"It doesn't sound weird at all. I talk to my grandfather."

"When did he pass away?"

"Three years ago."

"I'm so sorry."

"It is life. The unexpected losses are what open your eyes the most."

"They most certainly do."

Gabriel turned onto a winding dirt road, flanked by trees on both sides. Just like the ones I'd seen on the concert venue property yesterday, the trees here still had vibrant-colored autumn leaves clinging to them. The peak foliage kind of leaves that are admired and photographed during September in this part of the United States and are then typically gone by the first week in October. For whatever reason, that rule of mother nature didn't apply to this part of Essex County.

"Is that land your family's?" I asked, pointing out Gabriel's windshield.

"Yes."

"It's beautiful."

"I think it is too, especially during this time of the year. Springtime comes in second place."

"I can only imagine what it looks like when everything is coming back to life after a long winter."

Gabriel glanced at me and smiled. "You live in the city but really seem to love the country."

"I do love it. One day, I may just find myself a cute little house on the outskirts of Boston to call my own. I'd have a garden, maybe a cat or two. I'd dry my herbs in my kitchen, read by candlelight at night, and so on."

"Sounds rather witchy to me."

I poked Gabriel on his side, making him flinch, and we both giggled.

"It sounds divine to me," I said.

"Yeah...it does."

"Oh my God, is that your house ahead of us? I didn't realize you lived in a farmhouse. It's huge."

"There's a long history to it."

"Tell me about it!"

"It was built in eighteen-forty and has been home to several of my family members since that time. The last ones who lived in it were my mother's brother, James, his wife, Francis, and their three sons, Dayton, Michael, and Max. My cousins."

"How long ago was it that you moved in?"

"Six years ago, after my aunt and uncle moved to Boston."

"What made them decide to do that?"

"Two things: their sons are grown and living on their own, plus the maintenance of the house and land became too much upkeep. James and Francis are at retirement age."

"That makes sense, and good for them. They simplified their lives."

"They're really happy about having done it, too, but they do miss the farmhouse. They loved it."

"Where did you live before you moved into it?"

"With my parents."

"Does your sister still live with them?"

"Yes."

"Do you miss being at home with your family?"

Gabriel took off his sunglasses and looked over at me. "I miss being around my mother and sister, but not my father. He isn't the easiest person to live with."

"That stinks."

"It is what it is."

"How does your sister handle living under the same roof as your father?"

"Willow gives his BS right back to him. I used to do that, but with my father's temper and mine, it's not a good thing to do any longer."

I could tell there was much more to that part of Gabriel's story and wanted to hear the rest of it, but the timing wasn't right.

"I understand. Family can be the most difficult people we ever deal with."

Gabriel was pulling up to the farmhouse now and I started taking in more details. The exterior was red with white trim and there were lots of windows. The metal roof was high, making me wonder if there were two floors inside. There was an expansive deck on the left side of the house that I could imagine lounging on with a cup of coffee in the morning or a glass of wine in the evening. Just beyond the deck, I could see a garden area, birdhouses, and a pond. And just as Gabriel had told me, there were red roses growing wild in his yard.

"You have your own special kind of heaven out here," I said.

"It is special."

"I am so jealous."

Gabriel grinned at me and then started rounding the right side of his home. Sitting about fifty yards behind it, there was a large metal building. I knew it had to be where he made his wine. Off to the side of the building, there were rows and rows of grapevines well into their slumber for the season.

After parking in the garage, Gabriel walked around to my side of his Range Rover and opened the door. I handed him his birthday cake, and he motioned for me to walk ahead of him.

"After we go through that door, take a right," he said, nodding at it.

We entered his home and walked down a hallway that led into an open kitchen, dining room, and living room. I stood in the center and glanced around, already blown away by the interior beauty of the place. The floors were wooden and the cathedral ceiling was high. Seeing the ceiling, I realized there wasn't a second floor, but there was certainly more than enough room to breathe comfortably here.

"How many bedrooms and bathrooms do you have?" I asked.

"There were four bedrooms, but I made one of them into a workout room. So three bedrooms and two full baths. One is down that hallway," he said, pointing toward it. "The other is in the master bedroom."

"There is so much space in here."

"It didn't start out like this. The farmhouse was a lot smaller when it was first built. All of the family members who lived here over the years added on to it a little at a time and made the necessary plumbing and electrical updates, as well as needed structural improvements."

"Ah. Makes sense."

"I'm going to put my cake in the kitchen. Keep looking around if you want."

"I do want."

Gabriel searched my eyes for a moment, grinned, and then started heading toward his kitchen. I kept standing where I was, wanting to absorb a little more of the feeling inside this place. There was a spiritual peacefulness to it that was incredibly soothing.

I walked into the living room and set my purse down on the couch. After grabbing my brush out of it, I started working on getting the tangles out of my hair while checking out the room.

"Here," Gabriel said, startling me. I hadn't heard him walk up. He was holding out his hand toward me.

"May I have your brush?" he continued.

"Why?"

"Because I'd like to get rid of those tangles for you."

"Are you serious?"

He smiled. "Hundred percent."

"Have you ever brushed long hair before?"

"Willow's, when we were kids. She used to give me part of her allowance to do it."

"She liked having her hair brushed that much?"

"Yes. She's always reminded me of a cat that likes to be stroked, but on her strict terms. One wrong move and she'll claw you."

"Well, I'm tender-headed. One wrong move and I'll claw you too. Or bite."

"Don't threaten me with a good time," Gabriel chuckled.

I side-eyed him and then handed him my brush. He pointed at the floor with his free hand and twirled his finger. I turned around and seconds later, I felt him begin untangling my wind-blown hair.

He started at the bottom and slowly made his way up to the top of my head. In the few minutes that it took Gabriel to complete his mission, he remained quiet and focused on what he was doing while I focused on how it was making me feel.

The gentleness of his movements with my brush, along with the gentle way he'd randomly touch my hips, waist, sides, back, shoulders, neck, and head with his other hand to hold me still or to move my hair, made me feel as if there was an inferno burning inside me. I knew Gabriel hadn't intended to arouse me, but it happened anyway.

"That wasn't so bad, now was it?" Gabriel asked.

I took a deep breath and then turned around to face him, immediately seeing the smile in his eyes turn into concern.

"Harper, your cheeks are bright red. Do you feel okay?"

"Yes, um, I just had a weird wave come over me."

"Are you dizzy?"

"No. Just feeling a little hot is all."

"Would you like a bottle of water?"

"That'd be great," I said, feeling my cheeks.

Gabriel handed my brush back to me and I tucked it away inside my purse as he was going to get me the water. While he was gone, I smiled to myself about what just happened. There was no way I could've told Gabriel the truth about why my cheeks were red. I would've been embarrassed and he probably would've been too. But then again, maybe not.

"Here you go," he said, hurrying into the living room. Then he opened the water and gave it to me.

"Thank you."

"Of course."

I took a few sips and put the lid back on the bottle. "To answer your question—no, you brushing the tangles out of my hair wasn't so bad. It wasn't bad at all. I enjoyed it. Not one tug that hurt."

Gabriel smiled. "I do my best."

"At everything, I'm sure."

"Are you feeling better now? Cooler?"

"Yes."

"Good. Are you ready to see the rest of my home?"

"I am."

"Then come with me."

10
#turnedon

Harper

Just like Gabriel's kitchen, living room, and dining room, his three bedrooms had antique furnishings in them. The master bedroom, where Gabriel slept, was the last room he showed me and it felt the coziest. That was due to the larger size of the furniture inside it, as well as its color.

The wood in his bedroom had been stained a much darker brown than what I'd seen on the dressers, armoires, bedposts, headboards, and nightstands in the other rooms. The plush comforter and pillows in their array of sunset tones, neatly spread across Gabriel's king-size bed, also added to the coziness of this room.

"That's a really nice comforter you have," I said, grinning up at Gabriel standing beside me. He grinned back.

"Thanks. I think so too."

"It's identical to mine."

"I know."

"You bought it at Bed, Bath and Beyond in Somerville, didn't you?"

"I did."

"It's where I bought mine."

"You don't have to say it," Gabriel chuckled. "I already know what you're thinking because I'm thinking it too."

"I'm just not going to be surprised anymore when other likenesses show up between us. I expect them to now."

"Ditto."

"That's another one of my words."

"Do you mind sharing it with me?"

"You know I don't."

Gabriel showed me his bathroom next. There was a large glass stand-up shower in the far corner with a bronze rainfall shower head and a matching bronze handle. The cream-colored tiles on the shower floor were square like the showerhead. In the other far corner, Gabriel had a jacuzzi tub that two people could comfortably soak in.

His long double-sink vanity was cream-colored with bronze fixtures—the kind that I wished I had in my master bathroom. The waterfall faucets were unique, just like the rainfall shower-head.

Hanging on the light caramel wall above each sink was a large oval mirror trimmed with wood stained dark brown, the same as the wooden towel rack that sat next to the vanity with folded washcloths, hand towels, and bath towels on it. The colors of those towels were Gabriel's favorites: the ones you see at sunset.

The tile on the floor in the bathroom was the same shape and color as in the shower, and it had a mix of plush russet-colored rugs on it. A large rectangular one was in the center of the floor and smaller-sized rugs were next to the two vanity sinks, the shower, the jacuzzi, and the toilet. Gabriel's bathroom was warm and inviting, just like the other rooms I'd seen in his home.

Looking back at the vanity, I could see which sink Gabriel used, as well as his different toiletries sitting on top of the counter. Among them was a cobalt-blue glass bottle with a dropper top. The thought immediately came to me that it was the blend of essential oils that Gabriel made. Curious to see if I was right, I walked over and picked up the bottle, opened it, and took a whiff. Then I looked over at Gabriel. He was leaning against the doorframe, watching me.

"I thought this was probably that EO blend of yours," I said. "Which oils do you use?"

"Patchouli, bergamot, pine, and sandalwood in a carrier oil."

"Like jojoba?"

"That's exactly what I use. Sounds like you're familiar with all of this. Do you use any essential oils yourself?"

I nodded yes. "Rose or lavender whenever I soak in my bathtub."

"Those are good ones."

"I use citrus scents with rosemary in my diffuser."

"Add a little black pepper and those will keep you alert."

"How did you become interested in essential oils?"

"My mother introduced me to them years ago."

"I've never known any man who was into them, but I think it's great that you are."

"It's another extension of nature, and I'm kind of into natural things," Gabriel said with a small shrug. Then he started tugging at his bottom lip with his teeth while grinning at me.

"There you go again, being cute."

He kept grinning and gazing into my eyes like I was his. I could feel the tingling in my skin growing stronger as the heat inside me began rising again. Needing to distract myself, I took another whiff of the EO blend, tightened the lid on the bottle, and set it back down. When I turned around to leave the bathroom, I gasped: Gabriel was standing directly in front of me.

"I'm sorry," he said, gently touching my arm. "I didn't mean to startle you."

"How do you do that?"

"Do what?"

"Move so quickly and quietly. I didn't hear you walk up to me when I was in your living room, and I didn't hear you just now."

"Years of practice sneaking up on my mother and sister, I suppose."

"Were you trying to sneak up on me?"

"Goodness, no. I was just going to offer to let you take this home with you." Gabriel reached around me and grabbed the little bottle of oil off of the counter. "You really seem to like it."

"I do, but I'm not taking your only bottle."

"I have another one under the sink and can mix up more of the blend at any time."

"I can't wear it. It's a masculine scent."

"I didn't expect you'd wear it. I just thought you might enjoy smelling it on occasion."

"I would."

"Then the bottle is yours. I insist."

"Thank you."

"You're welcome."

Neither one of us said another word or moved from where we were standing. We were doing it again—this silent pausing and sharing a lingering look that spoke volumes.

As the seconds kept passing by, I could feel the sexual tension mounting between Gabriel and me. I knew he wanted to kiss me as much as I did him and wondered if he was about to make that move. But he didn't. He steered matters in a different direction by asking if I wanted to see his workout room, or bypass it and go to his wine building.

I believed the gentleman inside him thought that if he kissed me this soon, I'd think less of him, so he used the excuse of continuing our tour to be sure it didn't happen. But I wouldn't have thought less of him for giving in to his desire for me. I wanted him to. I was ready to taste those lips of his. So ready that my mouth was watering.

"I would like to see your workout room, and for you to show me a little of what you do to be in the shape that you're in," I said, looking him up and down. "How often do you work out?"

"Three times a week. It'll bump up to four or five this coming week since we brought my birthday cake over here," Gabriel chuckled.

"I wouldn't worry about it. Just enjoy the sweet treat."

"Oh, I will."

I put the EO blend in my yoga pants pocket as Gabriel started leading me to the bedroom that he'd turned into his workout room. The first thing I noticed was the pull-up bar in the doorway. Then I saw a set of free weights, a bench, a treadmill, a stair-climber, a leg-press machine, and a rower.

"You are serious about this stuff," I said, looking up at Gabriel standing beside me.

"I enjoy working out. It's a good stress reliever."

"Have you ever injured yourself?"

"No. I'm careful."

About me too, I thought to myself.

I walked inside the room and touched the different equipment. Then I went back over to the doorway and looked at the pull-up bar again. I reached for it but couldn't come close to touching it.

"Need a little help there?" Gabriel asked, grinning from the doorway

"Please. Short-girl problems."

"Raise your arms again."

I did as he'd said and then he grabbed ahold of my waist and lifted me up with ease. I was hanging from the pull-up bar now.

"We're eye-level," I giggled.

"How do you like it?"

"I like being able to look straight into your eyes."

"Shall I squat for the rest of the day then?"

I busted out laughing. "No!"

"Do a pull-up for me."

"I'll try."

I took a deep breath, pulled myself up to the bar, and then lowered myself back down.

"That's one. Can you do another?"

"Maybe."

"Keep going until you can't."

I kept doing pull-ups and could feel the muscles in my arms starting to burn. Then they started to shake and I had to stop.

"That was ten. Very good."

"Thank you. I probably won't be able to lift a thing tomorrow," I chuckled while still hanging onto the pull-up bar.

"Nah, you'll be fine. Just take some ibuprofen before you go to bed. Are you ready to go see my wine building now?"

"Yes."

Gabriel grabbed ahold of my waist again and lowered me back down to the floor. When he stood back up straight, he started looking at me like he'd done while we were standing in his bathroom. All of this sultry eye contact between us, all of the unspoken words full of so much meaning, and all of the gentle touches exchanged were such a turn-on. Standing here in front of this enchanting, charming, and incredibly desirable man, I realized I'd been in a constant state of arousal since he'd called me at noon. I could feel the wetness in my panties and needed to take care of it.

"Would you mind if I use your bathroom before we leave here?" I asked.

"Of course not. Take your pick of the two and I'll be waiting for you in the kitchen."

• • •

After using the master bathroom, I stopped in the hallway to take a closer look at the photos on the walls. We'd passed by them earlier, but I hadn't mentioned that I wanted to see them up close and personal.

There were some black and white ones that I guessed to be of Gabriel's great-grandparents and beyond. There were also some of Gabriel, Willow, and who I was certain were their mother and father because they all looked alike.

They'd gotten their father's black hair and eye shape, and their mother's smaller nose, high cheekbones, and the shape of her lips. Gabriel's amber eye color came from his father and

Willow's came from her mother. All four of them were beautiful people.

"I love the photos in your hallway," I said to Gabriel as I was walking toward him, leaning against the island in his kitchen. "The black and white ones are so unique. That was such a different time that all of our ancestors lived in."

"Life was simpler then but it was also harder, considering the amount of physical labor they had to do. We have it easy nowadays."

"We really do."

"I'm grateful to my ancestors for all of their sacrifices. They were the stepping stones that provided me with the life I have."

"You have such a reverence for them. It's admirable."

"I think it's important to know where you came from and to honor those past generations."

"Do you know where your people originally came from?"

"England. What about yours?"

"I don't have a clue."

Gabriel pulled his cellphone out of his pants pocket and held up his finger. "Bear with me for just a moment."

"Okay then."

I watched him typing on his screen and then he started slowly swiping up, reading something of obvious interest. Less than a minute later, he cut his eyes up at me.

"Harper Hewitt, your people also hail from England. At least they do on the paternal side of your family," he said.

"How do you know that?"

"I just Googled the surname Hewitt."

"Well, that was easy. I never thought about doing that. This kind of stuff is all so new to me."

"What is your mother's maiden name?"

"Ellsworth."

Gabriel held up his finger again and I anxiously awaited the result of what he was now looking up online.

"That's an English surname too."

"This is fascinating."

"It is. And it goes much, much deeper."

"How?"

"Science has now proven a thing called 'genetic memory.'"

"Never heard of it."

"Basically, some of our ancestors' ways and even their affections for certain things are in our blood and we experience them. Have you ever been drawn to a location and you don't know why? Or a place that feels familiar and you know you've never been there before? Or maybe you have a phobia it makes no sense for you to have."

"Are you messing with me?"

"No," Gabriel chuckled. "I know it sounds made up, but it's a real thing."

I leaned against the island and stared up at Gabriel standing next to me, thinking about what he'd just said. "I-I've always felt as if I don't belong here. That I should be living in a different time and place. I've dreamed about it and even did a sketch of what I saw in my dream," I said.

"Do you know which time and place?"

"It's during the Victorian era, but I don't know the place. I can see it clearly in my mind, though."

"Describe it to me."

"It's at the edge of a beautiful forest. I'm looking out at it from a balcony at night and can see the full moon high above the trees."

"It sounds like you're standing on the balcony of a castle."

"Maybe."

"Do you know what you're wearing?"

"Yes. I have on a long..." I glanced at Gabriel's shirt and grinned.

"A long what?"

"Teal-colored dress. Teal just like your shirt."

Gabriel grinned then.

"The dress is trimmed in black lace," I continued. "I'm also wearing a black lace choker with an oval-shaped red jewel in the center."

"Very interesting."

"In the last part of my dream, I'm suddenly wearing a black hooded cloak over my dress. It's like I'm about to go somewhere, but I always wake up at that point."

"So you've had that dream more than once?"

"Yes. I've had it several times. It seems so real, too. I can feel the texture of my dress and cloak and I can feel the wind blowing through my hair. I can also smell the richness of the forest."

"I just realized something about you, and I want you to consider its validity."

"What'd you realize?"

"That forest scent may be the reason why you like my essential oil blend as much as you do. Same for your perfume. Even though it has a touch of sweetness in it, it's still earthy."

My mouth fell open. "Holy shit, Gabriel."

He shrugged. "It makes sense to me."

"And now, it does to me."

I looked up at the ceiling, closed my eyes for a moment, and just breathed. Then I felt Gabriel's hand on my back, gently rubbing it.

"I know this is a lot to process," he said.

I looked back at him and nodded. "About places feeling familiar to me... That's never happened. But I do have a phobia that makes no sense for me to have."

"What is it?"

"A fear of the ocean."

"Hmmm. Perhaps one of your ancestors experienced a tragedy that involved the ocean and now you're dealing with their trauma."

"Yeah. Perhaps. Do you have a phobia?"

"No."

"You're lucky. I do love the sight and sound of the ocean and I really love the smell of salty air, but I am incapable of wading out into the water beyond my knees. It's like I hit an invisible wall. It's been that way for me since I was a little girl."

"Did your sister have the same phobia?"

"No. She had zero fear of the ocean."

I started fanning myself because I'd suddenly started feeling hot. "Whew."

"Another wave, huh?"

"Yes."

"Come here." Gabriel turned toward me, then lifted me up underneath my arms and set me down on the island. He watched me closely and even felt my forehead. About a minute later, I was back to myself.

"It's gone now," I said.

"I wonder what those waves are about."

"I know what the first one was about, but not this one."

"Why are you smiling?"

"Are you sure you want to know?"

"I wouldn't have asked if I wasn't."

"You aroused me when you brushed my hair earlier."

Gabriel's dark eyebrows shot up. "I did not intend for that to happen. My sincere apology, Harper."

"I know you didn't intend it and your apology isn't necessary. I'm not upset about the way you made me feel. You just can't brush my hair ever again is all."

Gabriel's smile matched mine now. "No promises."

• • •

"I never realized making wine takes this much equipment," I said.

"Yes, it is quite a bit. Come on and I'll show you the rest of this place."

Gabriel led me over to one of his vats of malbec and I couldn't have been more excited.

"This whole thing is full of wine?" I asked, placing my hands against it.

"No, it has Malbec grapes fermenting in it."

"Do you actually have any wine here or have you bottled all that you've made and taken it to the Raven's Cauldron?"

"I have plenty here that's waiting to be bottled once it's aged long enough."

"Where is it?"

Gabriel crooked his finger at me and then we walked around a corner.

"It's right there," he said, pointing at the far wall.

There were dozens and dozens of stacked oak barrels and I could hardly believe my eyes.

"Oh, my God. So many," I sighed. "How many gallons of wine does one of those barrels hold?"

"Sixty."

"How many bottles does that equate to?"

"Approximately three hundred."

"I cannot imagine the pounds of grapes that it takes to make that much."

"The general rule is eight hundred."

I looked back over at the oak barrels and shook my head in amazement. Then I asked Gabriel when the grapes were harvested.

"Late summer or early fall," he said. "A number of things factor into when they're ready."

"How in the world did you learn to do all of this?"

"I studied enology and viticulture in college and then decided to do what you see here. I was offered a job at a vineyard and winery closer to Boston but wanted something of my own. Even if it flopped, I had to give it a shot."

"Well, it obviously worked. Besides Malbec and Merlot grapes, which other varieties do you grow?"

"Cabernet Sauvignon and Chardonnay. An interesting fact about Malbec grapes is they aren't known to grow well in Massachusetts. Only in California, Washington state, and Oregon."

"So how do you get them to grow so well here?"

"I closely tend them like they're my children, because they are in a sense. I'm protective of them and give them all the nurturing care that I can. It is so very gratifying watching the grapes grow and thrive, harvesting them, and then making wine. Its history reaches back thousands of years and whenever I'm sipping on a glass of wine—mine or anyone else's—I always feel as though its history goes into me and enriches who I am," Gabriel said, placing his hand on his chest.

"Your passion for all of this is enviable."

"Are you not passionate about your job?"

I teetered my head. "I have been at times, and it was due to the patients who genuinely appreciated my help. They expressed their gratitude to me and many of them hugged me before they left the hospital. A few even sent me a thank you note afterward. It doesn't happen often. In my experience, most patients are pissy and unappreciative. They act like they're *owed* and I should be so honored to be helping them. It's the same situation with the majority of the doctors I've worked with and am currently working with. There's way too much ego in the white coats."

"I figure that comes with the territory. It's no excuse, but..."

"I know what you mean. The way that I feel about anyone with an oversized ego—man or woman—is they're actually insecure and because they are, they need a lot of accolades showered onto them by others. Lots of pats on the back to feel validated."

"I agree."

"With that in mind, I'd like to tell you what I did before I walked up to the wine bar and met you yesterday."

"I'm anxious to hear it."

"I stood back and watched you interacting with Millie."

"Where were you standing?"

"Across the room. Millie had been showing me all the vintage furniture and chandeliers and I didn't realize she had walked off because I was so enthralled with my beautiful surroundings. When I saw her sitting at the bar with a glass of wine in her hand, talking to you, I had a good idea of who you were. Millie had already mentioned Raven Crest wine to me, and that she personally knew who made it, and that he frequently tended the bar. She also told me the guy was super friendly, as well as one fine piece of eye candy. Quote."

Gabriel busted out laughing. "Leave it to Millie to say something like that! She's a funny lady."

"Yes, she is, and she's right about you. About both things she told me. Your reaction to what she said just affirmed to me, once again, what an amazing man you are. You don't have a conceited bone in your body when you so easily could, based on your appearance and also your vintner and business skills. You are a confident man and there lies the difference. When you're confident about who you are and what you do, you don't have to say a word to prove it. There's a humbleness to being that way and its foundation is gratitude. There are already so many things that I admire about you, but that particular personality trait of yours—I admire the most."

Gabriel's eyes had a serious look in them now and all that he was doing was staring at me. Then he wrapped his arms around me and hugged me so tight.

"Thank you for saying that. It means more to me than you realize," he whispered in my ear.

"I meant every word."

He squeezed me a little tighter as he let out a sigh. When he pulled back and looked at me, we smiled at each other, and then I asked him to show me his vineyard. As we were walking toward the rows of dormant grapevines, I asked him how old the vineyard was.

"Six years. I planted it right after I moved out here," he said.

"One thing that I hope to do at least once in my lifetime is attend a grape stomp. I think it'd be fun."

"They are a lot of fun, and they're messy too."

"So you've had them out here?"

"Yes."

"With your family, friends, and customers?"

"No, just my family."

"Did you actually stomp all of your harvested grapes?"

"Goodness, no. Some of the machinery that I showed you earlier does ninety-nine percent of it. I have the yearly grape stomp just for the sake of having it. It's symbolic to me."

"I can see that."

After Gabriel finished walking me up and down one of the long vineyard rows while explaining the grape-growing process in even more detail, he asked if I was getting hungry and I told him that I was. When we started making our way back up the hill to his farmhouse, he reached for my hand and laced his fingers through mine. I looked up at him and found he already had his eyes on me.

"Is this okay?" he asked.

I gave his fingers a squeeze and nodded yes.

11

#magic

Harper

"Do you have Crisco?" I asked Gabriel. "I do. It's right here." He reached into one of his kitchen cabinets and handed me the container.

"What about coarse sea salt?"

"Got you covered."

The salt was in the same cabinet.

"These two things make the best-tasting potato skin," I said, holding them up.

"That's my favorite part."

I smiled. "Mine too. I'll start working on our potatoes and salad while you're getting the grill prepped."

"You're a take charge kind of woman. I like that."

We both giggled, and then Gabriel walked outside to his deck. While he was gone, I got the potatoes ready and popped them into the oven. Then I started slicing the tomatoes, cucumbers, and radishes. I washed the lettuce, set it down on the cutting board, and took a moment to look all around me. I loved it here and I loved that I felt so at ease. Everything was free-flowing and harmonious within the high walls of this beautiful farmhouse.

I took a sip from the glass of Raven Crest malbec that Gabriel had poured for me and then got busy making the salad again while continuing to play music on my cellphone sitting on the counter. It was Gabriel's playlist that I was listening to. He'd sent me the link to it and I'd sent him the link to mine.

I heard the back door open and looked up to see Gabriel walking through it. He smiled as he rejoined me in the kitchen.

"You've already gotten the potatoes and salad done?" he asked, glancing at the oven and the cleaned-up counter where all the vegetables had been. "You're quick. Is there anything I can get for you?"

"No, I'm good. Thank you, though."

"Of course."

Gabriel grabbed his glass of malbec off the island and then came back over to me, leaning against the counter like I was doing.

"I'm really happy you're here. I've enjoyed all of this with you today," he said.

"Ditto." I took another sip of wine and then looked back up at Gabriel. "You and I have talked about several things since we met, but one thing we haven't talked about is our relationship histories. Would you like to get it out of the way?"

Gabriel grinned. "If you're ready, I'm ready. Mine won't take long."

"Neither will mine."

"Shall I ask the first question or do you want to?"

"I want to."

"Okay then."

"How many romantic relationships have you been in?"

"Three. What about you?"

"One," I said.

"How long ago was that relationship?"

"I ended it four months ago after a year. How long ago was your last relationship?"

"Two years."

"Have you dated anyone since then?"

"No. What about you?"

"I haven't either. I wasn't interested in going down that road again. Not until I met you."

Gabriel leaned over and nudged me with his shoulder. "Ditto."

"Two years is a long time to not have romantic companionship. Did you have a bad breakup the last time or something?"

"No."

"Then why such a long break?"

"It has to do with my father."

"What do you mean?"

"I'd barely started dating the woman when my father began pressing me to get married."

"What?" I asked, shocked.

"I know."

"That's nuts. Why would he do that?"

"Because I'm his only son and continuing our family name is on my shoulders."

"I get that, but what I don't get is your father's rush for you to get married. You're only thirty."

"He thinks I'm running out of time."

"I don't mean this disrespectfully, but he sounds very old-fashioned."

"He is. He's controlling, too, and that's why we butt heads. It's also why I called off my past relationships. My father started trying to stick his nose into them, and I didn't want the women to have to deal with him. It's embarrassing. After ending my last relationship, I just figured I'd live a solo life until... I didn't know when. I've just been floating along and keeping myself busy with work."

"So your past relationships didn't get the chance to become the slightest bit serious, did they?"

"Not really. They all ended during the initial fun stage of getting to know each other."

"Like you and I are doing."

Gabriel paused. "Yes."

I took a deep breath.

"What are you thinking?" he asked.

"I'm wondering why you asked me to go on a date. Going by your relationship track record, my time with you is limited."

"Not necessarily."

"What's the difference between dating me and dating those other women?"

"My mindset is different now. Meeting you is what made that happen. Should I be so lucky to have another date with you, and another and another, and also should my father get wind that I've met someone wonderful and am seeing her, then I'll deal with it. I will handle him."

"Is this your way of asking me to go on another date with you?"

"Maybe."

I smiled. "My answer is yes. But Gabriel, I don't want to be the cause of any conflict between you and your father."

"You'd never be the cause."

"I just had a thought come to me. We can keep things hush-hush if you want. For now. We don't have to do anything in the public eye, here or in Boston or anywhere else."

"I'm not keeping you a secret for now or ever."

I smiled again.

"I have a question for you," Gabriel continued.

"So ask it."

"Was your past relationship serious? I'm guessing it was since it lasted a year."

"It wasn't as serious as I thought, but I didn't realize that until the night I ended my relationship with Daniel. That's the guy's name."

"How did you not realize it until then?"

"I saw a side of Daniel that I'd never seen before. And in that moment, I accepted the truth about who he is and about my feelings toward him. I did care about him a great deal, but I wasn't in love with him. At least not the kind of love needed for a lasting relationship."

"This side of Daniel that you just mentioned... Do you mind telling me what happened between you and him?"

"I'll say it like this: he let me know in a very cruel way that he wasn't satisfied with our sex life."

Gabriel's face dropped. "I'm sorry, Harper."

"Thank you, but I'm not looking for sympathy. I'm no victim. I'm just someone who misjudged another's character and learned a big lesson from it."

"I still want to hug you."

"I'll happily take another one of your hugs."

Gabriel wrapped his arms around me and we held onto each other. Afterward, he started prepping our steaks with seasoning while I checked the potatoes.

"I'm going to set the table while you're getting that done," I said.

"No, I'll do it in a minute."

"Gabriel, I've got it. Just tell me which cabinet the plates are in."

He grinned at me and then pointed at the cabinet directly behind him.

"Thank you," I continued. "I'll find the rest of what I need. Go cook our steaks. I'm starving."

● ● ●

"That was so good, but I'm saving the rest so I have room for dessert," I said.

"I feel like a pig. I ate everything on my plate."

"You're a big guy and you need to eat. Besides, I enjoyed watching you."

"Is that so?"

"Yes, it's so."

"Would you like a slice of birthday cake now?"

"Only when you're ready for one."

"If you don't mind, I'm going to sit here for a few minutes and let some of my meal digest."

"That's fine. It's relaxing just sitting here and talking with you. Tell me about your ring," I said, nodding at it. "It's really unique."

"Willow made it for me. She does everything, art-wise. She's also made jewelry for our parents and tons of customers."

"She is so gifted."

"She has been since she was a little girl. She started drawing and painting all kinds of amazing stuff back then and it evolved from there."

I smiled and then pointed at Gabriel's living room. "Surely Willow didn't craft your fireplace over there, but someone did. It's a work of art within itself. Is it the original fireplace?"

"No, she didn't, and yes, it is."

"I love how it's made with all those old stones. I actually love all old things—homes, antiques, and the like. Touring around Salem with Millie yesterday really satisfied that part of me. I touched so many old things while wishing they could talk. They hold all the secrets of what they've been witness to over the decades and even hundreds of years, and I can only imagine their tales."

Gabriel reached for my hand and I rested it in his, on top of the dining room table. "You really love a good story, don't you?" he asked.

"Always."

"I do, too, so tell me about your childhood."

"Um...it was really good. Haley and I had everything we ever needed or wanted. Our mom and dad spoiled us in a lot of ways but they also kept a tight rein on us. They were strict and had my sister and me in church every time the doors were open, it seemed."

"Do you still attend church?"

"On occasion, I'll go to one that isn't very far from my apartment. I always sit in the back and just observe everything and everybody while listening to the sermon. Do you attend anywhere?"

"No. I wasn't raised religiously like you and Haley. However, I do feel like I attend church every time I'm outdoors."

"You sound like Millie. I don't think she'd mind my telling you that she's on a new spiritual journey. She used to faithfully attend church but then discovered the world of witchcraft and embraced it. She's shared quite a bit about it with me and I have to say that my eyes have been opened. It's not evil and there is no devil involved in it like I was taught by my parents. It's nature-based and about the energy of our thoughts, words, and actions. But you already knew that since you've read so much about witchcraft, among other things."

Gabriel smiled and nodded. "Yes, I already knew that. And changing the subject... I could use a slice of cake now. What about you?"

"Absolutely."

"Do you want a glass of milk too?"

"Like you've got to ask?" I chuckled.

"Come on then."

We got up from the table and took our plates into the kitchen, setting them aside on the counter next to the sink.

"I'll get our glasses of milk," I said.

"And I'll get our slices of cake."

"Deal."

Before Gabriel cut his cake, he swiped some chocolate frosting off the side with the tip of his finger and held it up in front of my mouth. After I parted my lips, he eased his finger into my mouth and I sucked the frosting off it, grinning. Gabriel grinned too, but we both knew what we'd just done wasn't only about frosting. It was the tastiest kind of flirting that I'd ever experienced.

"My turn," I said, swiping some frosting off the cake.

Gabriel parted his pretty lips and I stuck my chocolate-covered fingertip into his mouth, but then he grabbed hold of my hand and pushed my finger in even further. Between him staring into my eyes and feeling the suction of his tongue... Well, I could feel the heat rising up through me once again and it was rising quickly.

After slowly pulling my finger from his mouth, Gabriel licked his lips, looked down at mine, and then met my gaze again. The sexual tension between us felt palpable, thick, and on the verge of taking over both of us.

"Kiss me," I finally whispered.

"Like a gentleman? Or like I really want to?"

"Like you really want..."

Before I could finish my sentence, Gabriel had his lips on mine and his long tongue in my mouth. I wrapped my arms around his neck and his arms held my body against his. He was kissing me as hard and as deeply as I was kissing him and we both kept moaning between the breaths we were taking.

When Gabriel suddenly pulled his mouth away from mine, I didn't know what to think. Then he slid his hands down across my ass to the backs of my thighs and began lifting me up. I wrapped my legs around his waist and we started kissing each other again. My fingers were in his hair now and he had one of his hands in mine at the back of my head. He was pulling it tight and pushing me toward him, keeping my face exactly where he wanted it.

He stopped kissing me again, pulled my head to the side by my hair, and started smelling my neck. I closed my eyes and felt him run his tongue across my skin, up to my earlobe. After giving it a tug with his teeth, he began making his way back down my neck by peppering it with little biting kisses. Then he began sucking on the skin above my right collarbone.

"You smell and taste so good," he half-growled as he pulled back to look at me. Then he carried me over to the island and set me down on the edge of it.

I kept my legs wrapped around him and reached for the buttons on his shirt to undo them. I pushed his shirt behind his shoulders and he let it fall to the kitchen floor. I was expecting to see Gabriel's nipple piercings—but was shocked when I finally saw the full design of the tattoo below the center of his chest.

I didn't say anything as I stared at it but the wheels in my mind were spinning. Then I reached out and ran my fingertip across the straight lines and circle of the black pentagram on Gabriel's skin. When I was done, I looked back up at him.

"You're a witch?" I asked.

"I am."

"How long have you been one?"

"My entire life."

"Do you come from a long line of them, like Alex Kingston?"

"Yes."

"So your sister is a witch too?"

"She is."

"Why didn't you tell me?"

"Surprisingly, it's not the easiest thing to drop into a conversation."

I shrugged. "I just...I guess I'm a little shocked is all."

"Is it going to be a problem?"

"No."

"After you told me how you were raised, I wondered if it would be an issue. I knew this would come to light eventually. I just didn't think it'd be this soon."

"Why do you feel the need to hide who you are?"

"Although I'm from Salem and rumors have swirled around about my family and me for decades, I still have to be mindful of the businesses we run, and keep things as professional and neutral as possible. Most people readily accept the commercialized version of witchcraft, but not the real thing because they don't understand it. They'd rather keep it on the surface. Come to my hometown, explore, buy a souvenir, and then cackle all the way home."

"You sound resentful."

"That's not the right word. More like 'frustrated.' I wish more people took the time to find out where their ancestors came from and what they practiced, spiritually. Once upon a time, all of our ancestors were pagans and embraced the old ways."

I took a deep breath and slowly exhaled it.

"I'm overwhelming you. I apologize," Gabriel said, pulling back from me even more. I pulled him to me again with my legs still wrapped around his waist.

"I'm just processing all of this. It's a lot, but it's okay. I see you, Gabriel Grey, and accept everything about you, like I hope you do with me."

He canted his head to the side as his eyes danced across my face. Then he reached up and cradled it with his hands. "Accepting everything about you is no problem. You are some kind of wonderful, Harper Hewitt. I didn't see you coming and you are the last thing that I ever expected to show up in my life."

"Ditto." We grew quiet for a long moment, and then I asked, "What is this between us? I mean, our attraction to each other is obvious, but what I'm feeling is more than that."

"What are you feeling?"

"A strange energy that I experience only when I'm around you. My skin tingles all over. It started happening as soon as I looked into your eyes when we met, and the sensation didn't go away until after Millie and I left. Then it started happening again when you came up to Millie's car while she and I were waiting in line to get to the concert. It's happened every time that I've seen you since then."

"So you're experiencing it now?"

"Yes."

Gabriel didn't say anything. He just kept looking at me.

"What is it?" I finally asked.

"I felt the same energy when we met. It actually started affecting me before you walked up to the bar, and when I saw you, I immediately knew it was you who was making my skin tingle because the sensation grew stronger. But I was mistaken about why you were able to affect me in such a way."

"What do you mean?"

"Those who come from a long line of witches have exceptionally strong energy within them that radiates out several yards beyond their bodies. We also have the ability to sense another witch's energy. The tingling in our skin is how we recognize each other without having to say a word. Whether we speak or not, we always give a respectful nod. Your energetic effect on me in the bar and the nod that you gave me when we met led me to believe you were a witch like me. When I saw you and Millie in the car line, I still believed you were one because your presence made my skin start tingling again. But when I saw Alex Kingston wanting to give her necklace to you and then heard you ask her if she was a witch, I realized you weren't one of us."

I took another deep breath and kept staring at Gabriel while thinking about what he'd just told me. "Okay, um, so I'm not one of you. I guess I'm an alien."

Gabriel softly smiled. "No, Harper. You're not an alien. You're an extraordinary human being with your own special kind of life force. A life force that pulls me to you like a magnet."

"I'm pulled to you the same. So again, I'm asking you—what this is between us?"

"I don't know what it is, but I love how it feels."

"So do I."

I looked down at Gabriel's chest and reached out to touch it. After laying my hands on it, I held them in place just to feel this man standing in front of me who'd so willingly bared his soul to me only moments ago. I could feel his heart beating beneath my right hand, and the longer I held it there, the harder it beat.

"You and I have found ourselves in one complex situation, haven't we?" I asked, looking back up.

"How so?"

"The situation with your father being prone to sticking his nose into your dating life and the situation with my parents believing witchcraft and witches are so bad."

"You can keep me hush-hush. I don't want to be the cause of any conflict between you and your parents."

"This is my life, not theirs, and I'm not keeping you a secret just like you don't want to keep me one. You are the magic that I've been seeking and have needed for a long time."

"I feel the same way about you, Harper."

"Then kiss me again."

12

#closer

Gabriel

"The moon is still so bright and beautiful," Harper said, smiling up at it through my windshield. "Are you still feeling its effect?"

"Yes."

"I hope you get a decent night's sleep tonight."

"I'm not worried about it."

"But I am for you. You've got to rest, Gabriel."

I pulled my eyes away from the interstate again and looked over at Harper sitting in my passenger seat, looking brighter and more beautiful than the moon. Then I lifted her hand to my mouth and kissed it. We had been holding hands since I pulled out of my driveway to take her back to her apartment.

"I'll be fine."

As I was looking back at the flow of traffic, a song from my playlist came on and it couldn't have been more fitting for how I was feeling toward Harper.

"You're tugging on your bottom lip with your teeth and grinning again," she said, giving my hand a squeeze. "What's it about this time?"

"This song. It reminds me of you."

"It does, huh?"

"Yes. Have you heard of it before?"

"No. What's the title?"

"'Take Me Where Your Heart Is.'"

"Who sings it?"

"Q."

"Q?"

I glanced over at Harper and grinned once more. "Yes. He's an R&B artist."

"Yeah, I can tell. His song is soulful and all sexy-sounding."

"So you like it then?"

"A lot. Start it over for me?"

"Of course."

Harper leaned her head back against the seat, closed her eyes, and started swaying to the rhythm of the song while I quietly sang the lyrics. I kept stealing glances at her as she kept moving her body around and seeing her doing it made me feel like pulling off the interstate, driving down a side road, parking, and kissing Harper as I had earlier at my house. Twice.

Our accidental peck at her apartment had only whet my appetite for more of her and when I finally got more, I felt so goddamn high. I also felt how hard my dick was. I was certain Harper had too, since I'd been pressing myself into her through my jeans and her yoga pants while she sat on the edge of the island in my kitchen. I couldn't hide what she had done to me either time.

When the next song began playing, Harper leaned over and rested her head on my shoulder. I could smell the scent of her hair and wanted to bury my face in it. Harper's all-over body chemistry affected me unlike any other woman's ever had. If I could have, I would've bottled it up to have on hand whenever I needed a dose of Harper.

As the music kept playing, we were both quiet. My mind wasn't, though. I had started thinking about when Harper had seen my pentagram tattoo. The shocked look on her face wasn't surprising. I expected it. But what I did not expect was how easily Harper accepted who I was and what I did, especially considering her religious upbringing.

You never knew about people when it came to them finding out someone was a witch. As I had told Harper earlier, I kept things as professional and neutral as possible when in the public eye. But I was certain all of my employees at The Raven's Cauldron believed the rumors about my family and me. They had never approached me about them, but Willow had heard their whispers over the years and relayed them to me. She had also let me know their speculations about me being gay.

I assumed it wasn't my appearance, physical gestures, or speech that had led them to think that. It was probably due to the fact that they'd never seen me with a woman of romantic interest before. The three I'd dated before Harper, I kept away from Salem. They were all from Boston, where I'd met them while running errands, and I made a point to keep matters with them in that city. That was my game plan from the start: to have a buffer between my dating life and my father, although it didn't work for long. My game plan now, since meeting Harper, was to show her off to any and everyone. There'd be no more hiding this part of my life. Whenever my father got wind of it, I'd be ready to deal with him.

"I appreciate you explaining the elements and four directions to me earlier," Harper said, cutting her eyes up at me.

"Of course."

"When my Aunt Jenny told Haley and me about them, I was too young to understand the world that she was introducing to us. I didn't think much of what she said either because off-the-wall stuff coming out of her mouth was typical. She was so quirky but she was also a ball of fun. Haley and I loved her."

"I'm going to help you try to find her just like Millie plans to do. With three of us doing P.I. work, something good will surely come from it."

Harper held up her right hand and crossed her fingers. "Maybe this'll help."

"It will."

At Harper's apartment complex, we walked hand-in-hand to her front door as Josephine circled silently overhead. It was dark, but I could feel her presence and her mood.

Why are you cranky? I haven't asked you to do a single thing all day except keep your distance. I want to ease Harper into this, I thought to her. She let out a soft caw and landed in a nearby tree.

When Harper and I reached her door, we turned to face each other.

"Would you like to come inside?" she asked.

"Yes. But if I did, I would end up staying with you all night."

"That wouldn't be such a bad thing, now would it?"

I smiled. "It would be an amazing thing."

"What would we do if you stayed?"

"Whatever you wanted."

"What would you want to do?"

"Get closer to you in every way."

Harper raised up onto the tips of her toes and pressed her lips against mine. I let go of her hand and pulled her body against me, causing our kiss to ignite. The feeling of our tongues touching and the sound of Harper's breath-filled moans had me feeling like I was flying high again. I wanted this woman so much. I wanted to lay her down and fuck her until both our bodies were spent, but I knew it was too soon to do anything to her other than kiss her breathless.

I pulled my mouth away from hers and held her face in my hands while staring into her beautiful brown eyes. "You are driving me crazy," I said.

"Ditto."

"Go inside your apartment, close the door, and lock it. I beg you."

Harper giggled. "Okay then."

"I will let you know when I get home."

"You better."

We kissed one more time, but it was only a peck. After I heard Harper lock her door, I started walking back to my car and whistled for Josephine. Seconds later, she landed on my right shoulder and nibbled my earlobe.

"Good evening, my love," I said. I opened the driver side door and waited for Josephine to hop down onto the seat.

"Well? Do you need a written invitation?" I asked.

After I put my right hand up to her breast, she wrapped her feet around my first two fingers. Turning her to face me, I cocked my head to one side and asked her what was wrong. Then she looked down and stretched her neck toward me. While I was scratching the back of it, she softly cooed, but I could still sense sadness in her.

"If you're worried about being replaced by Harper, you are wasting your worries," I said. Then I put my left hand under Josephine's beak and brought her face level with mine. "*No one* can replace you, understand? You are my best friend. You are my heart flying around outside of my body. I love you, silly bird. Nothing will change that. Not even a girl. Not even *the* girl."

I kissed the top of Josephine's head and she began to softly purr.

"Now let's get you home. It's way past your bedtime."

• • •

I called Willow on my way home because I needed to talk about what was happening between Harper and me. I wasn't surprised that she picked up on the first ring. She knew that I had moved up my date plans with Harper to today and I knew she was anxious to hear all about it.

"Give me the juice, Gabe. Every detail," Willow said. That was how she answered my call, and I chuckled.

"I had a blast with Harper. She loves the farmhouse and my wine building. We cooked dinner together and talked about several different things. And get this—Harper surprised me with a chocolate birthday cake when I got to her apartment. She put thirty red candles on it, sang happy birthday, and then had me make a wish and blow out the candles."

"You got teary-eyed too, didn't you?"

"Yes. It was so thoughtful of her. She's big on celebrating birthdays, and celebrating mine in her surprising way was exactly what I needed. I just didn't know it until it happened."

"Does Harper know about you and our family?"

"She does."

"How did it come to light?"

"She saw my pentagram tattoo after she unbuttoned my shirt."

"Why did she unbutton it?"

"Nosy. She wanted more of me, like I did her. We'd just had our first real kiss."

"The sweet kind or the devouring each other's mouth kind?"

"The latter," I said.

"Good. How did it feel kissing a woman again after all this time?"

"I'll sum it up like this: Harper made me feel as if I'd had an entire bottle of malbec. I felt drunk while kissing her and no woman has ever made me feel that way."

"I know. You've never spoken of one like this until now. So tell me how Harper took finding out that you come from a family of witches."

"She took it with accepting ease. She also asked me if I would teach her about the craft."

"What did you say?"

"That I would."

"Does that include showing her all that you're capable of doing?"

I let out a long sigh before answering. "I don't know yet."

"What made her so curious about this?"

"Her friend Millie. She's talked to Harper quite a bit about our world."

"Is she a witch?"

"Not like us. She's new to the craft. A dabbler."

"What made you willing to teach Harper? You've never done that for anyone."

"I don't know. Something about her. I feel safe opening up this part of my life to her."

"But you barely know her."

"Part of me feels as if I've known her for years, though. It's strange."

"Gabe, I'm ecstatic about the happiness that I hear in your voice."

"I am happy. It's been a long time."

"I know. So when are you going to see Harper again?"

"Friday."

"Think you can wait that long?"

"I'm going to have to."

"Are you still worried about Father ruining all of this for you?"

"No, because I'm not going to let him. I know he's going to eventually find out that I'm dating Harper. Probably sooner rather than later, because I plan to show her off every chance I get. I'm taking your advice about living my life in exactly the way I choose. It's too short not to."

Willow and I continued talking until I pulled into my garage. We had moved on to other topics: Willow told me about a new painting she'd been commissioned to do, then asked when it was going to be time to bottle some more of my wine. It was a few weeks away. Then, like always, my sister would jump in to help me all she could.

As soon as Josephine and I went into my house, she flew off my shoulder and I knew where she was heading: the kitchen. Without question, she was starving from all the flying that she had done, following me to Boston to drop off Harper. After I'd prepared a large bowl of dried fruit and mixed nuts for her, she dove into eating it while I poured myself a glass of malbec. Then I went outside to the deck, pulled my cellphone out of my pocket, and sat down in one of my lounge chairs to text Harper.

Me:I'm home now, so no more worrying.

Harper:<smiley face emoji>

Me:What have you been doing since I left your apartment?

Harper:Thinking about you.

Me:I've been thinking about you too.

Harper:I looked over your Pandora playlist and know several of the songs.

Me:I'm not surprised.

Harper:There is one song, though, that I'd like for you to add. That is if you like it. I happen to love it and just got done dancing around to it while thinking about you.

Me:Before I ask you the title of the song and who sings it, you must tell me if you danced naked.

Harper:I did.

I took a gulp of my wine and then sat the glass down on the table beside my chair.

Harper:Did I lose you?

Me:No, I'm still here. I'm just imagining you dancing in your birthday suit.

Harper:Speaking of birthday suits... What about you dancing naked under the full moon? Were you just messing with me?

Me:No.

Harper:So you've done that all by yourself during the middle of the night or whenever?

Me:Yes. I enjoy communing with nature as I was made. Night or day, full moon or otherwise.

Harper stopped texting.

Me:Where did you go?

Harper:I'm here. I'm the one imagining things now.

Me:I hope you like what you're imagining.

Harper:"Like" is an understatement.

Me:Which song did you dance to?

Harper:I'll text you the link, then I've got to get some beauty sleep.

Me:I know you need to sleep but you don't need any more beauty. I couldn't take it.

Harper:Goodnight and sweet dreams, Gabriel Grey.

Me:I'll check on you tomorrow. Goodnight and sweet dreams to you, Harper Hewitt.

It was only seconds after my text-chat with her ended that I received the link to the song that she had danced naked to. "Addiction." Doja Cat. I had never heard of either.

After turning on my indoor/outdoor speaker system through the app on my cellphone, I took another gulp of wine because I had a feeling that I was going to need its calming effect after listening to this song. As the intro began, I knew I was right. The lyrics, along with the heavy bass rhythm, already had my mind racing with images of Harper moving her body around while her long hair swung back and forth across her face, shoulders, and arms, and her black tourmaline necklace bounced between her breasts.

When I heard the part of the song that mentioned going without "it"—which I interpreted as "sex"—and then heard the parts about breaking the curse of going without it and still believing in magic, I leaned my head back on my chair and looked up at the night sky. Of course, I was still picturing Harper, but I also had my hand on the outside of my jeans, holding my erect dick.

By the time the song ended, I was about to come unglued. I finished off my wine and went inside to get some damn relief. I walked straight to my bathroom, turned on the shower, and stripped down to nothing. After turning up the volume all the way on the speaker system, I started "Addiction" over. Then I laid my cellphone down on top of my vanity, stepped beneath the steaming water, and began jacking off while imagining Harper dancing naked around her apartment again.

My thoughts of her quickly moved into the two of us having sex. I imagined us in my bed, me on top of Harper, slowly sliding my dick in and out of her pussy. It was when I began imagining fucking her as hard as I could that I finally came. I shot off all over the shower wall in front of me. Coming that hard made my head spin and I saw stars. Then my knees buckled and I leaned against the wall behind me to catch my breath and wait for my vision to return to normal and my legs to regain function.

I didn't bother drying off with a towel. Instead, I walked over to the French casement windows in my bedroom and opened them, allowing the night air to cool me down. My mind was still preoccupied with Harper, and I knew the only way I was going to be able to get some sleep tonight was by taking some hits off a joint. So I walked over to my nightstand, grabbed the one that was inside the top drawer, and then went back over to my windows. About fifteen minutes later, I was relaxed enough to go to bed and start dreaming about Harper.

13

#tease

Harper

Gabriel was the first thing on my mind when my alarm woke me up this morning. I continued lying in bed while thinking about the day I'd spent with him and couldn't stop smiling. On my way to the kitchen to make myself a cup of coffee, my cellphone chimed, and I sighed when I saw who'd texted me.

Gabriel:Good morning.

Me:Good morning to you. <smiley face emoji>

Gabriel:How did you sleep last night?

Me:Heavenly.

Gabriel:Ditto.

Me:I woke up thinking about you.

Gabriel:I woke up thinking about you too, and the song that you sent to me.

Me:Did you like it?

Gabriel:More than I probably should have.

Me:Why do you think that?

Gabriel:Because the images of you that began running through my mind while listening to the song were quite vivid.

Me:Good. That's what I wanted to happen. <winky face with tongue emoji>

Gabriel:Mission accomplished. <fireworks emoji>

The same as when he and I were standing in front of each other and staring into one another's eyes, there was a quiet pause between us. But this time, it was in our texting. I had no doubt that Gabriel was smiling like I was and also having erotic thoughts about me again as I'd had about him last night while dancing around my apartment, and also while lying in my bed. I was having them at this very moment, too, and needed them to stop; otherwise, I was going to be late for work due to a morning date with my vibrator. So I steered things in a completely different direction.

Me:Have you got a busy day ahead of you?

Gabriel:Just a typical Monday, making sure all is back in tip-top shape at the Raven's Cauldron. I suspect your day will be busy.

Me:They always are at the hospital.

Gabriel:I won't keep you any longer. I'm sure you need to get ready for work.

Me:Currently standing naked in my bathroom, about to take a shower.

Gabriel:Thank you for that image that I won't be able to get out of my head now. <hot face emoji>

Me:You're welcome. It's fun teasing you.

Gabriel:I could tease you by telling you certain things about myself.

Me:Go for it.

Gabriel:Another time.

Me:Okay then.

Gabriel:I hope you have a good day.

Me:I hope you do too.

Gabriel:Please text me when you get home tonight. Or call me.

Me:I'll call you.

Gabriel:I can hardly wait.

• • •

As I was walking toward the nursing station, I saw Millie coming from the other direction. She smiled and waved, and so did I.

"You doing okay this morning?" she asked.

"Yes. I'm great! Why do you ask?"

"You have on your faded backup pair of scrubs."

"And?"

"You obviously didn't do your Sunday laundry as usual, so what did you do yesterday? Get lost in your new romance book?"

"Um, no. I got lost in something else. Or rather, *someone* else."

Millie side-eyed me and then her mouth fell open. "You got together with Gabriel yesterday, didn't you?"

"I most certainly did."

"And how did that come about?"

"He called me and asked if I wouldn't mind changing our Friday date plans. I was anxious to see him again, so I said yes to his request."

Another one of my nurse coworkers looked around the open doorway of the patient room straight across from the nursing station and said she needed to talk to Millie for a minute. Millie nodded at her and then looked back at me.

"You might want to put some concealer and powder on that hickey peeking out from under your neckline," she giggled, and I immediately covered it with my hand.

"I didn't think it showed."

"The edge of it does."

"Okay, I'll take care of it."

"Only if you want to."

"I don't need the staff whispering about it."

"How'd it feel getting it?"

"Incredible. It may seem high-schoolish but I don't care. It's my first hickey ever."

"Gabriel Grey has left his mark on you, my friend."

"In more ways than one."

"I want to hear the rest of this story but need to go for now."

"We'll catch up later."

"One last question... How was your first kiss with Gabriel?"

"Well, we accidentally peck-kissed each other after he came to my apartment to pick me up, and that's another story for later. But as far as our first *real* kiss is concerned?" I glanced around and then leaned closer to Millie. "It was so—fucking—magical. We were all over each other and if Gabriel had kept kissing me and pressing his body against mine, I think I would've...you know."

Millie grinned. "He probably would have too."

• • •

I was sitting in the breakroom, eating a late dinner, when I got paged. I gobbled down the last few bites of my leftover steak and baked potato from my dinner with Gabriel the day before and then headed to the nursing station. As I was approaching it, I saw Millie and a delivery sitting on top of the counter. I looked from it back to Millie and then came to a stop in front of her.

"Did you have me paged?" I asked.

"Yes. These are for you." She nodded at the delivery that I now recognized.

"Oh my God, those roses are from Gabriel."

"I know."

"Where is he?" I glanced up and down the hallway but only saw hospital staff.

"He left."

"Why?"

"You were with a patient when he got here. I told him that he was welcome to wait until you were free but he said no. He'll talk to you later. Sorry that I've just now let you know about this. It's been a crazy day."

"No, it's fine," I said, reaching out to touch one of the newly opened rose buds. "I just wish I could've seen Gabriel."

"Why don't you see what his card says?"

I looked back at the white envelope taped to the rim of the crystal vase, and grabbed it. As I was removing the card, I could tell there was something inside it. Something thick like a folded piece of paper. When I saw what it actually was, I gasped and then held the photo against my chest.

"What's wrong?" Millie asked.

"Nothing's wrong. It's Gabriel."

"Going by your reaction to that photo, I'm guessing it's a sexy one."

"It's borderline X-rated."

"I don't need to see it then. You just enjoy it."

"But I want you to see it if it won't be weird for you."

"It won't be weird for me. I was just thinking about you."

I looked all around Millie and me and then slipped her the photo. As soon as she flipped it over and saw the image of Gabriel, her signature Cheshire cat grin spread across her face.

"My oh my, Harper."

"I know."

Millie handed the photo back to me and I took another look at it. Gabriel was standing in front of his bathroom vanity, holding his cellphone in front of his chest with its camera pointing at the mirror above his sink. His hair was wet and tousled, and the towel loosely wrapped around his waist was low enough in the front for me to see not only the muscled grooves above Gabriel's hips but also the black hair on his lower abdomen that led down to his dick and, no doubt, surrounded it. Although the towel was covering Gabriel's manhood, I could still see its outline and I had been right. It was big. Really big. And it wasn't even hard.

When I looked back up at Millie, I let out a long sigh and then read Gabriel's card. I was so distracted by his photo at first that I hadn't thought to see what his card said.

Harper,

I'm getting you back for teasing me about you being naked in your bathroom this morning. I hope you like what you see.

Gabriel,

When I finished reading his short handwritten message, I started chuckling and cut my eyes up at Millie. "His sexy selfie was intended to get back at me."

"For what?"

"I teased him by text this morning by letting him know I was standing naked in my bathroom, about to take a shower. There's much more behind the whole naked thing, too, and it's yet another story to tell you later."

"I've really got to give it to Gabriel. He one-upped you big time."

"Yes, he did."

"And you're already thinking of how to get him back, aren't you?"

"You know it."

"What's happening between you and him is fast, furious, and fantastic."

"I think it is too. Gabriel isn't only courting my heart, Millie. He's also courting my soul."

"Are you concerned at all about getting hurt again?"

"No. I feel at peace and plan to keep journeying on with Gabriel, having as much fun with him as possible and kissing those pretty lips of his every chance I get. But I also want you to know that I'm not naïve about this situation. Okay? I watched things with Daniel turn on a dime, and I realize it could very well happen to me again because people are people. We're all human and life is complicated."

"Gabriel seems superhuman to me."

I smiled. "He is. I'll tell you more about that later too."

After Millie walked off, I put Gabriel's photo back into the card, slid the card into the envelope, and stuck the envelope in my scrub pants pocket. Then I focused on the bouquet of roses and leaned closer to breathe them in. They weren't average in any way. Their appearance was exotically robust and their scent was the strongest I'd ever smelled. Nothing about that surprised me either. All things Gabriel Grey were extraordinary.

I started to text him to let him know that I had received his bouquet, card, and photo but decided against it. I was going to make him wait for my response. I knew he was on pins and needles, wondering how I felt about his surprise delivery. I would've been if I was in his shoes. We had a game going on now. An exciting and sexy game that we could both win.

14

#touché

Harper

When I got home from work, I set my roses and purse down on my kitchen counter and then threw all of my dirty scrubs into the washer except for the pair I had on. Then, I poured myself a glass of Gabriel's malbec, plucked a handful of rose petals from my new bouquet, and headed to my bedroom.

Laying across my bed to relax for a few minutes, my thoughts were on what I was going to do this evening: take a sexy selfie to send to Gabriel. Turnabout was fair play.

I needed to get into a seductive frame of mind, so I grabbed my cellphone out of my pocket and started playing Isabel LaRosa's song "I'm Yours" on repeat while continuing to sip on my wine. When I began feeling the effect of both, I walked into my bathroom and took off my clothes. Then I loosely wrapped a bath towel around my waist, touched up my makeup, and placed the rose petals in my hair. Holding my glass of wine in front of my left breast came next, and then I held my cellphone in front of the other and took my photo in the mirror above the sink.

I had thought about giving Gabriel a full view of my breasts to really get at him but decided against it because it would've been pushing things too far, too soon. I was pushing them now, just as Gabriel had done earlier, and couldn't help but wonder how much further he was going to push things once he received my surprise. I had a feeling that this game of seduction chess between us was going to quickly ramp up. I'd be ready to make my next move whenever it did.

Looking at my selfie now, I smiled, and then added it along with "Your roses and wine... It doesn't get any better than this!" to my text thread with Gabriel. One deep breath later, I hit send and waited for his response. Almost immediately, he added exclamation marks to my image and then called me.

"Hi," I said.

"I almost dropped my phone when I saw your photo."

"Good. I nearly shit myself when I saw yours," I chuckled.

"How long have you been home?"

"Long enough to enjoy some of your malbec and take that sexy selfie. I know I told you that I'd call you as soon as I got here, but decided not to after I received your surprise today. I planned to get you back and intentionally waited to contact you via my photo. Hope I didn't worry you."

"You did a little. I wondered if I did the wrong thing by coming to your work with the roses, the card, and the photo."

"I apologize for worrying you. And no, you didn't do the wrong thing. I really wish I could've seen you in person."

"I wish I could've seen your face when you saw my photo."

"I wish I could've seen yours when you received mine."

"Are we going to continue playing this game, Harper?"

"I would like to."

"It's torturous."

"But the good kind of torture, right?"

"Yes."

"It's your move now."

"It is—and I hope you're ready for it."

"I am."

"Okay then. Listen, I know you're tired, so I'll let you go."

"Aren't you tired too? You've had a long day just like I have."

"It has been a long day and I am tired, but I won't be going to sleep any time soon, thanks to your photo. It's going to take me a while to cool down."

Before Gabriel and I hung up, I told him how much I appreciated his second bouquet of roses, as well as his card and sexy selfie. He said he really did want to give me more roses since I loved them so much.

I had just stepped out of the shower when I heard my doorbell ring, so I quickly dried off. Then I put on my robe, grabbed my cellphone off the vanity, and hurried to see who was at my apartment this late. It was almost 10:00 p.m. I was pretty certain that it was my neighbor from downstairs, Mrs. Crawford. She and her husband were both elderly, but Mr. Crawford was more frail. His wife had come to get me several times before to help her lift him off the floor. He was prone to falling and I guessed he had fallen again.

When I looked through my peephole, I gasped. It wasn't Mrs. Crawford standing on the other side of my front door. It was Gabriel. I kept staring at him while feeling my heart beating faster and faster, not only because he was here but also because I didn't have time to get dressed. Knowing I couldn't keep him waiting, I took a deep breath and then unlocked and opened my door.

"Hi," he said in his deep raspy voice as soon as he saw me. "How are you?"

"Um, fine. I just got out of the shower."

Gabriel looked me up and down. "I can tell."

"Is showing up unannounced at my apartment tonight your way of one-upping me in our little game?"

"No, I'm not playing our game at the moment. I'm here because I need to touch you, kiss you, and feel your body against mine again. I ache for you, Harper."

I didn't say anything else. I just started backing away from the doorway and Gabriel stepped through it, closing and bolting the door behind him. When he turned back around, he looked me up and down again and then started coming toward me like I was his prey. When he made it over to me, he grabbed my face and began kissing me so deep and hard. We melted into each other and kept slowly spinning round and round in my foyer, and then Gabriel walked me backward into my living room.

I lay down on the couch and Gabriel lay down on top of me. Feeling the weight of his body on mine and the heat of his kiss again sent a wave of arousal rushing through me and I moaned. Gabriel pulled back and searched my eyes, then started kissing my neck as he had the day before. I felt his soft lips, his gentle bites, and his long tongue gliding across my skin. He kept making his way down my body but stopped when he reached my breasts. They were fully exposed now because the top part of my robe had come undone. Gabriel looked up at me as if he was worried that things had gone too far.

"You don't have to stop," I whispered.

"Yes, I do. If I see any more of your bare beautiful body, I won't be able to stop myself from carrying you to your bedroom and..." He shook his head no to himself and sighed. Then he raised up, sat on the edge of my couch, and pulled the top part of my robe back together. "I didn't come here to have sex with you," he continued.

"I know you didn't."

"But I do want you so much."

"Ditto. What's happening between us reminds me of author Ella Frank's quote: 'The strongest drug that exists for a human is another human being.' I am addicted to you, Gabriel, and I've known you for only three days."

"I'm addicted to you, and I was having withdrawals earlier. I was walking around the farmhouse and felt like I was about to crawl out of my skin. I finally just gave in and did what my heart told me to do."

"I'm so happy you did. But what do we do now?"

"I don't know. Stay right here and gaze into each other's eyes?"

"Until we fall asleep?"

"About that... I know it's late and you need to rest, so I'm going to head back to Salem. I just needed to see you in person for a few minutes. Get my fix."

I reached up and ran my fingertips across the dark scruff on Gabriel's chiseled jawline and then encircled his mouth and touched his lips. "You're welcome to stay here tonight. You can sleep in my bed with me, but I'll wear baggy sweats and a T-shirt to keep us safe."

"I'm not certain that would work."

"It's worth a shot, don't you think?"

"Harper, I want to stay. You know I do. I appreciate your invitation, tremendously, but I've got an early start in the morning."

"Okay then."

"Let's raincheck me spending the night with you."

"Deal. Before you leave, though, I want to tell you something about myself that I think you should be aware of before things get any more physical between us. We both know they're going to if we continue seeing each other."

"There's no 'if' about us continuing to see each other but go ahead. What do you want to tell me about yourself?"

"I'm a virgin."

Gabriel's eyebrows shot up and he swallowed hard. "I…

"You had no idea. How could you?"

"But I respect you for being a virgin. And I apologize if I've done anything that made you feel uncomfortable," he said, sitting up even straighter.

"Stop. You've not done one thing that has made me feel uncomfortable. Do you hear me?"

He paused and then nodded. "I hear you."

"When I told you about Daniel telling me that he wasn't satisfied with our sex life, I meant he was no longer okay with us not having full-on sex. When he and I began seeing each other, I was upfront with him about the fact that I was a virgin. He was fine with it and completely supported me. He and I did everything but have actual intercourse, and he seemed to be fine with that. But when he asked me four months ago if it was going to take him marrying me for me to finally fuck him—quote—I realized I was mistaken about him. His true colors came out, and I knew right then that it was never going to work between us. I lost all respect for him that night and told him we were over. Now, I need to know if *you* are truly fine with me being a virgin."

"Of course I am," Gabriel said, reaching for my hand. "What I'm not fine with is Daniel saying that to you. He's immature, classless, and didn't deserve you, Harper. He's the type of man who needs to be checked up by a real one."

Gabriel's eyes had anger showing in them, so I put my hand on his chest to calm him. "I agree with everything that you just said."

"Does Daniel live in Boston?"

"Yes."

"Have you run into him since you two split up?"

"No. Not once. But I feel like if I did run into him, he'd turn around and walk off in the other direction."

"Okay then."

Gabriel grew quiet and kept staring at me. I knew there was more that he wanted to say but for some reason, he was holding back.

"Talk to me," I finally said.

"I want to ask you a question but am concerned that it might offend you."

"I'm not worried about that, so ask."

"Did your religious upbringing color your decision to remain a virgin?"

"No. I've remained one because I've never been in love. I'm talking about the kind of love that is so deep and real that it consumes you and the other person. It takes over your hearts and your souls and you find it hard to breathe whenever you're apart. Is that the hopeless romantic in me speaking? Sure. Why not? But I have seen love like what I just described in couples of all ages, and I won't settle for anything less. It's my prerequisite for giving my whole body to a man."

Gabriel leaned down and rested his forehead against mine. We were both quiet while absorbing everything that we'd just shared, and then he softly kissed me. Afterward, he got up, reached for my hand, and pulled me to my feet.

"Thank you for sharing more about yourself with me. More than that, thank you for trusting me enough to tell me," he said as he searched my eyes.

"I do trust you. A hundred percent."

"Ditto."

"Let me know when you make it home."

"I will. I'll see you on Friday, unless my withdrawal from you becomes too unbearable again."

I chuckled. "Mine from you may become too unbearable, and I may just show up on your doorstep."

"If it does, then bring an overnight bag."

• • •

After Gabriel left, I went into my bathroom to get ready for bed. I brushed my teeth, got the tangles out of my still-damp hair, and then applied some retinol oil to my face. When I walked back into my bedroom, I looked around and sighed because I wasn't sleepy due to seeing Gabriel. Feel-good endorphins with his name on them had flooded my bloodstream and were still flowing through it.

Wanting to feel the cool night air, I walked over to my bedroom window. When I pulled back the curtains, I was shocked to see a pair of eyes staring at me. Not those of a human but of an owl. He or she was perched on one of the branches of the tree closest to my window, clearly unfazed by my sudden presence or the fact that there was only about ten feet between us. I'd never seen an owl this up close before, nor had I ever seen a white one.

I got the sudden urge to talk to the nocturnal creature and slowly raised my window, hoping my doing so wouldn't scare it away. It was again unfazed.

"Hi, you beautiful thing," I whispered.

The owl ruffled its feathers and then hooted, which made me jump. I giggled and just kept watching my new friend. When I started getting drowsy, I told it goodnight, closed my window and curtains, and crawled into bed. Then I looked at Gabriel's sexy selfie again. When he called to let me know that he'd made it home, I was still looking at it.

"I feel like turning around and driving back to you," he went on to tell me.

"Then do it. We could call in sick tomorrow and spend all day together."

"Oh, how you tempt me."

"You do the same to me."

Gabriel sighed. "Harper, I'm crazy about you, although I'm certain you already know that. There are so many things about you that speak to me on the deepest level and I don't know what to make of it. But what I do know is your presence brings me so much happiness. Telling you all of this after knowing you for such a short amount of time is insane, I know—but I had to do it. I just hope it doesn't scare you away from me."

"It won't. Do you know why?"

"No."

"Because I feel the same way about you."

15

#imagination

Harper

"I'm good with us swapping shifts. We just need to get it approved," I told Misty. She was another nurse coworker of mine and my favorite one on the floor after Millie.

I needed to go check on a patient and after I was done, Misty caught up with me in the hallway to tell me that our shift-swap was a go. She needed to be off work on Friday for personal reasons and now, I was going to be off work on Thursday. I already had a surprise up my sleeve for Gabriel too. It wasn't sending him another sexy selfie. I was going to drive to Salem to see him.

My dinner break came late again because things were so busy at the hospital. I was sitting in the breakroom, texting Gabriel, when Millie walked in and sat down across the table from me.

"I know who that is," she said, nodding at my cellphone still in my hand. "Your smile gives you away. Tell Gabriel I said hi."

I sent him another text with Millie's message and also told him that I'd talk to him later. His reply was a heart emoji.

"You never finished telling me all the juicy details about your Sunday spent with Gabriel. Feel like sharing them now?" Millie asked.

I glanced at the other nurses on break and then motioned for Millie to come closer. After she leaned toward me, I began telling her more about my first date with Gabriel. I told her what he'd done the night before too, showing up unannounced at my apartment.

"Did he give you another hickey?" she chuckled.

"No, but I'm sure he will eventually. He likes smelling and tasting my skin. He nibbles on me and licks me and it feels so damn good."

"And where all has he done that to you?"

"On my neck and chest."

"Imagine it happening elsewhere."

"I already have."

Millie waved her hand at me and snickered.

"There's one thing about Gabriel that I haven't told you," I continued. "But you cannot mention it to him or anyone."

"You know I won't."

"I just had to say that for my own peace of mind because this is big. At least it is to me."

"What is it?"

"Gabriel is a generational witch."

Millie's jaw dropped. "Are you serious?"

"Yes."

"Did he tell you that he's one?"

"Yes—after I saw the black pentagram tattoo on his chest."

"So that means his family are all witches too."

"Exactly. Gabriel and I talked about it for quite a while and he's teaching me about the craft now."

"I've heard the longtime rumor about him and his family being witches, but dismissed it. There are several families in Salem whose ancestors were original settlers and the same rumor has circulated about them. They're all easy targets. My God, I just... I just never saw anything in Gabriel that would lead me to believe he was a witch."

"It's like you told me—they're as normal looking as anybody else. As normal-acting too."

"I've just relearned that lesson. So when are you going to see your magic man again?"

"Misty and I swapped Thursday and Friday shifts, so I'll see him on Thursday. He doesn't know it yet, though. I'm going to Salem to surprise him."

Millie smiled. "He'll love that. Do you know what I just realized? You got your wish to meet a male witch after all."

"I most certainly did. I just didn't know he was one until the next day."

"Has it made you view Gabriel any differently?"

"Yes and no. Of course, I'm fascinated by him being a witch and so anxious for him to teach me what he knows, but I still see him for who he is. He's a beautiful human being, inside and out, and has the kindest heart and gentlest soul."

"You've got yourself an amazing man. You lucky girl."

"That I am."

"Gabriel is lucky to have you too."

Millie was paged but before she left the breakroom, she mentioned that a new intern doctor was coming on board next week.

"Oh great. Another overinflated ego to deal with," I said.

"I'll handle it."

"Do you know his name?"

"Nicholas Clarke."

"*Dr. Clarke*," I spat out as sarcastically as I could. "Fingers crossed, he won't be an asshole like the others."

"He might not be since he's from England."

I jerked my head back in surprise. "Is he really?"

"That's what I was told."

"Hmmm. I wonder what his story is. Like why is he practicing here in the U.S.?"

"We'll find out soon enough. And if he is an asshole, then maybe his British accent will make him tolerable."

"Doubtful."

I called Gabriel when I got home from work and we chatted for over an hour about our days. I was so tempted to tell him about my plan to come to see him on Thursday but held back. I wanted to see his face when he saw me.

Before I went to sleep, I looked out my bedroom window, hoping to see the white owl again. To my delight, it was sitting on the same branch as before. When I raised my window and started talking to it again, it didn't ruffle its feathers or hoot. It began making its way down the branch, coming toward me, and I couldn't believe my eyes. When it stopped moving, amazingly, there was only about a yard of space between us. If there hadn't been a screen on my window, then I could've reached out and touched the owl.

When I told it goodnight, it ruffled its feathers and hooted, and I jumped and giggled like last time. I could hardly wait to tell Gabriel about all of this. I had already mentioned the owl being in the tree before, but what had happened tonight was unreal.

Once I was snuggled up with my extra pillow beneath the covers, it didn't take long for me to start drifting off to sleep. It was then that I heard movement in my bedroom and my eyes flew open. I turned on the lamp on my nightstand and looked around, searching for the source of the sound, but couldn't see anything.

I knew it wasn't an intruder in my apartment because if someone had entered it, my alarm would've gone off. More than likely, it was a mouse. I had dealt with one before and still had the trap underneath my kitchen sink. I decided to set it in the morning before I went to work.

I turned off my lamp and snuggled with my extra pillow again, pretending it was Gabriel that I had my arms wrapped around. Then I started imagining us having sex. I had a fairly good idea of what Gabriel's dick would feel like inside me because of my vibrator. It was long, thick, and even veined.

I let my erotic thoughts of Gabriel keep flowing and could feel his muscled body on top of mine as he slid his dick in and out of my pussy. Then I felt him start pumping his hips even faster. I was so aroused now and close to coming. All that it had taken to get me to this point was fantasizing about Gabriel.

I closed my eyes and imagined him thrusting himself into me even harder. Seconds later, I started to cum. When it ended, I kept my eyes closed and kept imagining Gabriel fucking me. I wanted him to cum and I wanted to hear all the sounds he made while he did it. He never did, though, and when I opened my eyes to look at him, I gasped because it wasn't Gabriel's face that I saw. It was my angel-man's.

I suddenly heard a loud jarring sound and sat straight up in bed. Then I realized it was my cellphone alarm. I turned it off and laid back down to give myself a minute to level out. My heart was pounding and I was covered in sweat.

Little by little, my heart rate slowed and my body cooled down. All my senses came back, too, but what I couldn't figure out was when my wide-awake thoughts of Gabriel last night had slipped into being a dream. They were all blurred together now.

Another thing that I couldn't figure out or understand was why my angel-man had come to me in my dream about Gabriel. And why did he touch me this time? Why did he fuck me? He'd only ever watched me from across the room with his piercing ice-blue eyes, never speaking a word.

16

#twoprinces

Harper

"What's bothering you?" Millie asked. "You've had a worried look on your face ever since you got here."

"I had a hell of a dream last night and can't shake it off."

"Come with me."

After stepping inside an unoccupied hospital room, Millie asked me to tell her about my dream. I didn't give her all the details but enough to paint a clear picture for her.

"I never took you as one for being into threesomes," she joked and I shoved her on her arm.

"Not funny."

"I'm just trying to snap you out of your current frame of mind. You had a dream, Harper. That's all."

"But it felt so real."

"When was the last time your angel-man appeared in your dreams, before last night?"

"Last week."

"This with him and Gabriel reminds me of a song from the early nineties, when you were just a wee little girl."

"Which song?"

"'Two Princes' by a band called the Spin Doctors. It's about a woman who has two men vying for her, just like you do. The difference with you, though, is that one of the men is real and the other is a figment of your imagination."

"But this time, my angel-man didn't just watch me. He fucked me after Gabriel did."

"So who was better?"

I shoved Millie on her arm again and started chuckling. "Just stop."

"Now that you're smiling, I will."

"Thank you."

"Take a deep breath. You are fine. Focus on the day ahead of you."

"You're right."

"By the way, the new doctor arrived early."

"He's here today?"

"Yes."

"Shit."

"I think you're going to be pleasantly surprised when you meet him. He's super polite and his British accent is *really* nice."

"Where is he?"

"Dr. Ward was showing him around earlier, but I don't know where he is now. You're bound to run into him at some point today, though."

I grumbled a couple more choice words, and then Millie and I walked to the nursing station. I had just started going over a patient's chart when Millie touched my arm and I looked up at her.

"What is it?" I asked.

She grinned and nodded over my shoulder. The moment I turned around, I dropped the chart onto the floor. The man in the white coat that I was staring at rushed over to me and bent down to pick up the chart. When he stood back up, he held it out toward me and I took it from him. Then he extended his hand for me to shake.

"Hello. I'm Dr. Clarke," he said in the most poetic-sounding British accent that I'd ever heard.

"Hi. I-I'm Harper Hewitt."

Our fingertips grazed each other's and then Dr. Clarke gently shook my hand.

"Lovely to meet you, Miss Hewitt."

"You too. Um, I saw you at Bambolina's in Salem on Saturday."

"I saw you, as well."

We both grew quiet but never looked away from each other. Seconds kept passing by and the longer they did, the more my mind was playing tricks on me. The last image of this morning's dream kept coming forth despite my trying to push it away. Still staring into Dr. Clarke's ice-blue eyes, all I could see was my angel-man on top of me, fucking me.

"I'm sorry but I need to go," I whispered. Then I took off running down the hallway.

• • •

"Come out of the bathroom stall," Millie said.

"I can't. I can't see Dr. Clarke again."

"Harper, stop this insanity. Listen, I see what you were talking about, about the resemblance between your angel-man and the man at Bambolina's who we now know was Dr. Clarke. I get it. But it's nothing more than a coincidence."

"A huge coincidence that's mind-fucking me majorly right now. And let's not forget what my drunk mind conjured up about Dr. Clarke while I was at Loreena McKennitt's concert."

Millie sighed. "I'm going to count to three and if you don't come out of that damn stall, I'm coming in to get you. Then I'm going to kick your ass like you're my bratty little sister. Do you hear me?"

I didn't say anything, but I did slowly open the stall door.

"Harper, you've got to get a hold of yourself," Millie continued. "You are going to see Dr. Clarke again. You're going to be working with him. We all are. So someway and somehow, you're going to have to separate your dream world from your reality.

Especially your reality here at Massachusetts General Hospital. You have a job to do."

I walked over to one of the sinks, turned on the cold water, and then bent down and splashed my face with it.

"Dr. Clarke probably thinks I'm the rudest American ever," I said, patting my face with a paper towel.

"No, he doesn't. He's concerned that he said or did something wrong to you and is waiting for me to let him know if you believe he did. He's also ready to apologize to you."

I sighed. "He didn't do anything wrong. I just wish he didn't look like my angel-man. I swear, he is identical to him."

After hanging out in the women's staff restroom for a couple more minutes, Millie and I walked out into the hallway. Dr. Clarke was standing a few yards away and appeared nervous. I waved and then walked over to him.

"Are you all right, Miss Hewitt?" he asked.

"Yes. I apologize for running away earlier. It's a long story that has nothing to do with you. Nothing at all. You just remind me of someone I know. You could actually pass as his twin."

"Is there anything that I can do to make this situation easier for you? I want you to be comfortable working with me."

"Well, you could wear Clark Kent glasses and a mask full-time when you're here," I said, partially grinning.

Dr. Clarke then gave me a full-blown smile that was as perfect and bright as Gabriel's. "I'm willing to do both if it would help you."

"I'll be fine. Thank you, though."

"You're most welcome, Miss Hewitt."

Millie walked up and told Dr. Clarke that she and I needed to get back to our patients. Yes, that was true, but she also knew I was still hanging by a thread.

"Of course," he said, holding out his arm for us to go.

Millie and I walked off but before we turned the corner at the end of the hallway, I looked over my shoulder. Dr. Clarke was still standing where we'd left him and he still had his eyes on me.

I had just made it to my car in the hospital parking garage when I remembered the Tupperware that I'd packed my dinner in this morning. I'd left it in my locker.

"Dammit," I mumbled to myself. Then I turned around and went back to the parking garage elevator. When it finally arrived and the doors opened, my breath caught in my throat.

"Lovely to see again, Miss Hewitt," Dr. Clarke said.

This was the first time I'd seen him since we'd spoken to each other earlier, after I came out of the restroom with Millie. He was alone.

"Um, hi."

"Are you returning to work?"

"No, I'm going back to get something that I forgot in my locker. Then I'm going home."

"The lift is all yours."

"*Lift?*"

The corners of Dr. Clarke's mouth curled up. "Elevator."

"Ah. British and American word differences."

"Yes."

As the lift/elevator doors were closing, he pushed the button to reopen them and then slowly stepped up to me.

"May I ask you a question?" I said, not feeling quite so nervous around him.

"Of course."

"Why are you here?"

"In the car park?"

"You mean *parking garage*?"

"Yes."

"I wasn't wondering about that, Dr. Clarke. I was wondering why you're here in America."

"I applied for the position of a resident doctor at this hospital and was offered it."

"So you wanted to move across the Atlantic Ocean just to practice your medicine?"

The corners of his mouth curled up again. "Yes, I wanted to move across the *pond*, as I call it, to practice my medicine."

"Your family must miss you."

"They do, as I miss them, but they understand my decision to come here."

"Do you have a spouse and children back in England that you're planning to move to Boston later on?"

"No. Do you have a spouse and children?"

I shook my head no. "I hope to one day, though. I've always imagined myself having a big family."

"So have I." Dr. Clarke pushed the elevator call button again to keep the doors open for me and then asked, "Do you have a sweetheart?"

"You mean *boyfriend*? I do."

"Lucky bloke."

"Thank you. I'm also lucky."

Someone texted me, so I reached for my cellphone in my scrub pants pocket. Dr. Clarke also reached for his, in his pocket, and then we looked at our screens and back up at each other.

"It was your phone that I heard. You and I have the same pulse text tone," I said.

The Englishman smiled and then stepped over to the elevator and held the doors open for me instead of pushing the call button again. "I must reply to this text. Plus your chariot awaits, Miss Hewitt."

I grinned, stepped into my makeshift chariot, and turned around. "I have one more question for you before I go. Why were you in Salem on Saturday?" I asked.

"The same as everyone else."

"Trying to get your witchy fix?"

"Something like that. Farewell."

17

#fairytale

Gabriel

"How was your day?" I asked Harper.

"It was fine. How was yours?"

"Uneventful, which is always good."

"Yes, always."

I noticed Harper wasn't as lively and forthcoming with her words, which made me wonder if something was wrong. Everything within me was telling me that it was.

"Are you okay?"

"I'm just tired."

"Okay then."

"I think I'll go to bed early tonight."

"I know you haven't been getting the sleep that you normally do since we met."

"It feels like it caught up with me too."

"I'm sorry."

"It's fine."

"Harper, what's going on? This is more than you being tired. I sense it, so I must ask."

"Is that one of your witch abilities? Keen senses?"

"It's a human ability."

"Gabriel, I had a long and taxing day. That's all. Patients will be patients and doctors will be doctors."

"I can only imagine."

"Just know that I miss you."

"I can be at your apartment in a flash."

Harper chuckled. "It's tempting. But you and I both know if you came here, neither of us would get the sleep we need."

"I beg to differ. It could very well be the best sleep we've ever had."

There was a lull in our conversation, and my senses were still telling me that something was wrong with Harper. Something more than her being tired and dealing with patients and doctors. I wasn't going to push her any further about all of this, though.

"Will you FaceTime me?" she suddenly asked, surprising me. "I need to see those dreamy amber eyes of yours."

"Hang up and you will."

The moment I saw Harper's face on my cellphone screen, I breathed a sigh of relief. She was smiling at me and I could sense her energy shifting back to what it normally was.

"There you are," I said.

"And there you are."

"I wish I could crawl through my phone to you."

"Ditto."

"I can hardly wait to see you on Friday. Do you still want to eat at Union Oyster Bar?"

"Yes! I love that place."

"Then it's a date."

"Do you mind if I have dessert after dinner?"

"Goodness, no," I chuckled. "You don't even have to ask. Get anything you want and as many desserts as you want."

"I only want one. Can you guess what it is?"

"Not right at this moment. After we hang up, I'll take a look at the online menu and then text you my guess."

"The dessert that I want isn't on Union Oyster Bar's menu."

I grinned. "Is that so?"

"Yes."

"Then where is the dessert that you want?"

"He's on my cellphone screen."

• • •

"What's up, Gabe?" Willow asked.

"Do you have time to talk on the phone for a few minutes?"

"I always have time for my brother, and more than a few minutes."

"Okay then. I just wanted to catch you up on things between Harper and me. You're the only one I can talk to about all of this and I've got to talk because I'm feeling so much."

"Then spill the beans."

"Things are quickly progressing."

"I gathered that from our last conversation."

"I surprised her last night at her apartment. She had no idea that I was coming over."

"So you saw her twice yesterday."

"No, just once. When I went to the hospital, she was busy with a patient. But I did leave the roses with Harper's friend Millie and she made sure Harper got them."

"Good."

"When I saw her last night, things became quite physical between us but I stopped myself from taking them too far. I didn't want Harper to think I came over to have sex because I didn't."

"Well, it is a bit early for that to happen."

"It's probably never going to happen between Harper and me."

"Why do you think that?"

"Because she's a virgin."

"What?"

"She's a virgin."

"Okay."

"Her reason for remaining chaste doesn't have anything to do with her religious upbringing that I told you about, though. It has to do with the fact that Harper has never been in love. She won't give all of her body away until she is—and not just your average love either. She wants the kind that's in romance books and fairy tales."

"Everyone does."

"You're right. What I have going on with Harper feels like a fairy tale. She and I aren't in love but we are crazy about each other."

"Given a little more time, you may just fall head over heels in love with her. She's like your Cinderella and you're her Prince Charming. Or rather, *Witch* Charming," Willow chuckled.

"Good one, little sister."

"Thank you. I crack myself up. So how do you feel about Harper being a virgin?"

"I respect it, and I respect her reasoning behind the decision."

"I get that, and I respect her too. What I meant was: how do you feel about being in a sexless romantic relationship?"

"I'm good with it."

"You know as well as I do that things are going to keep heating up between you and Harper, and I think it's going to reach a point where neither of you is good with not having sex. The temptation to go all the way is going to eventually come up whether you're in love or not. Human nature, Gabe."

"There are other things that Harper and I can do. She shared with me that she and her ex-boyfriend did them. She has experience. I saw it in her on Sunday and last night."

"I'm relieved for both of you. The passion between you and Harper is going to need an outlet. If it doesn't get one, then I can see both of you becoming victims of spontaneous human combustion."

I laughed. "It's possible."

"Are you still taking Harper on a date on Friday?"

"Yes. We're going to Union Oyster House."

"Yum! You'll have to let me know how the date goes."

"I will. Thanks for listening to me tonight."

"Any time. You know I'm just a phone call away."

"Ditto."

"I don't think I've ever heard you say that word before."

"It's one of Harper's words. I stole it from her."

"Now you need to work on stealing her heart. I can tell she's already stealing yours."

18

#bodyandsoul

Harper

Yesterday, Gabriel and I went through the same routine of exchanging good morning texts, texting on and off while we were at work, and then talking on the phone during the evening. Each time, he never failed to put a smile on my face. Same as now since I'd just received his Thursday morning greeting. I was also smiling because he had no clue that I was coming to see him today. I had texted him as if I was going to work.

After getting dressed, I was on my way to see my handsome magic man. I had no idea if he was going to be at the Raven's Cauldron when I arrived in Salem, but that was the first place I planned to check. I spotted Gabriel's black Range Rover in the parking lot and parked next to it. Then I went inside the Gothic building.

People were browsing in the bookstore while some sat in the lounge area, reading. There were lots of people in the coffee shop enjoying their cups of caffeine but from where I was standing, I could only see a few customers in the wine bar. I wasn't surprised, though, since it wasn't even noon yet.

I decided to not go inside right away because I wanted to try something first. I was curious if Gabriel would sense my presence before he saw me, as he'd done on the day we met. I peeked around the entrance but couldn't see him anywhere.

Then he appeared from the left, pushing a dolly stacked with crates of wine.

He was in the middle of unloading them when he stopped and glanced around with a perplexed look on his face. Then he stepped around from behind the bar and began walking toward the entrance. I jumped out in front of him and said, "Boo!" He gasped as he ran into me, then grabbed my shoulders.

"Harper! What are you doing here?" he asked, smiling so big.

"I came to see you."

"But you're supposed to be at the hospital."

"No. One of my coworkers asked me to swap shifts with her. I wanted to surprise you."

"You have surprised me! I cannot believe you're actually standing here in front of me."

"Well, believe it. You sensed me again, didn't you?"

"Yes. My first thought was there was no possible way that you could be here, but I had to take a look around anyway—and here you are."

Gabriel wrapped his arms around my waist and lifted me off the floor. I held his face in my hands, and then he pressed his warm lips against mine. I breathed him in, feeling as though I was exactly where I was supposed to be.

After he set me back down, I said, "I hope I'm not interrupting your work too much."

"You're not."

"Well, I saw the crates of wine that you started unloading."

"I can get one of my employees to finish it. It's not a big deal. Your coming here like this is such a gift and I'm taking full advantage of it. What would you like to do?"

"Gabriel, I didn't plan on pulling you away from your responsibilities. I just thought I could sit at the bar for a little while and sip on a glass of your amazing malbec while talking to you in between you waiting on your customers or whatever else you need to do."

He shook his no. "Not happening. Let's get out of here."

"Are you sure?"

"Yes. The only things that I need to do before we leave is touch base with my wine bar manager and go up to my office for a minute."

"Okay then. Um, I'll go wait in my car for you."

"Are you kidding? You're coming with me."

Gabriel laced his fingers through mine and we started walking into the wine bar—both of us smiling from cheek to cheek. I got to meet the manager that he had mentioned. Her name was Miranda Stevens and she was really nice. After Gabriel told her about his plan to leave work, she grinned while looking back and forth between Gabriel and me. Then she told us to have fun.

Gabriel and I continued holding hands until we reached his office door. He unlocked it and motioned for me to walk ahead of him. After locking it behind us, he turned around to face me.

We were standing several yards apart. He was still by his door and I was in front of his desk. Then, as if someone had shot a starting pistol at a track meet, Gabriel and I took off running toward each other and our bodies collided. We were wrapped up in one another's arms again and kissing without any restraint. Gabriel walked me backward over to the far wall of his office, never ceasing to taste my mouth with his.

When he pulled his lips away from mine, I opened my eyes and looked up at him. He grinned wickedly, grabbed my hands, and held them above my head, against the wall. Then he started gently biting the skin on my neck and running his tongue up and down it. I sighed as we both melted into each other even more.

"I crave you so much," Gabriel breathed into my ear.

"I crave you too."

He had just let go of my hands and was starting to pick me up underneath the backs of my legs when someone knocked on his office door. We both froze in place with a matching "Oh shit!" look on our faces.

"Gabe, it's me. I know you're in there, so open the door. I need to talk to you," a woman said, and I recognized her voice. It was Willow.

"Can't do that at the moment, sis."

"Why not?"

Gabriel kept looking at me as he stood up straight. "I just can't."

"Yes, you can."

"Unless it's an emergency, it's not happening. We'll talk later."

"No emergency here. But it sounded like you and Harper were on the verge of needing an ambulance called."

My jaw dropped, then Gabriel sighed and rolled his eyes.

"Go away, Willow."

"Okay. But we *will* talk later," she chuckled.

After she walked off, I asked Gabriel how she knew it was me in his office with him.

"Miranda told her that you're here or she heard you."

"I haven't said a word since I walked in here with you. Not until now. So Willow couldn't have heard me."

"But you did say something. You told me that you craved me."

"God, I did."

"Don't worry about it. I'm not."

"Wait. If Miranda didn't tell her that I was here, then how could she have heard me? Your office door is really thick wood and I was quiet just like you were."

"Willow can still hear. That's one of her abilities."

"What do you mean?"

"Her hearing is magnified. She can hear people talking from across a room if she focuses on them."

"Are you serious?"

"Yes."

"Are you capable of that?"

"No. But I can hear Willow's thoughts when I tune in to her. We have to be in close proximity to each other, though."

"That is...incredible."

Gabriel sat down in his desk chair and pulled me into his lap.

"Are you okay?" he asked.

"I'm fine."

"I just want to be sure."

"Don't worry."

"Okay then. What would you like for us to do today?"

"It doesn't matter to me."

"Well, it is dinnertime, so how about we go grab a bite to eat somewhere."

"That would be nice."

"What are you in the mood for?"

I teetered my head. "A deli sandwich if that sounds good to you."

"It does, and I know the perfect place. ChezCasa. There isn't a lot of seating room, but their sandwiches are worth the wait and so are their house-made potato chips."

"Why don't we get our dinners to go and eat at your farmhouse? I'd rather it be just us anyway if I'm being honest."

Gabriel tucked my hair behind my ear. "So would I."

Before we left his office, he filed away some paperwork that'd been sitting on top of his desk and put away a half-full bowl of mixed nuts and dried fruit into one of his desk drawers. I grinned because that was a favorite snack of mine too.

While we were walking toward the exit of the Raven's Cauldron, Willow approached and Gabriel officially introduced us. It went well; she was really friendly and kept grinning at her brother and me. After Gabriel told her what our plans were, she told us to enjoy our day and then flitted off like a little raven-haired fairy.

Gabriel had just walked me to my car and opened the driver side door when he remembered his office window was open.

"Harper, I apologize but I need to run back upstairs and close it," he said.

"No problem. I'll wait here for you."

"It won't take long."

After he returned, I followed him in my car to ChezCasa. While standing in line with him, I read the menu on the wall and also looked around at all the customers. A couple of them greeted Gabriel, and he introduced me as his girlfriend. When I heard him call me that, my skin tingled even more.

• • •

"Dinner was so good. Thank you again," I said.

"My pleasure. I still have some leftover birthday cake if you'd like a slice."

I rubbed my stomach. "Maybe in a little while. I am stuffed."

"Me too." Gabriel sat back in his chair and stretched out his long legs in front of him, underneath his dining room table. "So what would you like to do now?"

"Ask you a question."

"Okay then."

"I'll preface it with this first. When Millie and I were at the wine bar on Saturday, Willow walked by us as I was saying something about you and I am pretty certain that she overheard me because she cut her eyes at me and smiled."

Gabriel smiled then.

"Oh my God, she did hear me and she let you know what I said by thinking it to you, didn't she?"

"Yes."

"And you heard her thought while you were standing at the opposite end of the bar. You were going over paperwork on a clipboard but then stopped, looked up at me, and grinned while tugging on that luscious bottom lip of yours."

"Correct."

I buried my face in my hands and mumbled, "I knew it."

"Harper, don't be embarrassed."

I peeked through my fingers at Gabriel. "I can't help it."

"Full confession... I was having the same thoughts about you."

I took a deep breath and laid my hands back down in my lap. "That I might be a little lonely and in need of some hot and sweaty sex?"

"Yes. I hope you don't think badly of me now."

"I could say the same to you."

"I would never think badly of you."

I kept looking at Gabriel, sitting at the head of the table, while I sat to his left. Then I asked, "Was I right about you being lonely like me?"

"Yes."

"Are you still lonely?"

"Not since I met you."

"Ditto."

"Are you going to ask me about the other part?"

"I was thinking about it."

"Don't hold back now."

"Are you still in need of some hot and sweaty sex?"

"Yes, but the kind that's meaningful. Not just a fuck. That's all I've ever had and it's empty. I'm better off taking care of myself."

"Yeah. Me too." I glanced down at Gabriel's chest. "Did those women you dated before know you were a witch?"

"They asked me if I was one when they saw my pentagram tattoo, but I played it off. I told them that it symbolized my hometown and its history. Nothing more."

"You didn't want them to know what you are because you didn't trust them enough?"

"Correct."

"How long did you date each of the women?"

"About two months."

"Did they ever come here to your farmhouse?"

"No."

"Why?"

"I didn't want them here or in Salem. I kept all of my dealings with them in Boston."

"Because of your father, right?"

Gabriel nodded yes. "I was concerned that he'd instantly catch wind of my dating life if I brought it to Essex County. But I want you to also understand that my choice to not have any of my ex-girlfriends come to my home wasn't only about my father. Even if he wasn't invasive with my personal life, I never would've allowed the three women to come here. I go back to trust. Unless I totally have it with someone, they're not coming to my home. It is my most personal space and it is sacred to me."

"We met six days ago and I already know you're a witch. I know about your family dynamics. I've been to your beautiful farmhouse twice now. We've cooked a meal together here. You kissed me in front of the wine bar entrance today. You held my hand while introducing me to Miranda and your sister. You also did that while we were standing in line at ChezCasa—a local eatery in your hometown. You introduced me as your girlfriend to two of your acquaintances there, and I don't mind telling you that I really liked hearing you call me that. What is so different for you this time around, Gabriel, when it comes to dating someone? You've gone from one extreme to the other."

"It is you, Harper. You've opened a part of my soul that's never been opened before and you did it just by being you. I want this that's between us—whatever it is. I've never wanted anything more, and I would like to give us a chance to see where it goes. A real chance."

I could feel the sting in my eyes, then a tear rolled down my cheek and I wiped it away. Gabriel immediately got up from the table and came over to me. Then he picked me up underneath my arms and carried me over to his chair where he sat back down and I straddled his lap.

Gabriel said, "I've talked to my sister a whole lot about you. She told me that she could tell you were already stealing my heart away from me—and she's right. You are."

"You're doing the same thing to me. It scares me, too."

Gabriel reached up and pushed my hair behind my shoulders. "I'll never hurt you. I just want to love you—body and soul. I want to take care of you. Spoil you. Experience new things with you. I want it all."

19

#stay

Harper

The sun was getting close to setting when I told Gabriel that I should start heading back home. He remained quiet, but I could see in his eyes what he wanted to say. I wanted him to say it too. He never did, though. Instead, he got up from his couch, held out his hand for mine, and walked me outside to my car. As soon as he opened the driver side door, he closed it and turned to me.

"Stay with me tonight, Harper. Please."

And there it was. Exactly what I needed to hear, spilling from Gabriel's pretty lips.

"If I stay, what will happen between us?" I asked, thinking about how physical we'd already become with each other.

"Only what you want to happen."

"You know what I want to happen, but it can't. Even as much as you tempt me."

"What do you think you do to me?"

I stared up at Gabriel, standing only inches away. He was so close that I could smell his sweet breath and the masculine scent of his body. "I'll stay," I whispered.

Relief instantly washed across his face. "Thank you. You can sleep in my bed and I'll take one of the guest rooms. I just want you here with me."

"I'm sorry, but that arrangement won't work."

"Why not?"

"Because you'll be too far away from me. I want you lying beside me in your bed and I want to fall asleep in your arms."

"Okay then."

• • •

"Where on earth are you taking me?"

"It's not actually *on* the earth. It's on something else."

I side-eyed Gabriel and grinned. He was grinning too. Several yards later, we reached the back left corner of his wine building.

"Now we're going up that spiral staircase," he said, pointing at it.

"But it goes all the way up to the ceiling. Where do we go after we reach the last step?"

"Through the hatch."

I looked up again. "So that's what that is. What's on the other side of it?"

"The top of this building."

"And that's where you want to take me?"

"I do."

"To throw me off it?"

Gabriel busted out laughing. "You trust me, right?"

"I did, but I don't know now," I joked.

"We can turn around and go back up to the farmhouse if you'd like."

"No, I wouldn't 'like.' I am really curious about the view from the top of this building."

"That's exactly why I want to take you up there. Are you ready?"

I took a deep breath. "Yes."

"I'm going to lead us up the staircase. Just hang on to the railing or the back of my waistband, okay?"

"I choose your waistband."

"Thought you might."

We grinned at each other and then started walking up the stairs. When we made it about halfway, Gabriel asked, "How are you holding up?"

"Great!"

"Are you sure?"

"Yes. I've been focusing on the scenery."

"*Scenery*?"

"Your tight ass. It's really nice."

Gabriel glanced over his shoulder and smiled at me. "Glad you think so."

"I know so."

Unable to stop myself, I grabbed his left ass cheek and squeezed it, making him jump.

"Enjoying yourself back there, Miss Hewitt?"

"Thoroughly."

When we reached the top of the staircase, Gabriel unlocked the hatch and then pushed it up and out of the way.

"I'm going to step onto the roof and then I'll help you up," he said, glancing over his shoulder at me again.

"I'm excited."

"That's what I want to hear. I think you're going to really enjoy what we're about to do."

The moment I stepped onto the roof, I gasped at what I was seeing. There was an observation deck, several yards long and wide with solar lights encircling its entire perimeter.

"Oh my God, did you build that?" I asked.

"I did."

"It's incredible."

"Thank you."

"Do you come up here often?"

"Every chance I get. Come on."

Gabriel reached for my hand and then led me over to a section of the deck that had a large outside storage bench on it. He opened it and pulled out several blankets, as well as two pillows.

I stood back and watched him spread the blankets and place the pillows side by side. When he was done, he looked back at me.

"Care to join me?" he asked.

"I would love to."

He motioned for me to sit down and asked, "Would you like some malbec?"

"Don't tell me you have that up here too."

"But I do."

"You're always prepared, aren't you?"

"I try to be."

I sighed. "I would love some of your malbec."

"Then I shall pour a glass for you."

"Are you going to have some?"

"Of course. I'm not letting you drink alone."

Gabriel stepped back over to the storage bench and proceeded to get out a bottle of wine, an opener, and two glasses. After pouring some of his malbec into both, he handed me one. Then I looked at his glass.

"Harper, I know you're probably wondering why I have two glasses instead of only one. Willow has been up here with me many times before. My mother even hangs out with me on occasion to enjoy some wine and the night sky."

"You read my mind."

"No. I'd be wondering about the extra glass, too, if I were you, since I told you that I've never had any of my ex-girlfriends come to my home, which to me includes this building. It's like a second home for me in a sense, because I spend so much time in it."

"I appreciate your understanding."

"I totally understand."

Gabriel sat down next to me on the pallet and held up his glass. "Cheers."

We clinked our glasses together, took a sip of wine, and then Gabriel leaned over and softly kissed me.

"That was nice," I said, looking over his handsome face. "Everything you're doing and have done is nice. You know how to make a girl feel special."

"You are special, Harper." Gabriel smiled and then looked up at the sky. "Do you see those two bright stars?" he asked, pointing at them.

"You can't miss them because they're so bright."

"They're actually the planets Venus and Mercury. It won't be long before Mars rises."

"So you're into astronomy too?"

"I am. Humankind has always done as you and I are doing now: staring up at the heavens in wonder and fascination."

"It's a beautiful sight."

"If people would take the time—say, twice a week—to sit outside under the stars, I believe they'd feel a whole lot better about life and could handle its stresses easier. It has a way of putting everything back into perspective."

I shook my head back and forth. "You are part vintner, essential oil pro, songbird, chef, magician, astronomer, and philosopher. Is there anything else that you're into?"

"Nothing that I can think of," Gabriel chuckled. "But we all have different facets that make us who we are. There's more to you than being a nurse. Much more."

The way that Gabriel was looking at me, along with the way the starlight was illuminating his face, sent a wave of arousal rushing through me and I quietly sighed.

"Let's lie down and watch the sky for shooting stars," he said.

"I'd love to."

We both took another sip of wine and set our glasses to the sides of the pallet, and then Gabriel stretched out beside me.

"Come here. I need to feel you in my arms," he said, holding out his toward me.

I smiled and fell over into them, and Gabriel pulled me even closer and wrapped one of his legs around both of mine. I buried my face in his chest and breathed him in while he smelled my hair. When I looked up at him, he kissed me and then pulled one of the blankets over us. Only a few minutes had passed when we both spotted the same shooting star and pointed at it.

"Make a wish!" we both said and then laughed. A moment later, Gabriel told me about his wish. Not the one that he'd just made, but the one I'd watched him make before blowing out his birthday candles.

"My wish was to have you as my own, Harper," he said.

"I am yours."

"I'm yours too."

Gabriel kept staring into my eyes and then softly smiled at me. "How about we listen to some music?"

"Your playlist, not mine."

"Okay then. By the way, I added Doja Cat's 'Addiction' per your request."

"How many times have you listened to it since I first sent it to you?"

"Too many."

"Did you imagine me dancing naked to it?"

"Every single time."

"Good."

"I'd like for you to listen to a song that I added to my playlist while on my way to the Raven's Cauldron this morning. As you know, Pandora suggests songs that are similar to the ones that we already have, and the one that it suggested to me immediately made me think of you."

"Is it a sexy song like 'Addiction?'"

"No. But I think you'll like it anyway. At least I hope you do."

"Can't wait to hear it."

Gabriel pushed play and then laid his cellphone down on the deck by our heads. The first thing that I heard was the soft strumming of a guitar. As it continued, Gabriel held me in his arms while I rested my head on his chest and looked up at the autumn night sky. When the male singer began easing out the first lyrics with his smooth voice, I swooned. Not only because of the romantic stream of words, but also because Gabriel had quietly sung them too.

As the song continued playing and I kept listening to him speaking to me through it, I could feel myself falling for him even more. Was I still scared? Yes. Because I knew he was the one man who could shatter my heart into a million little pieces. He was a dream come true and too good to be true at the same time.

After he sang the lines "Spinning like a turning wheel. Looking like the way I feel. You can keep all that you steal because I want you now," I looked up at him and he stopped singing. For the remainder of the song, he gazed into my eyes...and I just kept falling for him.

As the next song on his playlist was beginning, I asked him about the one that we'd just listened to.

"The Paper Kites," he said. "'Nothing More Than That.'"

"You already know all the lyrics."

Gabriel nodded. "I cannot tell you how many times I've listened to them today. I put on my earbuds after I got to the Raven's Cauldron and kept the song on repeat until minutes before you surprised me at work."

"You and I both get lost in music, don't we?"

"Yes, we do."

"I can see why you got lost in 'Nothing More Than That.' It's a beautiful song."

"You're beautiful, Harper."

"So are you."

Gabriel smiled. "Come lay on top of me but with your back to me."

"Okay then."

As I stretched out my body on his, he slid his hands around my waist and held me tight. We were watching for another shooting star while talking when "Addiction" started playing. We grinned at each other, and then I started swaying my hips to the rhythm of the song.

"You're going to dance for me now?" Gabriel chuckled.

"Yes! I can't help it. This song just does it to me."

I didn't get up and give him a show. I stayed where I was and kept moving my body on top of his. He started running his nose up and down the side of my face and neck, smelling my skin. He was also running his right hand across my hip and upper thigh, squeezing them. I knew Gabriel was aroused, but it wasn't only what he was doing to me that let me know it. I could feel his erection pressing against my ass through his pants.

"Harper..." he breathed into my ear.

I didn't say anything to him, but I did move his right hand underneath my shirt, up to my breasts. Then he took over and started touching me exactly how I'd been longing for him to touch me.

He gently squeezed my breasts through my bra, then unclasped the front of it and began rolling my nipples between his fingertips, making me sigh over and over again. Wanting to feel his touch even more, I grabbed his hand and eased it down to the waistband of my yoga pants, but he stopped me from going any further.

"I don't want to go too far with you," Gabriel said.

"This is where I want you to go. I need you to."

He nodded and then took over again. He pushed his hand beneath my yoga pants and lace panties and immediately found my swollen clit with his fingertip. My body rose up at his touch and I moaned, then I started swaying my hips to the music again while Gabriel rubbed circles on top of my clit, driving me even wilder.

When he bucked his lower torso, I knew he was imagining fucking me. I was imagining him doing it, too, but it wasn't going to happen. There were other things that we could do, though, to relieve this ache between us.

What I needed from Gabriel now was for him to slide his finger deep inside me, but I knew he wouldn't do it on his own because of my virgin status. So I reached for his hand and pushed it further down, then I began pushing one of his fingers into my pussy. His fingertip had barely gone inside me when he pulled it back out. I stopped swaying my hips and looked at him.

"You won't hurt me," I said.

"If I do what you want me to do, I will most certainly hurt you."

"No, you won't. I have a vibrator at home."

A deliciously wicked grin spread across Gabriel's lips, and then he slowly slid his middle finger inside me and pulled it back out.

"You're so wet," he whispered.

"Because of you. Now finger-fuck me until I cum."

"Yes, ma'am."

As he began sliding his finger in and out of my pussy in a steady rhythm, I leaned my head back on his shoulder and closed my eyes. Seconds later, the tingling in my skin started growing in intensity, and Gabriel started finger-fucking me faster and harder. I turned my face toward him and opened my eyes again because I could feel myself on the verge of coming and wanted to look at him when I did. His eyes were half closed and his lips were parted like mine and we were both breathing fast.

As my body began releasing itself, Gabriel pressed his forehead against mine and I began moaning out all the pleasure I was feeling. It kept going on and on, making my legs tremble and my toes curl.

"I'm not done with you yet, so hang on, baby," Gabriel whispered against my face.

Then I felt a surge of hot energy expand through my pussy and lower abdomen, taking my breath away and making me arch my back. When it ended, I gasped for air and then melted on top of Gabriel. Once I'd caught my breath, I pulled back and looked at him. He was grinning.

"How was that, Miss Hewitt?" he asked.

"What did you do to me?"

"I directed my energy into you at the right time and it magnified everything you were feeling."

I stared at Gabriel. "You did it through your finger?"

"Yes."

"You're joking."

"No, I'm not."

"I've never cum that hard or long in my life. I'll never recover from it either. I don't want to."

"I don't want you to. I want you to keep coming back to me for more."

"Have you ever done what you just did to me, to anybody else?"

"No."

"Why me then?"

"I wanted you to feel exceptionally good. I knew you needed it and I wanted to be the one to provide it for you."

"Your finger is like a magic wand."

Gabriel smiled. "In a sense, yes."

"And you still have it in me."

"I know. I like it there. I've been wanting to touch you *and* taste you."

"Pull your magic wand out of me and you can taste me."

He removed his middle finger from my body, stuck it into his mouth, wrapped his lips around it, and then slowly pulled it back out. "Just like I thought you'd taste. You're sweet like honey," he said.

I kept staring into his eyes while thinking about not only what he'd just done to me but also about making him feel exceptionally good. I didn't have the ability to direct my energy through one of my fingers, but I did have an able mouth and a slick tongue.

"Where are you going?" Gabriel asked as I was getting up off him.

"Here."

I straddled his upper thighs and began unbuttoning his shirt. Then I pushed it open and looked at his chest and abs while running my fingertips across the muscled grooves. When I was done, I sighed. Gabriel was such a beautifully made man and he was mine.

After leaning down and kissing him, I tugged on his bottom lip with my teeth while he kept his eyes on me. I could tell that he was anticipating my next move, so I ran my tongue across his left nipple piercing and then sucked on his nipple, causing him to let out a low groan.

I kept making my way down his body by kissing and gently biting his skin and when I made it to the waistband of his pants, I sat back up and started unbuckling his belt. But he stopped me by placing his hand on top of mine.

"Harper, you don't have to do anything for me. I'm satisfied with having given you pleasure," he said.

"I want to touch you and taste you too. I've fantasized about it more than you know."

Gabriel grew quiet and stared at me. The gentleman inside him had just stepped forward, but I didn't want to see him. I wanted to see the wild man that I knew was inside Gabriel. Then he appeared.

He lifted his hand off mine and I continued doing what I wanted to do. I unbuckled his belt and then unbuttoned and unzipped his pants. When I saw the outside of his sports briefs, I smiled to myself because of the big bulge. Then I looked back up to see the wild man still staring at me.

"Are you ready?" I whispered.

He nodded yes, and I pulled his pants and sports briefs down to his upper thighs. When I saw his erect dick, I was surprised, but not because of its size. It was due to the tip of it being pierced. Perhaps I shouldn't have been surprised, considering Gabriel's pierced ears and nipples, but I still was. I really liked that he had his dick pierced, though. It was just one more thing about him that turned me on so fucking much.

I reached out and lightly ran my fingertip across the silver hoop and then swirled it around Gabriel's tip, making his stomach quiver. "Did it hurt?" I asked.

"Not too badly."

"Why did you get it?"

"Because it makes having sex feel better for me, as well as for who I'm with."

"It looks good on you. I like all of your piercings. I also like that your dick is leaking so much." I held up my fingertip and showed Gabriel his semen on it.

"That's how much I want you," he said.

I touched him again but this time, I wrapped my fingers around the end of his rock-hard dick and gently squeezed it. His body rose up like mine had done when he first touched my clit and then he relaxed again, still closely watching every move that I was making.

After wetting the inside of my hand on him, I began running it up and down all of his thick inches. Gabriel's lips parted, his breathing deepened, and his amber eyes blazed with desire. He was in such a vulnerable state with me and that within itself was its own special kind of turn-on.

I stopped pumping him, leaned over, and took the edge of his dick piercing between my teeth. When I looked back up at him, his teeth were clenched together. He was so aroused and it had me ready to go another round with him finger-fucking me.

Before I let go of his piercing, I gently pulled on it and watched Gabriel's body rise up and relax again. After licking the creamy saltiness off his tip, I started sucking on it. That was when Gabriel pushed his head back into his pillow and closed his eyes while his chest continued rising and falling with the deep breaths that he was taking.

After expanding my throat, I took the full length of him into my mouth which caused Gabriel to let out a deep groan that sounded more like a growl. Then I began running my mouth up and down him. A moment later, my magic man breathed out my name and I looked up to see him watching me again.

I started pumping him once more and also sucked on his smooth sack. As I began moving my hand faster, he began moving his hips in rhythm with me and quietly groaned with every deep breath that he was taking. I could tell that he was so close to coming. The concentrated look on his face, all the sounds that he was making, and the snakelike flow of his body gave him away. Gabriel was on fire and so was I.

I took my mouth off his sack and went back to sucking on his tip while still pumping him. Less than a minute later, his body stiffened and he began growling out a deep groan again. Then he filled my mouth with his warmth and I swallowed every drop.

As Gabriel's body began relaxing back onto our pallet of blankets, I took my mouth off him and looked up at his face. He was staring straight up at the sky, still trying to catch his breath, and then he focused on me again. I still had his dick in my hand and my mouth wasn't far from it. Neither of us said anything. We just kept gazing into each other's eyes. Then Gabriel motioned for me to come to him.

After I lay down on top of his body, he reached up and slowly ran his thumb across my lips.

"What you just did to me was..." he began saying.

"Was what?"

"Out of this world."

I smiled. "Good."

"Harper, I've never cum that hard or long in my life."

"Now we're even."

"I'll never recover from it either. I don't want to."

Gabriel was using the same words that I'd said to him earlier. Then I repeated his.

"I don't want you to. I want you to keep coming back to me for more."

"You can count on it," he said. Then he kissed me.

20

#sweetdreams

Gabriel

Before walking back to the farmhouse, Harper and I spent about another half hour holding each other and talking on the observation deck. What she and I had done up there, I hadn't planned on. I wasn't complaining, though. We didn't fuck each other, but my body felt as if we had. I felt incredible and even closer to Harper.

We were in my bedroom now and I had just told her to feel free to take a shower or a bath. I wanted her to make herself at home here within mine.

"Shower with me," she said.

I searched her eyes and nodded. I had never showered with any woman before, but I wanted to with Harper. I wanted to do everything with her.

After we walked into my bathroom, I turned on the water and adjusted it to the right temperature. Steam quickly filled the shower and rolled out of the top of it like clouds. When I looked back over at Harper, she had already taken off all of her clothes and was walking toward me. I looked her up and down and swallowed hard. She wasn't shy about her body and hers took my breath away.

"Let's get these clothes off you, Vintner Grey," she said as she was unbuttoning my shirt. Then she stripped me down to my skin. We stood in front of each other, both of us totally naked for the first time, and I'd never felt more bold and free.

After Harper and I stepped into my shower, I closed the glass door behind us. Then she smiled at me, backed into the stream of water, closed her eyes, and let the water run down over her face and body. I just kept watching her, taking mental photos of everything I was seeing.

When she stepped toward me, I told her to turn around so I could wash her hair and bathe her. It was all foreign territory to me, but I still wanted to do it because I wanted to touch Harper in this other intimate way.

I washed and conditioned her long hair, and she didn't flinch once nor complain that I'd hurt her tender scalp. After lathering up my hands with my bar of soap, I began bathing her. When I reached her breasts, I felt my dick twitch. I didn't need it to get hard again, but it was already starting to happen. Harper noticed, too, and grinned up at me.

"Taking a shower with you is dangerous," I said.

"I'm not scared."

"You should be, because what I'm imagining doing to you at the moment is..." I cleared my throat. "Never mind."

By the time I began bathing Harper between her legs, I had a full erection and she just kept grinning at me. When I finished bathing her all over and she had rinsed off, she turned back around to face me and wrapped her fingers around my dick.

"Let me take care of this for you," she said.

"You already have once today."

"You apparently need me to do it again."

She pushed me backward until my back was against the shower wall and then she started jacking me off. I watched her do it because I wanted to see the way she touched me instead of just mostly feeling it like I'd done while we were on the observation deck.

When I felt myself getting close to coming, I braced myself against the wall with my hands and planted my feet on the floor. Then it began happening. I closed my eyes, leaned my head back against the wall, and groaned through my clenched teeth. I felt like I was flying as Harper kept pumping my dick, making it shoot off everywhere, I was certain.

As I was coming down from my sexual high, I opened my eyes and looked back at Harper. My cum was all across her breasts and abdomen. She swiped some of it off her right breast with her fingertip and grinned at me again. Then she licked my cum off her fingertip.

"I love the way you taste," she said.

"You know I love the way you taste too," I said, still trying to catch my breath.

Once I'd balanced out, Harper rinsed me off the front of her body and then proceeded to wash and condition my hair and bathe me. She touched me so tenderly and I didn't want her to stop. Her touch was addictive. Everything about her was.

After we got out of the shower, we dried each other off. Then I pulled Harper into my arms. I wanted to feel her naked body against mine one more time before we got dressed and went to bed.

"Would you mind if I borrowed a shirt to sleep in and possibly a pair of shorts?" she asked.

"Of course I wouldn't mind, but my clothes are going to swallow you."

"I know, but I'd really love to sleep in one of your shirts. Also, my panties and yoga pants are quite wet in the crotch area, thanks to you."

"Let's go find something for you to wear then."

I pulled one of my T-shirts out of my dresser drawer, along with a pair of drawstring shorts. When I held them up in front of Harper, I started laughing. "My T-shirt could be a dress for you, and I don't think you can pull the drawstring on my shorts tight enough to keep them on your petite body," I said.

Harper looked at the shorts, but didn't take them from me. She did take my T-shirt, though, and slipped it over her head. "I'm fine just wearing this."

"Thankfully, it reaches the tops of your knees. I don't need to see you walking around here with that fine ass of yours showing."

"I could always flash you." I looked up at the ceiling and sighed. Then I returned my gaze to Harper's smiling face. "Yeah, you could."

After I put on a pair of sports briefs and the drawstring shorts that Harper couldn't wear, I asked her if she was hungry. We'd eaten the deli sandwiches and potato chips from ChezCasa earlier, but that was it.

"I could definitely eat a slice of your birthday cake."

"Me too. Let's go!"

We walked hand in hand to my kitchen and while I was getting our slices of cake, Harper poured two glasses of milk for us. We both sat on the island, feeding each other bites of cake and stealing kisses in between. Everything that we had done today felt so natural—as if we'd been together for years. I never knew a romantic relationship could be like this. That it could be this good.

After I rinsed off our dishes and put them into the dishwasher, I told Harper that I needed to show her something before we went to bed. She glanced down at my crotch and grinned.

"Not him," I chuckled.

"Okay then. What do you need to show me?"

I held up my finger. "Give me just a moment. I'll be right back."

Harper side-eyed me right before I walked off to the deck, but I didn't offer her any further info. As soon as I opened the door, I looked back at Harper.

"I'm about to introduce you to someone who is extraordinary and very, very special to me. Don't be scared when you see her, though. She won't hurt you," I said.

"*She*?"

"Yes. *She*."

I looked out the door and whistled. Seconds later, Josephine flew up and landed on my right shoulder. When I turned back around to face Harper, her eyes were huge and her mouth had fallen open.

"It's okay," I continued. "I promise you that Josephine will not hurt you."

"*Josephine?*"

"Yes. She's my familiar. Do you know what that means in the witch world?"

"No."

"She's a magical creature who watches over me. She's been with me since I was born. We're able to communicate with each other through our thoughts."

"But... she's a bird."

Josephine squawked and ruffled her feathers while Harper nearly jumped out of her skin. I chuckled and smoothed her feathers down while quietly shushing her, in her ear.

"It's okay, my love. Harper doesn't yet know how much that offends you." Looking back at Harper, I said, " Josephine detests being called a bird."

"I-I'm sorry. I didn't know."

"It's okay. She's a raven. A very unique one. She can be loud, but she's exceptionally intelligent and she's the best friend that I've ever had."

Josephine chattered quietly as she looked from me to Harper and back.

"Would you mind if Josephine and I come over to you? She would like to meet you."

"Did she just say that to you?"

"She did."

"Okay..."

"She doesn't want to scare you. She's been anxious to meet you for a while now."

Harper took a deep breath and slowly blew it out. She didn't appear to be as nervous as she'd been only a moment ago. "Okay. Please just take it slowly," she said.

I cautiously approached her, hoping she wouldn't take off running at the last second. I'd thought her seeing Josephine would freak her out, but not this much. She kept staring at Josephine.

"Gabriel, she is beautiful. I've never seen feathers so black and shiny."

Josephine made a soft noise in her throat.

"Josephine says 'thank you.'"

"I'm in complete fucking awe."

"Would you like to pet Josephine?"

"Yes, if she's okay with it."

"Hold out your hand so she can smell it."

"Like you'd do with a dog."

"Yes."

Harper turned her hand over, palm-up, and slowly held it out toward Josephine. It was trembling. I felt bad. This had really shaken Harper up, but she was quickly recovering. After Josephine touched her hand with her beak, she stretched out her neck.

"She wants you to scratch her on the back of her neck. It's her favorite spot," I told Harper.

She reached up and began scratching my spoiled pet. When Josephine started cooing, a smile stretched across Harper's face and her shoulders finally relaxed.

I needed to feed Josephine, so the three of us went over to the island. Josephine hopped down from my shoulder, and then I poured some mixed nuts and dried fruit into a bowl for her.

"Wait a minute," Harper said, pointing at the bowl. "You had that same mixture on your office desk earlier."

"I know."

"It was Josephine's and not yours, wasn't it?"

"Yes."

"So she was at the Raven's Cauldron when I got there? In your office?"

"Yes—until you and I began walking upstairs. I asked her to give us some space. I keep my office window cracked open and she went for a flight."

"Does Josephine go to work with you every day?"

"She goes everywhere with me."

"How have you kept her a secret from your employees?"

"I haven't. They all just think I'm eccentric enough to have a pet raven and I don't correct them. She only enters my office through the window and she never goes anywhere else inside the Raven's Cauldron. I do take food safety quite seriously and if word got out that there's a B-I-R-D hanging out where people eat and drink, I doubt the county health inspector or the local gossip mill would go easy on me."

"When you went back inside to close your office window earlier, did it have something to do with Josephine?"

I smiled at Harper. "I really did forget to close my window because I was a bit, uh, distracted. I had already let Josephine know our plans to go to ChezCasa and then my farmhouse."

"So what did she do? Follow us the whole time?"

"Yes."

"Wait a minute. I just remembered she was at my apartment complex, sitting on top of your car when we came out of the stairwell."

"Yes, she was."

"And I remember you acting like you were so annoyed by her. You deserve an Oscar for that performance."

I smiled again and took a bow. "Thank you."

Harper looked back at Josephine eating her dinner on the island. "Did she follow you to Boston to come pick me up?"

"No, she rode in my car with me."

"And then flew all the way back to Salem, following us?"

"Yes."

"That's such a long way for her to fly."

"She's a strong girl," I said as I reached out to scratch Josephine's back.

Harper sighed.

"I would've told you about her before now if I had thought you were ready to hear about her," I went on to say. "I've been easing you into my world, but when you agreed to spend tonight with me, I knew I would be introducing Josephine to you before we went to bed. I hoped you would take it well. She's very special to me and now, so are you."

Harper smiled at me and then looked back at Josephine. "She makes me wish I had a familiar. To have someone always watching over you would be amazing."

"It is."

Josephine finished eating and took off flying. I knew where she was heading: my bedroom. She normally slept in there, nestled at the foot of my bed, but that wasn't going to happen tonight.

When Harper and I walked into my bedroom, Josephine was in her usual spot. I shook my head at her and told her that I needed her to stay in the guest bedroom where Willow always slept when she stayed here late and didn't feel like driving back to our parents' house. Thankfully, Josephine didn't give me any grief about the change in her sleeping arrangement. After she flew out of my room, I closed the door behind her and walked over to Harper sitting on the edge of my bed.

"What a day," she said, smiling up at me.

"What an evening too."

"Yes, it has been. I'm just-just... I don't have all the words to describe how I'm feeling right now."

"I can describe how I'm feeling."

"I'm listening."

I took Harper's hands into mine and kissed them. "I'm happy. Genuinely happy and it's because of you. All of this between us has been an absolute whirlwind—but it feels right to me."

"It does to me too."

I reached out and brushed Harper's hair behind her shoulders. "Are you ready to go to sleep?"

"Yes. I need to. You need to. It's getting late and morning will be here before we know it."

"I've already got my cellphone alarm set to wake us up extra early so that you have plenty of time to get back to Boston."

"Thank you."

"Of course. I meant to tell you that I have a new toothbrush still in the package in my bathroom if you want to use it."

"I do want to. After eating that slice of your birthday cake and drinking the milk, my teeth feel like they have sweaters on them."

"That's a good way to describe it. Mine feel that way too. Shall we?" I asked, holding out my hand toward the bathroom.

"Yes, we shall."

Harper and I stood in front of the two sinks in my vanity and brushed our teeth together while grinning over at each other. It was a simple thing we were doing, but it felt good to be sharing a simple first with her. I looked forward to sharing more firsts with her and hoped she did with me.

After we returned to my bedroom, I pulled back the covers on the bed, and Harper crawled across my side to the other and lay down.

"Why are you looking at me like that?" she asked.

"As you were on your way over there, I saw your ass. I saw the other thing too."

Harper grinned. "*Thing?*"

"Yes...thing"

"You mean my pussy?"

"Well, yes."

"Can you not say the word?"

"I prefer not to, to you."

"Because you're trying to be a gentleman?"

"Yes."

"As wild as you and I got with each other earlier, you can say the word."

"I don't think so," I chuckled.

"Oh, come on! You can do it!"

Harper rose up onto her hands and knees and crawled over me. I was still standing next to my bed and could feel the redness in my face. Then I shook my head no.

"Gabriel, seriously. Say the word for me. It'd make my night."

I sighed. "Pussy."

"A little louder, please. You whispered that."

"Pussy!"

Harper rolled over onto her back and started laughing so hard. Then I jumped on top of her, straddled her hips, and held her arms above her head.

"You are so much fun," I said.

"It's so much fun teasing you."

"You know how to tease me in more ways than one. That's for certain."

"Look down between your legs."

As soon as I did, I swallowed hard and then cut my eyes back up at Harper. My T-shirt, that she was wearing, had risen up and her pussy was showing.

"Oops. Wardrobe malfunction," she said.

"What am I going to do with you, Harper Hewitt?"

"What do you want to do with me?"

"At this moment, it's a matter of what I want to do *to* you."

"Okay then. What do you want to do to me?"

"Taste you, but not by licking you off my finger. I want to run my tongue up and down the inside of your pussy and suck on your clit until you cum again. Besides, you're one orgasm behind me and I prefer to keep things even between us."

"Ditto."

21

#chances

Willow

I was on my way to my art studio this morning when I decided to stop by the Raven's Cauldron to see Gabriel. I figured he would've called me last night to let me know how his day with Harper had gone, but he didn't. I was so curious about them and thought they were adorable together.

When I walked into the wine bar, I saw Gabriel talking to Miranda by the register. Then he looked up and saw me coming toward him. He smiled with his whole face, and I chuckled. I knew that smile better than anyone and could hardly wait to hear what he was about to tell me.

Before I reached the bar, Miranda walked off to the backroom and it was only my brother and me. I sat down on one of the barstools and said, "Your face is already talking, but I need to hear the words. How was yesterday with Harper? I've been on edge, waiting to hear all about it."

"It was amazing. So was last night and this morning with her."

My jaw dropped. "Excuse me? Keep talking, mister."

"She spent last night with me. I asked her to. I didn't want her to leave."

I raised an eyebrow. "And? I know there's more to this story, so go ahead and spill it, Gabriel Grey. All of it."

"Stop doing that."

"Doing what?"

"Giving me that look."

"You and Harper totally messed around, didn't you?"

Gabriel looked down and shook his head back and forth, still smiling so big. I noticed lines on his face that I hadn't noticed before. They were so beautiful to me because I knew for the first time in a long time that my brother was truly happy. When he looked back up at me, he nodded yes to my question and I giggled.

"I knew it!" I told him. "After watching you and Harper together yesterday, I knew you guys couldn't physically resist each other for much longer. I could feel the chemistry and it was explosive, to say the least. You didn't do the whole deed, though, did you?"

"No, we didn't and we won't."

"I know you are trying to take things slow, Gabe, and I commend you for being such a gentleman. But I have a feeling that what is happening between you and Harper isn't going to be anything that either of you can control. You are as powerless with her as she is with you. You're each other's kryptonite."

Gabriel now had a look of both fear and acceptance on his face over what I had just told him.

"Everything you said isn't lost on me, Willow. I knew it when I first laid eyes on Harper. All I know is I'm crazy about her and there is no turning back now."

"I can tell that she's crazy about you too. I like her, Gabe. I really, really like her. It means the world to me to finally see you happy. You deserve all of this."

"Thank you."

I glanced around and still, no one was close to my brother and me. It was too early for customers and all of Gabriel's employees were elsewhere.

"So did you get to teach Harper anything?" I asked.

"No lessons, but I did introduce her to Josephine."

"Oh wow! That's a big step. How did it go?"

"Harper freaked out at first but got over the shock of Josephine and what she is rather quickly. Of course she had some questions that I was more than happy to answer. By the time Harper left, you would have thought she and Josephine were old friends."

"That's great. I wondered how Josephine was going to respond to Harper if you introduced them. She isn't used to sharing you."

"She's not used to a woman being at my farmhouse either."

"How was it for you, having Harper there with you again?"

"Wonderful. I like her being there. She loves the farmhouse and makes herself at home like I want her to."

"I love this so much for you, Gabe. I know Harper and I don't know each other well yet, but I have a feeling that she was destined to be part of our lives."

"I do too."

"When are you planning to see each other again?"

"Saturday."

"Is she coming back to Salem or are you going to Boston?"

"I asked her what she wanted to do and she told me that it was my turn to spend the night with her."

"Is Harper okay with Josephine tagging along and staying too?"

"She is. She's already planning to get some mixed nuts and dried fruit for her, to keep there."

"That's so thoughtful of her. Just like what she did by getting you a birthday cake."

"Harper is very thoughtful. It's a trait of hers that I adore."

My cellphone started ringing and I got it out of my purse.

"It's Mother," I said, looking up at Gabriel.

"So answer it."

After I said hello to her, the first thing out of her mouth was to ask me if the rumor about Gabriel dating someone was true. She knew how close my brother and I were and also that I would know the truth about him. It wasn't my place to tell her, though.

I would never divulge my brother's business, and our mother should've known that by now.

I was still looking across the bar at Gabriel when I said, "I plead the fifth, Mother." Less than a minute later, my conversation with her ended and I tossed my cellphone onto the bar. Then I told Gabriel that she knew about Harper.

"Did she call her by name?" he asked.

"No. She just asked me if I'd heard the rumor that you were dating and you heard my reply."

"Boy, it didn't take long for word to get around, now did it?"

"Not around here. I wonder if it's just Mother who knows or if Father knows too."

"If he does know, he would do well to take heed to my warning to stay out of my personal life."

"I hope he does, Gabe. I don't want to see things get any more volatile between you and him, and I really don't want to see your relationship with Harper go down the drain."

"Oh, it's not going anywhere but forward. I don't care how bad things get between Father and me. I will not allow him to ruin what I have with Harper. He will not get near her like he did the others."

"Then you may want to keep her out of Salem's public eye and even Boston's; otherwise, you stand a good chance of running into Father."

"I'll take that chance. I'm not hiding Harper."

"I've got your back if you need me at any time."

"I know you do. Thank you, sis."

"Of course. You're my only brother and I love you."

"I love you too."

"Let's take a deep breath and let all this shit with Father go. Focus on Harper, Gabe. I want to see you smiling with your whole face again."

Then that was what my brother did. He lit up as soon as his thoughts were back on his sweet Boston girlfriend.

After arriving at my art studio, I threw my hair into a messy bun, put on my smock, and lit a stick of sandalwood incense and some candles. Then I turned on some music—Austin Giorgio's song "Dangerous Hands." Listening to it on repeat was the only way that I was going to be able to make it through putting the last touches on one of my paintings. Not one that I had been commissioned to do. This one was for me, and I had been secretly working on it for a few weeks.

Sitting on my stool in front of it now, I stared at the hauntingly beautiful man's face on the canvas. I knew it well. I knew every laugh line and I had kissed those dimples a thousand times in real life. The painting was of my ex-boyfriend Damon. He was the only one that I'd ever had and he'd texted me "Dangerous Hands" after we started seeing each other. He said it reminded him of me.

We met last summer in Boston while I was running errands. I had just reached the exit of Gracenote Coffee with a nitro cold brew in hand when he opened the door. We immediately locked eyes and the blue in his pierced my soul. Frozen in place, we stared at each other for what felt like an eternity. Then another customer walked up behind me and broke our gaze. Damon stepped aside, I walked past him, and that other customer followed.

I had gone only a few yards when an overwhelming feeling to turn around came over me. I turned around and Damon was cautiously approaching me. When he came to a standstill, there was only about a foot of space between us. Then I felt his heartbeat sync up with mine. I thought it was surely a form of magic because I had never experienced anything like it before or since.

I was still staring into his beautiful blue eyes when he slowly leaned in and kissed me. Kissing him felt like coming home. We didn't even know each other's names, but it didn't matter. We *knew* each other. We knew what we both were, too: witches.

He came from a long line of them, as I did; however, the difference between his family and mine was they were "traditional." That meant that Damon was expected to marry a woman who'd been linked to him since her birth. He and I ignored all of that, though. All of the traditional bullshit went out the window the second we laid eyes on each other. I was certain that no force, worldly or otherworldly, could keep us apart. But I was wrong.

Damon was his father's firstborn male, which meant he was set to inherit the family dynasty. That, coupled with the fact that they were traditional witches, meant nothing would stop his father from making Damon's life a living hell if he disobeyed him. Because of that, we kept a low profile to prevent his family from finding out about us. It worked in our favor for ten of the most passionate months of my life. Although Damon's family learned of our secret relationship, no one in my family ever did, except for Gabriel because I told him about it from the start.

On the day that Damon's parents forced him to end things with me, he came to my art studio to break things off. He apologized, profusely, and begged my forgiveness while tears streamed down both our faces. I held him as tightly as I could and told him that I forgave him. He was torn between love and honor, and I understood. I knew that his life was not his own and that he had to honor the traditions of his family.

Before he left, I ran my fingers through his raven-black hair and slid them down to his lips. Then I pulled him closer so I could feel his heartbeat next to mine one last time. I wasn't at all surprised that ours were still in perfect sync. Just like on the day we met.

While Damon was kissing me goodbye, a tear fell from his eye and rolled down to our mouths. Then he told me, "I will love you until the day I die, Willow." I stared at him for a long painful moment and finally said, "I will never love another."

As Damon was leaving, I stood back and watched him—both of us still crying so hard. When he closed the door behind him, taking my heart with him, I fell to the floor and struggled to breathe.

I never saw him again. But on occasion, he'll visit me in a dream. His eyes still take my breath away, but there's a heavy sadness in them now. And I swear I can still hear that all-too-familiar heartbeat. Before each of those dreams ended, Damon kissed me, and after I woke up, I tasted the salt of a tear on my lips.

22

#mumstheword

Harper

While driving back to Boston earlier this morning, I'd gotten a text from Gabriel. As soon as I saw the song link to Nick Jonas' "Delicious," I started laughing. That was the word that Gabriel had used to describe how I tasted to him, between my legs. He'd gotten a really good taste of me last night before we went to sleep, and I could still feel his lips and tongue on me.

"What are you doing for dinner?" Millie asked me.

"My usual date with random snacks in the breakroom."

"Nah. Let's get out of here for a little while. Besides, I want to hear all about yesterday with Gabriel."

I smiled. "I'll go ahead and tell you that it was fantastic. So was last night and this morning."

"Shut up."

"Give me ten minutes and I'll be ready to go."

"Can't wait."

Millie winked at me, and then I left the nursing station to go check on a patient. Mrs. Miller was her name and she wsas the sweetest old lady. Eighty-one to be exact. She was recovering from pneumonia and doing well too.

When I walked into her room she was sleeping, and I quietly checked her vitals. Afterward, as I was looking at her peaceful face, I thought about my grandmother. My mother's mother. She passed away three months before Haley did.

My grandmother, or "Nana" as I called her, had ALS. There were fewer than 20,000 cases per year and men were the majority of who came down with the neurological disease. When Nana was diagnosed, of course, my family was shocked. After she passed away, my grandfather died a year later from a broken heart. I missed them both so much, but was happy knowing they were together again.

I was walking toward Mrs. Miller's hospital room door to leave when it opened.

"Lovely to see you, Miss Hewitt," Dr. Clarke said, coming into the room.

"Hi. How are you?"

"I'm well. Thank you for asking. How are you getting on?"

"Is that British for asking how I'm doing?"

"Yes."

"I'm fine. And thank you for asking."

"Of course. How is our patient getting on?"

I glanced over at Mrs. Miller. "She's good. Recovering quickly."

"Wonderful. She's a kind lady."

"Yes, she is."

Dr. Clarke stepped over to the wall mount of hand sanitizer, dispensed some into his hands, and started rubbing them together. When he turned back around, the top part of his face mask came undone and fell down. Then he looked at me.

"Would you please help me with this?" he asked, motioning at his mask with his sanitizer-covered hands.

"Um, yes. Absolutely."

I hurried over to him, raised up onto the tips of my toes, and wrapped my arms around his head to retie his mask. I could feel his eyes on me and was trying not to look at them, but the temptation became too much. I looked up at Dr. Clarke and froze as his eyes carefully moved across my face, pausing at my lips, and back across my face again. He was staring straight at me now and the only sound I could hear were the breaths we were taking. A moment later, I pulled my eyes away from him and finished retying his mask.

As I was stepping away from him, I lost my footing and began stumbling. Dr. Clarke caught me in his arms, though, and pulled me up against him. We began staring at each other again and the longer we did, the faster my heart beat. Seconds kept passing by and finally, the Englishman let go of me.

"Are you feeling all right, Miss Hewitt?" he asked.

"Yes. I-I just lost my footing. Thank you for catching me."

"You're most welcome."

As I kept looking into his eyes, my mind started playing tricks on me again. One moment, it was Dr. Clarke standing in front of me and then it was my angel-man.

"I've got to get out of here," I whispered.

Dr. Clarke nodded and then walked over to the door and opened it for me. As I was walking past him, he said, "Harper, if you need me for anything, please let me know."

I didn't respond to his statement. I just kept walking, wondering why he'd chosen to call me by my first name this time.

• • •

"I have plans tomorrow, Mom. Why don't you and Dad come to see me on Sunday?" I said.

"Okay. But it will be later in the day when we get there. We'll head your way after we get out of church. Are you and Millie doing something together tomorrow?"

"Um, yes. We're getting manicures and pedicures and then going out to eat somewhere."

"Sounds like fun."

"It always is with Millie."

"Are things still going well at work?"

"Yes. Busy as always too."

"Your dad and I miss you so much, Harper, and wish you lived closer."

"I miss you and Dad."

"You could always get a nursing job at the hospital here."

I sighed. "We've talked about this, Mom. I'm happy at Massachusetts General. I also like living in Boston."

"Okay. You always have a room here at home if you change your mind."

"I know, and I appreciate it. Hey, I'm pulling into my apartment complex now, so I'll let you go."

"Dad and I will see you in two days, sweetheart. I love you."

"I love you too."

After parking my car, I leaned my head back on the seat and closed my eyes. I hated lying to my mom about my Saturday plans. I couldn't tell her that they were with Gabriel, though. Neither she nor my dad had a clue that I was in a romantic relationship again and I didn't want them to know about it. At least not yet.

When the time came to tell them, they'd want to meet the man in my life and I had no doubt that they'd like him. But the fact that he was a witch had to be kept a secret. I really didn't know what my parents would say or do if they found out...and I didn't want to know.

I had almost made it to my apartment when I noticed a long white feather on my doormat. When I picked it up and took a closer look, I knew it belonged to the owl that I'd seen in the tree by my bedroom window. I didn't know how his/her feather ended up on my doormat but regardless, I was happy to find it and took it inside.

I locked the door and reset my alarm. After setting the feather and my purse on top of my dresser, I stretched out across my bed. I was mentally and physically zapped.

My encounter with Dr. Clarke earlier had really affected me. The way that he caught and held me against him after I started stumbling felt inappropriate. So did the way that he kept staring at me. I didn't want to believe that he'd intended to be that way. He really was such a polite man.

While eating dinner with Millie at Harvard Gardens, I didn't tell her about what happened with Dr. Clarke, but I did catch her up on Gabriel and me. I covered everything from when he first saw me at the Raven's Cauldron to when I left his farmhouse this morning.

When I mentioned Gabriel's *other* piercing to Millie, she gave me her Cheshire cat grin and then asked, "What do you think about that piercing?"

"I love how it looks on Gabriel's very large package. I also love how it feels on my tongue," I told her.

She started chuckling and called me a "dirty girl." I had never been called that before, but didn't mind. I'd get as dirty with Gabriel as he wanted.

Millie knew, just like he did, that I was a virgin. She'd also known what I meant when she and I were sitting at the wine bar at the Raven's Cauldron on Saturday and I made the comment about Gabriel maybe being a little lonely and in need of some hot and sweaty sex like me. There was more than one way to have it.

· · ·

When my cellphone ringing woke me up, I was disoriented for a moment and then realized I was still lying across my bed in my scrubs. I hurried to grab my phone out of my pocket and saw that it was Gabriel who was calling me. I also saw that it was almost 9:00 p.m.

"Hi," I said, answering my phone.

"Are you okay?"

"Yeah. I fell asleep right after I got home from work. That's why I didn't call you and I'm sorry. I made you worry about me again."

"I was worried. But hearing your voice has made me feel a whole lot better."

"Ditto."

"Where are you now?"

"Stretched across my bed still in my work clothes."

"I guess I kept you up too late last night. That has to be why you're so tired today."

"You didn't keep me up too late. I just had a really long day."

"Was it extra stressful or something?"

"Yes."

"Was it doctors, patients, or both that got to you?"

"Both."

"Care to go into it?"

"Not really."

"Okay then. Do you care if Josephine and I come to your apartment tonight?"

"Not at all."

"Good, because we're already on our way."

23

#home

Harper

When I opened my apartment door, I was expecting to see Gabriel with Josephine sitting on his shoulder. Only Gabriel was standing in front of me, though.

"Hi," I said, smiling. "Where's Josephine?"

"She's spreading her wings for a bit."

"Come on in."

I stepped back from the doorway, and Gabriel stepped through it with a small suitcase in his hand. He set it down, closed and locked my door, and walked over to me. Before I knew it, he'd scooped me up into his arms and was spinning me around. When he stopped, he leaned his head down and pressed his warm lips against mine. While we were breathing each other in, I breathed a sigh of relief because Gabriel was here. Just seeing him made me feel so much better about my day.

When he started walking down the hallway with me still in his arms, I smiled at him again.

"Where are you taking me?" I asked.

"You know where."

He tugged at his bottom lip with his teeth and grinned, and I just shook my head at him. After he laid me down on my bed, he joined me and then pulled me over on top of him and wrapped his arms around me.

"You feel like home," he said.

"So do you."

"I'm excited about spending tonight and the whole weekend with you."

"Um... I haven't had a chance to tell you that my parents are coming to see me on Sunday. My mom called me when I was on my way home from work. She first asked about coming here tomorrow, but I told her that I already had plans."

"With me?"

"No. I told her a little white lie and said that I was doing girly stuff with Millie. I do want her and my dad to know about us. Just not yet."

"I understand. This morning, I found out that my mother knows about us and I'm certain my father does too."

"How did your mother find out?"

"Word travels fast amongst the Salem locals and apparently some of them have been talking about you and me."

"Apparently some from ChezCasa."

"Yes."

"Are you worried about it?"

"No. What will be, will be with my father."

Gabriel tucked my hair behind my ear and kissed me again.

"Oh, I just thought of something," I said. "I don't have the mixed nuts and dried fruit for Josephine. I'd planned to go to the grocery store first thing in the morning."

"I brought some with me, Harper."

"Whew! Good."

"Are you ready for me to let Josephine into your apartment?"

"Yes. I'm curious how she'll be in here."

"She'll be fine."

"Then let's go let her in."

Gabriel and I got up from my bed and as we were walking by my dresser, he stopped and picked up the owl feather I'd laid on top of it.

"Where did you get this?"

"I found it on my doormat when I got home."

"It appears that the owl is still hanging around."

"I know."

"Have you seen it again since that first time?"

"Yes...but I forgot to tell you about it. I've had other things filling my mind, such as you."

"When did you last see the owl?"

"A few nights ago maybe. You won't believe what happened either. The owl actually came down the branch toward me and stopped just a few feet away. I could've touched him or her if there wasn't a screen on my window."

"Oh wow. It came that close?"

"Yes. I talked to it, like the first time, and it ruffled its feathers and hooted. It made me jump just like when Josephine squawked."

"Harper, please don't ever take the screen off your window and try to touch that owl."

"Why?"

"Its behavior is abnormal. Owls aren't naturally friendly creatures. Not unless they're your familiar, and you're not a witch, so..."

I stuck out my bottom lip. "But I like the owl. It's so pretty and unique."

"I understand, but please do as I asked. I don't want the thing to attack you and it very well could since something is apparently wrong with it."

"Okay then. I'll just admire it from the other side of my window."

"Thank you."

Gabriel set the feather back down on top of my dresser, and then he and I walked to my front door. After he opened it, he whistled for Josephine, and seconds later, she swooped in out of the darkness and landed on Gabriel's right shoulder. When he turned around and looked at me, he was smiling.

"And there she is," I said. "Hi, Josephine."

She clicked her beak twice and then took off flying around my apartment.

"Is it okay for her to check out your place?" Gabriel asked."Absolutely. I want her to make herself at home just like I want you to. I expect you to."

"Yes, ma'am."

. . .

I woke up this morning to the smell of bacon frying and Gabriel singing. I didn't know how long he had been up, but he was doing exactly as I'd wanted him to do. He was making himself at home, and I was glad that he was comfortable enough to do it.

I kept lying in bed, listening to him in my kitchen while also listening to the song that he was playing on his cellphone. I didn't know it, but I already liked it. It had Gabriel and me written all over it.

I got out of bed and grabbed his collared button-up shirt off the floor to put on. We'd both gone to sleep last night without a stitch of clothing on our bodies and now, I was curious about what Gabriel was wearing. His sports briefs, dress pants, belt, dress shoes, and socks were still on the floor.

I eased down my hallway and peeked around the corner to see him standing in front of my stovetop with a black pair of sweatpants on but nothing else. I started tiptoeing toward him. He didn't know I was awake until I wrapped my arms around his waist and hugged him.

"Good morning, beautiful," he said, smiling over his shoulder at me. "Are you ready for a cup of coffee?"

"Yes, please."

I unwrapped my arms from around Gabriel, and he walked over to my Keurig, placed a pod of French roast into it, and pushed the eight-ounce button.

"I have two questions for you," I said. "How did you know which coffee cup in my cabinet was my favorite and how did you know I prefer 8 ounces of coffee?"

Gabriel smiled over his shoulder at me again. "Traces of your lipstick are on the rim of this cup, and I guessed that your ounce preference was the same as mine since we have so much in common."

"Keen sight and keen guess. Hey, where is Josephine?" I asked, glancing around.

"She's spreading her wings again. After we eat breakfast, I'll call her back inside."

"I liked her sleeping at the foot of my bed last night."

"So did I."

My cup of coffee had just finished brewing. Gabriel walked over to my refrigerator with it, grabbed the carton of half and half, and added a splash to my wake-up juice. Yesterday morning at his farmhouse, I'd learned that only a splash was his preference too.

After coming over to me, leaning against the counter by my kitchen sink, Gabriel gave me a soft kiss. Then he handed me my coffee.

"Thank you," I said, grinning up at him.

"You're welcome."

"What was the song that you were singing right before I came in here?"

"'The Mates of Soul' by Taylor John Williams."

"You sing it as well as he does. I will definitely be adding it to my playlist."

"Good."

"Was it already on yours or is it a recent addition?"

"It was already on mine."

"You and I both have so many songs on our playlists about an ideal romantic relationship with someone, although we've never had it."

"Until now."

"Yes. Until now."

While Gabriel and I were eating breakfast, we went back and forth, throwing out ideas about what we could do this day. We considered making a day trip to Martha's Vineyard, but it would've consumed the entire day, so we decided against that idea. Then Gabriel asked me if I'd be interested in going on a Boston Harbor dinner cruise later this evening. I was interested, so he made reservations for us.

After breakfast, we cleaned up my kitchen, and then Josephine rejoined us. Gabriel poured some mixed nuts and dried fruit into a bowl for her and while she was enjoying it, he and I lounged in my living room, on my couch. He sat up and I laid my head in his lap, looking up at his handsome face.

"So when are you going to teach me some more about witchcraft?" I asked.

"When do you want me to?"

"Today would be nice."

"Okay then. Let's talk about spell-casting. The first thing is you don't need any props to cast a spell. You don't need candles, crystals, and such. However, they can help you focus your mind. Magic starts in your mind."

"Do you use any props?"

"I did at first, but not for long."

"Millie told me that casting a spell is akin to saying a prayer."

"She's correct. It's the same thing. You don't need to be inside a church with all of its props to say a prayer, do you?"

"No."

"You can pray or cast a spell anywhere. Source is always with us. It surrounds us and works with our energy and intentions."

"*Source?*"

"God, Goddess, or whatever you prefer to call what created this universe and all of us."

I paused to think about what Gabriel had just told me. It was simple yet profound. The parallels between his religion and mine were so clear.

"Do you have any other abilities besides hearing Willow and Josephine's thoughts and making my orgasms magical?" I asked, grinning.

Gabriel kept staring into my eyes but didn't say anything. Then he nodded yes. "Sit up and I'll show you."

"Okay then."

I was facing him now, sitting cross-legged on the couch, and he had his body turned toward me.

"You've experienced what it's like when I direct my energy. You're about to experience it again—but in a much bigger way," he said.

"I'm a little nervous now."

"There's no reason to be. I want you to close your eyes, take a deep breath, and be as still as you can."

As soon as I'd done what he told me to do, I heard a faint whirring sound begin. It quickly grew louder and began going round and round me. Then my whole body started vibrating. I took another deep breath, wondering what was going to happen next.

"I want you to look at me, but try not to freak out when you do," Gabriel said.

I nodded and then slowly opened my eyes. I was looking at Gabriel again but from a different angle. I was no longer on my couch. I was suspended in the air, a few feet above it, still in a cross-legged position. I never felt my body lift up and I'd never dreamed what was happening to me could really happen.

Gabriel was holding out his arms toward me, with his fingers spread apart, and the expression on his face was one of total concentration. I'd never seen his eyes so focused.

"I'm going to lower you back down now," he said, but I didn't say anything back to him. I could only keep staring at him.

As he began lowering his arms, my body slowly floated down to my couch and I was back in my original spot, sitting straight across from Gabriel. He laid his hands on the tops of my thighs and looked at me. I knew he could tell that I had freaked out after all. I was just keeping it inside.

"Welcome to my world even more, Harper."

"I-I..."

"I know. It's a lot."

"Yes, it is...but I love it. What else have you lifted up before?"

"A number of inanimate objects."

"No other people?"

"Only one. A thug in downtown Boston. He attempted to rob me in a parking lot. I knocked his gun out of his hand and threw him against a building a few yards away by directing my energy at him. Afterward, I called the police and when they arrived, they picked the man up off the pavement. He was still in a daze."

"Your energy is so strong."

"I've honed it over the years."

"Can Willow do what you just did to me?"

"No."

"Does she have other abilities?"

"Yes. She can cloak or hide herself from others."

"How?"

"She'll spin clockwise one time and disappear into thin air."

"Where does she go?"

"She's either still standing where you last saw her or she has gone elsewhere."

"Wow," I sighed. "I am completely fascinated by all of this. What other abilities do you have? I'm guessing you do."

"Your guess is correct."

Gabriel turned his head and began staring at the first bouquet of roses that he'd given me. A few seconds later, it slid across the top of my coffee table and stopped at the edge. Then Gabriel looked back at me.

"My God. You're capable of directing your energy through your eyes, just like your hands," I said, shaking my head in amazement.

"Yes. Are you up to seeing one more example of what I can do?"

I shrugged my shoulders. "Why not? My mind is already so fucking blown."

"Come sit between my legs, facing forward."

Once I was in place, Gabriel wrapped his right hand around mine. Then he held them both out toward the bouquet.

"Now spread your fingers apart," he said.

The moment I did, my hand started heating up and vibrating as my whole body had done only minutes ago. Then I watched the vase of beautiful red roses slide back across my coffee table to where it had originally been sitting.

"I can also direct my energy through others," Gabriel softly spoke as he was lowering our hands.

I leaned my head back on his shoulder and stared up at the ceiling. "Why do I feel so tired now?"

"It's due to what I did to your body and through it. It can be quite draining. How about we go take a nap?"

"Sounds good to me."

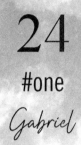

24

#one

Gabriel

Harper fell asleep almost instantly. I slept for about thirty minutes and woke up, but didn't get out of bed. I kept watching Harper lying beside me, lost in her slumber. She looked so peaceful and beautiful.

I looked down at Josephine at the foot of the bed and smiled. She liked Harper a lot and she also liked her home. I would've never imagined my pet adjusting to this new setting so quickly and easily. I credited Harper for it. She had her own kind of magic that put others at ease.

When Harper woke up, it was almost 3:00 p.m. I was sitting on the couch in her living room, watching TV, when she came walking into the room.

"There you are," she said with a sleepy smile.

"And there you are. Do you feel better?"

"Much better. When did you get up?" she asked, sitting down beside me.

"A while ago. I only slept for half an hour, then Josephine and I got up and came in here."

Harper looked around. "Is she outside, spreading her wings again?"

"Yes."

"Can you hear what she's thinking right now?"

"No. She's too far away at the moment."

"Okay then. I'm going to go make myself a cup of coffee and start getting ready for the cruise. Question about Josephine... Will she follow us while we're on the cruise?"

"Yes. We may not see her, but she'll be keeping an eye on us."

Harper got quiet and kept looking at me.

"What are you thinking?" I asked.

"About how happy I am because of you."

"I'm happy that you're happy."

"Are you as happy as me?"

"More."

"It's not possible."

"Yes, it is."

"No, it's not."

"Is this our first argument?"

"I suppose it is," Harper chuckled.

"How about we go fool around to make up?"

"I think we should. Now."

• • •

Harper and I were nearing the cruise ship when she squeezed my fingers tight and took a deep breath. Then it hit me. I remembered her fear of water.

"Come here," I said, pulling her into my arms. "I'm so sorry. I didn't think this through. We don't have to take another step toward the harbor. We can turn around and go do something in the city."

"No. Just give me a minute and I'll be okay." She looked over at the ship and then up at me. "Do you think they have any kind of life preservers or rafts?"

"My guess would be yes, but we can certainly ask."

Harper nodded, and we started walking toward the ship again. As soon as we boarded, I asked an attendant about the kind of safety measures they had in place. All passengers were covered in every way.

Harper seemed to relax a little at hearing that, and then she and I were escorted to our table. After we sat down, I told her that I was going to order her a glass of wine to calm her nerves.

"Are you going to have one?" she asked.

"Of course."

She smiled, and then picked up the wine menu off the table and started reading it. "I don't believe it. Your wine is listed here."

"Is it really?"

"Yes."

I looked at the menu and saw my malbec, chardonnay and cabernet sauvignon. "We're in luck. We'll get to have our favorite wine this evening."

Harper smiled at me again and I leaned over and kissed her. By the time the harbor cruise began, she was totally relaxed and I was relieved. I had wondered if her fear of water would start overwhelming her once more when the ship took off. Thankfully, it hadn't.

While enjoying our meals of oven-roasted salmon, cheddar scalloped potatoes, and Caesar salad, we got to see some waterfront landmarks outside the window by our table. The most impressive was the USS Constitution warship. As the sun was setting behind the Boston skyline, Harper leaned over and rested her head on my shoulder. A couple of minutes later, the D.J. on the ship began playing a song that I was going to have to dance to with my beautiful date.

"Come on," I told her.

"Where are we going?"

"To dance."

She grinned like I was doing, and then we got up from our table. After leading her over to the dance floor in the center of the dining area, I wrapped my arms around her waist and she wrapped her arms around my neck. As we began swaying to "Don't Fade" by Vance Joy, I gazed into Harper's eyes and quietly sang the lyrics to her. They encompassed how I felt about her.

As the song was ending, I kissed Harper and for a moment afterward, we held our foreheads together and breathed. Then we walked back over to our table and sat down. I was pouring more malbec into our wine glasses when Harper said she needed to use the restroom.

"I'll walk you," I said, starting to stand up.

"No, that's okay. I'm a big girl."

"I know you are."

"But the gentleman inside you can't help himself, right?"

"Right."

Harper shook her head at me and then said that she'd be back in a flash. I kept my eyes on her until she had left the dining area. While looking across it at the other passengers enjoying themselves, I noticed a man sitting alone at one of the tables, staring at me. I held eye contact with him, and then he smirked and looked away. I had no idea what his smirk was about. Regardless, the man's behavior was odd and borderline rude.

When Harper returned to our table and sat back down, I immediately noticed the shift in her mood. She was nervous again.

"What's going on?" I asked.

"Um, one of the doctors I work with is on this cruise."

"Okay then."

"I was coming back from the restroom and ran into him."

"And?"

"We spoke to each other and..."

"And what?"

"Nothing. That was it."

"Then why are you so shaken up?"

"The white coats always make me nervous."

"I don't understand. They're human like you, me, and everybody else."

"I know."

Harper's gaze slid to something behind me and when I looked over my shoulder, I saw the man who'd been staring at me. Then I stood up.

"May I help you?" I asked him.

"I simply wanted to introduce myself to you since you're in the company of Miss Hewitt. She and I work together at Massachusetts General Hospital."

I looked at Harper. "So this is the doctor you were just telling me about?"

"Yes. Hello again, Dr. Clarke," she said, turning her attention to him.

"Lovely to see you again."

When I turned back to face him, he was looking past me and smiling at Harper. I didn't like the way that he was smiling at her, either. It was too personal. Then he looked her up and down as if he was undressing her with his eyes.

"I'm Gabriel Grey," I said, holding out my hand toward the man.

He focused back on me and received my handshake while introducing himself. He also gave my hand a hard squeeze as I'd done to his. Then he asked, "Have you and Miss Hewitt been enjoying the harbor cruise?"

"Thoroughly."

"As I have. The food was surprisingly delicious and the view has been stellar. Especially on this side of the ship."

He looked back at Harper and smiled at her again as he was saying that last part. He definitely had balls to have not only made that indirect reference to her just now, with me standing by him, but to also keep eyeing her in the manner in which he'd been doing ever since he walked up to our table.

"Did you come on this cruise by yourself?" I asked him. He slowly turned his attention back to me.

"Yes. I prefer my own company and that of a few others," he said, looking at Harper and smiling yet again. His ego was as huge as it was entertaining.

"Well, you enjoy what's left of the cruise while Harper and I do the same," I said, stepping over into his line of vision of her.

"Thank you, Mr. Grey. You and Miss Hewitt have a good evening."

He smirked at me as he'd done earlier and then walked off. I watched him, thinking that he was going back to his table, but he didn't. He left the dining area. I kept staring in the direction he'd gone and then looked at Harper and sat back down.

"Are you okay?" I asked.

"Yes."

"I have never met anyone as full of themself as Dr. Nicholas Clarke."

"He's never acted like that around me before. I'm sorry."

"There's no reason for you to be sorry; however, there are several reasons that he should be. I started to call him out about the inappropriate way that he kept looking at you and smiling, as well as his indirect references to you. Then I decided against it because I didn't want to make you feel any more uncomfortable than you already were."

"I appreciate you not saying anything. I think it's best just to let it go."

"How long have you been working with Dr. Clarke?"

"A week."

"He's British. I wonder why he's here."

"He told me that he wanted to work at Massachusetts General Hospital. All of his family is still in England, though."

Right then, I realized Harper had engaged in another conversation with him. A personal one.

"His family? You mean a wife, children, or what?"

"No, he's not married and doesn't have any children. His parents and two sisters are in England."

I sighed while looking over Harper's beautiful face. "Tell me something."

"What would you like to know?"

"If I have anything to be worried about."

"What do you mean?"

"Exactly what I said. It is clear to me, as a man, that Dr. Clarke is very much into you, and it obviously doesn't matter to him that you're with me."

"I don't care if he is. I'm not looking for anybody else. I want you."

"Are you sure?"

"Gabriel, where is this coming from?"

I sighed again. "My insecurities. I've never been in love before, and now that I am, I cannot help but be even more protective of you, as well as territorial."

Harper's mouth fell open and she stared at me.

"Yes... I'm in love with you," I continued. "I feel you flowing through me and I see your face before everything I do now."

We both had tears in our eyes and our bottom lips were quivering. Then I heard the words that I was hoping Harper would say. She told me that she was in love with me too. And as she was saying it, I felt my heart absorb her sweet words and expand throughout me.

• • •

When the cruise ended, I glanced around the dining area for Nicholas Clarke as Harper and I were getting up from our table. I didn't see him anywhere, though, and hadn't since our earlier interaction. I had no idea where on the ship he'd gone, but was relieved that he'd disappeared somewhere. My feeling that way wasn't about me, it was about Harper. I didn't want her to feel uncomfortable again and knew she would have if she'd seen Dr. Clarke sitting at his table across the dance floor.

After Harper and I reached my car, I opened the passenger side door for her but before she got in, I pulled her closer to me and held her face in my hands.

"Thank you for taking me on the cruise," she said, smiling up at me.

"You're welcome. Is there anything else you'd like to do this evening?"

"Yes."

"What?"

Her eyes gravitated down to my mouth, and then she met my gaze again. "I want us to go back to my apartment, strip down to nothing, get in my bed, and have sex. Real sex. I need to feel you deep inside me."

She placed her hand on my crotch and held it there while I stared at her.

"Harper, I don't want you to do something that you're not ready to do," I finally said.

"But I am ready. You, Gabriel Grey, are who I want to give *all* of my body to...and I want all of yours."

I swallowed hard. "Then I'm going to need to stop by a CVS or Walgreens."

"You don't need condoms. I'm on the pill and have been since I was in high school due to irregular periods."

I took a deep breath and slowly exhaled it while continuing to stare into Harper's eyes.

"What is it?" she asked.

"I'm imagining what it's going to feel like to finally love your body the way that I've wanted to."

"Take me home and you won't have to imagine it any longer."

As I was driving us back to Harper's apartment, she leaned across the console and started kissing my neck, making my dick twitch even more than it already had been since we left the parking lot. Then she took off her seatbelt and crawled over into my lap, facing me, with her legs stretched out across the passenger seat.

I kept glancing at her and the road in front of me while wondering what she was going to do next. Then she unbuttoned my shirt and began sucking on my left nipple. The feeling of her tongue sliding over it and my piercing made me fully erect within seconds. By the time I parked my car in Harper's apartment complex, I was about to come unglued. I was burning up inside with so much desire for this woman who was still in my lap, driving me crazy with her mouth.

We both got out of the car on my side and hurried to Harper's front door. As soon as I locked the door behind us, we started pulling each other's clothes off, leaving a trail of them down the hallway to Harper's bed. Lying on top of her, I stared into her eyes, then grabbed my dick and started rubbing it up and down the inside of her pussy lips and over her clit, making her softly moan over and over again. I wanted to make her as wet as I could to lessen the pain of receiving all of me. Although she was used to using a vibrator, it couldn't come close to what she was about to experience.

"That feels so good," she breathed against my face.

I nodded and when I felt the wetness between her legs, I pushed the tip of my dick into her and pulled it back out. Then I pushed myself into her a little farther and pulled back out again. I kept going deeper into her and when she tensed up, I stopped.

"Does that hurt?" I asked.

"No. I just feel pressure because you're so big."

"Do you want me to keep going?"

"Yes."

I pushed my dick into her pussy again and went deeper than before. Harper closed her eyes and her breath caught, sounding like a pained gasp. I froze, then she wrapped her legs around me and pulled me all the way into her. She was so tight.

"Keep moving," she said.

I started sliding my dick in and out of her, slow and easy, and then she told me that she wanted to see me going into her. I raised up and we both looked down at our bodies joined together. We were one and it looked amazing. It also felt that way.

When I looked back up, Harper's eyes met mine. The fire burning in hers for me was almost too much to take. I could see how much she wanted me and how much she loved me.

"Go faster and harder," she whispered.

"Be careful what you wish for."

I started fucking her like she wanted me to and she fucked me back. When she closed her eyes and her body began rising up, I knew she was about to cum. Then it started happening for her.

"Harper, look at me," I said, and she did. She opened her eyes and stared straight into mine. I wanted her to see my face when she came. I was the first man to make it happen for her like this and I intended to be the last.

I started thrusting myself into her even faster as my body began releasing itself. As I was coming, Harper held my face in her hands and searched my eyes. In hers, I saw my future. I saw a lifetime with her.

After I came, I leaned my head down and kissed her. Then she pulled my body all the way down on top of hers and hugged me around my neck. When I heard her start whimpering, I looked at her. She was crying.

"What's wrong?" I asked.

"I-I just love you."

"I love you."

"You are my person, Gabriel."

"You're mine too."

I wiped her eyes and then asked her if she was hurting.

"No, but I'll probably be really sore later," she said.

"I'm sorry."

"No. Don't be. I'm not sorry."

"Was your first time what you thought it would be?"

"It was so much more. The way we move together is..."

"I know."

"What was it like for you?"

"Euphoric."

25
#surprise

Harper

When Gabriel and I got out of bed to take a shower, I looked down at the sheets and saw some spots of blood. Gabriel saw them too.

"It's sacred to me being your first," he said.

"It is to me too."

"Now that we've had sex, you and I are energetically tied to each other."

"What do you mean?"

"We merged our energies together when we had sex and a soul tie was formed. A bond. We already feel drawn to each other, but it will get even stronger now. I'll be able to sense your emotions whenever we're apart, and you'll be able to sense mine. We'll start having fleeting images of each other too. They'll just pop into our minds."

"You're serious?"

"Yes."

"Okay then. What about those three women that you dated before me?"

"I severed my soul tie to each of them as soon as I ended things."

"How?"

"A tie-cutting ritual. That's the only way to do it."

I stared at Gabriel. "I've never heard of any of this before."

"Most people are unaware of the energetic ties they form with others. When a relationship ends, they think that's it. It's over. It isn't, though. They'll be going about their day and their ex will come to their mind seemingly out of nowhere, and they can't understand why they're even thinking about them. It's the tie."

"You have blown my mind once again."

After we took a shower, Gabriel let Josephine back into my apartment, and then we all got a late-night snack and went to sleep. It was morning now, I was still lying in Gabriel's arms, and he was still sleeping. I kept watching him and when he woke up, he smiled and kissed me on the forehead.

"How long have you been awake?" he asked in that deep, raspy, sexy voice of his.

"Not too long."

"How do you feel this morning?"

"Down there?"

Gabriel grinned. "Yes."

"Like I thought I would. I'm really sore."

"Is there anything I can do to help?"

"No. I'll be fine in a day or two, though."

"We'll have to take it easy next time."

"We'll see," I chuckled. "Are you ready for some coffee?"

"Yes, but I'll get it, and yours."

"I like it when you make my coffee. For some reason, it tastes better than when I do it."

"Then let's go get you some."

As Gabriel and I were walking down the hallway, Josephine flew over our heads. She'd been sleeping at the foot of my bed again. Gabriel let her outside, and then he and I went into my kitchen. I was leaning against the counter, watching him brew my coffee, when he looked over his shoulder at me.

"Harper, do you work with Dr. Clarke every day?" he asked, surprising me.

"Um, no. Doctors rotate. Why do you ask?"

"Just wondering. I hope he never makes you feel uncomfortable at work like he did on the harbor cruise last night."

My heart was pounding because I was thinking about what happened with Dr. Clarke in Mrs. Miller's hospital room. I was still confused about it and didn't know how to feel. I just wanted to let it all go and move on.

After adding a splash of half and half to my coffee, Gabriel brought it over to me and asked, "When do you want me to leave today?"

"Well, I don't *want* you to."

"But you need me to. So when?"

"Two-ish. That'll give me time to get presentable and get things picked up around here before my parents arrive."

"You mean to get things picked up in your bedroom?" Gabriel chuckled.

"Yes, and in my bathroom too. Traces of us are everywhere."

"I know. I like it."

"Ditto."

"How about we get some donuts from Kane's?"

"That sounds delicious."

"I bet I know which kind is your favorite."

"I bet you do too."

"Chocolate covered with sprinkles?"

"It is," I giggled.

"It's also mine. Let's get dressed and go get our breakfast."

I took a sip of my coffee, set it down on the counter, and then took off running toward my bedroom with Gabriel chasing me and laughing like I was. After quickly throwing on some clothes, we began to leave my apartment, but Gabriel stopped us in my open doorway by kissing me. He was still kissing me when I heard a male voice say, "Good morning, daughter."

I gasped and turned my head to see my dad and my mom walking toward Gabriel and me.

"What are you doing here so early?" I asked them.

"We wanted to surprise you, but your mom and I are the ones who are surprised," my dad said.

I looked back at Gabriel, but his eyes were on my parents. He nodded at them and then held out his hand toward my dad. He and my mom were now standing directly in front of my new boyfriend and me.

"Hi. Gabriel Grey. Nice to meet you both," he said.

My dad shook his hand and introduced himself, and my mom was next.

"Harper and I were about to go get some donuts, but I'll go get them so she can stay here with you. Would either of you like some?" Gabriel asked them.

They both declined his offer, saying they'd already eaten breakfast. Things were getting more awkward by the second.

"Gabriel, don't worry about the donuts. Um, let's all go inside," I said.

Gabriel stood back, allowing me, my mom and dad to enter before he did. All four of us were now standing in my foyer.

"Gabriel and I are dating," I told my parents.

"Apparently," my dad chuckled. Then my mom asked me how long we'd been dating.

"A week."

"How did you two meet?"

"At Gabriel's business in Salem. It's a bookstore, coffee shop, and wine bar all in one. It's called the Raven's Cauldron."

"It sounds like an interesting place."

My mom looked from me to Gabriel, half-smiled at him, and then turned her attention back to me.

"Did you go to Salem by yourself?"

"No. Millie was with me. She invited me to go with her and she introduced me to Gabriel. She knows him through his wine. He's a vintner."

My mom looked back at Gabriel with a raised eyebrow.

"Is your wine good?"

I wanted to die.

"I think it is. I've received several awards for it," Gabriel said with a shrug as he stuffed his hands into his front pants pockets.

"Let's go sit in the living room," I interjected. I couldn't keep standing here like this.

"Harper, I'm going to head back home," Gabriel said, surprising me. "Enjoy your time with your parents. I'll call you later."

"Okay then."

"Mr. and Mrs. Hewitt, I'm very glad to have met you," Gabriel told them. They said the same to him, then he began walking toward my front door.

"Mom. Dad. I'll be right back," I said.

As soon as they nodded, I caught up with Gabriel and we stepped outside together with my front door closed behind us.

"Harper, I am so sorry," he said.

"It's fine. I'm not worried about it. Yes, when I go back inside, my parents are going to want to know even more about you."

He sighed. "Have they shown up like this before?"

"No. They were just really missing me is all. It's been weeks since I've seen them."

"My suitcase is still in your bedroom. Do what you need to do with it, and I'll get it back from you the next time I see you."

"When will that be?"

"When do you want it to be?"

"Tonight, of course, but I know we both have things we need to do to get ready for the work week."

"I don't mind driving back here tonight."

"I know you don't and I appreciate it, but stay home. Get Josephine settled back in. Yourself too."

Gabriel smiled, then leaned in and kissed me.

"I love you," he said, as he was pulling his warm lips away from mine.

"I love you too."

"I can hardly wait to hear about your conversation with your parents."

I rolled my eyes. "I swear, their timing..."

"Now all we need is for my mother and father to show up at my farmhouse when you're there."

"I am interested in meeting them one day. I want to see who you came from."

After giving me another kiss, Gabriel left. I stood by my door and watched him until he reached his Range Rover. Right as he reached it, Josephine flew down from somewhere, and then Gabriel opened his driver side door and let his beautiful familiar into his car.

"Mom and Dad, give me a minute. I need to use the bathroom," I told them after returning to my apartment. They were sitting at my kitchen table.

"Take your time," my dad said.

I really didn't need to use the bathroom. It was just an excuse that would allow me enough time to go put Gabriel's suitcase in my closet, make up my bed, and tidy up my bathroom. As soon as I was done, I joined my parents.

"So start asking your questions about Gabriel. I know you have them," I said.

"He's a very nice young man, Harper," my dad said.

"He's very handsome too," my mom added. "He doesn't need those earrings, though."

"I like them, Mom."

"So how was Salem?"

"Fun. Millie and I went to a concert. It was held on Gabriel's family's land on the outskirts of town."

"Last Saturday was Halloween. I suppose you saw lots of women dressed up as witches."

"I did. Millie and I were dressed up as witches too."

"Really?"

"Yes. We bought hats before the concert."

"Just keep in mind what your dad and I taught you about staying away from witchcraft."

I sighed. "Mom, don't worry about me. Millie and I went to Salem to have fun and that's exactly what we did."

"Okay. So is Gabriel from Salem?"

"Yes."

"Have you met his family?"

"Only his younger sister, Willow. She's really nice."

"You look happy."

"I am happy."

My mom was jumping from one subject to the other and I had a good idea of which one she was going to jump to next.

"Did Gabriel spend last night with you?" she asked.

And there it was. What she had been most curious about.

"Yes, he did."

"After dating you for a week."

"Mom, I'm twenty-four and this is my life."

She stared at me for a long moment. "You're right. As long as you're happy, Harper, then I'm happy. Just be careful with Gabriel. You can't really know someone after only a week."

"I know him well enough."

"He gave you the two bouquets of red roses," she said, glancing at the one sitting on my bar and then at the one on my coffee table.

"He did."

"They're beautiful."

"I think they are too. They grow wild all around his farm-house."

"So you've been there?"

"Yes, and I love it. It was built in eighteen-forty and only Gabriel's family members have lived in it." I looked over at my dad. "You're being awfully quiet. Do you have any questions for me?"

He grinned. "No. I'm just glad to see your face, daughter."

Both my parents were strict with Haley and me when we were growing up, but our dad was also our friend. Our mom was too, in her own way. She just held our feet to the fire more than our dad did. She was extra protective, and I knew she always would be. Both of my parents just wanted the best for me in life.

Before they left to go back to Northampton, they took me out to eat dinner at Carmelina's. We'd been there on three other occasions, so I already knew what I was going to order: their Sunday macaroni. It was penne pasta with meatballs, sausage, beef rib, tomato sauce, and a dollop of whipped ricotta—and it was to die for. I couldn't eat all of it, so I brought home my leftovers and planned to eat them the next day.

I talked to Gabriel twice after my parents left my apartment. When he and I talked the first time, I told him about my mom's mini-interrogation and he chuckled. He was relieved to know she and my dad liked him. When I mentioned that my mom had asked if Gabriel spent last night with me, he sighed and then asked me what I told her. I said, "The truth. It's my life and I'm not a child. She acknowledged that and said she was happy for me if I was happy. As a matter of fact, she pointed out that I looked happy."

Before we hung up after our second call, we made plans to see each other Friday through Sunday again, in Salem. Gabriel was going to have to work Saturday evening because Miranda needed that evening off, and I told him that I'd hang out with him at the wine bar. He really liked that idea.

After getting in bed, with my dried blood still on the sheets, I replayed in my mind having sex with Gabriel last night. The way that he was with me was exactly what I needed. I needed his gentleness, as well as his unbridled passion. He was an incredible lover.

I'd started to wash my sheets after I got my scrubs done earlier but decided against it because Gabriel's masculine scent was all over them and my pillows. The smell was comforting and made me feel like my magic man was here with me in a sense.

I was reaching over to turn off the lamp on my nightstand and thought about the owl. I was curious if it was in the tree by my bedroom window again, so I got up to check. It was there and was looking at me.

I didn't open my window due to what Gabriel had told me about something possibly being wrong with the owl. I would play it safe but could still admire the owl, and that's what I was doing when it started coming down the branch toward me again. But this time, it came even closer, and we spent about five minutes just looking at each other. When I told the owl "Goodnight," it ruffled its feathers and hooted, making me jump and giggle like before.

26

#men

Millie

When I saw Harper coming down the hallway at work this morning, she smiled and shimmied her shoulders at me. She had something major to tell me and I could hardly wait to hear what it was.

"Walk with me," she said. The two of us hung a right and stepped inside the supply room. When she turned and faced me, she just kept smiling.

"Am I going to have to force it out of you?" I asked.

"Gabriel and I were together Saturday night."

"You slept with him?"

"Yes."

I blew out a long breath. "Then you must be in love with him."

"I am. He told me that he was in love with me first and was choked up when he said it. I immediately was too, of course, and then told him that I was in love with him. We were on a dinner cruise in Boston Harbor."

"The next thing I want to know is how your first time was."

"Incredible."

"You've got to be so sore, though. Remember, I saw that sexy pic of Gabriel."

"I was really sore yesterday morning, but I'm fine now."

I hugged Harper and she asked me if I thought it was crazy for her to say she was in love with Gabriel this soon.

"I don't think it's crazy at all. Some people might think a person can't possibly fall in love so quickly, but I've seen it happen and I've seen that love last too. You're in the baby stage of love and it's a powerful thing."

"I never knew I could feel like this, Millie. I feel like I'm floating around everywhere."

I smiled. "You are."

"Oh, get this. Dr. Clarke was on that dinner cruise."

"Really?"

"Yes. He was by himself just like when I saw him at Bambolina's."

"Did he talk to you?"

"To Gabriel and me both. He came up to our table."

"How did it go?"

"It was tense. Dr. Clarke kept looking at me and smiling while Gabriel was talking to him. He also looked me up and down in a seductive way and made indirect comments about preferring my company and that I looked 'stellar,' as he put it. It was definitely a side of Dr. Clarke that I've never seen before and for a minute, I thought Gabriel was going to say something to him. I could tell by the look on Gabriel's face that he wasn't happy about it."

"That's what you get with two alpha males."

"After Dr. Clarke walked off, Gabriel and I were able to enjoy the rest of the cruise and never saw him again."

"That's probably a good thing."

"I agree. Hey, I'll tell you one more quick thing, then I need to get to work."

"I'm listening."

"Gabriel and I were standing in my open doorway, kissing, yesterday morning and my parents walked up. I knew they were coming to see me, but they weren't supposed to be at my apartment until mid-afternoon."

"Oh, my God. How did that meeting go?"

"It was so damn awkward at first, but it panned out. Gabriel introduced himself to my parents, we all chatted for a few minutes, and then Gabriel left to go back home. Afterward, my mom asked me all about him. My dad didn't seem too concerned. Anyway... There's more to that story, but I'll have to catch you up on the rest later."

"You had a very full weekend, my friend."

"You're telling me."

After Harper and I left the supply room, she went in one direction while I went in another. As I was going to a patient's room, I thought more about what Harper had said about Gabriel and Dr. Clarke. She was going to have to be careful with how she handled that situation with the two men. It could easily turn into a precarious one.

I hadn't seen Dr. Clarke be anything but polite to Harper. I could understand, though, him being attracted to her, and looking at her a little too much. I would be monitoring matters between him and Harper up here a little more closely now. Harper was so young, and not experienced in male matters like I was.

• • •

Harper's shift and mine had forty minutes left. I hadn't seen her in a while, so I asked Misty if she had.

"Yeah, I saw her sitting in the breakroom with Dr. Clarke a few minutes ago," she told me. "He is such a gentleman. I wish all the doctors up here were like him." Misty leaned closer to me and grinned. "I wish they sounded like him too."

"Right?" I chuckled.

"His British accent is impossibly intoxicating and God, his looks. I could just lick him. Don't tell my boyfriend that I said that."

I acted like I was zipping my lips, and Misty winked and walked off. I headed to the breakroom but didn't go inside. Instead, I stood to the side of the doorway and listened to Harper and Dr. Clarke. They were discussing a patient, and then, the dinner cruise came up. That was when I walked into the break-room, acting surprised to see them.

"What are you two up to?" I asked them as I was sitting down at their table, next to Harper.

"Hello, Ms. Dupree," Dr. Clarke said. "Miss Hewitt and I were discussing what a coincidence it was that we were both on the Boston Harbor dinner cruise on Saturday."

I glanced at Harper. "She mentioned to me that she saw you."

"I was able to meet her sweetheart, Mr. Grey. He's a nice bloke."

"Yes, Harper mentioned that to me, too, and Gabriel is very nice. Have you done any other activities in Boston?" I asked, intentionally changing the subject.

"No, the dinner cruise is all."

"You should check out the tea party museum and Martha's Vineyard sometime."

"Thank you for telling me about them."

"You're welcome."

Dr. Clarke glanced at his watch. "Oh, bloody hell. I lost track of time and have got to get going. I enjoyed our chat, Miss Hewitt. Ms. Dupree."

"Likewise," I said, as Harper told him goodbye.

As soon as he left, I looked at Harper and raised an eyebrow.

"He was fine. A perfect gentleman today," she said.

"But you don't look fine."

"My mind started playing tricks on me again, and it was like my angel-man was sitting here, talking to me. I'll shake it off in a minute now that Dr. Clarke is gone."

"I really hope as time goes on, your mind will stop doing that to you."

"So do I. Sooner than later."

I chuckled. "Dr. Clarke apparently got a different impression of Gabriel than Gabriel got of him."

"Or maybe he just said that for my benefit. I'm telling you, there was tension between them. More on Gabriel's part, though."

"Well, you are his."

"Yes, I am."

I got paged, but Harper and I both left the breakroom and went back to work. I stopped at the nursing station while she kept going down the hallway where Dr. Clarke and Dr. Ward were talking to each other several yards ahead. As Harper was passing by the two men, she and Dr. Clarke smiled at each other. After she had passed by him, he slowly looked her up and down. Twice.

27

#confidante

Harper

Haley, *I wish you were here. I need to talk to you. There's so much that I wish you knew. I've met two men and am in love with one of them. The second? I don't know how to feel about him. Nothing other than confused,* I thought to myself.

I was sitting in a traffic jam, trying to get home from work, and missing my sister so much. She was my greatest confidante. There wasn't anything that we kept from each other. I wanted to tell her all about Gabriel, and I also wanted to tell her about Dr. Clarke.

Millie and I were close friends, but there were some things that I didn't feel like I could tell her. The main thing was what had happened between Dr. Clarke and me in Mrs. Miller's hospital room, and also what had happened between us this afternoon, before I left work.

He and I were together again in a patient's room while the patient slept. I'd checked her vitals and Dr. Clarke asked me how she was "getting on." His face mask didn't come untied this time but there was a long moment when he stared at me from across the patient's bed. Then he said, "Miss Hewitt, I must apologize to you for what happened last week."

"For holding me in your arms longer than necessary, after you caught me when I stumbled?" I replied.

"Yes."

"I've been really confused about that and didn't want to think you had intentionally been inappropriate with me."

"I did not intend to be that way with you. It's simply that when I felt you in my arms, it did something to me that's difficult to explain."

"Try."

Dr. Clarke took a deep breath and then told me, "Holding you filled me with a sort of light that went away as soon as I let you go."

"I don't know what to tell you about that. But what I do know is you can't touch me as you did last week, ever again."

"I won't."

"Dr. Clarke, we're colleagues and I like you. You don't thumb your nose at the nurses and other staff as so many of the other doctors do. You're friendly and down to earth. I enjoy talking to you as I did in the breakroom earlier and also when you and I ran into each other by the parking garage elevator."

"I enjoyed those occasions, as well."

I could tell he was smiling because his eyes were crinkled around the corners.

"Friends?" he continued and then held out his hand to shake mine across the top of our sleeping patient.

"Friends."

"Thank you, Harper."

"You've called me by my first name twice. It happened last week in Mrs. Miller's room and now, here. Why do you not call me by it in front of others?"

"Because I don't want them to get the impression that we're anything but colleagues. Being on a first-name basis with someone in a work environment such as ours presents itself as being quite personal, I believe."

"You don't have a problem presenting it in that way to me, behind closed doors."

Dr. Clarke shrugged. "I think your name is pretty and I like the way it sounds. If it bothers you, then I will stop."

I paused to study his eyes. They were sincere.

"I don't care if you call me by my first name and no one else up here would either. That's the American way, Englishman. I just wanted you to clarify to me why you addressed me differently depending on whether we're alone with each other or not. I understand now."

"May I ask you a question?"

"Sure."

"Do I really remind you of someone you know?"

"Yes, you really do."

"Is he a past sweetheart of yours?"

"No. He's a man who visits me in my dreams."

Dr. Clarke and I didn't discuss my angel-man any further. Our focus turned back to our patient and we parted ways a couple of minutes later. I felt a lot better about our work relationship, but when it came to the friend part, I left the hospital room still feeling conflicted.

The more that I got to know Dr. Clarke on a personal level, the more intrigued by him I was. For a brief moment, while staring across our patient's bed at each other, I'd felt attracted to him, when I shouldn't have. I also felt guilty because of Gabriel and immediately shut out how I was feeling about the Englishman. It didn't last for long, though.

Friday

"Come here to me," Gabriel said as soon as he opened my car door. Then he pulled me into his arms and started kissing me. I'd just arrived at his farmhouse.

"I have missed you so much," he continued after our kiss ended.

"I've missed you too."

"Are you getting hungry?"

I chuckled. "A little. You're always trying to feed me."

"I like taking care of you."

"Ditto."

"The roast has about forty-five minutes to go. In the meantime, would you like a glass of malbec?"

"You know I would...but I need something else first."

"What?"

"This."

I grabbed Gabriel's dick through the front of his jeans, and he started grinning while tugging on his bottom lip with his perfect pearl-white teeth.

"It's yours whenever you're ready," he said.

"I'm ready now."

The moment he closed his front door behind us, he picked me up, threw me over his shoulder and began carrying me toward his bedroom—both of us laughing the whole way. After he sat me down on the edge of his bed, he began undressing me and when he was done, I took his clothes off him. He was standing in front of me now without anything on, and I could only sigh at the sight of him. His desire for me was burning so brightly in his eyes, his lips were parted, his pierced nipples were hard, and his pierced dick was fully erect.

"Lay down," he whispered.

Once I had, he got on his knees between my legs and stared down at me. A moment later, he lifted my right leg underneath my knee and placed my foot on his upper chest, over his heart. Then he kissed it and began making his way up my leg by gently biting my skin until he reached my pussy. After running his long tongue up it and sucking on my clit, he moved his body over the top of mine and slowly pushed his dick inside me. We both sighed and then started moving our bodies together.

Gabriel was gentle, but I needed more from him. So I grabbed his ass and pulled him into me as deeply as I could. Then he started fucking me like I needed him to. He began thrusting himself into me with so much force that I had to put my hands against the headboard to keep myself in place. About a minute later, he got off me, flipped me over onto my stomach, and then pulled me up onto my knees. My ass was in the air, Gabriel's hands were wrapped around my waist, and he was taking me from behind. When he pulled out of me again, I looked over my shoulder at him.

"Let's lay down on our sides now," he said.

"Okay then."

As soon as I backed up against him, he lifted my right leg again and pulled it across his waist. Then he grabbed his dick and slid it back inside me. With his hand gripping my thigh, he began pulling me into his thrusts while we searched each other's eyes.

"I love you," he breathed against my face.

"I love you."

"I could stay in bed with you for the rest of this day, doing what we're doing now."

"Ditto."

"You feel so good to me."

"You do to me too. And you're about to make me cum."

"I like watching you, so go right ahead, baby."

He started fucking me faster and kept his eyes on mine. A short moment later, I came. Like before, it was so intense and went on and on until I was breathless. As it was ending, Gabriel started coming. I liked watching him the same as he did me, and when he was done, we held each other.

After wrecking his bed and drenching his sheets with our sweat, we didn't shower. We put our clothes back on and ate dinner instead. Gabriel's roast, potatoes, carrots, and baked yeast rolls were out of this world. We stuffed ourselves and were still sitting at the dining room table when he brought up something of interest to me.

"I read an online article earlier about a way for new couples to get to know each other faster. It's a series of questions that I'd like for us to ask each other," he said.

"It sounds fun."

"I think it would be. Also enlightening."

I smiled. "Let's do it."

"Are you ready to start now?"

"Absolutely."

Gabriel opened the notes app on his cellphone and I saw the list of questions he'd copied and pasted from the article. The first one he asked me was: "What was your first thought when we met?"

"That you were fucking luscious," I said, and Gabriel busted out laughing. Then I asked him what his first thought of me was when we met.

"That you were drop-dead gorgeous."

"Thank you. Ask me another question."

"What's one thing that you'll never get tired of doing?"

"Drinking your malbec. What about you?"

"I'll never get tired of kissing you. You have the softest lips."

"So do you. I actually think yours are pretty because they're full and the top one has a cupid bow. It's just not fair for you to naturally have lips like that," I said, pointing at Gabriel's. "Women pay top dollar to have theirs injected to look like yours."

"What can I say?"

"You can ask me another question. It's fun doing this with you."

"I'm having fun too. And the next question is: what is your favorite thing about me?"

"God, I don't think I can choose just one thing." I stared at Gabriel while mentally going over all of my favorite things about him and finally settled on one. "Okay, I've got it. It's the way that you tug at your bottom lip with your teeth and grin. You melt me every time you do it."

Gabriel did it just to taunt me and I pushed his leg under the table with my foot, making him chuckle.

"Are you ready to hear what my favorite thing is about you?" he asked.

"You know I am."

"It was the way that you laugh."

"*Was?*"

"Yes. Then I heard you moan when I made you cum that first time."

I fell back against my chair and giggled. "That's seriously your favorite thing about me?"

"Today, it is."

"You crack me up, Gabriel Grey."

"And you just keep me turned on."

"Next question."

He glanced at his phone screen. "What were you like before we met?"

"Um... I was really lonely and needed intimacy with someone, but I needed it to be more than what I'd had in the past. Much more. I needed emotional and spiritual intimacy, along with the physical. Then I met you and you gave me everything I needed."

"As you did me," Gabriel said, reaching across the table and holding my hand. "Harper, I want you to know I fell in love with you on the day we met. I just didn't realize it until later because I'd never been in love before and didn't know how to decipher what I was feeling. You threw me for such a huge loop when I saw you at the wine bar because I could already *feel* you. Then I heard your voice. Then you looked into my eyes. Then I got to touch you when we shook hands. The longer we kept talking to each other, the more I wanted to keep looking at you and talking to you. I also wanted to touch you again, and after I did, it only increased my desire for you."

"What is this between us? We've talked about it before, but really... What is this? I've never felt anything so powerful and consuming in my life. This is more than love. It has to be."

"I don't know what it is. But I do know that I'm never letting you go."

28

#church

Harper

After Gabriel and I finished asking each other the list of questions, he asked me if I'd ever heard of Stonehenge. I told him that all I knew about it was that it was located in England somewhere and was some kind of ancient pagan site. Gabriel then went on to enlighten me all about it.

Stonehenge is located in Wiltshire, England. It was built 5,000 years ago. It took 1,000 years to build. Scientists believe the stones were a way to tell the time of the year. Nobody knows for certain how the stones were moved to Stonehenge, but in the 12th century, a rumor began going around about a wizard having moved them there. Also, current research suggested that they were once in Wales.

Another thing that Gabriel told me about Stonehenge was that at sunrise on the summer solstice each year, people gathered at the circle of stones. Then he went on to say, "Now, I would like to show you something before it gets too dark outside."

"Okay then."

Gabriel stood up from the table, took my hand into his, and led me outside into his backyard as Josephine circled overhead. I thought we were stopping there, but we kept walking, and it wasn't until we'd gone several yards behind his wine building, deep into the trees, that I finally saw what he was wanting to show me. It was a circle of stones that looked like a mini-Stonehenge.

Gabriel stood back as I walked over to the circle and ran my fingers across each stone. My mind raced, wondering how these stones got here and what their purpose was. After making the full circle, I went back over to Gabriel and stared up at him.

"Explain," I finally said.

"This location was discovered by my ancestor John Grey, after he purchased all of this land. My parents have his handwritten notes about it."

"Why did you want me to see it?"

"I wanted to show you where I go to church. I come here to celebrate the cycles of the moon, the changing seasons, and to honor my ancestors."

"How do you do all of that?"

"With fire and dancing."

Gabriel reached out his right arm toward the stones and splayed his fingers, causing a fire to instantly ignite and start blazing in the center of the circle. I gasped but Gabriel didn't look at me again. His eyes remained focused ahead of him and then he started walking toward the stones and fire. I just stood back and watched him while wondering what he was going to do next.

When he reached the ancient site, he stood still and stared at the fire. Then he raised his face and arms toward the sky. That was when I started choking back my tears. I realized this truly was Gabriel's church.

A moment later, I heard a distant drumming begin from somewhere even deeper in this forest of trees that I was standing in the midst of. It kept getting louder and louder until I was surrounded by the sound. There was no visible source of the drumming, yet I knew the source was here because I could sense it. My body felt electric, inside and out.

Gabriel lowered his arms and looked back at the fire while remaining still. Seconds passed, and then I heard a blend of women's voices begin trilling much in the way that Native Americans did when chanting. It was otherworldly and haunting—and it filled me.

It was when the rhythm of the drumming began growing faster that Gabriel moved from where he'd been standing. He started walking clockwise around the fire and when I finally saw his face, I noticed the change in it. But mainly in his eyes. There was a wild look in them that let me know he had entered another dimension, mentally and spiritually.

As the ghost-drumming continued and the trilling voices of the ghost-women remained, Gabriel's pace quickened and then turned into a mixture of running, leaping into the air, spinning around, and dancing while waving his arms in a rhythmic flow. It was beautiful, and I watched in awe as tears streamed down my cheeks.

It wasn't long before Gabriel pulled his T-shirt over his head and threw it into the fire, causing sparks to fly in all directions. When I looked back at him, I saw that his chest and back were covered in sweat and I wasn't surprised. He hadn't stopped moving and praising and worshiping whatever it was that he'd chosen to uphold on this November night.

He made two more laps around the fire and stopped, looked at me, and held out his hand in my direction. He wanted me to join him in his church and I wanted nothing more. When I reached him, with his muscled chest still heaving for air and that wild look in his eyes also still there, he took my hand into his and softly smiled.

"Are you ready?" he asked.

"You know I am."

"Then come with me."

As Gabriel began leading me around the fire, we walked at a slow steady pace at first. It didn't take long, though, for us to fall into the faster rhythm that Gabriel had previously been in. I was now running, leaping, spinning, and dancing while waving my arms in rhythm with the drumming and trilling—and I'd never felt more free.

Gabriel and I continued going around the fire. We were on this magical journey together now and I couldn't see it ever changing course.

Saturday Evening

"Would you like a little more of my malbec?" Gabriel asked me. I was sitting at the far right end of the wine bar, hanging out with him while he worked.

"Please."

As he was pouring wine into my glass, he asked how my new romance book was. I'd brought it with me to read whenever he was waiting on a customer.

"It's really steamy," I said.

"Care to give me specifics?"

I glanced at the couple sitting a few barstools down. They were talking to each other and paying no mind to Gabriel and me. I leaned closer to him anyway.

"So far, there's been a sexy shower scene between the hero and heroine, one scene in her bed, and then another where she put whipped cream on the hero." I looked down at Gabriel's crotch and then met his intrigued gaze again. "He was her dessert, you could say."

"Hmmm."

"Would you like to get a can of whipped cream from the grocery store later?"

"Yes...I would."

"Thought so."

We grinned at each other and then Gabriel looked across the bar.

"I'll be back as soon as I can. Customers await," he said. After he gave me a quick kiss, I watched him walk off to go help the three employees that he had working with him. Then I took a sip of wine and settled back into reading my romance.

I had just come to the end of another steamy scene when I felt the tingling in my skin start increasing. As the sensation began concentrating between my legs, I looked up to see where Gabriel currently was. When I saw him standing at the opposite end of the bar with his smiling amber eyes on me, I realized he was messing with me—energetically speaking—and I shook my finger at him. He chuckled and then continued arousing me.

Between him, his malbec, the steamy scene that I'd just read, and the sultry song coming through the speakers in the wine bar right now, it wasn't going to take me very long to do what Gabriel had set out to make me do: cum while he watched me do it in a roomful of people.

I looked back at my book, acting like I was reading it, and buried my face in its pages when I felt that intense erotic feeling start washing over and through me. It went on and on, and it took everything that I had to keep still and quiet. When my orgasm finally ended, I took several deep breaths and then slowly pulled my book away from my face. Gabriel was leaning on the bar on his elbows, directly in front of me.

"How was that, Miss Hewitt?" he asked, grinning devilishly.

"Dammit you and what you do to me."

"Shall I stop?"

"Never."

Gabriel glanced around and then moved even closer, staring straight into my eyes again. "My body is on fire for yours at the moment."

"Good thing you're wearing a bartender's apron. I'd hate for you to alarm your customers."

"Yeah, that wouldn't be good."

We both chuckled, and I set my book down and took a sip of wine.

"Tell me the title of the song that was playing while you were getting me off, and also who sings it," I said.

"Why? Did you like it?"

"A lot."

"It's called 'Inscape.' It's by the band Stateless."

"Wait a minute. Did you intentionally start streaming it when you started doing what you did to me?"

"Yes."

"Because you knew I'd like it?"

"Yes. I also figured it would help you."

I sighed. "You had every bit of this planned out for me tonight, didn't you?"

"I absolutely did."

"You enjoy pushing the limits."

"On this with you? Yes."

"Do me a favor and keep pushing them."

"Gladly."

29

#justsayyes

Harper

"I've been keeping a secret from you," I told Gabriel.

"Is that so?"

"Uh-huh. And I think it's time to let you in on it."

"Okay then."

I reached into my pants pocket and pulled out the penny that I'd stuck into it after getting dressed this morning. Then I placed the penny on top of Gabriel's kitchen island.

"Are you ready?" I asked.

Gabriel nodded yes, and I pointed my finger at the penny while focusing on it. I'd been thinking a lot about the energy in and around me and wondered if I worked on directing mine if I'd then be able to move something like Gabriel. Obviously not to the degree that he could. Just something small and light. I'd decided to give it a shot with a penny this past Tuesday evening.

Nothing happened that night, but on Wednesday, something did. I had been pointing at the penny sitting on top of my coffee table for almost a minute when it slightly moved. I gasped, then started jumping up and down in excitement. After settling back down, I gave directing my energy another try and moved the penny about an inch.

I continued practicing my new skill that night and then again on Thursday after I got home from work. It was the hardest thing keeping my news from Gabriel when we talked on the phone that night. I wanted to see his face, though, when he saw what I could do, so I didn't say a word.

Still focusing on the penny now, I moved my finger a little closer to it and concentrated even harder. Then it suddenly moved several inches across the island. When I looked up at Gabriel, his eyes were huge.

"I can do it too," I said.

"Ob-obviously," he stammered. "But you shouldn't be able to."

"I would think that anyone could. It really is all about energy and working with it. I understand that well now."

"Harper, I've never known any non-witch to move an object."

"There are probably lots of regular people like me who know how to harness their energy and direct it. They just don't talk about it. It is really strange being able to do this and isn't a conversation topic that most would address with another, I would think."

"And I think you're right," Gabriel said, looking back over at the penny. Then he picked it up and focused back on me. "You have blown my mind this time instead of me blowing yours."

I smiled. "Good."

"Now I want to see you move this penny again."

For several more minutes, I repeatedly showed him what I could do and he shook his head every time. Afterward, he held me in his arms while I rested my head on his shoulder.

"I'm going to start calling you 'my little witch,'" he breathed into my hair.

"Go right ahead."

"What am I going to do with you, Harper?"

"What do you want to do?"

"Keep you with me forever. We'll just stay here at my farmhouse and live off the land and our love."

"That sounds wonderful. If only we really could do that. We must work, though."

"Yes, yes, I know. Let me dream for a minute."

"I've already dreamed about staying here with you. I love your home better than mine and hate leaving. I hate leaving you."

"Look at me," Gabriel said, then I raised my head off his shoulder. "Stay with me for as long as you want. Live with me. I want you to."

"Wh-what?"

"Live with me."

"But..."

"I'm serious. My home feels empty without you in it."

I stopped talking because I didn't know what else to say. I was shocked.

"If living with me full-time is too much to ask, then I'm asking you to do it at least part-time," Gabriel continued. "Stay here every Friday through Sunday from now on and a day or two during the other part of the week. I'll keep your gas tank filled so that you can commute from here to Boston."

I kept staring at Gabriel, clearly seeing how serious he really was about me living with him.

"I did not intend for my mentioning that I'd dreamed about staying with you to cause you to open your door to me doing exactly that," I finally said.

"I know you didn't. We're both dreaming out loud., but I don't want it to be a dream. I want you here with me, Harper. I *need* you here with me."

I took a deep breath and blew it out hard. "Gabriel, I don't... How would it..."

"How would it work, concerning my family?"

"Yes."

"Like you've said about yourself... This is my life. This is also my home and having you live in it with me, part-time or full-time, is my business. Willow would never have a problem with you being here. As far as my mother and father are concerned? I don't know how they would feel, nor do I care."

"My greatest concern is causing conflict between you and your parents. I feel that living here would be inviting that conflict. Majorly."

"No, it wouldn't."

"I do want to live here with you in this beautiful farmhouse, fall asleep in your arms every night, and wake up still in them, in the morning. You know I do."

"Then tell me that you will. Just say yes. That's all you've got to do, to make this dream come true for both of us."

I took another deep breath as my heart continued pounding. Then I said, "Yes, I'll live with you, Gabriel Grey."

He picked me up around my waist and started spinning me around—both of us smiling and giggling. Then we kissed. When we looked back at each other, we had happy tears in our eyes. We really were going to live together. It was a first for Gabriel and a first for me too. We'd never lived with anyone except for our parents and siblings.

We talked about our living arrangement some more and agreed that doing it part-time for a couple of weeks would be best. It would give me the time to adjust to commuting to and from work. Gabriel and I also talked about the craziness of what we were doing and laughed about it. We'd known each other for only fifteen days.

Another thing that we talked about was me not telling my mom and dad about me living with Gabriel. At least not yet. They'd been shocked enough to find out last Sunday that I had a boyfriend. I was going to have to ease them into the rest of my reality with him.

Gabriel and I spent the remainder of Sunday doing what we did best: cooking a meal together, eating it, cleaning up the kitchen afterward, playing with Josephine, hanging out, getting to know each other even more—and having sex. This time we were both sitting upright in the center of his bed and facing each other. I had my legs wrapped around his waist, my arms around his neck, and he had his hands on my ass, pulling me into his thrusts.

There was something about having sex with him in that way that moved me so much. While he was loving my body with his and staring straight into my eyes, I felt as if he saw all of who I was for the first time and I saw all of who he was. Our connection to each other was undeniable, and I still didn't understand it. I just knew that I never wanted it to end.

30

#whoiam

Harper

"Lovely to see you, Harper," Dr. Clarke said, smiling. "You too."

He and I happened to be walking toward the hospital parking garage elevator at the same time.

"Did you have an enjoyable weekend?"

"I did. How about you?"

"I did as well. Thank you for asking."

Dr. Clarke pushed the call button for the elevator and then looked back at me, smiling again.

"Um, have you talked to your family lately?" I asked. It was all I could think of to say.

"Yes. I chat with them often."

The elevator arrived and after the three people occupying it stepped off, Dr. Clarke held out his arm for me to walk ahead of him. It was just going to be the two of us on the ride up.

As the doors were closing, we both reached for the button panel and our hands brushed. We pulled them back, exchanged grins, and then Dr. Clarke pushed the button for my floor and the button for a different floor.

"Working another section today, I see," I said.

"Only for a bit, then I'll be back in yours."

I nodded and pulled my eyes away from his.

"Harper, I've been thinking about what you said, about me not being like the other doctors up here."

I looked back over at Dr. Clarke. "And?"

"I appreciate your compliment. But tell me... Have any of those other doctors been rude to you?"

"Yes, but not only to me. They've also been that way to Millie and the other nurses. Millie stands up to them, though. She's called several of them out about their God complex."

"I will do the same should I witness any of them acting in such a foul manner toward you or any other hospital staff."

"Dr. Clarke, don't worry about it. At least not where it concerns me. I just deal with the assholes and then roll my eyes at them behind their backs."

"I am certain that you're capable of dealing with them; however, you shouldn't have to."

He looked down at my lips and right as he met my gaze again, the elevator jumped and came to a hard stop, causing me to fall against Dr. Clarke. He caught me in his arms and I looked up at him in shock. Then he unwrapped his arms from around me and I took a step away from him. He reached up and pushed a few buttons on the elevator keypad, but nothing happened. The elevator didn't budge.

"Th-this is really happening," I stammered after a minute.

"Yes. It seems the elevator is stuck, but it will be okay."

"How is it that you're not the least bit freaked out by this?"

"I've been stuck in an elevator before. They malfunction."

"How long were you stuck in one before?"

"Almost an hour."

"Oh my God," I said, glancing around. It felt as if the space around us was starting to close in.

"Harper, are you claustrophobic?"

"No."

"Are you certain? Your breathing has grown erratic."

"I-I know."

Dr. Clarke stepped up to me and placed his hands on my upper arms. "I want you to focus on my eyes and slow your breathing. If you don't, you're going to pass out."

I nodded and then did as he had said. I focused on his eyes and within seconds, a feeling of calm began filling me and my breathing automatically slowed.

"Better now?" he asked, gently rubbing my arms.

I nodded again and then leaned my head against his chest, realizing I was claustrophobic after all. I'd never been confined to a small space like this before, so I had no idea how it would affect me.

When I looked back up at Dr. Clarke, he gave me a reassuring smile.

"Thank you for helping me through this," I said.

"You're welcome."

"It came out of nowhere."

"If you start feeling claustrophobic again, simply focus on me. I will get you through the episode."

"Just get us out of here."

"We will get out. But we're going to have to be patient. A maintenance crew has more than likely been called to assist us already. In the meantime, let's have a seat."

I sighed. "Okay then."

We sat down across from each other, on the floor of the elevator, and started sharing more about our backgrounds. As Dr. Clarke was telling me about his family and what it was like for him growing up in England, it piqued my interest to travel there one day.

"I love history and your country has a very long one. Lots of historical sites too," I said.

"You should visit England sometime. There is much to see."

"Would you happen to have any photos of it? Your family?"

"Yes."

He pulled his cellphone out of his scrubs pants pocket and as he was looking down, scrolling across the screen, I really looked at him. I was finally able to completely separate him from my angel-man. In Dr. Clarke, I saw a British gentleman trying to make a life for himself here in my country, and he was doing it alone.

"This photo was taken a few months before I left England," he said, handing his phone to me. "It's my mum, dad, and sisters standing outside our family home."

"Oh, your parents look so sweet."

"They are."

"Your sisters too. What are their names?"

"Isabella and Olivia."

"You have a beautiful family, Dr. Clarke.," I said, handing his phone back.

"Please call me Nicholas."

"Okay—*Nicholas*."

We smiled at each other, and then he asked me if I had any photos of my family. I showed him one of my mom and dad, and also the last one that had been taken of Haley and me. When he saw it, sadness washed over his face. I had previously told him about her passing.

"Again, I am sorry about your sister," he said, looking back up at me.

"Thank you. I still feel her with me, though. I guess it's a twin thing."

"You and Haley were nearly identical."

"I know."

"What was she like?"

"Like me, and I was like her. Our personalities were the same."

"She was friendly and outgoing then."

"Yes, she was. Here, let me show you this one other photo of my sister and me. It's actually my favorite one."

I crawled over to the other side of the elevator and sat next to Nicholas. As I was scrolling through my photo album, he pointed at the screen.

"Go back to the one of you and Mr. Grey if you don't mind," he said.

I didn't mind, so I pulled up the selfie that Gabriel and I had taken together over the weekend. Nicholas stared at it for several seconds and then looked up at me.

"What is it?" I asked.

"How long have you and Mr. Grey been dating?"

"A little over two weeks."

"I got the impression that it had been for much longer."

"You're talking about seeing us together on the harbor dinner cruise, aren't you?"

"Yes. You appeared very familiar with each other, and very much in love."I nodded. "It all happened very quickly."

"Mr. Grey really is a lucky bloke to have you."

Nicholas looked down at my lips again and then slowly raised his ice-blue eyes back up to mine. A moment later, the elevator jerked and started going up again.

"Ta-da!" Nicholas went on to say, raising his hand into the air.

"Thank God!"

After we stood up, he asked to see my favorite photo of Haley and me.

"I'll show it to you some other time since we're out of time now," I said. Then we reached my floor and the elevator doors opened. Before I stepped into the hallway, Nicholas told me that he enjoyed chatting with me and I told him the same.

I was walking toward the nursing station when I saw Millie standing in front of it. Then she looked up and did a double take when she saw me. As soon as I reached her, she told me that I was late.

"I know. But what you apparently don't know is that I got stuck in the parking garage elevator."

Her jaw dropped. "I had no idea."

"Nicholas was on it, too. It ended up not being such a bad thing. I had a really good talk with him and got to know him even better."

"So you're calling him by his first name now?"

"He asked me to, but I'll only do it when it's just him and I, or you and me like this. I won't do it around the rest of the staff because I know they'd raise their eyebrows if I did."

"Yes, they would. It would come across as you and Dr. Clarke having gotten a little too personal with each other. It's funny how no one thinks anything about doctors calling us by our first names."

"I know."

Millie looked over my face. "About getting personal... What did you and Dr. Clarke talk about while stuck in the elevator?"

"Our upbringings. We showed each other photos of our families and childhood homes too. Why?"

"I just want you to be careful, Harper."

"Careful about what?"

Millie stepped closer to me. "I've already told you. Alpha males. You obviously have two who are very fond of you. You're in love with one of them and the one that you're not in love with is falling for you. I can see it in his eyes. What you don't realize is that I've been closely watching Dr. Clarke whenever he's around you or you walk by him in the hallway. He lights up every time he sees you and he also checks you out when you're not looking.

I stared at Millie. "That may be true," I finally said. "He may be falling for me, but there's nothing that I can do about it if he is. Plus, he knows I'm with Gabriel and also in love with him."

"There is something that you can do, Harper."

"What?"

"Don't be quite so friendly. I know that's not who you are, but under these circumstances, you're going to have to draw a hard boundary line between you and Dr. Clarke. Yes, you can still be friendly to him—but business-friendly. A man can easily misinterpret a woman's intentions when she's being personal-friendly and talking to him about her upbringing, sharing photos of her family, and so on."

"Millie, I can't be any other way than how I am. I will not be fake."

"I'm not suggesting that you be fake. Just reserved."

"I feel like if I change how I interact with Nicholas, it'll hurt our work relationship. I don't want that to happen. I like him a lot and we work well together."

Millie stared at me and finally nodded. "Okay. I only said what I did because I've dealt with men a lot longer than you have. I don't want to see this situation blow up in your face and affect what you have with Gabriel."

"It won't."

Nicholas walked by Millie and me right then, but he didn't say anything. After walking a few yards, he looked over his shoulder and flashed his bright smile at me. When I turned my attention back to Millie, she gave me a knowing look. Then I told her that Gabriel had asked me to live with him.

"And what was your answer?" she asked.

"Yes."

"You cannot be serious."

"But I am. It's what I want to do."

"Harper."

"Millie."

"I understand your urge to jump into it. Really, I do. But you're both going to start coming down from this new romance high as you begin settling into your relationship, and I don't want you to look back and regret that you said yes to living with Gabriel so soon."

"I won't ever regret it."

• • •

I was sitting in the breakroom, snacking on Josephine's favorite: mixed nuts and dried fruit. I'd also brought some yogurt to work with me today. Gabriel and I had just finished texting each other when Nicholas came up to my table.

"Lovely to see you again, Harper," he said, flashing his bright smile at me again.

"You too, Dr. Clarke."

His eyebrows drew together and I knew why.

"Allow me to educate you again," I continued. "It's okay for you to call me or any other hospital staff by our first name up here, but it's not okay for us to call you anything other than Dr. Clarke."

"Thank you for the clarification."

"You're welcome."

"Would you mind if I joined you?"

"Not at all."

He sat down across the table from me, and we began talking about a patient. It wasn't long before Nicholas moved into the personal side of matters between us.

"May I see your favorite photo of you and your sister now?" he asked.

I grinned and pulled it up on my cellphone. "That's it."

As soon as Nicholas saw it, he chuckled and looked back up at me. "That is great!"

"I know! Haley and I got into our mom's makeup drawer and had a lot of fun making ourselves into clowns."

"What a fantastic memory."

"It really is."

"Who took the photo?"

"My mom. She has the printed original. I took a photo of it with my cellphone years ago and have kept it ever since."

"I don't blame you. How old were you and Haley?"

"Six."

"Innocent babes."

"I don't know about that. We were always getting into some kind of mischief."

"A little mischief can be a good thing, now and then. No matter how old we are." The look in Nicholas' eyes was still playful, but it also had a hint of seriousness to it now.

"I agree," I said, taking another bite of my yogurt.

"Is that all you're having for dinner?"

"Yes. It's plenty. Have you eaten yet?"

"I have not."

"You're welcome to eat some of this."

I pushed my bowl of mixed nuts and dried fruit toward Nicholas. He grinned, then grabbed a handful and began eating.

"This is good. Thank you," he said. "You have a healthy lifestyle."

"Except for the amount of wine that I drink."

"How often do you drink it?"

"Nearly daily."

"How much do you drink?"

"Two glasses. Sometimes three."

Nicholas shrugged his broad shoulders. "That won't harm you. Wine is good for you in moderation and you're a moderate drinker, so don't worry."

"Do you like wine?"

"On occasion. I prefer beer."

"Which brand do you prefer?"

"Stella Artois."

"How often do you drink it?"

"Nearly daily."

"How many bottles do you drink?"

"Two. Sometimes three."

"That won't harm you. Beer is good for you in moderation and you're a moderate drinker, so don't worry," I said.

The mimicking of each other we'd just done had us both smiling from cheek to cheek.

"Tell me more about yourself," Nicholas said.

"What would you like to know?"

"What are some of your favorite things?"

"Gah! I have so many."

"List three."

"Wine, obviously. Autumn. Music. I love how music transports me into another dimension. It's my mental escape, along with reading romance books."

"I relate."

I jerked my head back. "To me reading romance books?"

"No," Nicholas chuckled. "To mentally escaping through music."

"Which genres do you like?"

"All kinds, but mostly classic rock."

"Like from the seventies?"

"Yes. And the eighties."

"Were you even born then?"

"In 1987."

"So you're thirty-six?"

"Yes. How old are you?"

"I'll be twenty-five on Christmas day."

"What a celebration that shall be."

I shook my head no. "My birthday isn't the same without my sister."

"I can only imagine. I hope you celebrate your birthday anyway, Harper. I, for one, am glad you came into this world."

"Thank you."

Nicholas reached across the table for my hand. After resting it in his, he gave it a gentle squeeze and then got paged.

"I must go, although I hate to. Conversations with you are quite enjoyable," he said.

"Ditto."

He kept looking at me and finally asked, "Have you ever heard of the English rock band Led Zeppelin?"

"Can't say that I have."

"They're my favorite."

"Are they a classic rock band?"

"Yes."

"I will check out their music then. I have the Pandora app on my cellphone."

"Search for 'Whole Lotta Love.'"

"Is that your favorite Led Zeppelin song?"

"It is."

"I can't wait to hear it," I said.

"I can't wait to hear what you think about it. Enjoy the rest of your dinner *and* your wine this evening."

"Thank you. Enjoy your dinner later *and* your beer."

Nicholas and I exchanged one last smile, and then he got up from the table and walked out of the breakroom.

Curious about the song, I picked up my cellphone off the table and searched for it. When I found it, I pushed play. Two other nurses were sitting across the breakroom and looked over at me. My guess as to why was because I was playing the song too loudly. So I turned it down, started it over, and held my cellphone to my ear.

Nicholas's favorite song was definitely a rock song. It opened with a heavy electric guitar and bass combo, and then I heard the male singer's voice. It was strong, gritty, and as raw as uninhibited sex. That was what the song was about: sex.

When I heard the fast drumming begin, I smiled because drums were my favorite. It wasn't long before the song took on a psychedelic sound that was both dreamy and nightmarish. I'd never heard anything of the sort before, but I liked it.

One of the last lines in "Whole Lotta Love" caught me by total surprise. As soon as I heard it, I shook my head to myself because it fit this situation between Nicholas, Gabriel, and me. The line was: "I wanna be your backdoor man." No, Nicholas hadn't stated that, but I was aware of his interest in me—just as Millie and Gabriel were.

When the song ended, I clicked off my cellphone and set it back down on the table. Millie was right. I was going to have to be careful with the two alpha men in my life.

31

#family

Gabriel

"I knew you wouldn't have a problem with Harper living with me," I told Willow.

"Of course I don't. You know how quickly things happened between Damon and me. No, we never lived together. Obviously. But everything else was just like it's been for you and Harper. I'm really happy for you and her, Gabe."

"But? I know there's more you want to say."

Willow gave me a backward smile. "I'm wondering how Mother and Father are going to take your new living arrangement. You know it'll get back to them."

"I'm not worried about it. Neither of them has said a word to me about me dating Harper. I still haven't spoken with Father in person or on the phone, but Mother and I have talked on the phone. She even stopped by here the other day just to say hello. She never asked me about Harper, though."

"Maybe they both realize how serious you are about them, or mainly Father, staying out of your personal life."

"It seems so. Willow, I really don't have an issue with Mother. The way she's been with me about my dating life is normal. She asks questions like any caring mother would do and she's never tried to force her will onto me like Father has done. I would tell her all about Harper if she ever asked me about her."

"She walks a fine line, being in the middle of you and Father."

"She just wants peace and harmony."

Willow held out her hand toward Josephine, who flew off her perch on top of my desk and to my sister. "I miss you being at the house, pretty girl," Willow told my spoiled bird. Then they nuzzled each other.

"How are your art projects coming along?" I asked.

"Good. I finished that painting that I told you about. And..."

"And what?"

"I've already started on the project that you asked me to do."

"I know it is going to be amazing, just like all the other pieces of jewelry you've made. However, I do think this is your best work of art yet." I held up my hand to show Willow my ring.

"No, the piece that I'm making for Harper will be my best."

"Okay then," I chuckled. "I'd rather her have it anyway."

"I'll have it done soon. But are you going to be able to wait to give it to Harper on her birthday?"

"It's going to be hard, but I really want to surprise her. Her birthday and Christmas are tough for her because of losing her sister."

"I'm sure they are. I better not ever lose you."

"Ditto."

Willow and I smiled at each other, and then she said that she needed to get back to her studio. Before she left my office, though, she asked me if I needed her help getting Harper moved in with me.

"She and I have it covered, but thank you. I'm meeting her at her apartment after she gets off work, then we're going to pack up her clothes and whatever else she wants to bring with her."

"Would you like to take a bet on how quickly your part-time living arrangement shifts into being full-time?"

"No, I'm not betting. I don't want to jinx anything. But I am hoping Harper decides to make it full-time quickly. It's hard being apart from her."

"I give it a week."

I chuckled, and then Willow left but not before hugging me. As I was watching her leave my office, I felt a tinge of sadness for her. I knew she was still missing Damon and always would. He was her one true love and she was his.

When he'd been forced by his parents to end things with my sister, it devastated him and Willow. I had her stay with me for a couple of weeks under the guise of redecorating my guest bedrooms, when it was actually to give her the time and space that she needed to begin grieving losing Damon.

Because our mother and father didn't know anything about him, Willow couldn't break down at home. She broke down at mine several times, and I just held her while crying along with her. I hoped to never feel the kind of heartbreak that she did. It'd surely end me.

Willow had been gone for only a few minutes when my cell-phone chimed.

Willow:Mother is on her way up to see you.

Me:Thanks for the heads up. I'll let you know how it goes.

Willow:<thumbs up emoji>

Before my mother got to my office, I opened the window and had Josephine go spread her wings for a while. When I heard the light knock on my door, I went to greet my mother.

"Hello, son," she said, smiling up at me.

"What a pleasant surprise to see you."

We hugged each other, and then she gave me a kiss on the cheek.

"Come on in," I continued, stepping aside for her.

I closed the door behind her and then went back over to my desk to sit down. My mother sat in one of the chairs in front of it.

"You know what I want to talk to you about, don't you?" she asked.

"Yes."

"But only if you're up to it."

"I am up to telling you about who I'm dating. You're going to love her."

"I can see that you already do. Your eyes have never shined like they are now."

"I do love Harper. Harper Hewitt. She's a nurse at Massachusetts General Hospital. We met each other at the wine bar on Halloween."

"You fell for her quickly."

"Just like she fell for me."

"Do you have a photo of her?"

I grabbed my cellphone and pulled up the selfie that Harper and I had taken over the weekend while standing on my patio at sunset. We were looking at each other and smiling.

"Harper is beautiful," my mother said.

"Inside and out."

"I can't get over the way you two are looking at each other in that photo. What exists between you and her is very apparent."

"I know."

"How old is Harper?"

"She'll be twenty-five on Christmas Day."

My mother took a deep breath. "Your father heard the rumor about you dating someone, then told me. He also said that he will not interfere in this part of your life again. He doesn't want to lose his only son. I don't want to lose you either."

"Mother, you'll never lose me. You're the normal parent."

She chuckled. "I hope you don't mind my showing up here like this. I just wanted to know if you were happy...and you are. I'll not stick my nose any further into this than I have today."

"I don't mind talking to you about my relationship with Harper. If you think Father can handle knowing what you know about it now, then tell him. But that doesn't mean I'm ready to talk to him about Harper. I need some more time before I go there."

"He will understand."

"I have one more thing to tell you and you may not like it. Father, as well."

"What is it?"

"I asked Harper to live with me. She's moving in tonight."

My mother's eyes got big. "Son, that's a huge step."

"I'm quite aware. I hate being apart from her, though, and literally ache all over whenever she's away from me."

"Your soul tie to her is exceptionally strong then."

"Yes, it is."

"You never said that about the other women that you dated. That you ached for them."

"Because I didn't. This with Harper is..." I dragged my hands down my face. "Unreal. It feels so right, too. It's hard to explain."

"I understand how you're feeling. When your father and I met, it was like what you and Harper have."

"Do you still love him?"

"I've always loved him, Gabriel. I stopped being *in* love with him for a long while and then fell back in after he worked out some issues within himself. We all have emotional baggage to varying degrees and we all handle it differently."

"True."

"I want you to know that I am very happy for you, but I'm still your mother and am protective. I don't want to see you get hurt. Harper is young."

"So am I."

"Yes, but you have more life experience than she does. The five-year age gap between you and her makes a difference."

"She's mature beyond her years, Mother, because of everything she's been through. But I appreciate your protectiveness and always have. You're just doing your job."

We smiled at each other, and then I continued telling my mother about Harper. I let her know that she was going to live with me part-time, starting out, so that she could adjust to commuting to work. Then I covered where Harper grew up, her family, and also how she was raised.

"Does she know about us?" my mother asked.

"Yes. She's accepted everything, too."

"Have you shown her any magic?"

"I have. She wants to learn all she can about our world, and I want to teach her."

"I know you'll be excellent."

"Thank you."

"How do you and Harper plan to keep our world from her religious parents?"

"They'll never see me without a shirt on. That's for certain. And unless Harper decides to tell her parents about me, you, Father, and Willow, they'll never know. Personally, I don't want them to. I feel that it would only cause friction between Harper and them. I don't want that for her."

"Neither do I."

My mother suddenly had a look come over her as if she'd remembered something.

"Halloween..." she said.

"What about it?"

"You came to the house and looked for the book with all the witch families listed in it. I remember you saying that you had met someone whose last name was familiar."

"Yes. Harper's last name was familiar to me."

"She wouldn't have been in the book, though, since she's not a witch."

"I thought she was at first, due to her energy. I felt it before she walked up to the bar. Later, I realized it was just her life force. It is so strong."

"Will I ever get to meet the woman that my son is in love with?"

I grinned. "Yes, Mother. You will."

32

#changes

Harper

"**I** noticed your hands trembling," Gabriel said.

"I know they are."

He set down the box that he was holding on my bedroom floor and took my hands into his. As he was brushing his lips across them, he kept his eyes on mine.

"Are you having second thoughts about doing this, Harper?"

"No. This is just a really big step that we're about to take, living together. Our lives have already changed so much since we met, but they really will now. I'm excited about what we're doing. Just a little nervous is all."

"Is there anything I can do to help ease how you're feeling?"

He grinned at me and I chuckled because I knew he was talking about having sex.

"That will come later."

"I'm going to make sure you do. That's for certain."

Gabriel softly kissed me, and then picked up the box of my clothes off the floor to go put it in his Range Rover along with the other boxes of my belongings. Not one of them was in my own car, because Gabriel wanted to haul them for me.

In addition to most of my clothes and a few pairs of shoes, I'd packed my bathroom toiletries, and some photos of Haley, my mom, and my dad. I didn't need to take another thing with me, such as my iron or ironing board, because Gabriel had that covered and seemingly everything else.

I had just locked my apartment door and turned around to see him staring at me.

"This is it," he said.

"I know."

"We'll be at the farmhouse in no time, and we'll get all of your things unpacked tonight. I think you'll settle into this big change a lot quicker that way."

"You don't seem the least bit nervous about any of this."

"I'm not. I'm just happy that you're coming home with me."

I followed him to Salem and parked in his garage, next to him. When he opened his door, Josephine flew out of his car and then out of the garage. She apparently needed to spread her wings. I looked back at Gabriel and smiled, and then we began unloading my boxes.

On the first trip inside, I saw a bouquet of red roses in a crystal vase sitting on the island in the kitchen, and another one sitting on the coffee table in the living room. There was yet another one sitting on top of the dresser in Gabriel's bedroom. I thanked and kissed him three separate times for the three bouquets, and then we went to grab some more boxes. Together, we got them quickly unpacked and every item put in its new place. Afterward, Gabriel came up to me, smiling from cheek to cheek.

"I really like seeing your clothes hanging next to mine, your shoes on my closet floor, the other half of my vanity with your things on it, and your romance book on your nightstand," he said.

"So do I."

"You don't seem quite so nervous now."

"I'm not."

"This feels right, doesn't it?"

"Yes."

Gabriel gave me a quick kiss and then asked if I was ready to go to bed. I told him that I was, but needed to take a shower first.

"Mind if I join you?" he asked.

"I expect you to."

Standing together under the steaming water, Gabriel held me in his arms while I rested my head on his chest. We stayed exactly like we were for several minutes and then began bathing each other. We both got aroused during the process but waited until after we'd gotten out of the shower and dried off to have sex.

We were in his bed now, he was lying on his back and grasping my waist with his hands while I rode him in a slow and steady rhythm.

"I cannot get enough of you," he breathed.

I nodded and kept looking at his face. The expression on it, whenever he was turned on, was such a turn-on to me. Between his brows being pulled together, the intoxicated look in his amber eyes, and his parted pretty lips surrounded by all that dark scruff... Well, I loved it.

Daniel's facial expression had always looked funny to me whenever we messed around. The only way that I knew how to describe it was by comparing it to the look on Forrest Gump's face when Jenny sits down next to him on her bed in her college dorm room, takes off her bra, and places Forrest's hand on her bare breasts which makes him cum. Nothing against the movie. It was amazing, just like Tom Hanks and Robin Wright's acting. My humorous issue was about Daniel. If he only knew how many times I'd come close to laughing while watching his face when he was aroused, and especially when he came.

"I would really like to feel your tongue on me," I told Gabriel.

"I'm most happy to oblige you. Come here."

I raised up onto my knees, eased up his body, and straddled his neck. When he stuck out his tongue toward my pussy, I inched up to it, and he licked the outside of me. I sighed, he grinned and then said, "Hang on to the headboard, baby. I'm about to make a meal of you."

One moment, he was sucking on my clit. The next, he was running his long hot tongue up and down the inside of me. I was so wet and could see it on his face. What we were doing was messy, but felt heavenly to me.

When I started coming, I grabbed onto the headboard even harder while Gabriel continued sucking on my clit and clenching my ass with his fingers. After my orgasm ended, I backed up and looked down at him. We smiled at each other and then he licked his lips.

"Would you mind bottling some of this honey down here for me, please?" he asked.

"I'm not doing that, but I will wipe it off your face. You're covered in it."

"Doesn't bother me one bit. I like having you on me."

"Ditto."

"Did I make you feel good?"

"You made me feel amazing like always. It's your turn to feel that way now, so what would you like for me to do for you?"

"I want you to ride me again, but look away from me. I want to see your fine ass bouncing up and down while I fuck your pussy."

"You said pussy without any hesitation this time."

"Because I'm currently not feeling very gentlemanly."

"I like this other side of you."

"Which one do you prefer the most?"

"The more I see this side of you, the more I'm starting to prefer it. Don't get me wrong, though. The gentleman inside you still speaks directly to my romantic heart. But there's a time for him to be here and there's a time for him to step back, to let the wild man inside you step forward."

"The wild man inside me is ready to cum, so turn around and get on my dick."

I grinned and then did as Gabriel had just ordered me to do. I started riding him with my back to him. He was digging his fingers into my hips and pulling me into his thrusts while he grunted out his breaths. When he came, it lasted for as long as it had for me. Then I lifted myself off him.

I was about to move over to lie down beside him when he dug his fingers into my hips again, stopping me from going anywhere. When I looked over my shoulder at him, his eyes were where his dick had just been.

"I'm dripping out of you," he said.

"I know. I feel it."

"I like the way it looks."

"I like the way it tastes."

Gabriel swiped some of his semen off me and held up his finger toward my face. I turned around and licked it clean, then pressed my lips against his. I could taste both of us in our kiss. It was salty and sweet. The perfect combination.

• • •

It was 3:00 a.m. when I woke up to find Gabriel no longer in bed with me. I glanced over at his bathroom but the light wasn't on, so I got up and put on my robe. Then I went to see where he was.

I looked all over the quiet farmhouse but couldn't find him. As I was approaching his back door, though, I saw him through the window. He was standing by the deck railing, looking up at the sky. I kept watching him and waiting to see if he sensed me—and he did. As soon as he turned around, I opened the door and went outside to join him.

"You caught me," he said as I was walking up to him. Then I saw what he was holding—and smelled it.

"How long have you been smoking marijuana?"

"A few years. It helps turn my brain off so that I can sleep."

"But you were asleep."

"Then I woke up."

"What woke you?"

"A nightmare."

"I'm so sorry. What was it about?"

Gabriel took a hit off his joint while continuing to stare straight at me. "I lost you, Harper. I saw you packing up all your things, and then you left me. I have no idea why, either."

He wiped his eyes because he'd been crying, but was trying not to now. Seeing him in this state crushed my heart.

"It was a dream. A really bad dream. Th-that's all," I choked out.

"It felt real."

"What's real is I'll never leave you, Gabriel. You are my one and only love."

"And you are mine."

He set his joint down on top of the railing and pulled me into his arms. That was when I felt the trembling in his body and hugged him as tightly as I could. We both breathed for a long moment and then he pulled back to look at me.

"I apologize for not telling you about my little habit," he said.

"It doesn't bother me. You do whatever you need to do to help your mind rest."

"Have you ever smoked marijuana?"

"No. I couldn't if I wanted to, either, because hospital staff are randomly drug-tested. My marijuana is your malbec."

Gabriel softly smiled which instantly relieved me. I started to kiss him, but he turned his head at the last second.

"I'm sure I taste like an ashtray," he said.

"It's fine. Just kiss me, and then we're going back to bed and falling asleep in each other's arms again."

"Okay then."

33

#healer

Harper

Gabriel: So much has been going on that I haven't thought to ask you about Thanksgiving. I assume you'll be going to Northampton to spend the holiday with your parents.

Me: Actually, that's a negative. I'm working on Thanksgiving, so my parents asked me to come to see them on Friday. My mom is going to wait to cook the turkey, stuffing, and everything then.

Gabriel: That's good.

Me: Would you like to go with me? I know my mom and dad wouldn't object.

Gabriel: Yes, I would like to.

Me: Okay then. I'll let my parents know.

Gabriel: Thank you for inviting me.

Me: No need to thank me. <heart emoji> Gotta go. Just got paged.

Gabriel: See you tonight. Let me know when you leave work to head this way, my sexy little witch.

Me: <laughing face emoji> Will do. Love you.

Gabriel:Do you really love me?

Me:Yes. And lust you. <biting lip emoji>

Gabriel:Ditto.

When I stood up from the table in the breakroom, I felt the warm trickle in my panties and sighed. I'd just started my period. Because so much had happened since meeting Gabriel, I hadn't paid attention to my cycle.

After hurrying to my locker and grabbing a tampon out of my purse, I went to the women's staff restroom around the corner. While doing what I needed to do, I noted how different the pain was in my lower abdomen this time. There hadn't been any leading up to starting my period, but now, the pain was coming on quickly.

I was walking down the hallway to go check on a patient when a sharp pain that took my breath away shot across my abdomen. I stepped to the side, pressed my hand against the wall, and closed my eyes. A moment later, I heard Nicholas's voice.

"Harper, what is wrong?" he asked.

I opened my eyes to see him standing in front of me. He'd seemingly come out of nowhere. "Um, being female is what's wrong."

His eyebrows shot up. "Right. I hope you don't mind my asking, but are your cycles always this painful?"

"No."

"Come with me."

He held out his hand for mine. I gave it to him, and then he led me into an unoccupied hospital room. He walked me over to the bed and turned to face me.

"Do you trust me?" he asked.

"Yes...I do."

"I need to examine your abdomen to be sure nothing serious is wrong."

"That's fine."

Nicholas nodded once, stepped closer, and picked me up into his arms. As he was laying me down on the bed, he stared straight into my eyes and there was no mistaking the concern that I could see in his. I wasn't surprised by it as I was surprised by him picking me up. It wasn't necessary, but I would never tell him that. I appreciated his gallantry, as well as his concern.

"I must lift up the hemline of your top and lower the waist-band of your pants a bit," he continued as he was retying his mask.

"Do whatever you need to do. I don't have anything that you haven't seen before."

"I have never seen anything like you before, Harper."

Right then, Nicholas stepped out of the professional part of our relationship and back into the personal part again. I wasn't going to say a word to him about it, just like his picking me up only seconds ago. Instead, I asked him to take off his mask. I'd stopped wearing one after they were no longer required, but Nicholas always had one on—partially or all the way.

"There," he said, putting his mask into his scrub pants pocket.

"Are you worried about catching something from me?"

"No. Putting on my mask when I go into a hospital room is a cautious habit. More for the patient than for me."

Another sharp pain hit me and I winced. "God, that hurts."

"Let me get to work."

Nicholas lifted up my top to my belly button and lowered my pants down to right above my pubic bone. As he began examining my abdomen—gently pushing here and there—he didn't look at me. Instead, he stared out the window next to the bed.

"Harper, do female reproductive issues run in your family?" he asked, meeting my gaze.

"Yes. My mom had a complete hysterectomy when she was thirty. My periods were irregular and heavy from the start until I got on the pill. It was the same for my sister. Why do you ask? Do you feel something inside me that's off?"

"No. But I am incredibly sorry that you're experiencing so much pain."

"You can add nausea to it now."

"Unfortunately, they often go hand in hand. Are you feeling as though you need to..."

"No," I said, cutting Nicholas off. "Not yet anyway. I'm hoping for some kind of miracle relief here before I get to the vomiting stage."

He remained quiet and kept staring at me. "I'm asking you again if you trust me, Harper," he finally said.

"You already know my answer."

"I need to hear it again. Please."

"Yes, Dr. Nicholas Clarke from London, England—I trust you."

"I'm going to give you the miracle relief that you want and need. But don't be scared."

I swallowed hard and nodded. I had no idea what he was about to do to me, but whatever it was, I was ready and willing to accept it because my pain and nausea were still mounting.

Nicholas looked back at my abdomen, placed his hands on top of it again, and closed his eyes. It was only a few seconds later that I felt his hands begin heating up, and then the heat from them began radiating down into my body.

As I kept watching Nicholas, I noticed sweat beads appearing on his face and his breathing growing deeper and faster. In less than a minute, all of my pain and nausea were gone...and I was speechless. I was also choked up, because I had just witnessed the man standing beside me perform a true miracle. The moment that he looked back at me, I saw that he was choked up too. His ice-blue eyes had tears brimming in them.

"Are you still hurting and nauseous?" he breathed out.

I shook my head no and wiped my eyes.

"I'm a healer," Nicholas continued.

"B-but how?"

"I don't know. I've been able to do that since I was a boy. The first thing I healed was a bird with a broken wing. I was ten. When I found it on the ground in the woods, I picked it up and held it in my hands. Then I had the sudden inclination to touch its wing with my dominant hand. I felt my hand begin heating up and not long after, I removed it from the bird and watched it fly away."

I covered my mouth to stifle my crying, and then Nicholas leaned down and held the side of his face against mine. I wrapped my arms around his neck and he rested his hands on my shoulders. After a long emotional moment shared between us, he stood up straight and looked at me.

"You have an extraordinary gift, but tell me..." I began. "Have you healed others? Like your patients?"

"Yes, but they didn't know it. I touched them while they were sleeping or sedated. Modern medicine serves its purpose, and so does what I'm able to do."

"Does anyone up here, other than me, know about your gift?"

"No."

"Why were you willing to let me see this part of you?"

"You desperately needed my help and I wanted nothing more than to take away your pain and nausea, Harper."

"You also took a gamble on my reaction to all of this."

"Yes, I did."

I took a deep breath and slowly exhaled it. "I feel like I'm living in an imaginary world because of what you and Gabriel are both able to do."

Nicholas canted his head to the side and looked over my face. "What is your sweetheart able to do?"

"Um... I-I can't..." I shook my head no, wanting to kick myself for mentioning Gabriel.

"That's okay. It isn't my business anyway."

We held steady eye contact with each other, and then Nicholas asked me for a favor. He wanted me to keep what he'd done for me between us. I agreed.

"Do you feel like getting up now?" he asked.

"Yes. I need to get back to work."

After I pulled the waistband of my scrub pants back up and my scrubs top back down, Nicholas helped me to sit up. I kept still for a few seconds to see how my bearings were, and then the kind Englishman went on to help me step down to the floor.

Staring up at him now, standing in front of me, I shook my head back and forth in amazement and smiled. "Thank you for healing me," I said.

"Thank you for allowing me to."

"Please excuse what I'm about to say, but what you did to me is the biggest mind-fuck that I've ever experienced in my life."

Nicholas started chuckling. Then the look on his face turned serious again. "You're my biggest mind-fuck, Harper."

I searched his eyes, seeing the sincerity in them once more, but I didn't know how to respond. Here we were again, teetering between being professional and personal with each other. Yes, we were coworkers, but we were also friends. Friends who shared a mutual respect for one another...and also an attraction.

Because of Gabriel, I again felt guilty about my attraction to Nicholas. I was also confused as to why my attraction to him kept growing stronger despite my efforts to stop it. When I wasn't around Nicholas, I was fine. But whenever he was near, his presence was like fuel to the desirous fire inside me. A fire that shouldn't have been there for him.

I was still staring up at Nicholas when he cleared his throat and said, "I guess we should get back to our patients now."

"Yes, we should before..."

"Before what?"

"Never mind."

Nicholas glanced down at my lips. "If you need me again, I'll be here. If you are unable to find me, then have me paged or call me. I would like to give you my mobile phone number to have on hand in case of an emergency, but only if you're comfortable having it."

I wanted to tell him that I wasn't comfortable—yet I somehow was, despite my tangled web of feelings toward him. After agreeing to his giving me his *mobile phone number*, I listed him in my contacts as "N.C." Then we left the hospital room, heading off in opposite directions.

I floated around in a half-daze because I still couldn't get over Nicholas's gift of healing. I had watched TV shows before with so-called "healers" on them, but I never could let myself believe they were real. Tricks could easily be done with cameras and editing. There was no film crew present, though, in that room with Nicholas. It was just the two of us alone while I witnessed him touch my body and take away my pain and nausea.

We passed by each other in the hallway a few times during the remainder of my shift and each time, he greeted me with his bright smile and also by calling me by my first name. I called him "Dr. Clarke" while smiling too.

I was walking to my car in the parking garage when I remembered the song that he had wanted me to listen to. The thought of letting him know that I had, and also liked it, hadn't crossed my mind until now. After I got into my car, I started listening to it again while resting my head against my seat with my eyes closed. When it ended, I grabbed my cellphone.

Me: Hi. It's Harper. Great song by Led Zeppelin, by the way.

I kept staring at the screen, waiting to see if he was going to respond, and then he did. He hearted my text and also sent his own.

Nicholas: So you really liked it?

Me: Yes.

Nicholas: I'm glad. Recommend a song to me?

I paused to think of one, quickly dismissing the first two that came to mind, and then remembered a song that had the same kind of dark feeling to it as "Whole Lotta Love."

Me: "Fuel to Fire" by Agnes Obel. It's my favorite of hers.

I had just sent that text when I looked out my passenger side window to see Nicholas grinning at me, his cell phone in his hand. I rolled down the window and asked him what he was doing.

"I was on my way to my car, heard this one running, and then recognized you," he said.

"Okay then. I just sent you a song."

"Yes, I got it. Thank you. I will let you know what I think about it. I already like the title."

I smiled.

"Are you still without pain and nausea?" Nicholas went on to ask me.

"Yes."

"Very good. Be careful going home, Harper."

"You too."

He walked off and I rolled up the window. Then I began driving back to Salem while listening to "Fuel to Fire" on repeat, fully realizing that the song had been, in my subconscious, about Nicholas for some time.

34

#peaceandwar

Gabriel

"It's good to see you, son. Thank you for coming," my father said as we shook hands.

"Are you ready to talk?"

"I am. Will you join me in the library?"

"Yes."

I looked over at my mother and Willow standing across the kitchen and gave them a nod to let them know that everything was okay. It wasn't only the fact that my father had called me on Tuesday and asked me to come over for Thanksgiving dinner, but also the fact that he had apologized for his past interference in my dating life. Our conversation didn't go beyond that, but we both knew a longer one was coming.

My father closed the library door behind us, and we sat down on the leather couch.

"You look good, Gabriel," he said, giving me a once-over. "Happy. Your mother told me that you were."

"I am very happy, and it's because of the woman in my life."

"Harper Hewitt."

"Yes."

"Your mother told me all about her and she sounds delightful."

"She is, and I'm in love with her."

"I know."

"She's living with me, too, Father."

He nodded. "I hope it's going well."

"It is."

"I want to apologize to you again...for everything."

"Thank you."

"I really mean it, son. I've had a lot of time to think about my past actions with you, and I've been wrong for putting so much pressure on you to get married. It's just that continuing our family name is very important to me."

"It's important to me, too, but I can't and won't marry for the sole purpose of continuing our name. To marry, I have to be in love with the woman. Real love. I've never had that until now."

"You didn't get a chance to fall in love with anyone before due to my past intrusions."

I paused for a moment and studied my father's eyes. "Even if you hadn't stuck your nose into my business, I never would've fallen in love with those three women that I dated before. I realize it now."

"What makes you say that?"

"Harper. The moment I met her, a feeling came over me that I've never experienced with any other."

"What kind of feeling?"

"Like I already knew her. She was familiar to me, and I didn't understand why. I still don't."

My father smiled and nodded his head. "I felt the same way when I met your mother. I believe my soul recognized hers because we had journeyed together before."

I was surprised to hear him say that. "You believe in past lives?"

"Yes."

"This is the first that I've ever heard you reference anything to that spiritual degree."

"I'm getting older, Gabriel. I want to be transparent with you about everything, and about who I am. We'll always be father and son, but my job is done and I'm interested in us being friends. Two Grey men."

"I would like that."

"So would your mother and sister," he chuckled. I did too.

"I want you and Mother to meet Harper."

"We certainly want to, but only when you decide the time is right."

"I will talk to her about it after she gets off work this evening."

"I didn't realize she was at the hospital today. I thought she stayed at your farmhouse so you and I could talk."

"No, she had to work. It's just how it panned out with her schedule. I'm going to ask Mother to prepare a plate for Harper for me to take to her. One must eat turkey and stuffing on Thanksgiving Day."

"Yes, they must."

My father asked me if I was ready to go eat the huge meal that my mother and Willow had prepared. I told him that I was. Before we left the library, he reached out his hand toward me, but I didn't shake it. I hugged my father instead.

• • •

Josephine rode with me to Boston and as I was pulling into the visitor's parking area at Massachusetts General Hospital, I asked her if she wanted to stay in my car or spread her wings while I was gone. She wanted to fly.

When the elevator doors opened on Harper's floor, Millie was standing in front of me.

"Well, happy Thanksgiving!" she said.

"Thank you. And same to you."

"What do you have there?" she asked, looking down at the covered plate I was carrying.

"It's my mother's Thanksgiving dinner. I wanted Harper to have some. If I'd known you were working today, I would've brought you a plate too.""I appreciate it, Gabriel. The hospital actually provided all the staff with turkey, stuffing, and dessert today. I stuffed myself on it, too, not long ago."

"I'm guessing Harper did, as well."

"No, I don't think she's eaten yet, which is a good thing. I have no doubt your mother's cooking tastes much better than what's up here and I'll bet Harper loves it too."

I smiled. "I hope she does."

"Walk with me to the nursing station and I'll have her paged."

"Okay then."

As soon as Harper rounded the corner and saw me, she smiled, and then ran up to me and gave me a kiss.

"Hi, beautiful," I told her. "I brought you a plate of my mother's turkey and stuffing."

"Oh, I'm excited," she said, looking down at the plate. Then she lifted up part of the foil and took a whiff. "God, that smells heavenly. Thank you so much for doing this. You didn't have to."

"I wanted to. You know I enjoy taking care of you."

"Yes, I do know."

She kissed me again, and I handed her the plate.

"Why don't you two go to the breakroom?" Millie asked.

I looked back at Harper. "Do you have time?"

"I do. Come with me, handsome."

"Millie, it was good to see you again. Don't be a stranger at the Raven's Cauldron," I told her.

"Oh, I won't be. As a matter of fact, I was already planning to go there on Saturday."

"I'll be there and will have your merlot waiting."

"Sounds great!"

On our way to the breakroom, Harper asked me how it went with my father. I let her know that all had been resolved between us and I was at peace about it.

"It shows too," she said, looking over my face. "I'm relieved for you, Gabriel. Actually, for your whole family. I know they've missed you coming around."

"They have."

"When do I get to meet your parents?" she asked, grinning.

"I was going to talk to you about that after you got home tonight."

"I'm excited to meet them but don't want to push you to do anything that you're not ready to do."

"I am ready for you to meet them and vice versa."

"What about on Sunday?"

"I will contact my mother later and ask if that works for her and my father."

"And you better text me as soon as she gives you an answer."

I grinned "I will."

"I hope Willow is there too. I'd like to get to know her better."

"She's told me the same about you."

Harper and I sat down next to each other at a table in the breakroom. "I can hardly wait to dig into your mother's cooking," she said, taking the foil off the plate. Then she touched the stuffing with her fingertip. "I'm going to warm this up in the microwave for a minute. Be right back."

"Okay then."

I smiled as I watched Harper walking across the breakroom. I liked seeing her in her work environment. She seemed to be having a really good day, too. She was glowing like always, but there was something *extra* about her. I liked to think it was because I had surprised her.

After warming up her food, she stepped over and grabbed a plastic fork and knife out of a tray on the counter. I had forgotten to bring utensils and was glad there were some here.

Harper had just started coming back over to me when she looked to her right. She kept looking, too, so I turned my head and saw who she was looking at. It was Dr. Nicholas Clarke. He was walking toward Harper, smiling. When they reached each other, they stopped. I couldn't hear what was being said between them, though. Nicholas's back was to me and he was standing directly in front of Harper, blocking my view of her.

When he looked over his shoulder in my direction, I knew Harper had just told him that I was with her. I was expecting him to smirk at me, walk over to shake my hand, and then begin another asinine conversation that I wasn't in the mood for and wouldn't tolerate this time. He didn't do any of that, though. He only waved and then stepped aside for Harper. As soon as her eyes met mine, I saw the concern in them.

"Um..." she said as she was sitting back down next to me.

"Relax. I'm not concerned about Dr. Clarke being here. Are you?"

"Yes and no. I don't want things to get heated between you and him should he come over to our table."

"As long as he minds his manners, things won't get heated."

Harper and I both looked across the breakroom and then back at each other.

"It's a miracle. He's gone," I said, grinning. "Has he been mannerly with you since the harbor cruise? I'm guessing he's been around you other than just now."

"He was a gentleman each time."

"Good. Now why don't you dive into my mother's cooking before it gets cold?"

Harper smiled. "Happily!"

Her first bite was of the stuffing. She closed her eyes and said, "Mmm. Delish." Then she looked at me. "You be sure to tell your mother that I said that, and also tell her thank you."

"I most certainly will."

As Harper was taking a bite of turkey, I stole a quick glance across the breakroom to see if Nicholas had slithered his way back in. He hadn't, and I was relieved. I didn't have a problem dealing with him. I simply didn't want Harper to get nervous again.

I laughed to myself about the timing of his coming into the breakroom right after Harper and I did. It was extraordinarily convenient, considering this was my first time here. I was glad that he'd seen me, though. I hoped my presence kept him on his toes, concerning his behavior around the beautiful woman sitting beside me.

When she finished eating, she walked me to the elevator and kissed me goodbye. I watched her as she was going back down the hallway and when she turned the corner, I stepped around the other one that I'd seen Millie go around right before Harper and I reached the elevator. Millie smiled when she saw me approaching, but it didn't last for long. She had noticed the stress on my face that I was no longer hiding.

"May I speak with you in private for a moment?" I asked her.

"Sure."

She took me to a small waiting room that had no one in it and then asked me what was wrong.

"Before I tell you, I ask that you keep this conversation between us. If you feel that you can't, then tell me now. Please."

"Whatever this is about, it stays between us. I promise."

"Thank you. Tell me what you know about Dr. Nicholas Clarke."

"Uhhh, he's a nice man. He's from England. He's a great doctor."

"Anything else?"

"Such as?"

"Have you seen anything occur between him and Harper that would concern you if you were in my shoes?"

"No. Why do you ask?"

I folded my arms across my chest and sighed. "I don't know if Harper told you about the harbor cruise we went on, but Dr. Clarke was there. He came up to our table and introduced himself, but that's not all. He kept smiling at Harper in a really personal way and looked her up and down inappropriately. He also made indirect comments about preferring Harper's company and said that she looked stellar to him. When it came to his interaction with me, he smirked and was just basically an arrogant ass. I started to say something to him about his behavior but decided against it because of Harper."

"I am so sorry, Gabriel. I've never seen Dr. Clarke act like you described."

"I just saw him again in the breakroom with Harper."

"How was he?"

"Polite. We didn't actually speak, but he and Harper did. When Dr. Clarke entered the breakroom he went straight to Harper, they spoke, and then he looked over his shoulder and gave me a quick wave. After Harper sat back down to eat, we both noticed Dr. Clarke was gone."

"I'm relieved it went well when you saw him again. And again, I'm sorry about the way he acted on the harbor cruise."

"Millie, he really is like two different people, and I don't trust him. Given the chance, I know he would take Harper from me."

"Even if he wanted to, you don't have anything to be worried about. Harper is in love with you as much as you are with her. Surely you know that."

I sighed and unfolded my arms, dropping them at my sides. "I do. But it isn't easy being in love with a beautiful woman, knowing how desirable she is to every man who sees her, but especially if they get to know her."

"So I'll require Harper to wear a sack over her head whenever she's at work from now on."

I started chuckling. "No, that won't be necessary."

Millie searched my eyes and then said, "I'm going to give you my number. I want you to call or text me if you ever need to talk about this situation again."

"Thank you."

"You are very welcome, Gabriel Grey."

35

#mine

Harper

I texted Gabriel to let him know I was leaving work and would see him soon. He ssent back a thumbs-up emoji and that was it. It was actually the only form of communication that I'd received from him since he left the hospital. I'd been hoping to hear from him, letting me know that his parents were good with me meeting them on Sunday. But no. Nothing.

When I walked into the farmhouse from the garage, I looked down the hallway and immediately noticed how dim the lighting was ahead of me. I called out for Gabriel and he appeared from around the corner but didn't say anything. He only stared at me.

"What's going on?" I asked.

"Give me your cellphone and purse."

"Why?"

"Because you won't need them again tonight. You won't need your clothes on either."

"Gabriel, you know I'm on my period."

"It doesn't matter to me. I need to be close to you."

He didn't have to tell me why he was so insistent on us having sex. I knew this was about Nicholas. Despite Gabriel's attempt to hide it, I had still noticed the traces of concern on his face when Nicholas had come into the hospital breakroom earlier. I had already learned his body language and could read him like a book. My alpha male needed to take me into his den for a while, to feel better about the other alpha male in the picture.

I tossed my cellphone into my purse and handed it to Gabriel, and then he took me by the hand and led me into the kitchen. After setting my purse down on the island, he asked me if I was hungry and I told him no. He had already poured two glasses of malbec, and he handed one to me. We clinked our glasses together, took a sip of our wine, and then I looked around.

"I wondered why the farmhouse was so dark when I walked in. There are only candles burning. I like it."

"I was hoping you would. And now, I'm hoping that you're willing to do something different with me in bed tonight."

"You want us to push things again, don't you?"

"Yes."

"Okay then."

"Come with me. I have everything set up."

When we walked into Gabriel's bedroom, I counted ten lit white candles on the two nightstands, on the dresser, and even on the floor. There were red rose petals scattered around the room as well.

"This is beautiful, but it doesn't look like we're going to be pushing anything tonight. This is a purely romantic setting," I said, smiling up at Gabriel standing beside me.

"I haven't shown you everything yet."

He softly kissed me and then started taking off my clothes. When he got to my panties, I told him that I needed to use the bathroom and he nodded. After removing my tampon and washing myself, I walked back into the bedroom to see Gabriel sitting on the edge of the bed with long strips of red fabric in his hand. Then I noticed the red towel that he'd spread out in the middle of the bed.

"Looks like you and I are about to get rather kinky in here," I said.

"I just need your permission first."

"You have it."

"If at any point you want me to stop, tell me and I will."

"I doubt that I'll want you to, but okay."

"Are you ready to begin?"

"Yes. Dominate me. Do whatever you want."

Gabriel set the strips of fabric down on his nightstand, stood up, and stared down at me with the most serious look that I had ever seen in his eyes.

"Lie down on the towel, don't move or say another word until I tell you that you can. If you fight me on this, I will make you do what I want anyway," he said.

The bad boy in him had just fully come out and I had no desire to fight him. I was happy to do exactly as he demanded.

As I was lying down, he started playing "Earned It" by The Weeknd on the speaker system in his farmhouse and he played it loud. I knew the song from watching the movie *Fifty Shades of Grey* and had just realized I had the Salem version of Christian Grey. The witch version. I thought he was sexier, too. So much fucking more.

When he began taking off his clothes, I watched him while he kept his fiery amber eyes on me. After he'd stripped down to nothing but his bare skin, I looked him up and down while thinking to myself, *How can someone look so deliciously sinful and beautifully holy at the same time?* But Gabriel pulled it off with ease. It was just who he was.

As he was picking up the strips of fabric off his nightstand, I wondered how far he was going to push things between us tonight. Then he grabbed my left wrist and tied it to his headboard, quickly followed by my right.

When he spread my legs apart and started tying my ankles to the footboard, he was more forceful than he'd been with my wrists. I didn't mind, though. I liked him manhandling me in this way. It was a huge turn-on.

He had one strip of fabric left and I already knew what he was going to do with it: blindfold me. But before he did, he set it down beside my head, on the pillow, and opened the top drawer of his nightstand. When I saw what he had grabbed, I shivered all over. The last thing that I was expecting to see Gabriel holding was a knife. Then he surprised me again when I saw a red apple in his other hand.

He looked back at me, got on his bed, and straddled my hips. Then he sliced the apple horizontally and held up one half for me to see. The core had a five-pointed star in it. A natural pentagram. Because I'd only ever sliced apples vertically, I had no idea about their symbolic centers.

Using the tip of the knife, Gabriel touched each point of the tiny star while saying, "Earth, air, fire, water, spirit." The elements. Then he held out that half of the apple toward my mouth.

"Take a bite," he said.

I again did as he had ordered me to do, and then he took a bite. Once he'd swallowed it, he set the apple halves and knife on top of his nightstand, grabbed the last strip of fabric off my pillow, and blindfolded me. Then I felt him lean down even closer to me, by my left ear.

"Don't think. Just feel, Harper," he breathed.

Within seconds, he was pouring some kind of oil on me that was rose-scented. He covered the front of my body, from my neck down to my toes, and then began rubbing it across my skin as he sat on the bed beside me. The moment he was done, he straddled my hips again.

The next thing that he did was touch the center of my stomach with one of his fingertips. Then I felt him begin drawing something on my oiled skin, all around my belly button. It didn't take me long to realize what it was: a pentagram.

I heard "Earned It" begin playing again and I also heard Gabriel begin whispering words that I couldn't make out. When he stopped whispering, he reached for something to his right. Seconds later, I felt the ice in his hand. He rubbed it across my lips a few times and then started encircling my nipples with it, making it difficult for me to stay still. I was so aroused from all that Gabriel had done to me up to this point and hoped he kept going, surprising me with even more teasing.

When he began dripping the ice in a line down the length of my torso, I shivered all over again. Then he started dropping little pieces of something light and soft across my face and breasts. It only took me a moment to figure out that it was rose petals from the roses that grew wild on Gabriel's land. Their strong scent was unmistakable.

Gabriel got on his knees between my legs next and surprised me when he grabbed both of my thighs and dug his fingers into them. Then he slapped them, making me wince, but I liked it. I also liked it when he began making his way up my body by gently biting my skin and then giving both of my nipples a tug with his teeth.

He surprised me yet again when he grabbed my face and bit down on my bottom lip. Not too hard, but just enough to cause that hurt-so-good sensation to race through my body again.

"Open your mouth," Gabriel said.

The moment I did, he stuck his thumb into it and told me to start sucking. I again did what he wanted, getting more and more aroused by the second. Then I realized what Gabriel was doing with his other hand. The slight movements of his body gave him away. He was masturbating, and I wished I could've watched him. It would've sent me over the top.

Gabriel pulled his thumb out of my mouth and straddled me across my breasts. Then I felt him start running the tip of his pierced dick across my lips. I already knew what he was going to ask me to do next, so I went ahead and did it. I opened my mouth and he immediately filled it with his thick inches. Then he ordered me to start sucking on them.

As I began doing it, he moved his hips back and forth, fucking my mouth, and kept groaning over and over again. The creamy saltiness that'd leaked out of Gabriel was inside my mouth and outside of it too. It reminded me of when I rode his long tongue and covered the bottom half of his face in my "honey," as he called it. I liked having the evidence of his arousal on me.

I had no idea if he was going to continue fucking my mouth until he came and didn't mind if he did. I could take it. But then he pulled his dick out and began easing down my body, to the foot of the bed. A moment later, I felt him blowing his warm breath against my pussy and I sighed. Then he pulled me apart with his fingers and licked me. I knew at once that he'd tasted my wetness *and* my blood.

As he began whispering words that I couldn't make out again, I started thinking about everything that he had done since I lay down on his bed and realized he was performing some kind of ritual/casting a spell. Take the BDSM out of it, it was still happening. Gabriel had just added his own kink to it. I didn't know what kind of spell he was casting, but I trusted him to do whatever he felt was needed.

When he started rubbing little circles on top of my clit, I couldn't keep still. Gabriel didn't scold or spank me, either. I swirled my hips around, matching my magic man's movements with his fingertip—both of us moving slowly at first and then faster and faster.

I was so close to coming when he stopped what he was doing and got on his knees. Then he started rubbing the tip of his dick up and down the inside of my pussy. Less than a minute later, he thrust it into me. I whimpered but not in pain. Only pleasure.

Gabriel immediately began fucking me fast and hard and I fucked him back the same. In no time, I was close to coming again and I could tell by the stiffening of his body that Gabriel was too.

"Cum with me, baby! Cum with me!" he breathed against my face.

Seconds later, it began happening for both of us and that was when Gabriel pushed my blindfold up so I could see him.

His eyes were ablaze with desire and he was groaning through his clenched teeth while staring down at me, still fucking me. Then I noticed some of my blood on the edge of his bottom lip and in the dark scruff below it. Seeing it moved me in a way that was hard to explain. All I knew was that this was the rawest and most animalistic sex I'd ever had—and I wanted to have more of it.

When we finished coming together, we both stopped moving our bodies but mine felt different. When I looked to my right, I gasped: I was no longer lying on the mattress. My body and Gabriel's were several inches above it, floating in the air. I looked back up at him, but he didn't say anything. He just kept staring at me, then we slowly floated back down.

Gabriel kept his dick inside my pussy while holding himself up with his arms on either side of my body and looking over my face, which still had a few rose petals stuck to it. A moment later, he leaned his head down and softly kissed me.

Then he said, "You—are—mine."

And I always would be.

• • •

I was right about Gabriel performing a ritual/casting a spell last night. Before we went to sleep, I asked him if he had and he readily admitted to it. He said it was a spell of protection for both of us. I didn't ask him to explain why he felt the need to cast it. I already knew why, just like I knew why he was so insistent on us having sex. Every bit of it was about Nicholas.

When I'd asked Gabriel about our bodies floating above the mattress, he explained that the energy we created together while coming at the same time was what caused it. That, along with his spell. He called it "sex magic." Although the floating had never happened to either of us before, we both understood the power of raised energy. Without question, the blend of ours was powerful.

"You are in my hometown now," I told Gabriel. We had just reached Northampton.

"This is my first time to ever see it. It looks really nice."

"It is. I have a lot of good memories here. Take a right at the next light, then you'll get to see where I went to high school."

"What was your mascot?"

"The Blue Devil. What's your high school's mascot?"

"A witch, of course."

I smiled. "Yes, of course."

After checking out my high school, we went to my parents' house, where my dad greeted us at the door. After hugging me and kissing me on the cheek, he shook Gabriel's hand and then Gabriel gave him the two bottles of wine we'd brought with us. One was his malbec and the other was his chardonnay.

"Thank you," my dad said.

"It's my pleasure."

"Is this the wine that you make?"

"Yes sir, it is."

"I am looking forward to trying both. You two come on in."

While my dad was leading Gabriel and me to the kitchen, I noticed Gabriel looking around at my childhood home and smiling. I could hardly wait to see his on Sunday. He'd told me that his parents would love to have us come over then, and also that Willow would be there.

"They're here!" my dad said.

My mom looked up from the bowl of cranberry-pear chutney she was stirring. "Ah! It's so good to see you."

She set down the spoon and walked over, hugging and kissing me like my dad had done, and then she turned to Gabriel. He held out his hand, but she didn't shake it. She hugged him instead and welcomed him.

"Thank you, ma'am. It's good to be here. What can I do to help?" he asked, glancing around the kitchen.

"Nothing at all, but thank you. I've got everything covered."

"Okay then."

"The oyster stuffing isn't quite done," my mom said, looking back and forth between Gabriel and me, "so if you're hungry now, feel free to snack on the clam dip."

I glanced over at it, sitting on the counter, with a bowl of potato chips next to it. "My mom's dip is to die for," I told Gabriel. "Would you like some?"

"Yes, please."

"And to drink?"

"Water works for me."

"Ditto."

While I was getting our drinks, my dad showed my mom the bottles of Gabriel's wine. She thanked Gabriel for bringing them and also complimented him on the label. That was when he told her that Willow had created it.

"She is quite an artist," my mom said.

"She did the label for me, she paints professionally, and also makes jewelry such as this." Gabriel held out his hand for my mom to see his ring.

"That's a Gothic design."

"Yes."

"Is that a ruby?"

"It's actually a garnet. I prefer the deeper red color."

"It is beautiful, just like your wine label."

"I will pass along your compliments to my sister. She'll appreciate them."

Gabriel, my dad, and I sat down at the breakfast table in the corner of the kitchen and snacked on the clam dip and chips. My parents began asking Gabriel about his family and growing up in Salem. I grinned while listening to him answer their questions because he was very careful about what he said, making sure to leave out anything that had to do with witchcraft. A couple of times, he cut his eyes over at me and nudged my foot under the table. It took all I had to keep from busting out laughing.

When my mom asked Gabriel and me how often we were able to see each other, I answered her.

"Two or three times a week. We have to work around both of our busy schedules," I said, looking from her to Gabriel and back. I couldn't keep my eyes on him because he was tugging on his bottom lip with his teeth and grinning. If I'd kept looking at him, I most certainly would've lost it. Both of my parents would've wondered why.

I still wasn't ever going to tell them that Gabriel and his family were all witches, but was going to eventually tell them that I was living with Gabriel. My lease was going to end in February, and I had the option to renew it. There was no need to, though. I was already living full-time with my magic man.

When Thanksgiving dinner was ready, my parents, Gabriel, and I went into the dining room and sat down at the table. I immediately noticed Gabriel looking at the extra place setting.

"It's for Haley," I told him.

"That is wonderful."

I could see tears already brimming in his eyes. Then he looked at my parents.

"Thank you for having me here in your home, Mr. and Mrs. Hewitt," he said.

They both smiled at him, and then my dad asked us to join hands so that he could say grace. My parents bowed their heads and closed their eyes. Gabriel and I stole a glance at each other and then did as my parents had done. While my dad was saying grace, I thought about the conversations that I'd had with Gabriel about his faith and mine. They really were the same.

After dinner, I helped my mom clean the kitchen while my dad and Gabriel sat in the living room, talking and enjoying another glass of wine. I heard them laughing several times and smiled to myself. The camaraderie between the two men in my life was wonderful to see and hear. It was the same between my mom and Gabriel.

While she and I were in the kitchen, she told me that she really liked him and that his pierced ears didn't bother her anymore. I just chuckled and thought to myself how she would stroke out if she knew about his other piercings.

Before Gabriel and I left, I showed him around my parents' house. While we were in the bedroom that Haley and I had shared, he got choked up again. The nightstand on her side of our queen-size bed was still as she had left it, with all of its items. Until I moved to Boston, I'd kept her nightstand dusted off just like I had with her side of our dresser and bathroom vanity. All of her clothes were still hanging in our closet.

"I'm going to pull over up here," Gabriel said, nodding ahead of us.

He had driven around the corner from my parents' house and needed to get Josephine back into his Range Rover. She had ridden to Northampton with us and had been flying around or hanging out somewhere the whole time that Gabriel and I were with my parents.

Gabriel whistled for her while standing next to his open driver side door and seconds later, she flew past him and landed on my lap, where she stayed for the rest of the drive back to Salem.

"Would you like to have a glass of wine with me?" Gabriel asked as we walked into his kitchen.

"Yes. But I need a kiss first."

"Okay then."

He walked over to me, picked me up underneath my arms, set me down on the edge of the island, and then pressed his warm lips against mine. It was a sweet kiss that he gave me and when it was over, he again told me what a great time he'd had at my parents' house.

"I'm so glad you did. They're going to want us to come back on Christmas," I said.

"Sounds good to me. I want to be with you on your birthday."

"I want you with me too. What will you tell my parents if they ask you why you're not spending Christmas with your family?"

Gabriel grinned. "I'll tell them that I'm pagan and already celebrated the winter solstice with my family."

"You will not."

"No, I won't...and you know that. If they question me, I'll say that I asked my mother and father to celebrate Christmas on the twenty-fourth so that I could be with you."

"That'll work."

36

#changeofplans

Harper

"How was your delayed Thanksgiving?" I asked Millie.

"It was great! How did it go at your mom and dad's?"

"It couldn't have been any better. They really like Gabriel and he likes them too. Speaking of parents...I was supposed to meet Gabriel's on Sunday, but his mother was sick to her stomach."

"Just like I was on Saturday. I was looking forward to seeing you and Gabriel at the Raven's Cauldron."

"We were looking forward to seeing you."

"Did you make plans to meet his parents again?"

"Yes. This coming Sunday."

I looked over Millie's shoulder and saw Nicholas coming our way. He was already looking at me and smiled. He said hello and kept walking as Millie and I returned his greeting. Then she said that she needed to tell me something, but in private.

After she and I went inside the supply room, she turned to me and I could see concern showing on her face even more than it had been only moments ago.

"I am about to break a promise that I made to Gabriel."

"What did you promise him?

"That I wouldn't tell you about him talking to me in private when he came up here on Thanksgiving. He asked me about Dr.

Clarke. He wanted to know if I'd seen anything happen between you and him that I would be concerned about if I were in his shoes."

"And what did you say?"

"That I hadn't seen anything. I also told him what a nice man and great physician Dr. Clarke is."

"That's all true."

"Not the part about me not seeing anything of concern. I saw you and Dr. Clarke come out of that unoccupied room together."

I sighed. "Millie, I started my period that day and the pain was atrocious. Nicholas saw me in the hallway, leaning against the wall. He asked me what was wrong, I told him, and then he led me into that room and examined my abdomen to be sure nothing else was going on. That's it."

"I'm guessing Gabriel doesn't know that happened."

"No, he doesn't. Nor does he know about me getting stuck in the elevator with Nicholas. I can't tell him about any of it because he doesn't like Nicholas. You are so right about them being two alpha males, but especially Gabriel."

"He knows that *Nicholas* would have you as his own in a heartbeat if he could, just like you and I both know it."

"So? It means nothing to me."

Millie paused. "The last thing I need to tell you is that I gave Gabriel my cellphone number. I told him to contact me if he needed to talk about this situation again. If he does, then I will let you know."

"Thank you."

"I should've already let you know about him talking to me on Thanksgiving and I apologize for not doing it before now. The timing wasn't right."

"I understand."

"Harper, I care deeply about you."

"I care deeply about you too."

"Please be so careful with all of this between you and your two princes."

"I am."

We were about to leave the supply room when Millie asked me if I'd had any more dreams about my angel-man. I told her that I hadn't and also that I hoped it remained that way. I didn't need to see him again because if I did, I knew it would make separating him from Nicholas a struggle for me once more.

Millie and I passed each other in the hallways several times after we went back to work, and made funny faces at each other each time. I was going to have to make plans to get together with her sometime in the near future because I missed our girl time.

I had just left the women's staff restroom when I received a text that surprised me and immediately turned around to go back into the restroom and sit in a locked stall.

Nicholas:I have another song for you. Have you heard of Fleetwood Mac? They're an American rock band.

Me:Yes, I've heard of them but have never listened to any of their music.

Nicholas:Listen to "Rhiannon."

Me:Is it your favorite Fleetwood Mac song?

Nicholas:Yes.

Me:Why is it your favorite?

Nicholas:You'll hear why.

Me:I'll let you know what I think.

Nicholas:<smiley face emoji>

Sitting on the edge of the toilet, I looked up "Rhiannon" on my music app, holding my cellphone to my ear so that no one would hear the music if they came into the restroom. Not even thirty seconds had passed before I realized why Nicholas wanted me to listen to this song. It was the line "And who will be her lover?" that said it all.

I didn't text Nicholas back after the song was over. I could clearly see that he wanted to get even more personal with me, and what better way to do that than through music? It didn't matter that I was just trying to be his friendly coworker. I was going to have to draw a hard boundary line between Nicholas and myself after all.

I was walking toward the nursing station when he rounded the corner. He smiled when he saw me looking at him and I did an about-face, going in the opposite direction. Within seconds, he was beside me.

"Is something wrong, Harper?" he asked.

I glanced up at him. "Yes."

"What is it?"

"I can't discuss it here," I said quietly.

"I know where you can."

He grabbed my hand and quickly led me into another un-occupied hospital room and closed the door behind us.

"Talk to me," he said.

"Nicholas, I like you a lot as a doctor and a coworker, but especially as a person."

"I feel the same way about you."

"There is a difference between how you and I feel about each other, though. I do not wish to get any friendlier with you but I know you want to, with me."

He took a deep breath and slowly exhaled it. "I do."

"But you know I'm with Gabriel."

"Yes, I do know. However, I've seen the way you look at me. Have I really misread it?"

"What you've seen in me at times is my seeing the man in my dreams in you."

"I don't believe that's all it is. I believe you're attracted to me as much as I am to you. It is possible to want two men at the same time, Harper."

"No, it isn't."

"Then tell me that you don't want me. Say it and I will leave you alone."

I searched his ice-blue eyes and finally allowed myself to accept the full reality of my feelings toward him. I was completely attracted to him. I wanted him, too, when I shouldn't have. I was happy with Gabriel in every way and felt so confused and conflicted about everything that was happening with Nicholas. Regardless, I couldn't deny how I felt about him any longer.

"I can't say it," I whispered.

He carefully reached up and held my face in his hands. Then he looked down at my mouth and began leaning in. I watched his lips part and right before they touched mine, an image of Gabriel raced through my mind and I pulled away from Nicholas.

"Stop!" I said, holding my hands up in front of me. "This cannot happen."

"It already is happening."

"No."

"Harper, please kiss me. I am begging you. I need to taste your lips."

"That's not going to happen, but I'll tell you what is. You and I are going to be strictly professional with each other from now on. That's the only way that I can continue working with you."

Nicholas's face saddened and he sighed. A moment later, he nodded. "Very well then."

I left him standing where he was and walked straight to my locker to get my purse. Then I rode the elevator down to the parking garage, got into my car, and started crying, wishing so much that I could talk to my sister.

37

#no

Gabrield

"Father, just tell me what is wrong," I said.

"Not over the phone, son. Your mother and I need you to come to the house. Alone."

"Whatever this is about, I don't care if Harper hears it."

"No, son. Neither of you is going to want to hear it."

"Okay then. I will be there soon."

When I hung up, I looked at Harper standing in front of me.

"What's going on?" she asked.

"I don't know. But my father is insisting that I come over... without you. He and my mother want to speak to me alone."

"I hope everything is okay. We can reschedule my meeting with them again. It's fine."

I sighed. "I told you the other day that I've had a nagging feeling that something bad was coming, and I think this is it."

"How has their health been?"

"Excellent."

"Well, you go see them and let me know what's going on as soon as you can."

"Of course."

After I hugged and kissed Harper, I headed to my parents' house with Josephine perched on my passenger seat. When I walked into the living room, my parents and Willow were sitting on the couch. As soon as I saw their faces, I knew whatever I was about to find out from them was indeed bad.

"Tell me what this is about. Now," I said to my father.

"Why don't you have a seat, son?"

"No."

He looked at my mother and she handed him the book that listed all of the witch families. My father opened it, turned it to where I could read it, and then pointed at two names that I could not believe I was seeing: Haley Eleanor Hewitt and Harper Claire Hewitt.

I looked back at my father. "I-I initially thought Harper was one of us," I stammered. "I sensed her energy when we met, but the world of witchcraft was completely foreign to her. So I told myself that I'd picked up on her strong life force. I was wrong, though."

"Harper is in the process of coming out of her dormancy. You sensed her energy correctly when you met her."

"Dormancy?"

"Yes. There are countless dormant witches."

"This is the first that I've ever even heard of them. Why didn't you tell me about them before now?"

I didn't see a reason to. We can't sense them when they're in their dormancy. I apologize for not telling you."

I ran my hands over my face and blew out a heavy breath. "Harper doesn't even realize what she is, nor what's happening to her."

"No, she doesn't."

"What made her dormant?"

"She was born that way, just like her sister. Their parents, grandparents, and extended family, as well. The dormancy in Harper's family began in sixteen-ninety-one, here in Salem."

"How do you know that?"

"It's all in this book," my father said, glancing down at it. "Harper's ancestors turned away from the Old Religion due to their fear of persecution if they didn't."

"The Witch Trials."

"Yes."

I shook my head in disbelief at everything that I'd learned since walking through my parents' front door. "Do you know why Harper is coming out of her dormancy?"

"It's because of you."

"Me?"

"Yes. You've been teaching her about witchcraft, along with showing her what you're capable of doing."

"So all that it takes to awaken a dormant witch is for them to be exposed to our world?"

"No. They must immerse themselves in it as Harper has done."

I looked over at Willow and then studied my mother's face. Their expressions were still as stressed as when I arrived.

"You have more to tell me, don't you?" I asked my father.

"Yes."

"So do it. I'm ready to get back home to Harper and break all of this news to her. The sooner she knows, the better."

"Although the Witch Council allows each witch family, worldwide, to decide whether or not to go by their marriage arrangements, they still assign mates—active and dormant. They do it to keep up with the generational ties that could be and could have been."

"And?"

My father stood up, flipped the pages of the book to the back, and then handed it to me. "Look there," he said, pointing at my name...and Harper's. "You two were linked together. You were deemed to be mates for life."

I was totally astounded. I couldn't stop staring at our names, side by side. Then I fully registered what my father was telling me. "But you spoke in past tense, not present," I said, looking back up at him.

"Yes, I did. You and Harper are no longer linked together."

"Is that why a red line is drawn through her name?"

"It is."

"First of all, I cannot get over the tremendous coincidence of the Witch Council assigning Harper to be my wife out of the thousands and thousands of female witches. Secondly, I do not understand why we were unlinked. Do you know why?"

"Yes, and to explain it, I must tell you about Harper's sister Haley. She was linked to the eldest son of the most powerful witch family in England. Because his family is strictly traditional, he would have come for her at some point, had she not died. She did die, though, and tradition states that a male witch is entitled to marry his intended mate's younger sister, should there be one. And there is."

I could feel my pulse throbbing in my neck. "What is the name of the most powerful witch family in England? I don't know this book like you do," I said, shaking it.

"Spencer."

"Show me Haley's tie to the eldest son."

My father flipped the pages to yet another section. Haley was to marry Nicholas Spencer. As soon as I read his first name, my stomach dropped.

"Now show me his family tree. I need to see his mother's maiden name," I continued.

My father flipped a few more pages, and I immediately saw what I had already suspected. Nicholas' mother's maiden name was Clarke.

I threw the book across the living room and then screamed as I aimed my hands at my reflection in the mirror on the wall behind the couch, causing it to shatter.

"I am so, so very sorry," my father said, placing his hand on my arm. "But you must let Harper go. If you don't, what will come raining down on us from the Spencer family will end ours. They're not only the most powerful but also the cruelest. They will see to it that Nicholas gets what he's entitled to."

I gulped for air and then began telling my parents and sister what they didn't know. "Nicholas Spencer is Dr. Nicholas Clarke at Massachusetts General Hospital. He and Harper work together. I've met him but never sensed that he was a witch."

"Because he didn't want you to. You most of all. His abilities are incredible."

I swallowed hard and shook my head no. "I will not allow him to take Harper from me."

"Gabriel, my only son—whom I love and am so very proud of. You have no choice but to end your relationship with Harper. You must allow Nicholas to do what he came here to do. I am telling you again that if you don't, you will have no family left. We will all be wiped out."

"But Father, I love Harper with every fiber of my being," I cried, holding my chest. "I thought about what you told me, about believing in soulmates and that Mother is yours. I have no doubt that Harper is mine. That's why I'm pulled to her so strongly and ache for her whenever we're apart. I cannot live without her. I won't."

My father shrugged his shoulders, then I looked over at my mother and Willow. The tears streaming down their faces matched my own.

"No!" I yelled, looking back at my father. "I will not let Harper go!"

"Son, you must."

• • •

When I turned onto the road that led up to my farmhouse, I pulled over to the side and got out so I could throw up. It was the third time that I'd done it since leaving my parents' house.

Leaning against my car now, I looked up at the sky and shook my head in anger at it. Then I cursed it. Why would Source do this to Harper and me? Why would it allow us to meet and fall so deeply in love, only to rip us apart?

I was trembling all over and could not stop crying. I did not want to do this. I did not want to tell Harper that we were over. But I had to.

Before I left my parents' house, my father had gone on to tell me that Nicholas had likely been in Boston for much longer than he'd been working at Massachusetts General Hospital. He had also likely been following Harper around for weeks, watching her, and using his magical abilities to pull her to him. I could see that it had already been happening and Harper didn't have a clue, just like she didn't have a clue that she was an awakening generational witch.

My father pleaded with me to *not* tell her what she was, who Nicholas really was, or what he had planned for her. Essentially, my father wanted me to throw her to the wolves. He said it was all part of letting her go and allowing her fate to play out. But I couldn't stop questioning my fate with her. She was supposed to be mine.

I got back in my car, slowly drove up to my farmhouse, and parked in the garage. Before I could open my door, Harper walked into the garage. As soon as I stepped out of my car, she gasped, because she could see the traces of how upset I'd been.

"Gabriel, what is wrong?" she asked, holding my face in her hands.

I kept staring into Harper's beautiful brown eyes, wanting so much to pull her into my arms and hold and kiss her one last time. I couldn't, though, because I had a roll to fill. A duty. And Harper was about to see a person in me that I was not.

I pulled her hands away from my face and said, "Let's go inside."

She nodded and I followed her to the kitchen. And when she turned around to look at me, I began letting her go.

"I have made a grave mistake about you and me," I said.

"What do you mean?"

"This is all wrong between us and I don't want it any longer. I am sorry."

Harper stared hard at me. "You messing with me like this isn't funny, Gabriel."

"I'm not messing with you."

"Yes, you are. I can tell that you're lying about not wanting us any longer. I see it in your eyes."

"No, you don't. You're seeing only what you want to see."

"I-I don't get this."

"You don't have to."

"What in the hell happened at your parents' house? What did they say to you?"

"Nothing."

"They must have said something, because you aren't the same person who left here earlier. I don't even recognize you now."

I shrugged. "So."

"You and I have shared so much! We love each other! Or at least, I love you. Were you ever really in love with me?"

I kept looking at Harper as her bottom lip quivered and tears streamed down her cheeks. "No," I finally said, feeling like I was going to throw up again.

She covered her mouth with her hand and started sobbing. "You played me! You fucking played me, Gabriel Grey, and you did exactly what you said you'd never do: hurt me. But you've done exactly that. You got what you wanted from me too, didn't you? You got my body, you goddamn son of a bitch!"

Harper pulled back her arm and slapped me across my face as hard as she could. Then she hurried over to the kitchen sink, grabbed the box of trash bags out from under it, and ran toward our bedroom. I knew what she was about to do—throw her belongings into the bags and leave our home for good.

I didn't follow her into our bedroom because I couldn't watch her. So I stayed in the kitchen as she began making trips to her car with the full trash bags and finally, her two suitcases. Before she left, she came up to me and threw my spare house key at me. Then she jerked the necklace that Alex Kingston had given her off her neck and dropped it at my feet.

"One day, you're going to reap what you've sewn here with me," she choked out. "You will fall madly in love with a woman, and then she is going to break your heart and crush your soul like you have mine. No amount of magic will take away your pain, either. You're going to feel it all, Gabriel—and you're going to think of me when you do. Goodbye."

I nodded, and then Harper turned around and left. Minutes later, Willow came running through my front door and pulled me off the kitchen floor, into her arms. She held me and cried along with me while my heart continued breaking from letting go of the love of my life.

38
#aftermath

Harper

"Millie, can you talk?"

"Yes. What's wrong?"

"Gabriel ended us."

"What?"

"We're over."

"Why?"

"He told me that he made a grave mistake and no longer wants us. He also told me that he never loved me," I cried.

"Where are you now?"

"On my way back to my apartment. I packed up all my things at Gabriel's and I have them with me."

"Harper, none of this makes sense."

"I know. Something happened at Gabriel's parents' house earlier. I was supposed to meet them today, but then Mr. Grey called Gabriel and asked him to come over without me because he wanted to talk to him alone. When he returned to the farmhouse, it was like a light switch had flipped inside him. That's when he told me. He was so cold about it too. If you could've heard the steel in his voice..." My breath was coming out in hard sobs now.

"Oh, my precious friend. I am so very sorry about all of this. My heart is broken for you."

"It feels like my soul has been ripped apart. I'm hurting so much."

"I know you are. Do you have any idea what happened at Gabriel's parents' house?"

"Not a clue. Millie, I really believed what Gabriel and I had together was real. He was the one meant for me and I was meant for him."

"I believed it too."

"I breathed all of him into my life and now, I don't know what to do. How am I supposed to live without him?"

"I will help you through this, Harper. How long until you get to your apartment?"

"Thirty minutes."

"I'll meet you there."

. . .

Millie helped me get all of my clothes hung back up in my closet and everything else that I'd taken to Gabriel's put back in its place. She stayed with me until right before dark.

We went back over all that had happened with Gabriel earlier, and still—nothing added up. We also talked about when Gabriel and I'd met in the wine bar to the present day, trying to recognize missed signs. Signs that would've let Millie and me both know Gabriel wasn't who we believed he was. We didn't recognize any, though.

I went into my kitchen to get a glass of water and noticed a half-full bottle of Gabriel's malbec sitting on my counter, in the corner. I grabbed it, pulled out the cork, and poured the wine down my sink. Then I threw the bottle into a trash bag and carried it to my apartment complex's dumpster in the parking lot. I didn't want anything Gabriel Grey-related in my home.

While walking toward the stairwell to go back to my apartment, I noticed something out of the corner of my eye and looked up, to the right. Then I stopped in my tracks. It was the white owl. It was perched in the tree closest to the stairwell, staring down at me.

I watched the beautiful creature for about a minute while wishing I too had wings. I wanted to fly away into the night to someplace else. A place that I'd never been to before, where no one knew my name.

After crawling into bed and setting my alarm to go to work tomorrow, I began scrolling through my photos of Gabriel, deleting them one by one while tears rolled down the sides of my face and into my ears. Then I deleted Gabriel's music playlist from my app, our text thread, and his contact info.

The last thing that I did was hug my extra pillow to my body. It still had Gabriel's scent on it, just like my sheets. I never did wash them after our first time together. I couldn't, and still didn't want to. They were all I had left that reminded me of the only man that I'd ever loved. I thought he was bigger, brighter, and more beautiful than a sky full of stars.

• • •

"How are you holding up this morning?" Millie asked.

"I'm okay."

"Your eyes are still so puffy and red."

I shrugged. "Can't help it."

"Is there anything that I can do for you?"

"No, but thank you. I just need to get busy."

Millie hugged me, and then I walked off to go check on a patient, my first of the day. She was another elderly woman recovering from pneumonia. She was sleeping when I entered her room, so I quietly checked her vitals. As I left to see another patient, I heard my cellphone chime but didn't recognize the number that the text had come from. I knew who'd sent it, though.

Willow:This is Gabriel's sister. I want to tell you how sorry I am about everything. I also want you to know something that no one else but Gabriel knows. I went through the

**same kind of heartbreak earlier this year. I lost the love
of my life due to circumstances beyond our control. I will
always believe he and I were meant to be together just
like you and Gabriel. Please take care of yourself, Harper.**

I was standing at the side of the hallway, still staring at Willow's message and grappling with whether or not to reply when I noticed someone walking toward me. It was Nicholas. His eyes immediately grew big, and I knew why. I looked like weathered shit. It wasn't only my puffy and red eyes. I hadn't bothered showering this morning or putting on makeup, plus I was wearing my faded backup pair of scrubs. My hair was dreadful too. It was the messiest messy bun I'd ever worn and I couldn't have cared any fucking less.

Nicholas cautiously came up to me. "Harper, how are you getting on?" he asked.

I shook my head and choked back my tears.

"As your concerned coworker, I am asking if you would like to go chat in private with me," he continued.

"I-I'm not up to talking, but thank you," I whispered.

"You have my number if you need me...for anything."

I nodded and then stepped around Nicholas to go back to work. This day couldn't end fast enough.

39

#time

Harper

It had been twelve days since Gabriel and I parted ways. My parents still had no idea that I was single again. When my mom had called me the other day, asking how Gabriel and I were doing, I lied and told her that we were doing great. I would eventually tell her and my dad the truth. Just not yet.

My owl friend had visited me every night since the night that I saw it in the tree by my apartment complex's stairwell. On the other occasions that it showed up, it sat perched in the tree outside my bedroom window. I had been so tempted to open it but kept thinking about Gabriel's warning. However, I threw caution to the wind last night and welcomed the owl to come closer to me without any barrier between us. Not even the screen.

It immediately began making its way down the branch and stopped about two feet away from me. We stared at each other for the longest time and then I braved touching the owl. It allowed me to do it. I ran my fingertips across some of its soft white feathers and then stopped. When I did, it ruffled its feathers and hooted. I jumped and actually giggled. It felt good to laugh.

It was now Friday, and I was off work and had no plans. I was considering going to the indie bookstore around the corner, to find something new to read since I'd never finished the book that I bought at the Raven's Cauldron. I couldn't finish it because of where I'd bought it and also because of what the story was about: witches and magic.

I had just finished eating a bowl of tomato basil soup for dinner when someone rang my doorbell. I looked through the peephole and saw a young woman holding a vase of roses. They weren't red and even if they had been, I knew they wouldn't have come from Gabriel.

"Hello. Are you Harper Hewitt?"

"Yes."

"These are for you."

She handed the bouquet to me, I thanked her, and she left. But I kept standing in my open doorway, staring at the roses. They were blush-pink and delicate and there were two dozen of the beauties.

As I was carrying them to my kitchen, I couldn't imagine who had sent them to me and there was only one way to find out: open the card. When I saw the hand-drawn smiley face and the initials N.C. below it, I sighed. This surprise gift was from Nicholas.

After setting his card down on the counter, I stared at the roses again. I wondered how my English coworker had gotten my address, but I didn't wonder why he had sent something so personal. I knew exactly why he had dared to step over the professional line. He was concerned about me, and his concern hadn't left his eyes since he'd seen me so upset at work on the Monday after Gabriel ended our relationship.

I never did tell Nicholas what had happened between Gabriel and me. It probably wasn't hard for him to figure out, though. There was only one reason why a woman would appear so broken.

I pulled my cellphone out of my sweatpants pocket and opened my text thread with Nicholas. The last entry was a smiley face emoji from him. The entry before his was mine telling him that I'd let him know what I thought about Fleetwood Mac's song "Rhiannon." Wanting to hear it again, I opened my music app and started playing it. When it ended, I kept leaning against the counter, trying to decide what I should do. I wanted to let Nicholas know that I had received his bouquet of roses, thank him, and also let him know what I thought about the song. Then I decided to do just that.

> **Me:Thank you for the roses. They're beautiful. And BTW, I really like "Rhiannon."**

When I saw his chat bubble appear, it made me happy. Maybe it shouldn't have but so what. This little bit of personal connection with him was nice to have again.

> **Nicholas:You're most welcome for the roses. I simply wanted to make you smile again. I'm thrilled you like the song.**

> **Me:<smiley face emoji>**

I didn't receive another text from him. For all I knew, he could've been at work and had to return to his patients.

Feeling lighter in spirit, I decided to go to the indie bookstore. Getting lost in a romantic story that actually worked out was something that I needed. Would it make me cry? More than likely. But I could still appreciate the hero and heroine's love and happiness.

. . .

"Harper," I heard a familiar voice say from behind me. When I turned around, the man nervously smiled.

"Daniel. Hey," I said, shocked to see him.

"How are you?"

"I'm okay. Trying to enjoy my day off work. How are you?"

"I'm okay too. Thank you for asking."

I nodded but didn't say anything else. As Daniel kept staring at me, it became apparent that he did have more to say.

"I want to apologize to you for what I said that night. I was wrong in every way and disrespected you, terribly."

"Yes you did."

"I don't blame you for ending us, Harper. You deserve the best and it's not me."

I again grew quiet and Daniel stared once more. Then he asked if I would accept his apology. I told him yes.

"Thank you," he said, clearly relieved. Then he glanced down at the book in my hand. "I see you're still a reader."

"Always. You're not a reader, though, so what are you doing here?"

"Oh, um, my girlfriend is back there, looking for a book," he said, thumbing over his shoulder. "She's a lot like you."

"Is she a virgin?"

Daniel cleared his throat. "No."

"I'm no longer one either. Goodbye, Daniel."

He turned around and walked away, and I looked up at the ceiling of the bookstore and sighed. The odds of running into Daniel in this particular place were so low—yet he was here and with a woman that he could fuck.

I put the book that I was holding back on the shelf and left. When I made it to my car, I looked a few parking spaces over and did a double take, shocked again by who I was seeing. It was Nicholas. He had just closed his car door and was now walking toward a coffee shop a few businesses down from the bookstore. He was still in his scrubs, too, which let me know that he had been at work when we'd texted earlier.

I grabbed my car door handle, but then let go of it and looked back at the coffee shop. Then I decided that was where I was going next. When I walked in, Nicholas was in line behind one other customer. As I was approaching him, with his back to me, I took a calming breath to prepare myself to greet him.

"Nicholas," I said, instead of "Dr. Clarke."

The moment he turned around and saw me, he smiled and so did I.

"Harper. Lovely to see you."

"You too. I was leaving the bookstore down the way. I thought I'd say hello and thank you in person for the roses."

"Hello to you, and you're most welcome again. Might I interest you in a cup of coffee or tea? My treat."

"Oh, I'm..." I smiled again as my cheeks bloomed red. I wasn't expecting Nicholas' question. "Sure. Why not?"

He nodded and then motioned for me to step ahead of him in line. I stood beside him instead.

"What will you be having?" he asked, glancing up at the menu on the wall.

"Coffee with half and half. What are you going to have?"

"Yorkshire tea with milk."

"Hot tea with milk in it. I can't imagine."

"You should try it sometime. You may like it better than coffee."

"You talked me into it. I want what you're having."

"Very well," he chuckled.

Nicholas ordered for both of us and as we were walking away from the register with our very English drinks, I asked him if he was going home now and he said yes.

"Where do you live?" I continued.

"Not far from here."

"Neither do I. My apartment is literally around the corner, but you already knew that. How did you get my address to send the roses?"

"Your friend Millie."

"And how did it come about that she gave it to you?"

"At the hospital this morning, I asked her how things were with you. She wondered why I was asking, and I told her that I knew you had recently gone through something tragic and was still visibly upset by it. I have been worried about you, Harper, so I asked Millie if she knew of something that I could do to make things better for you. She suggested sending you some flowers. I told her that would be unprofessional of me, but she said that you wouldn't take it as such and would appreciate my gift."

I stared into his eyes while thinking about what Millie had done. It wasn't a bad thing. It was a really good thing. Her past warnings for me to be careful when it came to Nicholas no longer applied because the other alpha male was out of the picture. She knew it as much as I did and wanted to allow Nicholas the opportunity to bring me a little happiness. I could hear Millie telling herself, "This will get Harper over the hump." It was already in the process of happening.

"I'm glad that you took Millie's suggestion," I finally said.

"So am I." Nicholas took a sip of his tea and then nodded at my cup. "Give yours a try. I want to know what you think."

I grinned and took a sip. "Wow. That is surprisingly good."

"I may make an Englishwoman of you yet."

We both chuckled as we walked back outside.

"I guess this is farewell until I see you at work next week," Nicholas said, looking over my face.

"It doesn't have to be. You're welcome to come over to my apartment to see the roses if you want. They're really beautiful."

"I would very much like to see them, but don't want my coming to your apartment to backfire on me. I am walking a fine line with you, Harper. Professionally and personally."

"You don't have to walk a fine line with me anymore. I'm no longer with Gabriel."

Nicholas sighed. "So that is what has had you so upset."

"Yes."

"I am sorry."

I shrugged. "Relationships are messy."

"They certainly can be."

I kept staring up at Nicholas and then asked, "So are you coming with me or not?"

He smiled and nodded yes.

40

#somethingjustlikethis

Harper

As Nicholas was following me to my apartment, I looked in my rearview mirror at his car a few times. It was a sporty silver Mercedes with a sunroof and I thought it fit him perfectly. Right before we turned into my apartment complex's parking lot, I stole one last glance at his car. Nicholas was closer to me now, and I saw that his sunglasses had dark round lenses and that he was grinning. I was too.

For whatever reason, I felt completely at peace about what we were doing. The timing felt right. Even so soon after Gabriel had exited my life like he did.

How long was it supposed to take to get over a broken heart? I believed it was an individual thing, and several dynamics played into it. Was I over Gabriel? I was just steadily trying to block him from my mind and focus on the present. It hadn't been easy, though. Fleeting images of him had started popping into my mind as he'd said would happen. I had started feeling waves of different emotions, too. At first, they confused me because seconds before I felt them, I was fine. Then I realized I was sensing Gabriel's emotions—also like he'd told me would happen.

The images of him, along with what he was feeling, didn't add up. All of it was sad. Full of regret and grief. That wasn't what I witnessed in Gabriel on the day he tore my world apart by ending us. My ability to see and sense him was probably flawed and painting the wrong picture.

If I had to guess, Gabriel was blissfully happy. He was free to move on to another woman and probably had. Since he was such a highly sexual man, he'd likely already formed a soul tie with his latest fuck. What I couldn't understand was why he hadn't severed ours. Gabriel knew how to ritually do it. I didn't.

As soon as Nicholas stepped through my doorway, he stopped, closed his eyes, and took a deep breath. Then he looked back at me.

"It smells and feels good in your home," he said.

"Thank you."

"I'm big on the scents and energy of places."

"So am I."

We smiled at each other and then I led him into my kitchen.

"There they are," I said, holding out my hand toward the bouquet sitting on the counter.

Nicholas walked straight over to them with a pleased look on his face. "I wanted to go to the florist to pick them out myself, but couldn't pop out of the hospital," he said, looking back at me. "But the lady I spoke with assured me they were English roses and that they were pristine."

"I didn't know they were English roses. And they are pristine."

"Yes, they are. Like you."

As Nicholas kept staring into my eyes, my skin started tingling and then stopped. It was strange because that sensation had only ever happened when I was around Gabriel. The fact that it had just happened again was probably nothing more than his lingering effect on me and I wanted it to go away. Permanently.

"Would you like to stay a little longer?" I asked. "If you're hungry, I'm happy to cook something for you."

"Or we could pick up something to eat."

"So that's a yes?"

"Yes," Nicholas chuckled.

"What are you hungry for?"

"Tell me what you would like."

"Um, there's this little Italian restaurant a couple of miles from here that has amazing cheesy breadsticks with marinara sauce. Does that sound good to you?"

"It sounds delicious."

"All I have to drink here is water, of course, and some milk and orange juice. No wine or anything."

"We can stop by a liquor store if you wish."

"And get some Stella Artois for you."

"And some wine for you."

Nicholas and I were both grinning from ear to ear. On our way downstairs, he asked me if I wouldn't mind us taking his car. I told him that I was hoping we would. He opened the passenger side door for me and after I got in, he made sure that my seatbelt was secure. People said that chivalry was dead, but it wasn't. Not by a long shot.

In the liquor store, walking toward the wine section, Nicholas asked me what kind of wine I preferred.

"Malbec," I said.

"Any particular brand?"

"Um, no, but I'll find something good. Then we'll get your beer."

As we were going down the red wine aisle, I spotted some Raven Crest cabernet sauvignon on the shelf and took a quiet deep breath. I took another when we reached the malbec section. Gabriel's wine was in front of Nicholas and me, and he had just picked up a bottle of it. The fucking irony.

"What a lovely label on this one," he said.

"Yes, it is."

"Would you like to try this wine?"

"Actually, I've changed my mind. I want to try your beer. You made me a fan of hot tea with milk in it, so..."

Nicholas smiled. "Are you certain you don't want some malbec? You may not like my beer."

"If I don't, then I'll have water."

We had just left the liquor store to go pick up our food at the Italian restaurant when Nicholas asked me if I was familiar with the British rock band Coldplay. I told him that I was but only knew a few of their songs.

"Is one of them 'Something Just Like This?'" he asked.

"No. I've never heard of it."

"Coldplay collaborated with the Chainsmokers on the song. Are you familiar with them?"

"Can't say that I am. Is that song another one of your favorites?"

"Yes."

"Then play it. I'd love to listen to it."

The intro immediately grabbed ahold of me because it talks about reading old books about legends and myths. Achilles, Hercules, Spider-Man, Batman. Then the singer sings about not seeing himself upon that list. In the next part, a woman is introduced, saying that she's not looking for somebody with superhuman gifts or a superhero or some fairytale bliss. She just wants somebody she can kiss.

When the chorus began, I looked over at Nicholas. He wasn't singing, but he was grinning at me. Then I grinned, pointed at his stereo, and nodded. This favorite song of his was now one of mine.

• • •

"What are your Christmas plans?" I asked Nicholas.

We had finished eating an hour earlier and were now sitting in my living room, on the couch, with only a couple of feet between us.

"I'm flying home to see my family."

"How long of a flight is that?"

"Six and a half hours."

"That isn't too bad. Are you excited to go?"

"Yes. I guess you will be seeing your family at Christmas for the holiday and your birthday."

"Yes, I will be."

"I remember what you said about it not being the same without your sister."

"It really isn't."

"Before I leave for England, I would like to do something special for your birthday...if you would allow me."

"You don't have to do anything for me."

"I want to."

I stared at Nicholas and then nodded. "Okay. I'm thanking you in advance."

"You're most welcome," he chuckled. Then he looked at his watch.

"You need to go, don't you?" I asked.

"Yes. I wish I could stay longer. This has been very enjoyable."

"I think it has been too."

"I would like to see you again, Harper."

"That would be nice. You and I both know that no one at work can know about..."

"How personal we're becoming?"

"Yes."

"I'm well aware."

"This is risky."

"You're worth it to me."

"So are you, to me."

We smiled at each other and then got up from the couch. As I was walking Nicholas to my front door, I remembered his beer in my refrigerator and asked him if he wanted to take it home.

"You like it, so keep it and enjoy it," he said.

"I do like it. It tasted really good and it affected me differently than wine."

"How so?"

"Are you sure you want me to tell you?" I giggled.

"Yes."

I looked down at the floor and then back up at Nicholas, standing by my door now. "Wine relaxes me and your beer did too, but it also made me feel..."

"Feel what?"

"Lusty."

"It has the same effect on me."

I kept grinning and opened the door as Nicholas stepped outside onto my doormat. When he turned around, he canvassed my face with his eyes but didn't say anything. I knew what he wanted. He had begged me for it on that day in the unoccupied hospital room. He wanted my kiss. So I went up to him, put my hands on his chest, raised up onto the tips of my toes, and pressed my lips against his.

He sighed, and a moment later, he cradled my face in his hands and began sweeping his warm lips back and forth across mine. His touch was so light and feathery and also burning with his desire for me.

Our kiss remained a sweet and gentle one. I was good with it. I didn't want to rush things between Nicholas and me. Gabriel and I did that and I'd learned a hard lesson from it. I wasn't looking for anything from Nicholas except for a little bit of his time, because I greatly enjoyed his company. I greatly enjoyed looking at him and listening to him speak, too. Between his extremely handsome appearance and British accent... Well, I couldn't help but swoon over him. Any woman would have.

I watched Nicholas drive out of my apartment complex parking lot through the window by my front door. When I could no longer see the taillights of his Mercedes, I went into my kitchen, grabbed another one of his Stella Artois out of my refrigerator, and began listening to the song by Coldplay and the Chain Smokers that he'd played for me earlier. When it ended, I pulled up my text thread with Nicholas.

Me:I listened to "Something Just Like This" again and realized something. The lyrics fit you and me. Mostly. You actually do have a superhuman gift that amazes me. As for me in the song? I just want somebody that I can kiss. That somebody is you.

Nicholas:You've got me, so kiss me as much as you want.

41

#manipulate

Nicholas

Iwas perched in the tree next to Harper's bedroom window, waiting for her to check to see if I was here. She was predictable, innocently curious, and gullible, but she was only twenty-four years old. Twenty-five on Christmas Day.

Like clockwork, she peeked around her curtains, saw me, smiled, and then opened her window. I eased down the branch toward her as she was greeting me and then stopped, leaving a couple of feet between us. Harper had taken the screen off her window again and reached out to stroke my feathers. She didn't do it every time. Sometimes, she just sat back and stared at me.

I couldn't read her mind when she was awake and wished I could have. I didn't have that ability, but I was able to enter her dreams and had been doing it for months. She called me her "angel-man," but I was no angel. I was the eldest son of the Spencer witch family in England and we were all quite wicked. We had become that way over time as a means of survival.

After Harper told me goodnight, closed her window, and drew the curtains, I flew back to my condominium and landed on the patio. Then I turned back into my human form and went inside to go to bed. However, I didn't go to sleep. I focused on Harper and then entered her dream as soon as she began having it.

I didn't let her see me right away this time, because I wanted to see where her mind traveled to first. At the moment, she was replaying coming up to me in the coffee shop—an encounter I had planned. I knew Harper would take the bait.

She had just fast-forwarded to us standing in the wine aisle at the liquor store. I was holding a bottle of Gabriel's malbec and asking her if she wanted to try it. Harper was shaken up, as I had intended. I was going to continue doing whatever was necessary to keep her angry at Gabriel and wanting to get closer to me.

Through the witch grapevine, I'd found out Gabriel's parents, Stefan and Victoria Grey, had searched for Harper's name in the book of witch families and immediately realized she was one of us. They also realized who she was to Gabriel *and* to me. That was when Stefan told Gabriel that he had no choice but to end his relationship with Harper.

The Witch Council originally had me linked to her sister, Haley, for marriage. That was until she tragically died in a car wreck. Prior to then, I had been watching her from afar for years, as well as up-close. I'd made several trips to Massachusetts from England so that I could see her in person. She was gorgeous, intelligent, personable, and so desirable. The same as Harper, yet different.

The difference for me was that I was drawn to Haley. Strongly. It wasn't due to the Witch Council linking us together, though. They didn't do that between mates. My draw to Haley was something I had no explanation for. I didn't know why I felt it.

The one and only time that Haley and I had ever come face to face with each other was on a spring morning, in her college library. I'd planned that occasion because I wanted to look directly into her eyes. I wondered what her reaction would be when she looked into mine. My hope was that she would feel drawn to me as much as I was to her.

I walked up behind her as she was scanning over some books on a shelf and when she began reaching for one, I also did. The same one. Our hands brushed, causing a spark to fly up into the air from in between them and a rush of energy to race through my body. I was certain that Haley had experienced the same thing, because she jumped and quietly gasped while pulling her hand back at the same time as me. It was the first time that we'd ever touched and it was powerful, just as I had always believed it would be.

When Haley turned her head and looked up at me, it was powerful too. The moment we made eye contact, we experienced another rush of energy. It was evident in the all-over shiver that we both made.

As she was turning to face me, I recognized the curious and desirous look that filled her beautiful green eyes. It was the same as mine. She was drawn to me after all.

"Hello," I said to her.

"Hello."

"I'm Nicholas Clarke."

"I'm Haley Hewitt."

"It is lovely to meet you."

"You too."

"I apologize for startling you. That was not my intention."

"It's fine. I'm fine. You're welcome to that book," she said, glancing over at it.

"I don't want it."

"Then what do you want?"

"For you to marry me."

Haley smiled. "But we just met, Mr. Clarke."

"I don't care, Miss Hewitt. I'm in love with you."

She kept smiling while I kept watching her.

"So you believe in love at first sight?" she finally asked.

"Yes. Do you?"

"No. I believe in lust at first sight."

"Are you in lust with me?"

"I don't know you."

"You don't have to know me to want me."

Haley chuckled. "Mr. Clarke, this has been fun. But I must get back to my studies."

"Very well. Before I let you be, would you please do something for me?"

"It depends on what it is."

I glanced down at her lips. "Kiss me."

"Kiss you?"

"Yes."

"Mr. Clarke, I can't do that."

"But do you want to?"

Haley took a deep breath while keeping her eyes glued to mine. "I can't believe I'm about to say this—but yes. Yes, I want to kiss you even though you're a complete stranger to me."

"Do I feel like a stranger to you?"

"N-no."

"Neither do you, to me."

It was at that moment that I took a huge risk. I stepped even closer to Haley, cradled her delicate face in my hands, and then slowly leaned in and began kissing her. As I had hoped, she kissed me in return.

The passion between us quickly grew. I was tasting her tongue and holding her body against mine while she kept quietly moaning. Then she suddenly pulled away from me as confusion and alarm filled her eyes. I knew there wasn't time for me to say or do anything other than to erase her memory of me and all that had occurred between us. So I placed my hand on top of her head and did what was necessary. Then I left the aisle.

Wanting one last glimpse of Haley, I peeked around the corner. She had turned back toward the bookshelf and was reaching for the book that we'd both started to grab. After looking her up and down, I left the library as everything inside me screamed for me to return to my intended mate. But I couldn't.

Harper was replaying our first kiss now. While I had my lips on hers earlier, I imagined I was kissing Haley. Because the two sisters were so similar in appearance, it wasn't hard to do.

Just like it wasn't hard for me to imagine what it'd be like to have sex with Harper while again picturing Haley.

Harper had just moved to another scene in her dream. I didn't want her there, either. It was the night that she gave all of herself to Gabriel at her apartment. I could see her crying afterward and Gabriel holding her, but her tears weren't from feeling sad. She was happy.

The energetic tie that she formed with Gabriel on that night was still there and would be until I fucked her. The instant that my tie with Harper was formed, it would sever Gabriel's. No ritual or spell was needed. Until then, I knew Harper and Gabriel would continue feeling pulled to each other and dreaming about each other, as well.

I finally allowed Harper to see me in her dream. As I'd done in the past—except on one occasion when I briefly transformed Gabriel's face into mine as Harper was dreaming about him having sex with her—I sat in the corner of the room that she was in, in her mind, and watched her. I also wore the usual attire: men's Victorian clothes with a black top hat included. I could've willed it to be modern-day clothing or anything else, but I knew how appealing the Victorian era was to Harper and wanted to play right into it.

"You're back," she said, staring at me.

Instead of remaining in the corner as usual, I walked over to where she was standing, took off my hat, and held out my hand for hers. She hesitated to place it in mine, but for only a moment. After wrapping my fingers around her hand, I lifted it to my mouth and kissed it while staring into her dark brown eyes.

"Talk to me, angel-man. You never have. I need to hear your voice," she whispered.

It was my turn to hesitate. If I said one word, it would've been in my voice. I couldn't change that about myself in Harper's dream, so I shook my head no and watched disappointment wash across her face. Then I cautiously leaned in and kissed her cheek. She woke up at that point, but I continued lying in my bed, staring up at the ceiling.

I had just looked over at the clock on my dresser when I noticed out of the corner of my eye a dark shadow racing across the outside of my bedroom window. I jumped up and ran over to it, smiling as soon as I saw the raven's feather on the ledge. I knew it belonged to Gabriel's familiar. She was watching me for him, which meant that she was also watching Harper.

I opened my window and peered into the night, but couldn't see Josephine anywhere. I had no doubt that she was still close by, though.

"Tell your master that he's made a very foolish move," I said to her. Then I closed my window and went to grab a Stella Artois out of my refrigerator.

• • •

Good morning, Dr. Clarke," Harper said, smiling.

It was Monday morning and we were walking beside each other, going to the lift in the car park with two other hospital employees ahead of us.

"Lovely to see you. How was your weekend?"

"Wonderful. And yours?"

"The same."

I quickly reached for Harper's hand and pulled it to slow her pace. We both fell back, allowing the others to get in the lift without us. When the doors closed, I glanced around and didn't see anyone else near Harper and me. Then I reached for her hand again and pulled her over behind one of the supports in the car park where we wouldn't be seen by anyone.

"Why did you bring me here?" she asked, grinning up at me.

"I wanted a moment alone with you before our day got started."

"I see."

"I also wanted to do this."

I stepped closer to her, took her face into my hands, and kissed her as I had done on Friday before leaving her apartment. When I looked at her again, she stared straight into my eyes without uttering a word. Then she finally told me what she was thinking.

"I want more of a kiss than that, Nicholas," she whispered.

This time, I pushed her back against the support, pressed my body against hers, and began giving her what we both wanted. The moment our tongues touched, Harper quietly moaned into my mouth and I started kissing her even more deeply.

My dick was already hard and getting even harder. I knew Harper could feel it pressing into her. What she and I were doing was happening right on schedule. The spell that I cast on her at Bambolina's was working. She was being pulled to me, more and more, and desiring me the same.

When our kiss ended, we looked at each other and smiled. Then Harper glanced down at the front of my scrub pants.

"That is what you do to me," I told her.

"I'm glad that I can."

"It must go away before we leave here, but I don't know how quickly it will, with you standing here and looking so beautiful."

"I have an idea. I'll go up first, and then you can catch the next elevator...um, *lift*."

"Excellent idea."

"Before I go, I'd like to quickly tell you about something that happened to me last night."

"Please do," I said, adjusting my erection and making Harper giggle.

"Um, the man in my dreams returned. It had been a while since I'd seen him."

"How did it make you feel seeing him again?"

"I was happy. It was like you were there in my dream. I know you're two different people—one imagined and one with a heartbeat—but I still enjoyed seeing my angel-man's handsome face and your handsome face in one."

"Angel-man?"

"Yes. That's what I call him."

"Why?"

"Because of his blondish hair color and ice-blue eyes. They're the lightest blue that I've ever seen. His. Yours."

"Do you mind explaining to me why blondish hair and light-blue eyes equate to an angel for you?"

"No, I don't mind explaining at all. I grew up going to church, and every angel that I ever saw in the Sunday school books I read or saw in one of the paintings inside my church had hair and eyes like yours."

Listening to what Harper had just said, I was reminded of her young age and also the stark difference between our childhoods. She was innocent and sweet. So much so that I felt like I should be kneeling down before her due to my depravity that she had yet to see. She was good, gracious, and full of light. I was not.

"Why are you staring at me and not saying anything?" she continued.

I cleared my throat. "I was simply touched by your angelic explanation."

She smiled. "I'll see you soon, Dr. Clarke."

Harper stepped up to me, gave me a quick kiss, and left. Upstairs, fifteen minutes later, I saw her coming toward me down one of the hallways. She glanced at the front of my scrub pants and grinned like I was doing. When we reached each other, we spoke politely but kept going. This charade that we were playing was entertaining, to say the least.

While we were eating lunch together in the breakroom with Millie, I noticed Harper's water bottle move slightly toward her hand when she reached for it. She saw it, too, and looked across the table at me. I shook my head one time to let her know that she didn't need to say anything about what had happened. Thankfully, Millie hadn't noticed it.

Harper and I were in a sedated patient's room now and after doing our duties, I motioned for her to step aside with me.

"Why did you not freak out when you saw what happened in the breakroom?" she asked.

"There was no reason to freak out. You obviously have your own gifted hands. Now it's just a matter of you learning to work with your gift."

"You mean my energy?"

"Yes."

"Nicholas, I've been able to get a penny to move away from me but never have it come back. Today, without even thinking, I somehow called my water bottle to me. Well, a little."

"You certainly did."

"I've seen people on TV do that type of thing before and thought it was all staged. I have since realized it wasn't. It's the same with your gifted hands. I've watched shows with supposed healers on them, but questioned if they were fake. Because of what you did to me, I'm a believer in all of this now, but can't help but wonder what I'll do next without even thinking about it. I don't want anyone to witness me moving objects, just like you don't want them to witness what you're capable of doing."

"I can help you with your concern."

"How?"

"I will teach you how to control your energy."

"Thank you," Harper sighed.

"You're most welcome."

"Do you ever feel like you're an alien or something?"

I quietly chuckled. "Yes. I feel like I'm from an entirely different world."

"So do I."

42

#returnhome

Willow

A little over two weeks had passed since my brother ended his relationship with Harper. It had been hell on him, too. I'd been staying with him at his farmhouse as a means of emotional support and to also keep an eye on him, especially during the evening. Something about its arrival tripped Gabriel up. Majorly.

I totally related to him on that. I went through the same thing after I lost Damon. What I worried about the most, concerning my brother, were his darkest thoughts. I had them after Damon was gone and had thought about ending my life several times. Hell, it was a tremendous struggle to simply breathe without him. At the time, I couldn't imagine moving on. Then I eventually worked through it with my brother's help and learned to breathe again.

Last night was the first night that Gabriel hadn't sat on his patio and gotten wasted on his malbec wine while playing one song on his speaker system, on repeat. I used my Shazam app to find out the title and who sang it. Appropriately, it was called "Intoxicated" by Black Atlass. Although the lyrics were about a man's love for Los Angeles, California, I recognized the parallels between it and Gabriel's love for Harper. I understood exactly why he was clinging to the song while grieving the same fucking loss that I'd experienced with Damon. My brother and I had both lost our soulmates due to circumstances beyond our control.

Our parents had been keeping a close eye on Gabriel, as I'd been doing. They called and texted him several times, and had also stopped by the Raven's Cauldron to check on him. On each occasion, Gabriel was all business—unless we stepped inside his office and closed the door. Then and only then would he take off his professional mask and show his true emotions. Although his employees hadn't seen him break down, it wasn't hard for them to figure out why he was now so reserved and no longer cheerful. Harper's sudden absence in his life was apparent.

Needing a break from everything, I went to Boston today to shop or whatever. I was driving by Gracenote Coffee and did a double take at a man walking toward the entrance. I couldn't see his face. Only the back of his body. But I knew that body *and* that black hair. The man was Damon.

I hadn't seen or talked to him since the day we said goodbye. I hadn't been back to where he and I met, either. It would have hurt too damn much to go there. I had no choice but to go now, so I made a quick U-turn and parked in the lot beside the building.

I got out of my car and glanced around, relieved there weren't any people close by. That was how I needed it to be, to cloak myself. I didn't want anyone to see me suddenly disappear into thin air, but I especially didn't want Damon to see me walk into Gracenote Coffee.

I stood next to the entrance and looked through the window. Damon was standing in line behind a couple of other customers. My heart was beating so fast as I stared at him, and I was already choked up over what I was about to do.

Once inside the building, I continued watching Damon from a few yards away. Being physically close to him again was nearly overwhelming. I could feel myself being pulled to him and it was so hard to stay back.

When he ordered two nitro cold brews, I realized the second one was more than likely for his wife. Although she hadn't walked in with him, she had to be somewhere near. She was probably waiting for Damon in his car, anxious for him to bring her what just so happened to be his favorite kind of coffee and mine.

I kept watching him as he paid for the drinks, then he turned around to leave. But he didn't leave. He sat down at one of the round bistro tables and peered out the front window. Right then, I realized he was waiting for his wife to join him. But why would he want to be here with her? This was our place. I couldn't bear to see him with his wife, so I started heading toward the exit.

To leave Gracenote Coffee, I was going to have to pass by Damon. It was going to be so hard to do, too, because I didn't want to pass by him. I wanted to walk up to his table and sit down across from him. I wanted him to pierce my soul again by looking straight at me with his beautiful blue eyes. I wanted to hear him say my name and hold my hand. I wanted him to tell me that he loved me and then kiss me. None of that was going to happen, though. Not ever again.

I was nearing the exit when I decided to throw caution to the wind at the last second. I walked up to Damon's table and stood across from him just so that I could get a good look at his handsome face. He was still peering out the front window. But then he turned his head in my direction and slowly pushed one of the nitro cold brews to the other side of the table.

"I know you're here, Willow," he quietly said, shocking me. "There is no mistaking it. I sensed you before you walked in. Will you show yourself to me?"

I was torn over what to do. What if I reappeared? What then? Would Damon and I have a long talk? There was no point in us having one. It wouldn't change our circumstances. It would only bring more pain to him and to me.

"Willow, please. I need to see you," he continued. Then he looked up from the table and began scanning the space that I was standing in. That was when I noticed the tears brimming in his eyes.

I glanced around at the other customers. They were all doing their own thing, oblivious to what was taking place between the seen and unseen that was Damon and me. Being so, I decided to give Damon what he needed and uncloaked myself next to his table. The moment he saw me, a tear rolled down his cheek at the same time that one rolled down mine.

"My eyes have missed you," he breathed.

"Mine have missed you."

"Will you sit with me?"

"You don't have someone meeting you here, such as your wife?"

"No."

"I thought you did. You bought two drinks."

Damon nodded at the nitro cold brew that he'd pushed across the table. "One for you and one for me?"

I nodded and sat down. Then we spent a long moment just staring at each other. When Damon held out his hand for mine, I noticed it was trembling. My hand was, too, as I rested it in his. The moment we touched, we both drew in a sharp breath and then slowly exhaled it.

"You still have the same powerful effect on me," Damon said.

"Likewise. Obviously."

He softly smiled. "Tell me how you've been."

"I have good days and bad days. What about you?"

"The same."

"I have dreams about you."

"I dream about you every night, Willow."

We paused our conversation and took sips of our drinks. Then I told Damon that this was the first time I'd come to Gracenote Coffee since we went our separate ways.

"It isn't mine," he said, surprising me. "I often come here to relive meeting you. My whole life changed on that day."

"Both of our lives changed."

He shook his head in agreement. "What I'm about to ask you is going to be really forward, but I must know. Are you dating anyone?"

I half-laughed. "No. I'm not interested in dating."

"I understand."

"How's married life?"

"I'm married, but I'm not."

"What do you mean?"

"Celeste and I are friends and that's it. We never consummated our marriage."

My jaw dropped. "Why not?"

"Because she's in love with somebody else. She didn't want to marry me any more than I wanted to marry her."

"Are your families aware that you two have never slept together?"

"No, they're not. Celeste and I act like a happy couple in front of them and they believe it."

"Okay, I'm going to be really forward now. Where do you see things going with your marriage? The whole point of it was to continue your family name by having a son."

"That's not ever going to happen with Celeste. As a matter of fact, she and I have a combined meeting set for tomorrow with our parents. We're going to tell them the truth about our relationship. Then we're going to ask them to let us out of our marriage and to also give us the freedom to choose our spouses. If they don't, then they'll have no choice but to accept that they'll never have grandchildren come from Celeste and me."

I was speechless. I was also hopeful. Hopeful that Damon and Celeste's families would agree to what they desperately wanted. If they did, then Damon could return to me and Celeste could return to the man she loved.

"Should things not turn out as I want them to, in tomorrow's meeting, I still want you back in my life, Willow. I need you in it," Damon went on to say. "Even if it's just us being friends and meeting for coffee on occasion—I'll take it. It's better than not having you at all."

I covered my mouth and started crying again. Damon immediately got up from the table, stepped around it, and pulled me into his arms. I buried my face in his neck and breathed him in while feeling the synchronized beating of our hearts.

"I love you so much and have missed you," Damon whispered in my ear. "Yes, I've missed looking at you. I've also missed hearing your voice and your laughter. I've missed feeling your touch, tasting your lips, and loving your body with mine. I have never stopped craving you."

I raised my head and looked up at him. "I love you and have missed every single thing about you. I've never stopped craving you, either. And Damon?"

"Yeah?"

"I could never be just your friend."

His blue eyes danced across my face and stopped at my mouth. Then he leaned in and kissed me. Reconnecting with him didn't stop there, though. He slid his hand down my left side and over my hip, to where my ass and the back of my upper thigh met. He was staring straight into my eyes now and had just pulled my body into his even more. I could feel his erection pressing against me and I sighed.

Neither of us had to say aloud what we needed the most from each other. We already knew what it was: to be physically intimate again. It was the one thing that would jumpstart the healing of our broken hearts. So Damon and I walked out of Gracenote Coffee together, holding hands, and got into his car.

He began driving to one of the secret locations on the outskirts of Boston that we used to steal away to, to be alone. On the way there, I couldn't keep my hands off Damon and started rubbing his dick through his jeans. He was hard as a rock and kept groaning as I kept touching him. Waiting to be with him again was such a struggle. I remembered exactly how it felt to have him inside me. It was heavenly.

Damon glanced at me as his eyes continued flickering with desire. Then I leaned over, unzipped his jeans, and began sucking on his throbbing dick until we reached our secret location.

As soon as he parked in the camouflage of the trees, he pushed his seat back as far as it would go, and I straddled his lap.

Wanting to touch even more of him, I took his T-shirt off him and ran my hands down his muscled chest. Then he unbuttoned my blouse, unsnapped my bra in the front, and pushed them behind my shoulders. When he saw my breasts, he gently cupped them in his hands. Seconds later, he leaned his head down and started sucking on my left nipple. My hands were in his raven-black hair, my eyes were closed, and I was exactly where I was supposed to be.

When Damon looked back at me, I took a moment to study his eyes and could see how lost he already was in our combined passion. He was burning up inside and wanting more, just like I was. So we got into his backseat, took off the rest of our clothes, and lay down together.

As my lover was pushing his long dick into my pussy, we both moaned. Then we started fucking each other like it was going to be the last time, although it wasn't. We kissed while moving our bodies together. We cried some, too, and I tasted the salt in Damon's tears as I had before. Also like in the past, when I started to cum, he came with me—both of us breathless and even more in love.

• • •

"I'm driving into Salem now. Do you need me to grab anything from the grocery store before I come to your farmhouse?" I asked Gabriel.

"No, I'm good. Thank you."

"Okay."

"How was your Boston getaway?"

"It was...shocking."

"How so?"

"I'm hesitant to tell you because I don't want to upset you."

"Willow, what happened?"

"Nothing bad. It was actually wonderful. I saw Damon going into Gracenote Coffee as I was driving by."

"I suppose that was quite shocking to you."

"The story doesn't end there. I turned around and went back so I could see Damon up close. I cloaked myself and went inside the building, and then Damon sensed me and pleaded with me to let him see me. So I did, and then we had a long talk while sitting at one of the tables and sipping on nitro cold brews.

"And?"

"Gabe, are you sure you can handle hearing all of this, after what happened with Harper?"

"Yes, I'm sure. My current emotional state doesn't prevent me from being happy for someone when they're happy. I can tell that you are. I hear it in your voice."

I smiled. "I am happy. Damon and his wife, Celeste, are meeting with their parents tomorrow to tell them about their marriage."

"What about it?"

"They never consummated it. Celeste is in love with another man and didn't want to marry Damon, just like he didn't want to marry her. They've been acting like a happy couple whenever they've been around their families, but can't do it any longer. They're going to ask their parents to let them out of their marriage, and to also allow them to choose who they want in a spouse."

"Willow, I don't see that situation ever working out. I'm sorry, but I just don't. I believe you and Damon are going to get badly hurt again."

"Regardless of what his parents and Celeste's parents decide, Damon and I have already agreed to continue seeing each other. He's willing to risk having to face his father's wrath, as well as losing his inheritance. He said none of it matters to him anyway. I'm the only thing that does, just like he's the only thing that matters to me—other than you, our parents, and Josephine."

Gabriel let out a long sigh. "How did things end between you and Damon, when you left the coffee shop?"

"They didn't end there. Damon drove us to one of our secret locations. We had sex in his car."

Gabriel grew quiet and kept being quiet.

"Are you still there?" I asked.

"Yes."

"Did your little sister just disappoint you?"

"No. I envy you. You got to be with your soulmate."

43

#extraterrestrial

Harper

Nicholas and I went through the same routine at the hospital today as we did yesterday. We played our professional roles in front of others, but all of that ended when our shifts did.

I'd been home from work for about thirty minutes when Nicholas arrived at my apartment with pink and white balloons, another big bouquet of English roses, and a card.

"Happy early birthday!" he said, flashing his bright smile at me.

"Oh, this is too much!"

"No, it isn't."

I shook my head at him while mirroring his smile, and then he handed my gifts to me.

"Come on in, " I said, stepping back.

After Nicholas closed my front door, he came up to me and leaned in for a soft kiss. Then we walked into my living room. Once I'd set the roses down on my coffee table and tied the balloons to one of its legs, I opened my birthday card and read it. It was the prettiest and sweetest one that I'd ever received.

"Thank you...for everything, Nicholas," I said.

"You're most welcome. I have one more gift for you, though."

"Now you've really done too much!"

He grinned, reached into his scrub pants pocket, and then presented me with something that made my jaw drop.

"Th-these are airline tickets," I stammered.

"Yes, I know. They're ours. I would very much like for you to go to England with me, to celebrate your birthday and Christmas."

"But..."

"You don't have to give me an answer right now. All I ask is for you to think about it. We would have an extraordinary time. You could meet my family, I could show you my childhood home, and since you love history and old things so much, I would be most thrilled to be your London tour guide."

"Oh, Nicholas, this really is too much."

"No, it really isn't. I want you with me."

"I would love to go. It would be a trip of a lifetime, but I have my mom and dad to consider."

"I understand. If you decide that you want to join me, we will leave on the twenty-third."

"That's in four days."

"Yes, I know."

"When will we come back?"

"On the thirtieth. We will be in England together for a week."

I took a deep breath and slowly exhaled it. "I cannot believe you did this for my birthday."

"You're special to me and I enjoy seeing you smile as you're doing now."

"I'm really considering going with you. I can only imagine what it's like in your country."

"It is quite magical."

For a moment, I was taken aback by his statement. The word "magic" was something that he'd never said to me before. The last person who did was Gabriel.

"The photos that you showed me of England on your cellphone were quite magical."

"I'm hoping you have a passport."

347

"I do and…"

Nicholas side-eyed me and raised an eyebrow. "And what?"

"My answer is yes."

"Are you certain this is what you want to do?"

I looked at our airline tickets once more and nodded to show that I was absolutely certain. Nicholas wrapped his arms around my waist, picked me up off the floor, and started kissing me again. Things between us kept getting more and more heated and carried over to my couch where Nicholas lay down on top of me—kissing me yet again. Then we started slow-grinding each other.

I could feel his hard dick pressing against my pussy through our scrubs, but I wanted to feel it bare, with my hand. When I moved to do just that, Nicholas let me. He was as big as Gabriel. He was also leaking.

As I began playing with his tip, he groaned against my face while continuing to stare straight into my eyes with his ice-blue ones. Then he said, "I thought all you wanted was someone to kiss, Harper."

"I did. Now I want more from you."

"I want more from you, as well. I need it. I need you."

"Don't need me. Just want me. That's all I can handle at this point."

"Very well. May I show you how much I want you?"

"Yes…you may."

Nicholas got up and straddled my thighs. Because he'd changed the position of his body, and also because my hand was still wrapped around his hard dick, the front of his scrub pants had been pulled down. I could see all of his veined inches now and they were throbbing.

"That's not what I meant by showing you how much I want you," Nicholas said.

"Then what did you mean?"

"This."

He took his top off and then took my top and bra off me, dropping them onto the floor. He looked at my breasts while I looked at his muscled chest and abs. The dark blond hair covering them reminded me of a lion's mane that I wanted to run my fingers through. Then I started doing it while Nicholas watched me.

When I took my hands off him, he put his on me again by cupping my breasts. It wasn't long before he leaned over and started kissing them and sucking on my nipples.

He continued showing me how much he wanted me after he moved down to the end of the couch and took my shoes, socks, scrubs pants, and panties off me. He didn't remove the rest of his clothes next and start fucking me like I'd thought he was going to do—like I was willing to let him do, although I wasn't in love with him. I was willing to give all of my body to him because I thought it might lessen my pain of losing Gabriel. But Nicholas was apparently more interested in performing oral sex on me at the moment.

He began eating my pussy like a starving beast—licking it, biting it, and sucking hard on my clit until I came. It was long, intense, and made my body tremble all over. When it ended, the Englishman between my legs looked up at my face, swirled his tongue around his lips, and smiled.

"You needed that. An orgasm is the best stress reliever," he said.

"I know. Now it's your turn to get some stress relief."

He got off the couch and quickly stripped down to nothing. After repositioning himself between my legs, he began rubbing his still-erect dick up and down my pussy while staring into my eyes.

"I want you to say my name when you feel me entering you," he whispered.

The moment I nodded, he thrust himself into me and I sighed "Nicholas." I didn't do it only because he wanted me to. It was also due to the fact that it felt incredible to have him inside me.

"God, you're tight as ever," he breathed. Then began moving his hips back and forth, sliding his dick in and out of me.

GINA MAGEE

Several seconds passed as we continued fucking each other, and then he asked me how it felt being one with him.

"Like I knew it would," I said. "Amazing."

The corners of Nicholas' mouth curled up as he continued sliding himself into me—slow and then fast, slow and then fast again. He lasted for the longest time before he came and when he finally did, he threw his head back, closed his eyes, and groaned with his teeth clenched together. Afterward, he kissed me and then rested his body on top of mine.

"You don't want me to need you...but I do. I can't help it, Harper," he breathed against my neck.

I wrapped my arms around him even tighter and nodded. It was only an acknowledgment of what he'd said and nothing more. It didn't mean that I needed him, because I didn't. Did I want him? Yes. I desired him, tremendously. If I could just stop the images of Gabriel from popping into my mind and feeling his contradictory emotions, it would've been great. Experiencing the two made it difficult for me to stay present and focused on Nicholas whenever we were together.

Before he left my apartment, I thanked him again for my birthday gifts. Then I hugged and kissed him goodbye. As soon as I closed and locked my front door behind me, I saw another image of Gabriel and gasped. It wasn't like the others that I'd seen. This time, it was a close-up of his face and he was staring straight at me with tears in his otherworldly amber eyes.

I had almost made it to my kitchen when I gasped again, but not due to another fleeting image of Gabriel. I heard him say my name as clearly as if he'd been standing beside me and spoke it directly into my ear. He hadn't told me that would happen. Only that I'd see images of him and sense his emotions.

Feeling mine quickly rising, I ran to my bathroom and took off my scrubs top and pants that I'd slipped back on after Nicholas and I had sex. Then I got into my shower and stood beneath the warm water while crying and wishing I knew how to sever my soul tie with Gabriel. As long as it was there, it was going to continue fucking me up and keeping me from truly moving on with my life.

"How did your mom and dad take the news?" Millie asked.

"Not well. They're sad about Gabriel and me being over and they're also angry at him for how he ended our relationship. My mom repeated what she told me after she and my dad showed up early at my apartment and caught Gabriel and me here. She said a person can't really know someone so soon. Then I told her and my dad about Nicholas and where he was taking me for my birthday and Christmas."

"What did they say?"

"Nothing at first. They just got quiet. Then my dad told me to be careful and to take lots of photos. My mom then told me that she supported and loved me. That was all that I needed to hear to feel okay about going to England with Nicholas. After that, I got up from the couch, hugged my mom and dad, told them that I loved them, and left."

Millie blew out a heavy breath. "It'll be okay, Harper. Just live your life."

"I intend to. I need a grand adventure and am about to go on one with Nicholas."

"That's putting it lightly. Of course I'm excited for you, but I also want you to be careful."

"I will be."

"This thing that you have going on with Nicholas is fast, furious, and fantastic just like it was with Gabriel."

"I know it is, but it's also different. I'm not in love with Nicholas. Lust? Definitely."

"You're not in love yet. I don't think your romantic heart can help itself."

"Once upon a time, I would have agreed with you. But not anymore. Gabriel has left a deep wound in me and I don't care to get remotely close to getting hurt like this by a man again. One can only hurt me if I allow myself to fall in love with them, and that's not in my plan with Nicholas."

"He's already in love with you, though. He tries to hide it at the hospital but I see right through his masquerade, especially when you walk by him in the hallway and smile at him like you do."

"He's not in love with me, Millie. We're just two horny people who are very attracted to each other."

"Whatever you say. And on another note... I can't believe you were able to get the time off for your trip to England on such short notice."

"I said a prayer and crossed my fingers when I requested it."

"Either that did the trick or Nicholas put in a word for you. Everyone adores him at Massachusetts General."

"What's not to adore?"

"Right?"

I chuckled. "Hey, I want to tell you about one more thing and then I need to go. I'm not done packing yet."

"Okay."

"I had a dream last night."

"About your angel-man?"

"No. My sister. She and I were stretched out across our bed in our old bedroom at our mom and dad's house. At first, we were just talking to each other like we were back in high school. We had on the style of clothing from during that time, and then everything fast-forwarded to the present day. Haley and I were sitting in my living room at my apartment, and she told me, 'I'm always with you, Harper. Don't be scared.' I woke up after that."

"I am covered in goosebumps."

"So am I from thinking about my dream again," I said.

"It sounds like Haley was trying to warn you about something."

"I have no idea what it could be. You know, part of me believes she really did visit me last night. But the other part of me struggles to believe it really happened. That it's possible. Either way, I was comforted by seeing her face and hearing her voice again."

"Harper, I believe a hundred percent that our deceased loved ones are capable of coming to us in our dreams and outside of them, as well. My grandmother has come to me many times when I've been asleep *and* awake."

"Did you see her ghost or something when you were awake?"

"I always see a misty image of her from out of the corner of my eye that disappears as soon as I turn my head to look directly at it. Then I always hear a faint tinkling sound. The kind that a little wind chime would make. My grandmother loved wind chimes."

"Okay, I'm covered in goosebumps again."

"So am I."

"Thinking about what you just said about your grandmother makes me lean more toward believing that I really did see my sister in my dream last night, and also that she really is always looking out for me."

"Why don't you go ahead and lean all the way into believing it?" Millie asked. I could hear the smile in her voice.

"I believe I will."

"Good! You better get your packing done and you better let me know when you and Dr. Nicholas Clarke make it to London, England."

"I will."

"Love you bunches, my sweet friend."

"I love you too."

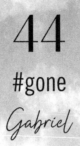

44

#gone

Gabriel

Me: Millie, this is Gabriel. I need to talk to you.

Millie: There is nothing to talk about.

Me: Please. I'm desperate. I've been trying to reach Harper but she must've blocked my cellphone number.

Millie: Do you blame her?

Me: No. But there is so much that she isn't aware of and needs to know before it's too late.

Millie: Where are you?

Me: Walking toward the entrance of your employer.

Millie: I'll meet you downstairs in the lobby.

Me: Thank you.

In less than two minutes, Millie and I were standing in front of each other.

"What I'm about to tell you is going to be shocking," I began.

"Are you going to tell me that you're a generational witch and can do all kinds of magic? Because I already know."

354

"I figured you did since you and Harper are so close. But yes, that was the first thing that I was going to tell you."

"What's the second?"

"Harper is also a generational witch."

Millie jerked back her head and scoffed. "Like hell, Gabriel."

"I promise you that she is. Harper's sister was too. Haley was dormant and Harper remained that way until recently. She is beginning to wake up and doesn't understand what's going to happen to her."

"Okay, you're starting to scare me."

"You should be scared. I know that I am, and so is my family."

"Keep talking."

"There's a book that lists all of the witch families, worldwide. It also lists who is to marry each other."

"Wait. There are arranged marriages in your world?"

"There are, but most witch families don't adhere to that old tradition. They have the option. However, there is one family in particular that does adhere to it. Strictly. It's the Spencer family in England. The eldest son was linked to Harper's sister, Haley, before she died. Because she did die, tradition states that if there is a younger sister, then she moves up in line. Haley was born two minutes before Harper, so Harper is now to marry the eldest Spencer son. You know him as Dr. Nicholas Clarke."

Millie's mouth fell open and she stumbled backward, but I caught her and steadied her.

"My God. Did you just figure all of this out?" she asked.

"No. I figured it out on the day that I ended things with Harper. It's why I ended them, Millie. I want you to know that my heart is totally shattered from letting her go. I had no choice but to do it, though, because of the power of the Spencer family. To oppose them would end my family."

"Gabriel, I never saw anything that would've clued me in as to who Nicholas really is."

"He does that by design. He's very polite and charming on the outside but underneath, he is sly and conniving. A master manipulator. One of the hardest things for me to choke down about all of this was when I found out who Harper was originally betrothed to by the Witch Council. It was me. Because my family isn't traditional about arranged marriages, I didn't know that Harper was originally supposed to be mine. But my mother zeroed in on two statements that I made to her about Harper, which led her to wonder if she was a witch and wasn't aware of it. There are many dormant witches out there in the world, so my mother researched Harper's name and got her answer."

"I cannot believe this."

"Believe it, because I am telling you the truth. Now... Will you tell me if Harper is working today?"

"She isn't, Gabriel."

"Is she at her apartment?"

"No."

"Her parents' residence?"

"She's not there, either. She's with Nicholas."

"At his residence?"

Millie took a ragged breath. "She's on her way to the airport with him. He's taking her to England."

My stomach dropped. "No!"

Millie nodded yes as tears filled her eyes. "I'm so sorry, Gabriel."

"Do you know which airline and flight?"

"I do."

"Give me the info. Please, Millie."

"But you just said you can't oppose Nicholas and his family."

"I'm going to risk doing it anyway. I have to reach Harper and tell her the truth about who she is, who we are to each other, who Nicholas really is, and what he's planning to do to her. He's going to keep her in England and force her to marry him."

"That's kidnapping."

"I know."

"When Harper doesn't come back here, her parents can report that she's missing and tell the authorities where they last knew she was going and who she was with."

"Millie, it won't matter. You don't realize the power of Nicholas's magical abilities. He will do whatever is necessary to get what he wants."

"So he's more powerful than you?"

"Yes, because he's remained strictly tied to witch tradition and has honed what he can do."

"If you're able to reach Harper before she and Nicholas board the plane, don't you think Nicholas would make a scene? Use his abilities on you and Harper?"

"No. He won't make a scene in the airport with so many witnesses. He is strong, but not strong enough to wipe all of their memories clean."

"What if he focuses solely on you? What if he hurts you?"

"Whatever happens, happens. I will lay down my life to try to save Harper's."

Tears trickled down Millie's cheeks as she was giving me the flight information. Then I asked her if she would text Harper for me.

"Of course. What do you want me to say?" she choked out.

"Tell her that you spoke with me at length just now and things are not as they appear with Nicholas. Also, tell her that I'm on my way to the airport and to not get on her plane. The last thing I want her to know is..." I was choking on my own tears now.

"Is what, Gabriel?"

"That I lied when I told her that I didn't ever love her. She's owned my heart since the day I met her and she always will."

Millie nodded and we hugged each other, then I ran back to my car. While speeding to the airport, I called the airline that Harper and Nicholas bought their tickets from and bought my own for the same flight. I knew I was going to need one to get through security.

After getting through it, I began running to the terminal as fast as I could, hoping I could reach Harper before she boarded the plane. I figured she was going to do it regardless of my text through Millie.

As I was approaching the terminal, I didn't see one passenger in the waiting area and looked at my watch. Oddly, it had stopped working and that had seemingly resulted in me miscalculating how much time I had to try to save Harper.

I went up to the airline employee at the desk and asked her if there was anything that she could do to help me get on the flight. She said no and then apologized while pointing out the window behind her. The plane carrying my soulmate was pulling away.

I walked over to the window and watched it continue to back up until it had lifted into the air and I could no longer see it. Then I whispered Harper's name and dropped to my knees.

THE MAGIC DOESN'T END HERE.
THE SEQUEL IS COMING.

Love this author? Read her other romance novels, *Twisted Roots, Fall Into Me,* and *Ocean of Stars* today.

Acknowledgements

TO MY READERS—a great big Texas hug and thank you from me to y'all for loving my stories like you do! You spur me on to continue creating fictional worlds that feel oh-so-real.

TO MY CO-AUTHORS—Brittany Lammerts and Savannah Tyler—this writing gig with y'all has been a crazy trip and it ain't over yet! I love what you brought to the pages of LA LUNE. I'm also proud of you two amazing women!

TO MY FAMILY & FRIENDS—thank you, BIG TIME, for your unending love and support of me! Mike Smith (my lil' brother) and Misty Hockman (my spirit-daughter), I greatly appreciate you combing through the rough draft of LA LUNE, and then giving me your critique. You were able to see what I couldn't at the time, because I was so close to Harper & Gabriel's story. You helped me to fill in the gaps and balance everything. XO.

TO MY BOOK COVER ARTIST—Murphy Rae—you made the cover of LA LUNE more magical than I ever could have imagined! As always, you've blown me away. You're so darn good at what you do.

TO MY EDITOR—Lilly Schneider—thank you so very much for putting your keen eyes on the manuscript of LA LUNE. You helped me to tighten the storyline and make it flow even better. And yes, I've got you down for the sequel!

TO MY BOOK FORMATTER—Elaine York—I absolutely love all the unique artistic touches that you've put on the pages of my books. My readers do, too! Thank you for everything.

About the Authors

GINA MAGEE is a romance author who sprinkles the supernatural into the storyline of the books she writes. She's currently working on her next book and is enjoying making it just as magical as the others. The East Texas Piney Woods is where Gina resides with her husband and two very spoiled Pembroke Welsh Corgis—Gypsy Willow and Sir Chesney.

Follow me:
Instagram: @ginamagee_author
TikTok: ginamagee_author
www.facebook.com/ginamageeauthor
www.amazon.com/author/ginamagee

BRITTANY LAMMERTS was born a writer, but had her skills refined thanks to a very patient AP English teacher throughout her high school career. An avid reader from an early age, she enjoys captivating stories of mystery, adventure, magic, and a dash of romance on occasion. When she's not writing, she can be found teaching her children, gardening with her husband, singing while she bakes, or planning her family's next grand adventure.

SAVANNAH TYLER is a romance author from a small town in Texas. She is a lover of words and enjoys writing/reading stories about forbidden love between soul mates. Stories where the characters fight mercilessly over every obstacle meant to keep them apart. Savannah enjoys photography and is a world traveler. Some of her favorite adventures include exploring castle ruins in Ireland, roaming the halls of the Tower of London, driving through the French countryside, walking the beaches of Normandy, standing beneath Juliet's balcony in Verona, exploring

Roman ruins, and catching a sunset on a cliff in Santorini. But her most favorite adventure of all is being a wife to her high school sweetheart and a mother to their two children. Savannah's adventurous life has given her much to draw from for writing suspenseful love stories.